**Praise for *New York Times* bestselling author
Lori Foster**

"Storytelling at its best! Lori Foster should be on everyone's auto-buy list."
—#1 *New York Times* bestselling author
Sherrilyn Kenyon

"Count on Lori Foster for sexy, edgy romance."
—*New York Times* bestselling author
Jayne Ann Krentz

"Foster's writing satisfies all appetites with plenty of searing sexual tension and page-turning action."
—*Publishers Weekly*

**Praise for *New York Times* bestselling author
Brenda Jackson**

"Brenda Jackson is the queen of newly discovered love…. If there's one thing Jackson knows how to do, it's how to pluck those heartstrings and stir up some seriously saucy drama."
—*BookPage*

"[Brenda] Jackson is a master at writing."
—*Publishers Weekly*

Lori Foster is a *New York Times* and *USA TODAY* bestselling author with books from a variety of publishers, including Harlequin, Berkley/Jove, Kensington and St. Martin's. Lori has been a recipient of the prestigious *RT Book Reviews* Career Achievement Award for Series Romantic Fantasy and for Contemporary Romance. For more about Lori, visit her website at lorifoster.com, like her on Facebook or find her on Twitter, @lorilfoster.

Brenda Jackson is a *New York Times* bestselling author of more than one hundred romance titles. Brenda married her childhood sweetheart, Gerald, and has two sons. She lives in Jacksonville, Florida. She divides her time between family, writing and traveling. Email Brenda at authorbrendajackson@gmail.com or visit her on her website at brendajackson.net.

New York Times Bestselling Author

LORI FOSTER

TREAT HER RIGHT

◆ HARLEQUIN® BESTSELLING AUTHOR COLLECTION

ISBN-13: 978-1-335-80427-3

Treat Her Right

Copyright © 2019 by Harlequin Books S.A.

The publisher acknowledges the copyright holders of the individual works as follows:

Treat Her Right
Copyright © 2001 by Lori Foster

In the Doctor's Bed
Copyright © 2011 by Brenda Streater Jackson

Recycling programs for this product may not exist in your area.

HARLEQUIN®
www.Harlequin.com

Printed in U.S.A.

CONTENTS

TREAT HER RIGHT

Lori Foster

To Morgan Arce. This one's for you!
Not only did I enjoy our chats on the phone,
but all the information you shared made
the research on this book a lot of fun!
Thank you so much.

Chapter 1

"Damn you, Conan! That's it!"

Zack Grange jerked upright in his bed, heart pounding, muscles coiled. His sleep-fogged brain felt in a jumble. He'd been dreaming, a very hot dream about a sexy lady—faceless, but with a gorgeous body—and then he'd heard the loud female shout. Caught between drugging sleep and abrupt wakefulness, confusion swamped him.

He looked around his shadowed bedroom and found it as empty as ever. No one lurked in the corners, certainly not the lady he'd been dreaming of, yet the voice had seemed to be right upon him. Heart still tripping, he strained to hear, and caught male laughter floating in through his open window. He frowned.

A glance at the clock showed it to be only seven-thirty. He'd barely been in bed at all, not long enough to recoup from the strenuous night. Certainly not long enough to finish that tempting, now elusive dream.

The deep female voice came again.

"It's not funny, you moron, and you know it," the woman groused, showing no consideration for those people still trying sleep. "I can't believe you did this to me."

"Better you than me, sweetheart." Then, "Ouch! Now that hurt."

Zack threw off his sheet. Wearing only his boxers, he went to the window to look out. He shivered as the morning air washed over his mostly bare body. The mid-September nights were getting cool, but he preferred the fresh air for sleeping. He stretched out aching muscles, still cramped from all the lifting he'd done just a few hours ago, scratched his chest, then slid aside a thin drape and peered down into the yard behind his house.

His was a larger, more private corner lot, and the street behind him ran perpendicular to his own. His bedroom window, at the back of his house, faced the side lot, so that he could see both the front and backyard of the home behind him.

New neighbors, he thought with disgust, noticing the For Sale sign now lying flat, and cardboard boxes piled everywhere around the yard. Squinting against the blinding red haze of a half-risen sun, his tired eyes gritty, he searched for the source of the screeching.

When his gaze finally landed on her, he stared in stunned disbelief.

Extremely curly brown hair was only halfheartedly contained in a sloppy ponytail. He couldn't see the details of her upper body beneath an overlarge, misshapen sweatshirt, but her shorts showed off mile-long, athletic legs and dirty white tennis shoes. Zack surveyed her top to bottom, and because a lot of distance stretched between those two points, it took a good minute.

As a basic male, he immediately considered those long strong legs. With the erotic dream still dancing around the corners of his mind, he pictured them twined around him, or perhaps even over his shoulders, and speculated on how tightly they might hold a man when he was between them, buried deep inside her.

As a discriminating man, he wondered why her hair looked such a wreck and what her upper body might present once out of that awful sweatshirt.

And lastly, as a neighbor, he wanted to groan at the lack of consideration that kept her squawking and carping in a voice too deep and too loud to be called even remotely feminine. The future didn't bode well, not with her living behind him.

"Daddy?"

Zack turned with a smile, but he felt ready to commit murder. Evidently, the noise had awakened his daughter, which meant there would be no going back to bed for him. Exhaustion wrought a groan in protest, but he held out a hand, smiling gently. "Come here, sweetheart. It looks like our new neighbors are moving in."

Rubbing her eyes with a small fist, Dani padded toward him, dragging her favorite fuzzy yellow blanket behind her. Her wee bare feet peeked out from the hem of her nightgown. Standing out around her head, her typically mussed blond hair formed a halo, and one round cheek was creased from her pillow. She reached him and held up her skinny arms. "Let me see," she demanded in her adorable childish voice.

Obligingly, Zack lifted her. His daughter was such a tiny person, even though she was now four. Petite, as her mother had been, he thought, and hugged her close to his naked chest. He breathed in her little girl smell, rubbed his rough cheek against her downy soft hair, kissed her ear.

She liked to be held, and he loved holding her.

As usual, Dani immediately gave him a wet good-morning kiss on his whiskered cheek. She wrapped her arms around his throat, her legs around his waist, and looked out the window. Her blanket caught between them.

Zack waited for her reaction. Dani never failed to amuse him. For a four-year-old, she was very astute, honest to a fault, and he loved her more than life itself.

Most of the kids her age asked constant questions, but not Dani. She made statements instead. Other than two days a week at a preschool, she was always in the company of his friends. Zack assumed her exposure to adults accounted for her speech habits.

"I see her butt," she said with an exaggerated frown.

Startled, Zack lowered his head to peer out the window again, and sure enough, the woman bent at the waist, her legs straight and braced apart for leverage as she tugged on a large box. Her shorts were riding rather high and he could just see the twin moons of her bottom cheeks.

Nice ass, he thought appreciatively, lifting one brow and looking a little harder. Dani poked him, and he shook his head, remembering that this woman had just awakened him from a much-needed sleep and a pleasantly carnal dream. "Wait until she stands up, Dani."

The woman tugged and pulled and when the box broke apart, she fell backward, landing on that nice behind. From somewhere on her porch, a man hooted with loud laughter and called out, "Want some help?"

Zack fancied he could see some of her curly brown hair standing on end. She all but vibrated with temper, then snarled in a voice reminiscent of an enraged cat, "*Go away,* Conan!"

"But I thought you wanted my help?" came the innocent, taunting reply.

"You," she said back, standing up and dusting herself off with enough force to leave bruises on a less hearty woman, "have done enough."

Zack tried to see the mysterious Conan, but couldn't. Her husband? A boyfriend? What kind of name was Conan anyway?

As the woman gained her feet, Dani said in awe, "She's a giant!"

Chuckling, Zack squeezed her. "She looks as tall as me, doesn't she, honey?"

His daughter nodded, watching the woman unload the box with jerky, angry movements, rather than try to move it again. Dani laid her head on Zack's chest, quietly thinking in that way she sometimes did. Zack rubbed her back, waiting to see what she'd say next.

She shocked him speechless by suddenly leaning forward—leaving it up to him to balance her off-balance weight—and cupping her hand to her mouth, she shouted out the window, "Hello!"

The woman turned, looked up with a hand shading her eyes, searching. She spotted them and her frown was replaced by a bright toothy smile. She waved with as much enthusiasm as she'd used to dust her bottom. "Hello there!"

In his underwear, Zack quickly ducked behind the

curtain. *"Dani,"* he said, ready to muzzle his daughter. "What are you doing?"

She wrinkled her little nose at him. "Jus' being neighborly, like you said I should."

"That was to the old neighbors. We don't even know these people yet."

She wiggled to get down, and when he set her on her feet, she said, "We'll go meet 'em now."

Zack caught her by the back of her cotton nightgown as she started to barrel out of the room. "Hold on, little lady. We have breakfast and chores and washing up to do first, right?"

Again, she wrinkled her nose. "Later."

He almost grinned at her small, sweet hopeful voice—a voice she only used when trying to wrap him around her itty-bitty finger. "Now."

Disgruntled and grumbling under her breath, she trod back to the window and yelled, "I'll be out later!"

The woman laughed. It was a nice rich husky sound, much better than her screaming. "I'll surely still be here."

Zack looked out, feeling as if he'd landed in the twilight zone. Now that his daughter had drawn attention to them—and the neighbors knew they'd been watched—he couldn't very well ignore them.

The man from the porch sauntered into the yard, smiling. Zack blinked with yet another surprise. *Massive* was the only word for him. Built like a large bulldog, he stood a few inches shorter than the woman, but was twice as thick and all muscle. He lifted an arm as stout as a tree trunk and waved.

"I'm Conan Lane," he called out, "and this squawking shrew is Wynonna."

To Zack's amazement and Dani's delight, the woman elbowed Conan hard, making him bend double and wheeze, then she corrected sweetly, "Call me Wynn."

Seeing no hope for it, Zack shouted back, "Zack Grange, and my daughter, Dani."

"Nice to meet you both!" And then to further exasperate him, Wynn said, "Since we're all awake and it's such a beautiful morning, I'll bring over some coffee so we can get acquainted."

Zack stammered, unsure how to deny that audacious imposition, but she'd already turned and hurried into her house, the enormous Conan following her. He frowned down at Dani, who shrugged, grinned, and said, "We better get dressed." And off she dashed, her blanket dragging behind her.

Zack dropped to the side of his bed and scrubbed his hands over his face. He was badly in need of a shave and a long shower. At the moment he had no doubt his eyes were more red than blue. He'd worked twelve grueling hours last night, tended two especially trying emergencies, and he was starved as well as fatigued.

Luckily, this was his day off, which he'd intended to spend shopping with Dani. Because his daughter liked to play hard, and paid no mind at all to the knees of her jeans or the elbows of her shirts, she was desperately in need of new fall clothes.

He did not want to be bothered with outrageous neighbors.

Especially not neighbors who'd awakened him too early and were too damn large. And loud.

Shoving himself off the bed, he determined to get through the next few minutes with as much politeness and forbearance as he could muster.

The doorbell rang not three minutes later. He'd barely had time to pull on jeans and a sweatshirt. He picked up his running shoes, carrying them loosely in his hand. On his way to the door, he peeked in at Dani. She stood there in a T-shirt and blue-flowered panties, surveying her closet with a studious frown.

Zack leaned on her doorframe. "Dress warm, honey."

She nodded, frowned some more, and looked through her clothes. Zack bit back a grin and asked, "Hard decision?"

She was so intent on her choice, she didn't answer.

Because jeans were a given, he said, "How about a sweater?" preferring that over what she might have chosen otherwise—a ratty sweatshirt. He posed it as a suggestion, rather than an instruction, because he knew she liked to make her own decisions—about everything— any time he gave her that option.

She nodded agreement. "Okay. What sweater?"

He walked into the room, reached into her closet and pulled out a soft red sweater with multicolored buttons. "This one is nice," he suggested, trying his best to sound serious and sincere.

She studied the sweater, considering, until the doorbell rang again. Snatching it out of his hand, she pushed at him and said, "Go! Go get the door, Dad!"

Zack laughed as he walked away. His daughter, the social butterfly. Most times, Dani didn't give two cents for how she dressed. She'd pull on the same clothes from the night before if Zack didn't get them out of her room and into the hamper fast enough. But let them have company and she agonized. Not that she wanted to wear dresses. Heaven forbid! And anything other than sneakers or boots repulsed her four-year-old sensibilities.

But she did like color. Lots and lots of color. Often if left to her own devices, she'd clash so horribly it'd make his eyes glaze.

Still sporting a grin, Zack bounded down the stairs and went to the front door. He turned the locks and opened it, wishing he didn't have to do this today. He'd wanted nothing more than to sleep in, then take a long leisurely soak in the hot tub, eat an enormous breakfast, and spend the day with his daughter.

Now he had to be neighborly.

The second the door opened, the woman looked at him and her smile faded. "Oh dear," she said. "We woke you up, didn't we?"

Zack went mute and stared.

Up close, she seemed even taller, and she did indeed look him in the eye. At six feet tall, that didn't happen to him often. His two best friends, Mick and Josh, were both taller, Mick especially, who stood six foot three. But then they were both guys. They were *not* female.

A light breeze ruffled her flyaway hair, which seemed to have been permanently crimped. The color was nice, a soft honey-brown, lighter around her face where the sun had kissed it. Curls sprung out here and there and everywhere, like miniature springs. He doubted such unruly hair could ever be fully contained.

A soft flush colored her skin—high across her cheekbones, over the bridge of her narrow nose and the tip of her chin—either by the warmth of the day, her exertions, or the bright sunshine. Zack suspected the latter.

Sporting a crooked smile, she stared right back at him with the most unusual hazel eyes he'd ever seen. So light they were almost the color of topaz, they were fringed by thick, impossibly dark lashes, especially given the

color of her hair. After a silent moment, her arched brows
lifted and her smile stretched into a full-fledged grin.

Zack caught himself. Good God, he'd been staring
at her as if he'd never seen a woman before. He'd been
staring at her...*with interest.* He shook his head. "What
gave me away?"

"What's that?" She now appeared confused.

"How could you tell that you woke me?"

"Ah. The hair standing on end? The all-night whiskers? Or it could be the bloodshot eyes." She made a
tsking sound. "Have you slept at all?"

He ran a hand through his hair and mumbled, "I
worked pretty late last night," and left it at that. He
wasn't with it enough yet to start rehashing the past
evening's events. He pushed the screen door open and
stepped aside. "Come on in."

She looked behind her. "Conan will be right along.
He's getting some muffins out of the oven. He's a terrific cook."

Conan-the-massive cooked?

The woman held up a carafe. "Fresh coffee. French
vanilla. I hope that's okay?"

He hated flavored coffees. "It's fine," he lied, "but
totally unnecessary."

"It's the very least I can do now that I know I got
you out of bed."

If she hadn't, he thought, perhaps he'd have finished
that sexy dream and not been so edgy now. But as it was,
he couldn't quite seem to get himself together.

She hesitated at the door. "I really am so sorry. This
is my first house and I'm equally stressed and excited
and when I get that way, I unfortunately get—" She
shrugged in apology. "—loud."

Her honesty was both unexpected and appealing. Zack forced a smile. "I understand."

Yet, she still held back. "I don't mean to barge in. If you have some cups, we could sit here on your porch. We'll share one cup of coffee, chat a little, and that's all, I promise. It's a beautiful morning and we are all awake now, right?"

Great. If he kept her and her husband outside, he could probably get rid of them quicker. "Good idea. Have a seat and I'll go get some cups."

Just then, Dani came dashing down the steps. Zack turned, saw her small feet flying, and said softly but sternly, "Slow down."

She skidded to a halt on the second to the bottom step, gave him a quick, offhand, "Sorry," and looked up at the woman as she finished approaching. "Hi."

Wynn's face lit up with her smile, making those golden eyes glow and the color in her cheeks intensify. "Hello there!" Kneeling down in the doorway, she said, "It's so good to meet you." She held out a hand that Dani took with formality. Zack watched in awe. "I hadn't realized I'd have another female for a neighbor. The Realtor only told me that a single man lived here."

"I'm Dani. My mom died," Dani said, "so it's jus' me and Dad."

Given half a chance, Dani would voice anything that came into her mind. Normally he didn't mind, but this time it rankled.

Her sweater was hiked up in the back and the left leg of her jeans had caught on a cotton sock. Zack smoothed the sweater, tugged the jeans into place, and frowned at her hair. His daughter, bless her heart, had the most impossible baby-fine, flyaway blond hair.

Then he glanced at Wynn again and revised his opinion. Dani had difficult hair, but definitely not the worst.

Softly, probably because she realized Dani had touched on a private topic, Wynn said, "Well, I'm very glad to have you for a neighbor, Dani." She glanced up at Zack warily. "And your dad, too, of course."

Zack took his daughter's hand, not about to leave her alone with a virtual stranger, and said, "Wynn, if you'd like to make yourself comfortable, we'll get the mugs and be right out."

Wynn stood again, stretching out that long tall body. Zack's gaze automatically dropped to her legs, but he quickly pulled it back to her face even as a wave of heat snaked through him. She was married, he thought guiltily, and he had no intention of ogling a neighbor anyway.

Rather than looking put out by his quick, intimate perusal, Wynn smiled. "Sounds good," she murmured, her eyes warm. She turned back to the porch, giving Zack a back view of those strong shapely legs and tight bottom, and the screen door fell shut behind her.

Dani stared up at him, but he shook his head, indicating she should be quiet for a moment. When they reached the kitchen, he plunked her onto a chair opposite him and took a moment to pull on his shoes. That accomplished, he looked at his daughter. "Juice?"

"Apple." Dani swung her feet, then tilted her head. "She's not taller than you."

"No, not quite," Zack said, locating a tray beneath the sink and loading it with three mugs, a glass of apple juice and a bowl of cereal for Dani. "It's close, though. She looked me right in the eye, but she had on thick-soled shoes and I was still barefoot."

Dani squirmed. "I want my hair in a ponytail like hers."

He smiled. Maybe a female neighbor, even a very big one with corkscrew hair, wouldn't be a bad thing. Eloise, Dani's sitter during Zack's working hours, was a very kind, gentle and attentive woman. But she was old enough to be Zack's grandmother, with bluish hair and support hose—not a woman to inspire a young girl.

Zack's company was mostly limited to Mick and Josh, and though Josh knew everything there was to know about legal-aged females, he knew next to nothing about four-year-olds. Since Mick had married, Dani got to visit with Delilah now and then, and the two of them had really hit it off, which proved to Zack that Dani needed a woman around more often.

For Dani's sake, he'd decided he needed a wife. But finding someone appropriate was proving to be more difficult than he'd thought, mostly because he had so little time to look.

When he did have time, he didn't run across any suitable women. A wife would need to be domestic, neat, lovable, and she'd have to understand that his daughter came first. Period.

"A ponytail it is," Zack said, forcing his mind away from that problem. He stroked his big rough fingers through Dani's fine hair. "Why don't you go get your brush and a band, and then come out to the porch?"

"Okay." She slid off the chair and ran from the room again. His daughter never walked when she could run. She was never quiet when she could talk or laugh, and she always fought naps right up until she ran out of gas and all but collapsed. She exuded constant energy, and she had an imagination that often left him floored.

She was his life.

Wynn and Conan were arguing again when Zack

opened the screen door. He stalled, uncertain what to do as Wynn poked the bulky bruiser in the chest and threatened his life.

Ignoring most of her diatribe, Conan said, "Ha!" then flicked her earlobe, hard.

Zack's mouth fell open, seeing the physical byplay.

Before he could say anything, Wynn lit up like a live wire, clutching at her ear. "That *hurt!*"

"Well so does your pointy little finger trying to bore holes in my chest."

"Bull." She leaned in to him, nose to nose, and deliberately gave him another, harder prod. "You can't feel anything through that layer of rock and you know it."

Conan rubbed his chest, opened his mouth to say God-only-knew-what, then noticed Zack. He scowled. "You're making a spectacle of yourself in front of your neighbors, Wynonna."

Frozen half in, half out of the door, Zack just stared. Domestic troubles? God, he didn't want to be involved in this.

Wynn rushed forward and took the tray from him. "Just ignore Conan," she said, "he's a bully."

Conan ran both hands through his blond hair, which Zack noticed wasn't the least bit frizzy, and growled. His eyes turned red and his face blue. "Wynonna, I swear I'm gonna—"

He reached for her and Zack, without really thinking, stepped between them. The tray in Wynn's arms wobbled, but she maintained her grip.

"Look," Zack said, not sure if the woman would need any help or not, "this is none of my business, but—"

Wynn rudely pushed her way around him. "You're gonna what?" she taunted Conan. "What else can you do?"

Conan reached for her again, and Zack grabbed him. *"That's enough,"* he roared.

Zack hadn't had enough sleep, he was still disturbed by the calls he'd made the night before, and he had no tolerance for petty bickering.

And he absolutely, positively, would not put up with a man hurting a woman, not even a pesky too-big neighbor woman he barely knew and who looked like she could damn well defend herself.

Silence fell. Conan, with one brow raised, stared at Zack's hand wrapped around his thick wrist. Zack had big hands, but still, his fingers barely touched.

Conan's gaze shifted to Wynn, and he made a wry face. "A gallant in the making?"

Wynn set the tray down and rushed to put herself between the two men, facing Zack. Her fingers spread wide on his chest, pressing, restraining although he could have easily moved her aside and they both knew it. Wedged between the two of them, she was so close to Zack he felt her breath and the heat of her body. He twitched.

Wynn stared into his face with an expression bordering on wonder, patted him, and then said with quiet sincerity, "Thank you, but Conan would never hurt me, Zack. I promise. He just likes to needle."

Conan, still caught in Zack's unrelenting grasp, snorted at that. But he replied easily, "She's right, you know. I might want to swat her every now and again, but I wouldn't hurt her."

Swat her? Zack peered into Wynn's large golden eyes and imagined all kinds of kinky sexual play between the two of them.

He wasn't sure if he was disgusted or intrigued,

and his indecision on the matter was unacceptable. He frowned, feeling very put upon.

Then Conan continued lazily. "Wynn, however, has never shown any such consideration. She's been kicking my ass since we were both in diapers."

Wynn gave Zack an apologetic nod. "It's true. Conan is such a big lug, he's always let me practice up on him."

Conan tugged on his hand, and Zack, feeling numb and rather foolish, and for some damn reason, relieved, released him.

Brother and sister?

"She's so big," Conan continued, "she's always looked older than her age. When she was in ninth grade, college guys were hitting on her! She needed to know how to fight off the cretins. So I've been her personal punching bag for longer than I care to remember."

Still with her hands pressed to Zack's chest, Wynn glanced over her shoulder and smiled. "Not that he feels it," she said to her brother, "regardless of how he carries on." Facing Zack again, she explained, "A steamroller could go over Conan and he's so thick with muscle he wouldn't notice."

Zack inhaled and breathed in the scents of vanilla coffee, fresh blueberry muffins, early morning dew on green grass—and Wynn. She smelled…different. Not sweet. Not exactly spicy. It was more a fresh scent, like a cool fall breeze or the forerunner to a storm. His muscles twitched again.

Damn, but this day was not going at all as planned.

And he could only blame one very big, and somehow very appealing, woman. A woman who was not only his neighbor, but still touching him, still looking at him with a mixture of tenderness, humor, and…hunger.

He'd known tall women, hell, Mick's wife Delilah was tall. But he'd never known such a...*sturdy* woman. Her open hands on his chest were nearly as large as his own. Her shoulders were broad, her bones long. Unlike Delilah, Wynn wasn't delicate.

But she was sexy.

He needed some sleep to be able to deal with the likes of her. And he needed more time.

And most of all, he needed sex, because he knew when he started getting turned on by a loud, pushy amazon, it had been far, far too long.

Chapter 2

Gathering his scattered wits, Zack looked at both Wynn and Conan, then stepped out of Wynn's reach. "I see," he said, for lack of anything better. His brain was all but empty of responses. This had not been a memorable morning.

Wynn fought off a smile, at his expense. "I do appreciate your consideration for my welfare, though."

The way she said it made him feel ten times more foolish. He could see why Conan thought she needed a good swat. At the moment, he wasn't totally averse to the idea himself.

Conan saved the awkward moment by pouring the coffee. The rich aroma of vanilla intensified, but Zack could still smell *her*. She'd been working and her skin was hot, dewy with her exertions.

He growled low in his throat, hating his basic response to her.

Thankfully unaware of the source of his disgruntlement, Conan said, "Sit down, Zack. You look like we've wrung you out already. And I have to tell you, it's only going to get worse."

How in the hell can it get worse? Zack accepted the coffee and seated himself in a padded chair. Conan sat across from him, Wynn on the settee. Mustering a tone of bland inquiry, Zack asked, "How so?" while eyeing the golden brown muffin, bursting with ripe blueberries, which Conan passed his way.

Nodding to his sister, who had reverted back to frowning, Conan explained, "Mom and Dad are moving. They needed somewhere to stay for two weeks and since Wynn just got this place, I convinced them she was a better choice than me." He flashed a wide, unapologetic grin.

Wynn huffed. "Not that I don't love my parents, but when you meet them you'll understand why I'm considering wringing Conan's neck."

Zack didn't want to meet her parents. He hadn't even wanted to meet her. With any luck, from here on out he'd successfully avoid the Lane clan altogether.

"But hey," Conan said, and punched Zack in the shoulder, nearly making him spill the distasteful coffee. "I like it that you wanted to protect her. Knowing she'll have a neighbor looking out for her makes me feel better about her living alone."

Conan had fists like sledgehammers, and not enough sense to temper his blows. The muscle in Zack's shoulder leaped in pain. He refused to show any weakness by rubbing it.

And he refused to become Wynn's protector, though God knew with a smart and loud mouth like hers, she'd likely need a battalion to shield her from retaliation. But before he could find words to express his thoughts, Dani appeared. She hesitated, showing unaccustomed shyness, her soft-bristled brush clutched in one hand, the other on the screen door.

Setting aside his coffee, Zack held out his hand and she skipped to him. He put her on his knee and began brushing her silky hair. "Dani, Conan is Wynn's brother."

Dani leaned close to his ear and whispered loudly enough for the birds in the trees to hear, "What do I call 'em?"

Wynn answered for him. "Well, neighbors can't very well stand on formality, now can they? So, if you don't mind us calling you Dani, you can just call us Wynn and Conan. Deal?"

Dani twisted, stuck out her hand, and said, "Deal."

Conan laughed and enfolded the diminutive fingers with his massive paw. Muscles flexed and rolled along his arm, yet Zack couldn't help but notice that he was very gentle.

After Wynn shook Dani's hand, too, Dani stated, "Your hair looks funny."

"Dani." Her habit of speaking her mind was often humorous, but this wasn't one of those times.

She blinked at her father uncertainly. "It doesn't?"

It did, so what could he say? He settled on, "You know better than to be rude."

Far from insulted, Wynn laughed out loud and shook her head so more corkscrew curls sprang wild. "It feels funny, too. Wanna see?"

Dani looked at Zack for permission, and he could only shrug. Never in his life had he known a woman who behaved as she did, so how was he supposed to know how to deal with her?

Dani reached out, nearly falling off Zack's knee, and put her fingertips to the bouncing curls. She gave a tentative stroke, and then another. Her brow furrowed in concentration. "It's soft." And then to Zack, "Feel it, Daddy."

Zack nearly choked. "Uh, no, Dani…"

Conan must have had a wicked streak, because he taunted, "Ah, go ahead, Zack. Wynonna won't mind."

"Wynonna will loosen your jaw if you don't stop calling me *Wynonna!*"

Dani laughed. Zack was a little bemused to realize his daughter recognized the lack of threat in their repartee while he'd been alarmed by it.

"My name's Daniella, but no one calls me that. 'Cept Dad sometimes when he's mad."

Wynn gave a theatrical gasp. "Your father gets mad at you?" she teased, holding one hand to her chest. "Whatever for? Why, you're such a little angel."

Dani shrugged. "Not all the time. Sometimes I get into mis…mis…"

"Mischief," Zack supplied, "and don't make me sound like an ogre to our new neighbors."

She beamed at him. "He's the best dad in the whole world."

"Much better." Zack smiled and kissed her soft plump cheek. "She has her moments, and if angels can be rowdy and rambunctious, then the description does fit."

Conan laughed, but Wynn gave him another of those tender, intent looks. He frowned and turned away.

"You don't really fight with Conan," Dani told Wynn, as if Wynn might not be aware of that fact herself.

"I would never take a chance on hurting him," Wynn boasted. Then, pretending to share a confidence, she added, "Besides, he's my brother and I love him."

Dani sat back against her father's chest and crossed her arms. "I want a brother."

Zack choked.

Conan handed him a napkin, again staving off the awkward moment. "If you want to hear the real joke about Wynn's hair," Conan said, "then you should know that our father is a coiffeur."

"What's that?" Dani asked.

"A coiffeur," Wynn explained, "is just another word for a hairdresser."

Again and again, they took him by surprise, Zack thought. "That's…interesting," he remarked, and gulped down more of the awful vanilla coffee.

Wynn chuckled. "The fact that I won't let him touch my hair makes him crazy. Which is why I won't let him touch it, of course. Every time he sees me, he wails like he's in pain."

"And when she says wails, she means wails." Conan sipped his own coffee before setting the cup aside. "My dad is likely to be the only flaming heterosexual you'll ever meet."

Zack stared. *Flaming heterosexual?* Did these two know any normal or mundane conversational tidbits? Couldn't they go on about the weather or something? Together, they were the strangest people he'd ever met so he had no doubt the parents had to be beyond odd as well. He kept silent.

His daughter did not.

"Does that mean hairdresser, too?" Dani asked.

Wynn quickly swallowed her bite of muffin. "No, Dani, that means he likes to dress in silk and lots of gold chains and he has this enormous diamond earring."

Oh Lord, Zack thought, and wished he could escape.

"Our mother, on the other hand, is the original hippie. She's into all things natural and doesn't wear any jewelry at all except for a plain wedding band."

"But," Conan interjected, casting a sly look at Wynn, "she loves my father enough to let him keep her hair trimmed."

"Daddy would have a heart attack if I asked him to do my hair now. You know that. Besides, he likes to have something to gripe at me about."

"Does your mom's hair look like yours?" Zack heard himself ask, curious despite himself.

"Heavens no! I got my hair from some long-deceased ancestor."

Conan leaned forward in a conspiratorial manner. "And believe me, we're all beyond grateful that he is long deceased."

Wynn shoved at him. "My father's hair is brown and sleek, and my mother's hair is blond like Conan's, but longer—all the way to her waist."

Dreading the answer, Zack asked, "When are they supposed to join you?"

"Next week," she mumbled, sounding despondent and resigned. "And I was so looking forward to living on my own."

"You lived at home until now?" As Zack asked that, he finished brushing the tangles from Dani's hair, smoothed it back and expertly wrapped the covered band around it, securing it in place. She bobbed her head a bit, making the ponytail bounce, then smiled and kissed him again. Zack gave her an affectionate squeeze—and noticed the silly smiles on his neighbors' faces.

He now felt conspicuous, all because he'd fixed his daughter's hair. It was no big deal, nothing elaborate, just a ponytail. And it wasn't like there was someone else to do it. Anything his daughter needed, he supplied. Except female company, but he was working on that.

"No," Wynn said, still looking too soft and female and approving, which for her was a gross contradiction. The contrast…intrigued him.

No, it did not!

"At twenty-eight," she continued, oblivious to his inner turmoil on her femaleness, "I've been out of the house for a while. But I had two roommates, and they were both awful slobs. I'm sort of what you'd call…"

"Fanatical," Conan supplied, toasting her with his coffee cup. "She likes to keep an immaculate, organized house. Drives me crazy."

"Dad's fatical, too," Dani told them. "Mick and Josh tell him he'll make a good husband for some lucky woman some day."

"Is that right?" Amused, Conan eyed Zack.

Wynn drank more coffee, cleared her throat as if embarrassed, and finally put her cup aside. "Well, I can't stand having things thrown just anywhere. Busy people need to be organized."

Since Zack felt the same way, he could empathize with her. Other than Dani's toys, which he left scattered around so Dani wouldn't feel stifled, he liked to have a place for everything and everything in its place. He kept the house clean and once a month a service came to do a more thorough job, getting the baseboards and the ceiling and the air ducts—all the places he seldom had time to tend to.

The idea that they might have something in common was a little alarming, so he didn't belabor the point.

Dani slid off his lap to sit beside Wynn. She situated herself in the exact same pose as the neighbor, shoulders back, spine straight, head tilted just so. Except that Dani's legs hanging over the edge of the padded settee didn't even come close to touching the ground, while Wynn's not only touched, they folded so sharply her knees were practically in her face. Zack shook his head. He'd never seen legs so long. Or so nicely shaped.

Dani gave Wynn a toothy grin, then picked up her bowl of cereal and dug in.

"Conan falls into the slob category." Wynn handed Dani a napkin almost without thought. Zack wondered if she was around children often, then decided it didn't matter to him one iota. "Which is probably why my folks decided to spend their two weeks with me. It's far too easy to get lost in his cluttered apartment. He keeps newspapers around for weeks, and there's always something rotting in his refrigerator."

Zack couldn't stop his shudder of revulsion. Watching him, Wynn nodded in perfect accord. "It's disgusting," she confirmed.

To change the subject, Conan asked, "What do you do for a living, Zack?"

Both he and his sister stared at Zack with expectant expressions.

Dani answered for him, saying around a mouthful of cereal and milk, "He saves peoples. He's a hero."

Settling back in her seat, Wynn slowly nodded. "Mmmm. I can see that." She eyed Zack up and down…

and up again, letting her gaze linger here and there. He
felt that interested gaze like a lick of fire and wanted
to groan.

"Your dad," she said, "has all the right makings of a
hero. Big, muscular, handsome and kind." And then with
an impish, very intimate and inviting smile, "I'm glad
he's my neighbor."

It was the most curious sensation, Wynn thought,
as if her heart had started to boil the second she'd seen
him. Then, when he'd held his daughter on his knee and
patiently brushed her hair, her heart outright melted.
She'd never felt anything like it. She'd never seen anyone like him.

And she was all but bowled over with a mixed jumble
of emotions.

Dani herself caused part of the effect; Wynn couldn't
imagine a more adorable little girl than the one sitting
primly beside her, milk on her upper lip and her riotous
hair neatly contained in a bouncy ponytail. The child
had an impish demeanor that proved she was both smart
and precocious.

Most of the effect, though, came from Zack Grange.
Wowza. She hadn't believed one man could carry such
a sizzling emotional and physical wallop, but Zack did.
He stood the smallest bit taller than she, maybe an inch
at most. Which meant he must stand a flat six feet. Her
height, however, apparently didn't distress him.

No, before he'd recalled himself, Zack had looked at
her with male appreciation, and she liked it. A lot.

She wished she hadn't worn the bulky sweatshirt with
the stretched out neckline and the hem that hung midway

down her shorts. Her upper body was as toned as the rest of her, and she wondered how he'd look at her there.

When she'd first dressed, the early morning air had carried a nip, but she was nowhere near cool now. In fact, she felt a little overheated. Maybe downright hot.

She guessed Zack to be around thirty, given the age of his daughter and his overall physique. It was his physique that had her doing more than her fair share of ogling. The man was put together just fine.

He wasn't a muscle-bound behemoth like her brother, but lean and toned, with an obvious strength that was partly innate male, partly specialized training. His chest was wide, his shoulders wider. He had narrow hips, long straight legs and large, lean hands and feet. There was no fat on his middle, no slouch in his stance.

Light brown hair, bone straight and disheveled from being roused out of bed, complemented gentle, intense blue eyes. His brows and beard stubble were darker, his jaw hard and stubborn.

But it was when he looked at his daughter that his gorgeous blue eyes held the most impact.

Only seconds after seeing Zack, she'd wanted him. The man exuded raw sexuality tempered with gentleness and caring. A highly potent combination.

Being around him felt…comfortable, in a dozen different ways.

With an acquaintance not quite an hour long, she knew enough to respect him. She'd already learned that he loved his daughter, was a natural defender of women, and showed politeness even when rude neighbors pulled him from a much-needed sleep.

She sighed, earning a strange look from both men and Dani.

"Sorry," she mumbled, wishing she could crawl over onto his lap now that Dani was no longer in it. But a big hulking girl like herself didn't sit in laps. In fact, she couldn't remember the last time a man had held her. "So what title applies to your heroic deeds, Zack?"

He rubbed his hands over his tired eyes while explaining. "I'm an EMT paramedic. Dani thinks Mick, Josh and I are all heroes. Actually, I believe she has Mick's wife, Delilah, in that category now, too."

"They're heroes," Dani insisted with a child's love and devotion.

And Zack responded, "Don't talk with your mouth full, sweetheart."

"So you drive an ambulance, huh?" Conan leaned forward with interest. "Who do you work for?"

"The fire department. Josh is a fireman there. We've known each other forever."

Wynn tipped her head, recalling the other name he had mentioned. "And Mick? What does he do?"

"Mick is a cop. His wife, Delilah Piper-slash-Dawson is a—"

"Novelist!" Conan finished for him, surging to the edge of his seat with excitement. "Are you kidding me? You know Delilah Piper?"

"Don't forget the 'slash-Dawson' part or Mick will have your head." Zack grinned, showing even white teeth and a dimple in his left cheek. *A dimple!* Wynn's melting heart thumped so hard, she nearly missed the rest of Zack's explanation. "Since she and Mick married, he's been understanding about her name already being well known. He's proud of her career, but insistent that those of us who are familiar remember she's a married woman now."

"Possessive, is he?" Wynn asked.

And Conan said, "Are you nuts? She's *Delilah Piper*." He snorted. "I'd be possessive, too."

"You always are," Wynn said with a shake of her head. Her brother drove his present girlfriend crazy with his possessive, overbearing ways.

"I take it you're a fan?" Zack asked.

"I just finished her newest. That scene at the river was incredible."

"I can get your books signed for you if you want."

Wynn watched in disgust as her muscle-bound brother looked ready to get up and dance a jig. She glanced at Dani, and they shared a woman-to-woman smile. Dani even shook her head and rolled her big blue eyes, causing Wynn to chuckle.

While the men continued to work out the details of the books, Wynn turned to Dani. "So you're close to Josh and Mick and Delilah?"

"She wants to be called Del, only Mick won't. I think it's jus' to tease her."

"And Mick and Josh?"

"They're fun. Josh has lots of ladies, but he says none of 'em are prettier than me so he can't marry 'em."

"Smart man."

"Yeah." She nodded with a look of pity for the poor unwed Josh and the not-pretty-enough women. "Dad wants to get married, too, but he's gotta find a wife first." Dani scrunched up her face, studying Wynn.

Wynn squirmed under such close scrutiny. *From a child!* Luckily, Dani whispered to her father that she had to go in to the potty. After she went in, Zack returned to his conversation about Del Piper, keeping Conan enthralled.

Wynn looked at Zack. So, he wanted a wife, huh? Or was that something Dani had misconstrued?

How in the world was it that he hadn't already remarried? A man like Zack probably had women by the dozens. But then…she rethought that and shook her head at herself. Zack was very dedicated to his daughter, and she knew EMTs worked long shifts, sometimes up to sixty hours a week. That wouldn't leave him much time for dating, much less cultivating a lasting relationship.

He must have felt her gaze, for he glanced at her while Conan waxed poetic about Ms. Piper's remarkable talent. Their gazes met and held and Zack frowned. He glanced away, then back again. Wynn blinked at him, feeling soft and hot and excited.

She stared, knew she stared, and couldn't seem to help herself. Zack shifted, glaring at her then crossing one ankle over a knee.

He had thick ankles. And wrists. And long fingers and…one thought led to another and she couldn't keep herself from peeking at his lap. His jeans were old and faded and appeared very soft. They cupped him lovingly, outlining a bulge that proved most noticeable, even without him being aroused.

Her heart dropped into her stomach and began jumping erratically. Her palms tingled, craving to touch him, to weigh him in her hands—

"Stop that!"

She blinked hard and looked up at him. Conan went silent, confused. A red flush crept up Zack's neck. He cleared his throat and stood.

"The coffee and muffins were great. Thanks."

As dismissals went, it wasn't the least bit subtle, but Conan didn't seem to find anything amiss. He shook

Zack's hand, saying, "I'll bring the books to you soon, if you're sure she won't mind signing them."

"Delilah's great. She won't mind." Zack didn't look at Wynn at all, and she had the feeling his avoidance was deliberate. But then, he'd caught her staring at his crotch, all but salivating.

She blushed. She'd known the man one hour, and already she'd behaved like a shameless hussy. Or worse, like a desperate spinster.

Oh God! Maybe that was how he saw her. After all, she was twenty-eight and single. The only male helping her move in was her brother; no fiancé, not even a boyfriend. He couldn't know that it was by choice, because she hadn't yet met a guy who…made her blood sing, not like he did.

Damn, damn, damn.

Not being of a shy or withdrawn nature, she stuck out her hand, daring him to continue ignoring her. She wouldn't allow it.

His jaw locked. With a false smile pinned to his tired face, he took her hand. His touch, his look, was beyond impersonal, and she hated it. "Welcome to the neighborhood, Wynn."

"Thanks." He tried to take his hand back, but she held on. "I'm sure we'll be seeing each other again."

After she said it, she winced. It sounded like a threat! Then she realized he was trying to tug his hand free and here she was, doing the macho "grip" thing. Good God, she was making things worse by the second.

She turned him loose and put her hands in her pockets so she wouldn't be tempted to get hold of him again. Conan gathered up the carafe and the muffin plate.

Feeling like an idiot, she said, "Well, thanks again. And really, I am sorry we woke you."

Dani bounded back outside, then skidded to a disappointed halt. "You can't leave."

Zack put his hand on the top of her silky head. "I'm sure Wynn wants to finish unpacking, sweetheart. And you and I are going shopping."

Dani groaned, wilted, all in all acting like a child being sent to the woodshed.

Barely hiding a smile, Zack said, "None of that. We'll have lunch out and it'll be fine. You'll see."

Conan gave a crooked grin. "I gather she doesn't like shopping?"

"Not for clothes, no. But she's about worn out everything warm she has."

"Sounds like Wynn. She hates shopping, too."

Dani's eyes widened. "You do?"

Wynn shrugged. "I know it's supposed to be a girl thing, but I've never understood it. Thank goodness I don't need a lot of clothes."

Conan leaned forward. "She used to outgrow her wardrobe daily, but we're hoping she's done growing by now."

Wynn elbowed him, caught Zack's look of disapproval, and wanted to throttle her brother. Zack didn't approve of their physical sparring, and she'd meant to cease it in front of him. But Conan had a way of egging her on. "I quit growing ten years ago. And with my job, casual clothes are perfect."

"What do you do?" Zack asked, then looked like he wanted to bite his tongue off.

"I'm a physical therapist. I work two days a week at the high school, two days a week at the college." She nodded toward her brother. "Conan owns a gym and I sometimes help out there, too, when the bodybuilders overdo it."

Zack looked dubious, but nodded. He said to Conan, again ignoring her, "A gym, huh?"

"Small, but it's all mine and I'm a good trainer. I do a lot of private stuff." He winked. "The clientele is as much female as male."

Bristling at Zack's disregard and her brother's caveman attitude, Wynn said, "Rachael will get you if she hears that particular leer in your tone."

Conan shrugged, unconcerned with the warning. "Rachael is my current girlfriend, not my wife. And speaking of Rachael, I should get going." He gave one last wave and headed off.

Wynn gazed after him, watching him go down the steps and then around the porch toward her new house. She sighed. "Me, too. I've got a lot of unpacking to do yet." She turned to Zack, who appeared anxious to finish the goodbyes. "Being as we're neighbors," she thought to say, "feel free to borrow if you ever need to. You know, the proverbial cup of sugar or whatever."

"Thanks." Zack's tone was dry. "I'll keep that in mind. And thanks for the coffee and muffins. They were…great."

With nothing left to say, Wynn stepped off the porch with a lagging step. "Okay, well…bye."

"Goodbye, Wynn."

She glanced over her shoulder to see Zack escaping into his house. He closed the door behind him, and she heard the lock click. Well, hell. His goodbye had sounded entirely too final.

That just wouldn't do. She wanted him. One way or another.

Chapter 3

"Look, dad!"

Zack pulled the car into the driveway and put it in Park. He didn't want to look. Because of the direction Dani pointed, he already knew what—or rather who—he'd see. And he wanted to keep her out of his mind, not dwell on her further. He'd done enough dwelling.

All day long, his mind had wandered to her, and he didn't like it. Even while buying miniature jeans with butterflies sewn on the pockets, and lace-up brown boots meant for a boy that had his daughter begging for them, he'd thought of Wynn. While hauling armloads of shopping bags filled with pastel sweatshirts and soft sweaters and long-sleeved T-shirts, he'd remembered the way Wynn had stared at him—*where she'd stared at him*—and he'd been distracted.

Not just distracted, but edgy with a sort of vague arousal.

Well, not really vague, either. More like…acute.

Damn, damn, damn.

He'd been forced to fight himself all day. And all that did was add to his exhaustion and detract from the pleasure he usually enjoyed while spending special time with Dani.

He'd pictured Wynn in his mind as they ate lunch in the food court, and he'd missed most of the matinee movie because his brain not only conjured what had already transpired, but what might yet come if he were to be friendlier to her.

And that wouldn't do! She was a neighbor living right behind him, so anything casual, *like hot, gritty, satisfying sex,* was out of the question. And anything less casual, like friendship, would only make him want the sex more.

Wynn came nowhere near meeting his requirements for involvement, so it'd be best if he stayed clear of her altogether.

"Dad, *look.*"

Dani, with her insistent, squeaky voice, gave him little choice. Zack glanced up to where she pointed, even as he said, "We need to get all these clothes put away…" His words died as he took in the sight of Wynn, now wearing a soft beige halter top, struggling with a long flat box. His driveway was at the side of his house, leading to an attached garage, which gave him a clear view of her house. Her yard was now empty of the packing boxes; it was the huge department store box that held her attention. Zack couldn't see the picture on the box to determine what she'd bought, but then, he wasn't exactly focused on the box.

Beneath the hot early-evening sun, Wynn's broad, toned shoulders looked dewy with perspiration and flexed with feminine muscles. Her belly... He swallowed hard. Her belly was flat, taut with her straining efforts, her waist lean and supple, dipping and curving. She looked sexy and healthy and strong and so utterly female his muscles cramped.

The effect of those long legs had nearly been his undoing that morning. Now seeing her upper parts more bare than covered was enough to make him sweat along with her. He just adored female bellies, and hers was especially enticing.

He felt Dani's hand on his arm and managed to wipe away the gleam of lust before looking down at her.

"You should help her," Dani declared.

Oh, no. Zack had no intention of getting anywhere near Wynn. He shook his head and finished undoing Dani's car seat. By age, Dani was old enough to forego the special seat, but by size... His daughter was so petite it'd probably be another year before he felt comfortable with only a seat belt for her protection. "We've got our own work to do, Dani."

But no sooner did he have his daughter free from the seat than she opened the car door and slithered out. "Hello, Wynn!" She waved both arms, drawing the neighbor's attention.

Wynn stopped struggling with the box and looked up. She wiped a forearm across her brow, squinted in their direction, then broke out in a smile. Even from the distance, Zack could see the open welcome in that smile.

He cursed, but silently.

Cutting across the yards, Wynn headed toward them.

He wanted to groan. He wanted to ignore her and go inside.

He wanted sex, damn it. With her.

No.

"Hey, you two!" She stopped by Dani's side of the car, hands on her hips, legs braced apart. "How'd the shopping go?"

Dani tipped her head way back to grin up at Wynn. "We bought lots of stuff. And we saw a movie, too."

Wynn automatically went to her knees. Zack remembered her doing that earlier, too, when she'd spoken with Dani. Was it an allowance she made for her height? A man wouldn't be expected to do that, but a woman?

Or did she just like kids enough that she wanted to greet them on an eye level?

"A whole new wardrobe, huh? Terrific." She glanced up at Zack. Her hazel eyes looked warm and welcoming, even intimate, at least to his overeager imagination. "Got it all taken care of?" she asked.

He cleared his throat. His brain was already in sexual overdrive, his body too long deprived, and now Wynn got on her knees in front of him. Her face, her beautiful mouth, were level with... No. It was too much.

Zack turned away and began yanking bags out of the car. "She should be all set for fall."

"I went shopping, too," Wynn told him, her voice now sounding confused by his dismissal. "I bought a hammock for the backyard."

Zack froze with his arms loaded down. Slowly he turned to face her. "A hammock?" Surely she didn't expect to lounge around in a hammock. Not where he could see her? "Where do you intend to put it?"

She pointed. "Those are the only two trees big enough

and close enough together to work. I always wanted a hammock, almost as much as I wanted my own house. After I finished unloading boxes, I couldn't resist. This weather is perfect for lying around outside and reading or napping."

A thousand questions went winging through his mind, but he heard himself ask, "You went shopping in *that?*" The way he was staring at her halter, which looked far too enticing molded over soft, heavy breasts that were in perfect proportion to the rest of her big body, he knew she knew just what he meant.

Then when he realized what had come out of his unruly mouth, and how incredibly possessive he'd sounded, he quickly added, "You're talking about in *my* trees?" Both yards had an abundance of shade, but the trees she'd pointed at were the ones edging his property.

She'd be right there, visible to him, flaunting herself to him, wearing on his determination. He couldn't handle it. He'd never had a problem with temptation before, but he'd never met Wynn before, either.

She blinked those awesome hazel eyes at him, and even that seemed provocative, deliberate. Hell, her breathing seemed designed to drive him nuts.

Her expression intent, watchful, she came to her feet. He didn't mean to, but his gaze switched to her legs, then quickly lifted back to her belly. She wasn't overly muscular there, not in the least mannish, just very smooth and lithe and softly rounded just as a woman should be.

His heart punched into his ribs.

Hands on her naked waist, one hip cocked out enticingly, she waited for his gaze to finally rise up to hers. It took him far too long to get there, but then, she had a lot of skin showing.

When their eyes met, Wynn smiled, but there was nothing friendly in the tilt of her lips or the narrowing of her eyes. "I changed when I got home," she informed him, "before getting the box out of the car. And the trees are actually mine. I specifically asked before buying the house. The Realtor checked the property line just to be sure."

Zack wanted to howl. He wanted to tell her that he didn't give a damn about the trees or whom they belonged to. He wanted to put his daughter down for a nap, then drag his neighbor off to bed—or to the floor or the ground or against one of those stupid trees...

He managed his own strained smile. "I see."

Dani, not understanding the sudden tension between the adults, reached up to tug on the hem of Wynn's shorts. "We got pizza for dinner."

Wynn's smile was genuine when she looked at his daughter. "Sounds like you've had a wonderful day." She ruffled Dani's hair, then saluted Zack. "I better get back to work. I want to get the hammock set up."

"You can eat with us!"

Zack cursed softly at his daughter's invitation, but not softly enough. Wynn heard.

Even though her chin lifted and her eyes were direct, she looked hurt. And that hurt *him*. Damn it, he didn't want to insult her, but neither did he want to be further forced into her company.

"Thanks, sweetie," Wynn said to Dani though she continued to look at Zack, "but I've got too much to do."

"Don't you like pizza?" Dani asked, stubborn to the core and always determined to get her own way.

"I do, but it's been a busy day, and I'm not done yet. Maybe another time, okay?"

Wynn turned away and almost stumbled. For the first

time, Zack noticed the weariness in her long limbs, the slight droop to those surprisingly wide, proud shoulders.

Suspicion bloomed, with it annoyance. Using the same tone that always worked for his daughter, Zack uttered, "Wynn."

She paused, turned to face him with one brow raised.

He stared at her face and noticed the exhaustion. Damn it. "When did you eat last?"

"What?" She couldn't have looked more confused by his inquiry. Beside him, Dani all but jiggled with excitement. She knew her father too well and knew he'd just made up his mind.

"Did you have lunch?" Zack demanded, and got a blank expression. He sighed. "Have you eaten anything since the muffins and coffee this morning?"

Rather than answer him, Wynn replied, "I appreciate your concern, Zack, but I'm sure you've got more important things to do than keep track of my meals." Again, she turned away.

He should just let her go, Zack thought, watching her leave and doing his best to keep his gaze off her ample and well-shaped rear end. But his daughter watched him with a look she'd probably picked up from him, one that showed extreme disappointment in his behavior. Dani no doubt expected him to rectify his bad manners, and he knew he should. Even with the womanly sway to her hips, Wynn looked ready to drop, her feet dragging.

She'd been neighborly and friendly and he'd been a surly jerk. All because he hadn't had a woman in too long and she appealed to him on some insane yet basic level. That couldn't be blamed on her.

Zack bent low and said to Dani, "Start carrying the bags up to the porch and I'll be right back."

With a severe look, Dani ordered, "Talk her into eatin' with us."

He sighed. "I'll try."

Dani pushed against him. "Go! Before she's all the way home."

Wynn had nearly made it before Zack reached her. She had to have heard his approach, but she ignored him. He caught her arm and turned her around to face him. "Wait a minute."

Seeing he was alone, she barked, *"What now?"*

He couldn't help it. He smiled, then actually laughed. "Without Dani listening, I get the full brunt of your temper? Is that it?"

"Don't kid yourself." She looked furious and still hurt. Pushing her wild hair out of her face, she sneered, "If you had my full temper, you'd be flat on your back right now."

Her threat brought with it an image of him on his back, her over him, riding him slow and deep. Her legs were so long and so strong he had no doubt her endurance would be endless, mind-blowing. He glanced down at her breasts, thinly covered by the soft material of the halter. Without his mind's permission, he imagined them naked, her nipples puckered, begging for his fingers, his mouth. Her chest glistened from the heat, her skin was radiant and so very soft looking.

No words came, no reply, but she must have read his mind because she drew back and her anger melted away. "I didn't mean that," she whispered in a shaky voice.

He couldn't stop himself from asking, "Mean what?"

She hesitated, their gazes locked, then she shrugged with a blatant challenge. "Sex. That's what you were thinking. Though I suppose you'll deny it now."

Zack rubbed his face. "No, I won't deny it." His neck

and shoulders were still sore from the night before, when he'd dealt with two very unusual crises, and now his body throbbed with sexual tension. "Look, Wynn…"

"Hey, I understand. Dani is a sweetheart, but kids have a way of speaking out of turn. No harm done, and I really do have plenty more work to do."

He dismissed what she said to ask, "You've been working all day, haven't you? I bet you haven't eaten at all except for that muffin at dawn."

"It wasn't exactly dawn—"

"Close enough."

"—and my eating habits aren't your concern."

Why did he have to have the most frustrating woman in creation move in behind him? Why did he have to find her so appealing that even his teeth were aroused? He was tired, achy, sexually frustrated, and now he had to deal with this.

Knowing Dani would only show so much patience before she decided to come help him out, he admitted, "I want you. That's why I was rude."

Those golden eyes opened so wide, she looked comical. He heard her swallow. Her mouth opened, but nothing came out.

Zack looked toward the trees where she planned to hang her hammock. "Between Dani and work, I don't get a lot of chances to date and it's been a long time—too damn long—since I've been with a woman. I didn't get enough sleep last night or I'd probably show better restraint today, but I'm running on four hours tops, and all my understanding and restraint is saved up for my daughter."

She said, "Oh."

"I don't want *you* to worry that I'm going to come on to you—"

"I'm not worried," she rushed to assure him.

"—because I have no intention of doing that."

She said, "Oh," again. This time with regret, if his tired ears didn't deceive him.

"Yeah, oh." He shook his head. "Come and eat with us, then I'll help you get that box to the backyard and from there we can be sociable, but not overly friendly. Okay?"

"Not overly friendly," she repeated, "because you don't want to want me?"

"That's right." Talking about it wasn't helping. He felt like an ass, more so with every word that left his mouth. "It wouldn't be a good idea what with us being neighbors and everything."

"I see."

She looked perplexed. Zack sighed again and looked around to see his daughter watching intently, arms crossed and foot tapping. He turned back to Wynn. "You understand, surely. Being neighbors is one thing. But it could get awkward if we took it any further than that."

She nodded. "Awkward."

His eyes narrowed at her patronizing tone. "That's right. Relationships have a way of complicating things, especially if they don't work out, and since I'm not looking to get involved—"

"It couldn't work out?" She smiled. "Well, you got me there."

What in the world did she have to smile about? *He* wasn't amused. In fact, he was getting close to annoyed. "We'd still be living next door to each other."

"I'm sure not planning on moving!"

"And then we'd both—"

"Feel awkward." She gave a sage nod. "I see your point."

Zack ground his teeth. "Will you join us for pizza or not?"

She licked her lips and tilted her head. "Can I clarify something first?"

"Make it quick. Dani will be on us any minute now."

"I'm standing here all sweaty and hot and my hair looks worse than usual and yet…you say I'm turning you on?"

Zack wanted to throttle her. Not wanting to hurt her feelings, he'd tried being honest with her, and now she felt free to provoke him.

She did look hot and sweaty—like she'd just been making love most vigorously. He stiffened his resolve. "Let's not belabor the point, okay?"

"Okay." She searched his face. "I just wanted to be sure."

Together they started back toward Dani. Zack could feel the heat of Wynn at his side, could smell the intensified scent of sun-kissed feminine skin, of shampoo and lotion and woman.

"How long's it been?" she asked with unparalleled nonchalance, as if that wasn't the most personal topic around.

Of course, he'd brought it up. He didn't look at her. "Long enough."

"For me, too." She smiled toward Dani and waved. "Although I don't think that's why you turn me on." She glanced at him, her long lashes at half-mast, her lips slightly curled. She leaned closer and breathed into his ear, "I think it's your gorgeous bod that's doing the trick."

Zack stumbled over his own feet, which left him standing behind Wynn. She walked over to his yard, took Dani's hand, and together they marched around front to the porch. He heard Dani say, "I can show you my new clothes!"

And Wynn replied happily, "Right after we eat. I'm starved."

Wynn finished off her fourth slice of pizza and sighed. She hadn't realized she was so hungry until she'd taken the first bite. Then she'd had to be careful not to make a glutton of herself. "That was heavenly. Thank you."

Zack just grunted, but Dani said, "You ate as much as Dad."

"Not true! He had one piece more than me." Then, eyeing Zack, she added, "But he has a lot more muscle so he naturally needs more to eat."

Zack choked on the drink of cola he'd just taken, and slanted her an evil look. It was all she could do not to laugh.

He wanted her.

He didn't want to want her, but he did. That was a good start. She could work with that.

On her end, she was crazy-nuts about him already. Not only was the man handsome and well built, but he had a soft streak for his daughter, an outrageous honesty, and his house was spotless. She'd never known a bachelor who enjoyed cleanliness as much as she did.

"Your house is set up different from mine." She looked around, admiring the orderliness of it.

Zack lounged back in his seat. "It's basically the same, I just had a few walls taken out to open things up."

She'd have done the same if she could afford it, but for now, having her own home more than satisfied her. "It's bigger, too."

He shrugged. "Not by that much. I added on to the dining room when I got the hot tub, and had the patio doors put in."

Wynn had noticed the large hot tub right away. It sat outside his dining room, to the left of his kitchen at the edge of the patio, and was partially shielded by a privacy fence.

The sliding doors really made the dining room bigger and brighter. Her house only had the one kitchen door that opened to the side yard. Wynn had noticed that from Zack's kitchen or his patio doors, he could look at the entire side view of her house, and see into her front and backyard. The only thing that would obstruct his view were the trees.

This topic didn't have him grinding his teeth, so she pursued it. "The landscaping in the back is gorgeous." He had as many mature trees as she had, with one especially large tree close to the house. Long branches reached over the roof and shaded the kitchen from the afternoon sun. Zack had hung a swing from one of those sturdy branches for Dani.

Around the patio, he had a lot of lush ground cover and shade-loving flowers bright with color. It took a remarkable man to plant flowers, but then she'd already made that assessment about him.

"Thank you. I needed the covered deck so we could get to the tub in the winter without plodding through the snow."

"You use it when it's cold?" Imagining Zack mostly naked and wet made her tongue stick to the roof of her mouth. It'd be great if he offered to share, but she wouldn't hold her breath.

He shrugged. "Off and on all year."

Wynn cleared her throat and steered her mind to safer imaginings. "I like the way you've decorated. It's nice and casual and comfortable." Everything was done in mellow pine with shades of cream and greens. There were a few plants, lots of pictures of Dani, and a couple of photos she assumed to be of his deceased wife. The woman was pretty, fair like Dani, but with longer hair. She looked very young, and Wynn made a point of not looking at the photos too long, despite her curiosity; she didn't want to dredge up bad memories for Zack. When she asked him about his wife, it would be without Dani listening.

"Can Wynn and me be excused now?"

Zack said, "May Wynn and I. And yes, you may. Wash your hands first, though."

Dani ran to the sink, used the three-step stool in front of it, and turned on the water. Over her shoulder, she said to Wynn, "My stuff's in my room."

Wynn watched Zack push back his chair. He didn't quite look at her. "I'll go carry that box to the backyard for you while Dani shows you her new clothes." He paused beside Dani, bent and kissed the top of her head. "I'll be right back, okay?"

She nodded. "Okay."

He went out the kitchen door and was gone before Wynn could agree or disagree.

When Dani dragged Wynn upstairs, she got a peek at the rest of his house. There wasn't a speck of dust anywhere. Not that she was looking for dust, but the complete and total lack of it was evident, and impressive.

Everything was neat and orderly, except for Dani's toys scattered here and there. She noticed two pine chests in the family room, one opened to reveal an assortment of dolls and games inside. The top of a desk was littered with crayons and construction paper and safety scissors.

She passed Zack's bedroom at the top of the stairs and, hoping Dani wouldn't notice, she peered in. More polished, heavy pine furniture filled the moderate size room. The bed was made up with a rich, dark-brown down comforter. A slight breeze wafted in through the open window, through which Wynn could just see Zack, in the corner of her yard, the large box hefted onto his shoulder.

They were of a similar height, but the difference in their strength was notable, and arousing. The box had been heavy and cumbersome to her, yet Zack handled it as if it weighed no more than a sack of flour.

She watched him for a long moment before it dawned on her that if she could see him now, he could see her... anytime she was in the yard.

She asked Dani, "Is this where you and your dad were when we first said hello, today?"

"Yeah, 'cept Dad was still in his underwear then 'cuz he'd just woke up."

"I see." Boy, did she see. Not wanting to give away her interest by lingering, she allowed Dani to hustle her along to her room. This time the furniture was white, with a pale yellow spread and yellow-striped wallpaper on the bottom half of the wall, topped by a white chair rail. An enormous corkboard hung behind the bed, filled to overflowing with pictures Dani had drawn.

With Dani's bedroom on the same side of the house as Zack's, Wynn was tempted to peek out the window again. Instead, she concentrated on the multitude of bags tossed onto Dani's bed.

When Dani began pulling out the clothes, Wynn

couldn't help but laugh. Other than small detailing here and there, the clothes could have been for a boy. No frills for Dani, evidently. Wynn approved.

She and Dani spent a good fifteen minutes looking at everything, paying special attention to a tiny pair of rugged lace-up brown boots that would look adorable on Dani's small feet.

Wynn commented on Dani's obvious artistic talent, after which Dani determined to draw Wynn a picture. Since she didn't want Wynn to watch, Wynn headed back downstairs. She found Zack in the kitchen, cleaning up the remains of their dinner. She picked up two glasses and carried them to the dishwasher. "I was going to help you with this."

"No need." He moved around her to the table and spent an inordinate amount of time crushing the pizza box.

It amused Wynn that he wouldn't look at her. She leaned back against the sink, her hands propped on the counter at either side of her hips. "It's the least I could do after imposing on you. Twice."

Again, he moved around her to the garage door. He put the garbage in a can, secured the lid, and came back in. "You were invited."

"Grudgingly."

Zack paused, rubbed the back of his neck, flexed as if trying to rid himself of tension. When he looked at her, his eyes were a very dark blue. "I explained that, Wynn."

"Indeed you did." She crossed her ankles and watched his gaze flicker toward her legs and back again. How odd for him to be attracted to her while she was such a wreck. Odd, but exciting. "About the hammock…"

"What about it?"

"If you don't want it in the trees, I can return it. We're neighbors and the last thing I want to do is cause any hard feelings. I realize the trees are almost smack-dab on the borderline."

He shook his head. "It's not a problem."

"That's not the impression I got when I mentioned it."

Head dropped forward, hands on his hips, he stopped. He stared at his feet for a long moment, then lifted his gaze to her face. "Look—"

The ringing of the phone made him pause. He took two almost angry strides to the phone on the wall and picked it up. "Hello?"

Wynn tried to look like she wasn't listening, but it was apparent he was speaking with a friend. The infamous husband to a famous novelist? The lady-killer Josh?

A lady-friend of his own?

She didn't like that idea at all, and went about wiping off the table, closing up the dishwasher. Zack watched her as he spoke casually, saying, "Sure, I could use the company. That'll work. All right, fifteen minutes." He hung up.

Dani bounded into the room, a colorful picture held in one hand. "Who was it?"

Zack scooped her up and held her to his chest. "Mick and Josh are coming over. If you want to get your bath a little early, you'll have time to visit before bed."

Mick and Josh must be very special to Dani, Wynn assumed, given the way her sweet face lit up.

She leaned around Zack to see the picture. "Is that for me?"

Suddenly looking shy, Dani said, "Yeah," and held

it out. Zack looked at it first and chuckled. Then Wynn had it and she held it out, studying it.

Dani had drawn the two trees in the backyard, Wynn and her hammock. Wynn grinned when she saw that she and the trees were the same lofty height, and her hair was accurately portrayed as a tornado. "It's beautiful, Dani." She held the picture to her chest, curiously touched, and smiled. "I love it."

Dani laid her head on Zack's chest. "Really?"

With a strange lump in her throat, she nodded. "Really." Wynn wished she could hold the little girl, too, that she could be the recipient of that adoring hug. She'd never thought much about kids before, but now she did, and an insidious yearning filled her. "May I keep it?" she asked, feeling overly emotional. "I'd like to put it on my refrigerator so everyone who visits me can see it, too."

This pleased Dani a lot. "Okay." And with a distinct lack of subtlety, the little girl added, "I could even visit you and see it sometime."

One look at Zack told Wynn that he didn't consider it a good idea. Tough, she thought. There was no way she'd hurt Dani's feelings just because Zack had some strange hang-up about getting friendly with her.

Feeling defiant, she said, "I'd like that a lot."

And on impulse, she leaned over and kissed Dani's cheek. Zack reared back, well out of reach, but Wynn still felt the sizzle of being so close to him.

She told Dani goodbye, winked at Zack, and let herself out through the kitchen door.

The sun had almost completely set, leaving long shadows over the lawns. If she hoped to get her hammock up in time to enjoy it tonight, she'd have to get a move on. She went in her house first to retie her hair. It was for-

ever in her face, making her nuts. She found her small
box of tools and headed back out.

Fifteen minutes later, when she'd almost finished,
she heard the car pull into Zack's driveway. Curiosity
got the better of her, and she peered toward the house.
A floodlight mounted over Zack's garage door lit the
area. Wynn saw two men get out, both of them tall and
handsome. One had dark coloring, like a fallen angel,
and the other was a golden Adonis. Mick and Josh, she
decided, and it was easy to figure out which was which.

Sheesh. Living next door to Zack-the-hunk would be
hard enough without him having other impressive hunks
over to distract her. She should have been immune to
gorgeous men, considering she helped out at Conan's
gym and saw well-built muscular guys every day, often
in nothing more than skimpy shorts and athletic shoes.
But these three…what a visual variety!

The golden one looked up just as she started to turn
away, and he kept looking. *Busted!* He knew she'd been
eyeing him and no doubt knew why. His type—tall,
sexy, well-built and handsome to boot—expected female adoration.

His companion turned, too, then propped his hands
on his hips and did his own share of staring. Good Lord,
her first day in her own house and she kept making a
spectacle of herself.

Seeing no hope for it, Wynn summoned up a friendly
and hopefully casual wave, which both men returned.
The dark one looked merely polite and curious, but the
other watched her with interest.

A second later Zack's door opened and both men got
yanked inside.

Chapter 4

"Get away from the damn window," Zack growled.

Josh, still holding aside the café drape on the small window over the kitchen sink, peered over his shoulder at Zack. "Who is she?"

"Nobody. Just a neighbor."

"She's Wynn." Dani, perched in royal splendor on Mick's thigh, showed none of her father's reservation. "She's our new neighbor."

Josh lifted a brow. "Is that right?"

"She had breakfast with us." Dani smiled after that statement.

Mick shared a look with Josh. "Breakfast, huh?"

Zack threw ice into three glasses. "Quit jumping to conclusions. She woke me up this morning, that's all."

Josh dropped the curtain and turned. "Long, tall and sexy got you out of bed, and you say that's *all?*"

Mick choked on a laugh.

Zack, after casting a quick glance at his daughter, scowled. Luckily, Dani was busy singing and drawing Mick a picture, which Mick pretended to attend to when actually Zack knew he was soaking up every word. "It's not like that!" He caught himself, shocked at his own vehemence, and explained more calmly, "She and her brother were making a racket moving in. When she realized she'd awakened us, she brought over coffee and some muffins."

"Nice neighbor," Josh muttered, and turned back to the window.

"She had pizza with us, too, and I drawed her a picture."

"Drew her a picture," Zack automatically corrected, and realized his daughter had been all ears after all. When she looked up at him, he thought to add, "A beautiful picture, honey."

She held up her newest endeavor. "This one is, too."

Mick leaned back to see it, pretending to dump Dani, which made her squeal. "It's incredibly beautiful," he confirmed. He hugged her close and kissed her cheek.

Zack shook his head. His daughter had more than her fair share of male role models. Now she needed a female role model—preferably one who wasn't loud and pushy and too damn big.

Josh said, "Damn, does she never stop working?"

"Not that I've noticed." Unable to keep himself from it, Zack went to the window and peeked out. "What's she doing?"

"Hanging a clothesline. Hell, the moon is out. She's working from the porch light."

Dani said quite seriously, "You cuss too much. Hell and damn are bad words."

Wincing, Josh muttered, "Sorry."

Zack had long ago explained to Dani that while grown men might say certain words now and then, she was still a little girl and was strictly forbidden to do the same. He forgot his daughter's bossiness as he watched Wynn go about her business. "What in the world is she hanging up?"

Josh narrowed his eyes. "Looks like her laundry. Like—" he smiled "—her underwear."

Mick came out of his chair in a rush and crowded into the window. Being that he still held Dani, it was a tight fit. He snorted. "You're both lechers. You should give the woman some privacy."

None of them moved.

Dani said, "We saw her butt today."

Both Josh and Mick turned to stare at him. Zack frowned, ready to explain, then he saw Wynn toss a nightgown over the line and clip it into place with a clothespin. It wasn't a sexy nightgown, but rather what appeared to be yards and yards of material. 'Course, for a woman her size, it'd take a lot of cloth to cover her.

For some stupid reason that thought made him smile.

Moonlight played over her flyaway hair and the slant of the porch light made exaggerated shadows on her body. Why was she hanging her laundry at night? For that matter, why hadn't she worn down yet? She'd been working all day, non-stop, and it was too damn distracting. The woman must have inexhaustible energy, and that thought did more than make him smile. It made him wonder how she might put all that energy to use.

Through the open window, they all heard her begin to whistle.

"This is pathetic," Mick groused. "You've got me here playing peeping Tom when I'd really rather be playing cards."

Josh explained, "That's because you're blissfully married and therefore immune to fantasies."

Zack glared at him. "Don't tell me you're interested in her?"

And before Josh could answer, Dani braced herself between Mick and Josh, leaned forward toward the screen, and yelled through the window, "Hello, Wynn! We's peeping Toms!"

They all three ducked so fast, their heads smacked together.

Mick, on the floor with his back against the sink cabinet, flipped Dani upside down while laughing and said, "I ought to hang you by your toes for that!" He tickled her belly and they both laughed.

Josh looked at Zack and said, "Do you think she heard?"

"That one? She hears everything." Then to his daughter, "Sweetheart, you don't tell people when you're looking at them."

"Why not?"

Josh crept up the edge of the sink and peeked out. With a resigned expression he completely straightened and called out, "It's a little late to be doing laundry."

Realizing Wynn must have been looking toward the window, Zack stood, too. He heard her soft laugh, then, "My new washer and dryer won't arrive for a few more days. I needed clean stuff for tomorrow."

To Zack's disgruntlement, Josh smiled, walked to

the kitchen door, and continued right on outside and around to Wynn's house. He should put up a damn privacy fence.

Dani pulled away from Mick and followed. Mick shrugged at Zack, hauled himself to his feet, and followed suit.

Groaning, forced into the situation he'd wanted most to avoid, Zack went along.

When Wynn saw them all approaching, she dropped an item of clothing back into her basket and walked to meet them halfway. Though the night had grown considerably cooler, she was still in the halter and shorts and Zack wanted to strip off his shirt and cover her with it. But it was too late. Josh had already seen her, and was already in charm mode.

Wynn held out her hand when he reached her. "Hello. Wynn Lane."

Josh took her hand, but not in a handshake. He held her fingers carefully, as if she were fragile. "Josh Marshall," he murmured, and his tone alone gave away his thoughts on seduction. "Nice to meet you."

Zack wanted to kick him.

Wynn tried to tug her hand free, but Josh wasn't being reasonable about it. She snuck a glance at Zack and then back to Josh. "You're the fireman, right?"

He looked briefly surprised, and Zack explained, "Dani told her all about both of you."

To Mick she said, "My brother is a big fan of your wife's work."

Mick reached out, took Josh's wrist and pried their hands apart, then indulged his own handshake. At least his was entirely casual and quick. "Mick Dawson. Nice to meet you, Wynn."

She looked at Zack. "I hope I wasn't disturbing you again?"

"We were peekin' at you," Dani informed her.

Wynn just laughed and petted her hand over Dani's hair in a show of affection that Zack felt clean down to his gut. "Well," she said with a wide smile, "I imagine anyone doing laundry by moonlight is sure to draw attention." And to Zack, "The thing is, I'm still too keyed up from moving in to relax, and I actually brought laundry with me from my apartment, so I figured I might as well get it done. Stuff dried on the line always smells so good, don't you think?"

Zack thought *she* smelled good. Working all day had intensified her natural scent, making it more potent, more intoxicating.

He snorted at his own ridiculous fancy and told her, "There's a Laundromat a couple of miles away, next door to the grocery."

"You could use our washer and dryer," Dani offered.

Feeling his smile freeze, Zack said, "Or you could use our washer and dryer."

Wynn was already shaking her head. "No, I don't mind using the line."

Josh stepped in front of Zack. "I'm not that far away. Feel free to use mine until yours arrive."

Zack considered strangling him. It wasn't that he cared personally, because he *didn't*, but it'd be almost as awkward for Josh to get involved with her as it would be for Zack. Josh wasn't ready to settle down, and in fact, since Mick's wedding, he'd been overindulging in a big way. Zack did *not* want him overindulging with his neighbor.

Mick said, "If you're about done, we were just getting some drinks. You could join us."

She took a step back. "Oh no, but thanks anyway."

"Join us, join us!" Dani sang, bouncing up and down in renewed energy.

"You," Zack told his daughter, "are about to go to bed."

Before Dani could summon up a temper about that, Wynn said, "Actually, so am I."

All three men stared at her.

She cleared her throat. "That is, I need to get showered and…" She looked from one fascinated male gaze to the other and coughed. "I'm a mess. I've been working all day."

In a feminine gesture that took him by surprise, considering he hadn't seen much in the way of femininity from her, Wynn attempted to smooth her hair.

Josh tipped his head. "You look fine."

His voice was low and appreciative and again Zack wanted to strangle him.

"Her hair is soft," Dani informed Josh in a loud whisper, then poked him in the thigh.

"Is that right?" Showing none of the reserve Zack had exhibited, Josh reached out and fingered a bouncing curl at her temple before gently tucking it behind her ear. "You're right, Dani. It's very soft."

Wynn twittered and took another step away. "I've got to finish up here. But it was nice meeting you both. Dani, sweet dreams!"

Josh murmured low and suggestively, "You, too."

She gave another ridiculous, girlish twitter and turned to hurry away. Josh stood there, hands on his

hips, watching her go with his gaze southerly enough
to singe her backside, until Zack elbowed him. Hard.

They all trooped back into the kitchen, Josh rubbing
his ribs as if he'd been mortally wounded. Dani now had
her head on Mick's shoulder and she yawned. They were
all three aware of how quickly Dani would collapse into
a sound slumber, and they shared smiles.

Zack scooped his daughter into his arms. "Time for
you to hit the sack, sweetie." Once Dani started fading,
she went fast. She'd run right up until she ran out of gas.

She blinked sleepy eyes at Josh and Mick. "G'night."

Josh bent and kissed her nose. "Night, princess."

Mick tickled her toes. "Good night, honey."

As Zack turned to leave the kitchen, he saw Mick sit
at the table, and Josh go back to the open window. He
grumbled under his breath as he hauled his small bundle upstairs. He was just lowering Dani to her mattress
when she said in a low, drowsy voice, "Josh likes her."

Pausing, Zack said, "You think so?"

Dani nodded. "I like her, too. Don't you?"

"She's fine." Zack pulled the sheet up to Dani's chin,
smoothed her hair and kissed her forehead. That didn't
suffice, so he kissed her again, then cuddled her close,
squeezing her until she gave a protesting squeak. "I love
you, baby."

"I love you, too, Daddy."

"Do you need to potty?"

"Nope." She rolled to her side, cushioned her cheek
on one tiny fist, and let out a long deep breath.

With a last peck to her brow, Zack stood. Dani was
already snoring softly. For a long minute, he just looked
down at her. She was by far the most precious thing in
the world to him. It seemed every time he looked at her

it struck him anew how much he loved her. That she was his, a part of him, was beyond remarkable.

Josh was still at the damn window when Zack reentered the kitchen. "You look like a lovesick pup."

Mick choked on a laugh. "As compared to you, who's playing the part of the snarling junkyard dog?"

At Mick's taunting words, Zack paused, but only for a second. He knew his friends, and if they had half an inkling of how Wynn affected him, he'd never hear the end of it. Casually, a man without a care, he took his own peek out the window. Wynn was nowhere to be seen, thank God. Out of sight, out of mind.

He grunted, then dropped into his seat, sprawling out and rubbing the back of his neck.

"No comment, huh?" Mick asked.

"I don't know what you're talking about." Ignorance was a lame defense, but he was too tired to think of much else at the moment.

Mick leaned forward over the table and whispered, "Possessiveness."

Josh turned. "She went in just a few seconds ago." He took his own seat. "Did you see the legs on that woman?"

"Since they're a mile long," Mick said, "they'd be a little hard to miss."

Josh lifted a brow. "She's put together right, I'll say that for her."

"You didn't have to put up with her first thing this morning." Wishing he could bite off his tongue, Zack took a long cooling drink of his cola.

Saluting him with his glass, Josh said, "She can get me up anytime."

"Ha ha." Mick shook his head at the double entendre, but amusement shone clear on his face as he looked between the two of them. "You have a one-track mind, Josh."

"And it's definitely on track right now."

Zack growled before he caught himself. "I hate to curtail whatever fantasy you're indulging, but she's off limits."

Josh hesitated with his drink almost to his mouth. "Says who?"

"Says me. I have to live by her. I'll be damned if you're going to date her, dump her, then leave her to me to deal with." Zack shook his head in adamant finality. "No way, so forget it."

Mick nudged Josh with his foot. "Besides, he's got his own plans."

Zack did bite his tongue this time. The more he said, the more they'd read into it, so denials would do him no good.

Eyeing Zack, Josh asked, "Is that right?"

"No, it is not right." He hoped like hell he sounded more definite than he felt. "Now can we talk about something else?"

"Because I can back off if you're making a personal claim."

Through his teeth, Zack said, "I'm *not* making a personal claim, but you *will* back off."

Josh stared at him a moment, then chuckled and switched his gaze to Mick. "I think you're right."

"Are we going to play cards or sit here mooning over women?" Zack barked.

"All right, all right," Josh soothed. "Don't get all fired up. We don't have to moon."

"Speak for yourself," Mick grumbled. "I'm mooning. I'd much rather be home with Delilah right now."

Josh shook his head in pity. Even Zack managed a credible chuckle. "You're still a newlywed, so you're allowed."

"And," Josh added, "Delilah is enough to make anyone moon."

Predictably, Mick bristled. Why in hell Josh continued to make those types of comments, Zack couldn't figure out. He knew there was a time when Josh had fancied himself taken with Delilah, too, but since she'd married Mick—an event Josh had supported wholeheartedly—Josh had roamed from woman to woman with a near insatiable appetite.

Mick half came out of his chair. "I wish you wouldn't speak so intimately about my wife."

Josh looked supremely unaffected by Mick's ire. "I was only agreeing with you."

"You—"

"Sheesh, men in love are so touchy," Josh complained. "First Zack breathing fire on me, and now you. A single man can't make a legitimate observation anymore."

"Zack isn't married, *I am.*"

"Zack wants to be married," Josh pointed out. "It's almost the same thing." Then he redirected his comments to Zack. "Is that it with Wynn? You considering her suitable wifely material?"

"No."

"Did you really see her backside?"

"No."

Josh grinned. "I'll take that first 'no' at face value. No way in hell am I accepting the second without some kind of explanation."

If he knew it wouldn't wake Dani, Zack would consider knocking Josh off his chair. Resigned, he gave up with a sigh. "She was bent over…" He faltered, unsure how to explain.

Josh protested his hesitation by saying, "I'm all ears."

"Actually," Mick admitted, "so am I."

"She had on short shorts—"

"I noticed that."

"So did I."

"Do you two *want* to hear this or not?" Zack glared at them both, waiting, but they now held themselves silent. "She was bent way over trying to drag a box into the backyard and her shorts rode up. That's all there is to it. I didn't see her whole behind." But he'd seen enough to know her backside was as delectable as her legs.

"A half moon, huh?" Josh made a tsking sound. "And here I missed it."

Zack gave up and explained in full the extent of his association with Ms. Wynn Lane. He told them about her family who'd soon be moving in, her brother who was built like a chimney, and her penchant for being outspoken and brazen and pushy.

"She is not," Zack reiterated, "wife material."

Josh had listened quietly, but now he waved away Zack's disclaimer. "Why do you want to get married anyway? I mean, just because Mick here found the perfect woman—"

Mick growled.

"—and *he's* blissfully happy, doesn't mean we all need to stick our necks into the noose. I know a lot more divorced couples than I do happily married ones."

Now that the cannon had been redirected, Zack relaxed and began shuffling the cards. "Dani asked me about feminine napkins the other day."

Both Mick and Josh froze, then gave near identical groans of emotional pain. "Commercials?" Josh asked.

"Yeah. She was watching cartoons when *bam*, there was a commercial for napkins. Can you believe it? She wanted to know what they were for and why women who used them got to go horseback riding and climbing and stuff."

Chuckling, Mick shook his head. "I can just imagine this conversation."

"Whatd'cha tell her?" Josh asked with interest.

"I fumbled my way through it." Actually, he'd made a total mess of things, but Zack wasn't about to admit that. "She wasn't ready to hear about the whole reproductive cycle thing—"

"Neither am I," Josh joked.

"—so I just told her women used them like they used perfume and makeup and panty hose."

Mick snickered. "Let me guess. She wants some."

"Yup. So you see, this is why I need a wife. I foresee stuff like this coming up all the damn time. I mean, what the hell will I know about fashion trends for teenage girls, or buying training bras?"

Josh considered that a moment, then said, "I could handle it if you want help. I wouldn't mind."

"Oh God, that's all I need! I can see the headlines now, Womanizer Extraordinaire Attempts Parenting 101."

"A female is a female is a female."

Mick tapped his fingers on the table. "Delilah would have something to say about that sentiment."

Josh grinned. "I know. She loves to give me hell."

"Girls start this puberty stuff earlier than guys, as early as eleven or twelve," Zack pointed out. He was

amused despite himself, at the picture of Josh sorting
through adolescent underwear. It was a far cry from
lingerie, which admittedly, Josh knew a lot about. He
bought enough of it for his girlfriends.

"I could handle it." Josh looked thoughtful, then
grinned. "Hell, it might even be fun. I do enjoy shopping you know."

Zack did know. Every Christmas and every birthday,
Josh took Dani shopping. They'd make a whole day of
it, and Josh would spoil her with gifts and a movie and
the amusement park. It was surprising, given Josh presented the world with only his preference for bachelor-
hood, yet Zack trusted him completely with his daughter.

In many ways, both Josh and Mick were pseudo-
daddies, picking up the slack whenever Zack ran short
on time. And they did a great job. They'd helped him
get through the loss of his wife, and helped even more
in the transition from grief to thankfulness, because despite losing his wife, he still had Dani, and that was a
lot, more than he'd ever asked of life.

Zack had inadvertently wandered down a maudlin
path, so he changed the subject while dealing out the
cards. "Mick, did Josh tell you his station is making a
charity calendar?"

"What's this?" Mick asked.

Josh picked up his hand, rearranged the cards a few
times, then said, "Some pushy promotions broad is or-
ganizing the whole thing. She wants a bunch of the men
to pose in some cheesy way to go on the calendar, then
they'll sell it and the proceeds will benefit the burn center."

"Pushy promotions broad," Mick repeated slowly, as

if savoring the words. "Does this mean she had the audacity to exclude you from modeling?"

"I never gave her the chance. Anyone who was interested was supposed to call her to set up an appointment." He peered over his cards at Mick and Zack. "To get ogled, no doubt. Can you believe that?"

Frowning, Zack asked, "Have you met her?"

"I don't need to. I heard all about her from a friend at a different station. She's a rich daddy's girl who plays at this charity stuff out of boredom."

Mick and Zack shared a look. Mick laid his cards facedown and crossed his arms on the table. "Since when do you care about a woman's character?"

"Yeah," Zack said. "I thought it was the size of her bra cups that attracted you."

Josh suddenly looked harassed and annoyed, not that Zack minded after what he'd just been through. About time someone else took a turn on the hot seat.

"She's supposedly really beautiful, okay? And I've had it with women like that. I want someone more like Delilah."

Mick choked and his face turned red.

"Oh for God's sake." Josh quickly got out of Mick's reach and explained, "I wasn't—not for a second—saying Delilah's not beautiful! She is. Flat-out gorgeous."

Mick stood, looking far from placated.

"But she doesn't go in for all the props. When was the last time Del painted her nails or colored her hair? Never, right? She's genuine. Well, that's the type of woman I want." He waved a hand toward the window. "Wynn what's-her-name would do, too. I want a natural woman, not a glamour doll who thinks she can crook her little finger and a guy will come running."

Mick subsided, but he looked far from appeased.

Zack shook his head. "Mick, you're going to have to get a handle on these jealous tendencies of yours. You know Josh won't poach."

"As if it'd do him any good to try!"

Zack sighed, but it turned into a laugh. "I wasn't suggesting it would. And seeing as you know that, why do you let his every comment rile you? You know he doesn't mean anything by it. It's just how he is."

Mick grumbled, "That wasn't your sentiment when he was trying to seduce Wynn."

It was Josh's turn to choke. "I wasn't trying to seduce the woman! Hell, all I did was hold her hand."

"You're both nuts," Zack concluded out loud. "Let's forget Wynn and the calendar and women in general. Mick, you can go on pining for your wife since I know you can't help it." He grinned. "Now, let's play cards."

Three hours later Zack was ready to call it a night. His neck was still stiff and his mind refused to pay attention to his hand, so he'd lost more than he'd won. Mick, too, was yawning, and mumbling that Delilah had likely finished writing for the night. Josh, the only one to look fresh, decided to call a woman from Zack's house and made plans to visit her that night.

Mick and Zack both shook their heads.

The night was cool and crisp and black as pitch when Zack waved goodbye from the doorway. He stood there until the headlights had disappeared out of the driveway, then he locked the door and tidied the kitchen.

On his way through the house, he picked up toys and drawings and a lone frilly sock peeking out from beneath a chair. He checked all the locks and headed upstairs.

Dani slept peacefully, her small body barely visible beneath the sheet. Zack smiled and pulled her door closed.

On his way to his own room he stripped off his shirt and stretched his aching arm and shoulder muscles. He kicked his shoes into the closet, then sat on the edge of the bed to remove his socks. After he turned out the light, he went to the window, breathing in the night air as he unzipped his slacks.

And from there, in a shaft of moonlight, reclining in the damn hammock like a sexual offering, he saw Wynn. For a single heartbeat lust raged through him, making his blood churn and his imagination grind.

Then a clearer picture formed; she looked to be sound asleep, which nearly made his mind explode with incredulity. She was a single woman, alone, in a new neighborhood, and she was stupid enough to pass out asleep outside, unprotected.

Jaw locked, Zack left his room with a stomping stride and iron determination. He'd known the moment he saw her that she was going to be nothing but trouble, both to his sanity and his libido.

Chapter 5

The well-trimmed grass was wet and slippery beneath his bare feet, and a gentle evening breeze stirred his hair. His temper remained hot; it rose in degrees as he closed in on her.

Wynn didn't so much as move an eyelash when he stood directly over her lush, limp body. She had one arm above her head, palm up, her fingers slightly curled. The other drooped over the side of the hammock, almost touching the ground. Those mile-long legs of hers were crossed at the ankle, her feet bare.

She'd changed clothes.

Zack surveyed her, at his leisure. Without those piercing hazel eyes watching him or her sharp tongue challenging him, he felt steady, more in control, free to look his fill.

The halter and shorts were gone, replaced by a long,

loose white nightshirt that almost reached her knees. Or at least he thought it was a nightshirt—until he read the front. Lane's Gym—Workout For A Better Body. Obviously an advertisement for her brother's gym.

Clouds drifted across the moon, darkening the sky so that only the faint light from her porch illuminated her. Her lashes looked feathery in the dark shadows, her mouth very, very soft.

The scent of shampoo and lotion rose from her warm body to mingle with the damp night scents.

Zack felt himself reacting to the sight of her, and it angered him. "Wynn."

She didn't move.

He didn't want to touch her. "Damn it, Wynn, wake up."

Her lashes stirred and a soft sound escaped her slightly parted lips, causing his abdomen to clench, his pulse to race. Then she resettled herself with a husky groan.

Zack's eyes flared. His stomach knotted with carnal awareness. He reached down and caught her shoulder for a brisk shake. "Damn it to hell, Wynn, will you get your ass awake before I—oompf!"

One moment he'd been indulging his temper and the next he found himself flat on his back in the dew-covered grass, the wind knocked out of him and Wynn's knee in his chest. Her fist was drawn back, ready to clout him.

Zack reacted as suddenly as she had, grabbing her legs and holding on as he flipped them both, putting her flat out beneath him. "What the hell is *wrong* with you?"

Both her knees came up to shove in his ribs and he groaned. Taking advantage, she pushed him face-down to the side and crowded in close to his back. Her elbow locked around his throat. He could hear her frantic breaths directly in his ear. "Just *what* did you think you were—"

Swallowing down a roar of anger, Zack reached back, caught her by the head, and flipped her over his shoulder. Her grunt was much louder than his and she wheezed, trying to catch her breath. She held still, not moving, just staring up as if to see if she'd broken anything.

Zack took immediate advantage, and this time when he covered her he did so completely. He held her wrists high over her head and pinned her legs with his, not about to risk his poor body again. Her knees had caught him so hard it felt like she'd broken his ribs. He'd always known her legs would be strong, but...

When she started to wiggle he squeezed her so tight she gasped. "What," he asked through his teeth, "the hell is the matter with you?"

He hadn't meant to yell, but never in his life had a woman attacked him physically. And absolutely *never* had he thought to attack a woman! Thank God there weren't many women like her.

When Wynn didn't answer, he leaned closer to try to see her face, now afraid that he'd hurt her.

She spoke barely above a whisper. "I didn't know it was you."

Zack grunted. So she'd thought she was defending herself? He was far from appeased. If she hadn't fallen asleep outside, it wouldn't have been an issue.

"Do you realize," she continued, "that I'm letting you do this?"

Disbelieving her gall, Zack reared back. "*Letting* me?"

Her head moved in a slight nod. "I could have bitten your face just seconds ago. Even your jugular."

"Of all the—"

"Even now," she taunted, "if I wasn't afraid of hurting you, I could toss you."

In that instant Zack became aware of her long lean body beneath him, the cushion of her plump breasts, the giving dip of her wide pelvis, the strong, sleek thighs... He had hold of her wrists—not delicate wrists, but large-boned for a woman—and he lifted them above her head, keeping her in a submissive position.

So he could control her.

Oh yeah, his body liked that a lot. Too damn much. He had no doubt she'd already noticed his hard-on, being as it was pressed rigidly into her soft abdomen. Well too bad. Zack leaned closer again so he could see her face. He looked at her lush mouth, open now as she struggled for breath, and then to her incredible hazel eyes. Damn she had sexy eyes. In nothing more than scant moonlight, they were the eyes of a wolf, and they stirred him. "Try it," he offered, and waited with his own breath held.

"Oh, no." She stared at his mouth, and he felt her attention like a hot lick. "I don't want to hurt you—now that I know it's you."

Without meaning to, Zack pressed into her. Only the thin cotton of her nightshirt and his slacks separated them from entry. He closed his eyes, tipped his head back and moved against her rhythmically.

The alignment of their bodies was perfect, chest to breasts, groin to groin. He could kiss her and ride her at the same time, and never miss a single deep stroke. That realization made his muscles ripple.

Her nipples had puckered and he felt them rasping against his bare chest. She shifted her thighs, maybe trying to accommodate him, but he refused to take any chances. Her arms hung limp in his grip, in no way fighting his hold. Still he secured her, stretching her out a bit more, aware of her strength, and her yielding.

He felt on fire. *"Wynn..."*

She lifted her head, as brazen as ever, and that was all it took. Zack had never been a man controlled by lust, never been a man to experience all that much lust.

But this...what else could it be called? Mere lust didn't seem adequate for the bombardment of sensations on his senses. He felt her everywhere, on his body, in his lungs, in his head and his heart.

She licked his mouth, making a sound of excitement and acceptance and hunger. He caught her tongue and drew it deep, then gave her his own. Their heavy breathing broke the quiet of the night, mingling with the faint sounds of crickets and rustling leaves. He switched both her wrists into one of his and brought his hand down to wedge between their bodies, cuddling her breast.

In reaction to his touch, her hips lifted so strongly she supported his weight off the ground for a suspended moment of time. It took one rough thrust for Zack to crush her down again.

He kissed his way to her throat and heard her ragged whisper. "Zack... Let me go."

"No." He thumbed her nipple, stroking, teasing.

A raw groan and a burst of movement later, Wynn had him on his back again. The woman was forever taking him by surprise. Zack almost wanted to laugh.

Until her thighs straddled his and she became the aggressor. Her hands opened wide over his bare chest, she stroked him and moaned with the pleasure of it. She nuzzled at his throat, then bit before licking and sucking and making him crazed.

The open vee of her thighs cradled his erection, and made him strain for more. He caught her behind in his hands, relishing the resilient feel of her, her softness in contrast with her feminine strength. He explored her, sliding his fingers over the silken material of her panties, pressing inward to touch her from behind. He found her panties damp, her body incredibly hot.

Cradling her hips, Zack urged her into a rough, slow roll that simulated sex and brought him dangerously close to the edge.

He was ready to take her, more than ready to get the ridiculous man's shirt off her body and touch her everywhere, kiss her everywhere.

Only he didn't have protection with him. And...

Reality dropped on his head like a ton of bricks. He actually groaned aloud with his disappointment, with the awareness of his responsibilities.

They were acquaintances of only a day, and not even a full day at that.

They were outdoors, in the open, and if he'd seen her through his bedroom window, his daughter could see them both if she should wake up and look out. Granted, that wasn't likely to happen, not the way Dani slept, but he didn't take chances with his daughter, not ever.

They were on the wet ground, mindlessly entwined and it was so unlike him, so unlike what he wanted for himself as a responsible father and server of the community, he felt appalled and embarrassed and rightfully angry.

At Wynn.

He caught her wrists again and held her hands still to enable him to gain control of himself. "Wynn."

His tone of voice had no effect on her. She wiggled free and attacked his mouth, kissing him so thoroughly he almost forgot his resolve. He turned his head aside. "No."

"Yes," she insisted. She grabbed his ears and held him still. Then, "God, you're incredible. So hard and sexy and sweet."

Sweet? Zack rolled to the side, literally dumping her off him, but the second she was flat, he stood. His chest worked like a bellows and his brain cramped at the effort it took to resist her. When he turned to look at her, his damn knees almost gave out. Her shirt had hiked up and he could see her panties, could even see her navel.

He stared—until she held out her arms to him and the sight of her offering herself, wanting him, looked so good, so right, he couldn't stand it.

Jerking around, Zack said, "Get up."

He didn't watch to see if she did as he asked. He couldn't. Finally he heard a slight creak and turned to see her perched sideways on the hammock, her feet on the ground, her hands beside her hips, her gaze direct and waiting and unapologetic.

Zack drew a deep breath. "I'm sorry."

After a heavy beat of silence, she said, "Yeah, me, too." She smirked and shook her head.

That drew him up. "Sorry for what?"

Wynn pushed to her feet and faced him eye to eye. "At the moment, I'm pretty sorry for everything." She turned away. "Good night, Zack."

He was so stunned by the dim sight of her wet back, the cotton shirt clinging to her behind and upper thighs, that he almost let her get away. He shook himself. "Wait a minute!"

"No point in waiting. Believe me, I understand."

Zack caught her arm and whirled her around. In the next instant she was on tiptoes and huffing in his face.

"Don't think for a single second that you bested me, buddy!" She poked him in the chest, making him stagger back a step. "The second I realized it was you, I went half-go. Besides that, you caught me asleep and sluggish. Now I'm wide awake and you're done kissing and you're acting all nasty and hateful again, so do *not* try manhandling me."

Zack had at least a dozen questions for her, but what came out of his mouth was, "You actually think you could best me in strength?" He was so incredulous he barely knew what he said.

Wynn snorted. "I've trained all my life. I know exactly what I'm doing."

And she thought…what? That he was a marshmallow? She'd called him *sweet.* What the hell had she meant by that? Through his teeth, Zack heard himself say, "No way, lady. Not on your best day." Then he wanted to smack his own head for challenging a woman! *What was he thinking?*

With a look of utter disdain, she said, "You keep living that dream if it makes you happy, big boy." And again she turned to walk away.

"Wynn." Even to his own ears, her name sounded like a warning. But then it had been strained through his clenched teeth.

Arms spread, she whipped around to face him and demanded, *"What?"*

He was a reasonable sort, Zack reminded himself. He was logical and calm and a pacifist. He absolutely, under no circumstances, wrestled with women, not even big bold pushy ones.

One slow deep breath helped a little. The second breath pushed the red haze out of his vision so he could see her clearly, or as clearly as the night-dark sky allowed. "Why," he asked, sounding more like a sane man, "were you sleeping on the hammock?"

She looked at the hammock as if to verify which one he meant. Then she shrugged. "I'd worked all day, I was hot and sweaty and after my shower I just wanted to rest my tired bones and get some fresh air. Only I nodded off. I didn't mean to fall asleep."

Zack clasped his hands behind his back to keep from reaching for her. Brows raised in inquiry, he said, "Do you, by any chance, know how risky that can be for a woman?"

"You mean with crazy neighbors lurking about ready to throw me on the ground and kiss me silly and paw me until I'm all excited and ready and then stop with no warning?" She gave him a smug, distinctly mean smile. "Yeah, I do now."

"I meant," he said, inching toward her, but watching her closely at the same time, "because of strangers who would do things to you without a second's hesitation. Men who would rape or murder or…"

"Rape and murder about covers it. No reason to go overboard."

"This is not a joke, damn it!"

She crossed her arms under her breasts and cocked one hip. It shouldn't have been a seductive pose, but damn, it made him sweat.

"Did I just say it was an accident, that I didn't mean to fall asleep? I thought I did, but given your attitude, I can't be sure."

Tension mounting, Zack flexed his shoulders and rolled his head on his neck. "It was irresponsible."

"Well, thank you, Mother, for your concern."

"Wynn, I know you're excited about your new house—"

"And my new neighbor? My new neighbor who likes to tease and lead women on, then pull away and act as if his finer sensibilities have been lacerated by my coarse and carnal behavior?"

Zack was again caught between wanting to shout with anger, and the urge to laugh. From the moment he'd met her, Wynn Lane had been too outspoken and honest for her, or his, own good. He rubbed his neck and concentrated on not smiling. "I didn't mean to tease."

"Oh? You call what you did—given the fact you pulled up short—fulfillment?" She shook her head. "You poor, poor man. You're missing the best part."

"Look, Wynn, it was a mistake for us to do—" he gestured at the ground "—this. I don't know about you, but I'm not in the habit of indulging in one-night flings."

She didn't confirm or deny what her habits were, which only made him edgier. Little by little his neck and shoulder muscles tightened into a painful cramp. He'd strained something at work the night before, and arguing with Wynn only exacerbated things.

Her eyes narrowed and she strode toward him. "What's the matter with you? Did I hurt you?"

His hand fell away from his neck. "Of course not."

"Ha! You're in pain, I can tell."

He started to say *she* was the pain, but held it in. It was past time he listened to himself. They were neighbors, no refuting that fact. They needed to get along in some civil but distant and detached way.

With that decision made, he waited until she stopped directly in front of him, then explained, "I dealt with two pretty nasty emergencies last night. The first was a case of domestic violence." His tone sounded raw even to his own ears, but the emotional devastation of the night still lingered. "I took a woman in with two broken ribs and multiple contusions. The bastard who'd worked her over had gone to a bar. Luckily, the cops caught up to him there."

Zack had to be grateful that the man had been gone when he got there. He wasn't at all certain he could have contained himself otherwise.

Wynn, evidently sensing his turbulent emotions, reached out and smoothed her hand over his arm. It was a soothing touch, and it helped him to recall himself.

He shook off his lingering anger and reminded himself that the woman had pressed charges. That wasn't always the case, but luckily this particular woman had had enough. He'd left her in the hands of the social services.

"Then there was a car wreck. We had to cut the door away to get to the woman inside. She was in shock, covered in blood from a head wound, and getting her out wasn't easy, especially since she wasn't exactly a small woman."

"She was big like me?"

Zack's temper jumped a notch. "I could handle you easily without straining a thing."

She smirked.

"No, this woman was obese." Wynn remained quiet and waiting so he continued. "The reach was awkward, and I strained something in my neck and shoulders when I lifted her out."

"Hmmm. Sounds like you strained a trap. That happens a lot in clumsy lifts. Turn around."

He stalled. "What?"

"Trapezius muscle," she explained.

And Zack said, "I know what it is. I just didn't…"

Grabbing his upper arm, she forcibly turned him—something he allowed—and then began pressing her fingers into his neck, his shoulders, his spine. Zack groaned. Her touch had an electrifying effect that both soothed and excited.

"Right there?" she asked, her thumbs now working some hidden muscle that reacted by going limp.

"Yeah." And then, "You're good at this."

"I'm good at a lot of things."

His eyes shot open.

"Have you been using any moist heat?"

God, everything she said sounded sexual to his beleaguered brain. *Moist. Heat.* He was such a goner. "No," he croaked. "I haven't had a chance."

"Bull. You're a paramedic, you know better than to ignore injuries. If need be, you make time. Maybe instead of hanging out with your friends you should have soaked in your hot tub."

His brain took a leap from her suggestion, to a vivid fantasy of them both in the hot tub, steam rising and flesh wet… "I will later."

"When is later?"

Her persistence annoyed him. "Maybe after work tomorrow."

Her hands continued to massage and work his aching muscles. He felt like butter—like *aroused* butter.

"What hours do you work?"

That, at least, was a safe enough topic. "We're all on a

rotating schedule. Ten-hour days, four days a week. My hours are usually eight to six. The three days off vary and are almost never grouped together, but at least that way everyone gets a weekend now and then. And there's always overtime, so my hours end up fifty or over more often than not."

Leaning around to see his face, Wynn asked, "Who watches Dani while you work?"

"There's a lady two blocks down, Eloise. She's a real sweetheart, in her early seventies, on a fixed income. Dani adores her, and vice versa. Dani thinks of it as her second home."

"Any friends her own age?"

He shrugged. "She goes to preschool two days a week, but Dani tells me most of the kids there are 'babies.'"

Wynn chuckled. "Yeah, I can see her thinking that. She's used to adult company, isn't she?"

"Too much so. I thought the preschool would help, and she does enjoy it. One of her classmates lives in the neighborhood and she's had Dani over for birthday parties and special outings and things like that."

"Mmm. Sounds like fun for her." Hands splayed wide, Wynn worked her way down Zack's back, over his lats, then his obliques. It was all he could do to remain standing.

Zack didn't mean to, but he felt so relaxed, so boneless from her massage, he heard himself confiding before he could censor himself. "She has a hard time fitting in with other girls."

"Oh?"

Zack closed his eyes, but now he had no choice except to explain. "She's...not into the same things as other little girls her age. The whole idea of playing dress-up revolts her, and she's outraged by the idea of frilly dresses and tights." He grinned, remembering the last time Dani had worn a dress. It had been for Mick and Del's wedding, and she'd only agreed because Del had helped her pick it out, and Del wasn't into lace and frills, either.

"I was the same when I was a little girl," Wynn said.

Zack teased, "You mean you were little once?"

Her thumbs pressed deep enough to make him jerk in pain. "Hey, ouch! All right, I was just teasing."

"I wasn't born an oaf, you know."

For the briefest moment Zack wondered if he'd hurt her feelings, then decided the massage must have softened his brain as well as his muscles. Wynn wasn't the type of woman who indulged fragile feelings.

On the tail of that realization came another, more startling one. Good God, was there a chance his daughter would grow up to be like Wynn? Wrestling in her yard, argumentative and loud and far too bold? The very idea made him shudder. He *had* to find a wife, a nice delicate feminine wife who adored Dani and could, with patience and a calm quiet demeanor, guide her into being a young lady.

"If you work fifty hours," Wynn said, breaking into his thoughts, "I imagine some of those nights it's pretty late when you get home."

"True."

"Do you bring Dani home?"

"Of course." He started to look at her, but she stilled him by working a particularly achy knot in his right deltoid. Damn, but she had wonderful fingers. "I was blessed with a real slughead for a daughter," he told her around a heartfelt groan. "It takes a lot to wake her before she's ready to wake. I just bundle her up and bring her home and tuck her into her own bed."

"If Eloise is in her seventies, how much longer do you think she can continue to baby-sit?"

"I've considered that," he murmured, his reserve now as limp as his muscles. "I'm thinking of leaving field-work."

"Yeah? To do what?"

Her fingers found just the right amount of pressure, and he groaned low before he could work up the energy to answer. "Maybe be a supervisor," he said, "or an operations manager. Or maybe I'll instruct. I think I'd like that."

Wynn made a sound of interest, and her hands moved lower, over his gluteus medius, then his gluteus maximus...

Damn, but her fingers were magic...marvelous... *intimate!*

Zack jerked around to face her. "You're seducing me!"

She tried for an innocent expression and failed. "Naw, just copping a feel of your nice tight buns."

He sputtered, both outraged and stupidly compli-mented, and, if he was honest, vaguely turned on. Okay, more than vaguely. He felt mellow and ready. Primed even.

She had the gall to laugh in his face, then pat his chest. "Relax, Zack, your virtue is safe with me. And you do feel better now, right?"

He flexed, rolled his shoulders in experimentation; she was right, damn her. He gave a reluctant nod.

"Good." She patted him again, this time ending with a caress of his pecs. "If you tighten up again, come see me."

He was tight already, just not where she meant.

"It probably wouldn't hurt to use a little ultrasound on the affected muscles, and I can do that at the gym."

"I'll be fine," he croaked.

She rolled her eyes. "You're a regular superhero, aren't you? Impervious to the needs of your body, both sexual and physical?"

Being pushy probably came naturally to her. She'd likely been born making demands and causing conflicts. "I'm trying to do what's right for both of us and you know it. We're neighbors. Anything beyond a friendly association would be too difficult."

She gave a heavy sigh, saying, "Whatever," and turned to leave.

"I hope you understand," Zack called out, watching her as she walked into the light from her back porch. His body felt relaxed but zinging with life, too. An odd mix. A *carnal* mix.

She sent him an airy wave without looking back. A second later she went through the door and it closed with a click that echoed around the empty yards.

Damn irritating woman.

He'd made the right decision, despite his still raging hard-on. But then why did he feel so pissed off with himself? Why did he hate the right decision?

An upstairs light came on in her house, and through an open window Zack heard her begin to whistle again. She was a woman without a care, while he still stood there in the yard churning with a riot of emotions and physical needs. He stared at her window hard, willing her to move into view, but then the light went out and he knew she had gone to bed.

From now on, he'd just have to be very careful to avoid her. Given his hours, that shouldn't be too hard to do.

Wynn watched through her dark bedroom window as Zack tipped back his head and stared up at the moon. He looked so rigid, every line of his body denoting frustration, that she half expected him to howl, but all he did was turn on his heel and head back to his own house.

Her massage had been a waste, she could see that now; the man was determined to be tense. She sighed.

What a twist of fate, she thought, her heart sinking a little at the sight of his retreating back. Her hands were still tingling from touching him, from feeling all those smooth hard muscles and hot skin and vibrating tension. She huffed. The first man who really pushed her buttons, who made her feel like gelatin on the inside and made her breathe too fast just being near, and he was a blasted prude.

Her thought process crashed there and she was forced to face the possibility that he wasn't a prude at all. A man as big and sexy and intelligent and responsible as Zack was more likely suffering disinterest than moral restrictions.

Why would he be interested in *her*?

She'd done nothing but make a fool of herself since meeting him, and her naturally forceful personality had been in rare, suffocating form. But he brought out the extremes in her, and half the time she didn't even know what she was going to do until she did it.

She closed her eyes on a wave of remorse and embarrassment. God, she'd accosted him at every turn, provoked him and even rolled on the grass with him. She'd called him names and insulted him, and here she was, wishing he'd want her just a little?

Wynn shook her head. She was a complete and utter dolt.

She left the window and moved blindly toward the hall. She needed another shower—this one preferably ice-cold to chase away the lingering hunger. She knew she wouldn't sleep tonight, not after feeling him atop her, not after inhaling his aroused scent.

She had to get herself together, and she had to give the man some space. Rushing him was not the best tactic. No, Zack was a subtle man, when he wasn't challenging her. He was a father, and his sensitivity toward his daughter only made him more attractive. He was the hero Dani had described him as being, and by far the most appealing male Wynn had ever met.

Zack needed time to get used to her, to get to know her.

She'd *ease* her way in, she'd be charming and sweet and polite...because knocking down his defenses sure didn't seem to be working.

Chapter 6

Zack saw her every damn day. He woke up in the morning and she was outside working in the yard or cleaning her driveway or chatting with the other neighbors.

He got home from work and she'd just be coming in or going out.

He ran into her at the grocery store and once while they were both taking out their garbage. Dani chatted her up every time, like she was a long-lost and valuable friend. And Wynn was forever sweet and attentive—to Dani.

It irked him, especially since she lounged in that hammock every damn night. Before bed, he'd find himself standing at his window, watching for her like a lost soul. And sure enough, she'd come traipsing out, her long legs bare and her stride sure to the point of being almost mannish. Not that anyone would ever mistake Wynn Lane for a man. She was too curvy, too soft and…she smelled too good to be male.

His whole body would go taut watching her as she relaxed back in that hammock and stretched out the length of her sexy body. Damn if he didn't get aroused every time.

Sometimes she read until the sun went down. Sometimes she just swayed, music feeding into her ears through a set of headphones. She sometimes dozed and she sometimes whistled, but not once had she fallen into a sound sleep again.

He almost wished she would, so he'd have a legitimate excuse to seek her out, to touch her.

She no longer intruded. In fact, she seemed to have lost interest in him. Always she'd be cordial, give a wave or a friendly hello, and then she'd move on. She treated him the same as she did the other neighbors, and he didn't like it.

He'd never known himself to be such a fickle bastard before. But he missed her. He barely knew her and already he'd grown accustomed to her.

As had Dani.

Even now his daughter sat on the kitchen door stoop, wistfully staring at Wynn's house, waiting for her to appear. Dani missed her. She wasn't at all appeased by the short friendly chats or casual waves, and that wasn't something Zack had counted on.

It tore his heart out.

"Dani," he called, "come on in and eat your sandwich."

Two seconds later Dani peered in the door. "I'm gonna eat it out here."

Normally Zack would have been fine with that, but he didn't want his daughter turning melancholy. "Dani…"

"Wynn'll need a sandwich, too."

Zack went still and a strange emotion, one he refused to study too closely, swirled through him. "Is she out there?"

"She's with a bunch of big men."

Before his brain and feet could make a connection, Zack found himself at the door looking out. Sure enough, there was Wynn, surrounded by bodybuilders—three of them. All massive, all handsome.

All fawning over her.

He scowled, thinking to duck back inside before she or her cursed boyfriends spotted him.

His traitorous daughter did him in once again.

Dani took two bounding steps down the stoop to the lawn and waved her arms like a windmill. *"Hey, Wynn!"*

Wynn looked up and her seven-watt smile shone brightly. She patted one of the guys on the chest, swatted at another's immense back and started in Dani's direction. Zack couldn't deny the pounding of his heart. It had been a week since he'd really talked to her, really been close to her. Deny it all he liked, he'd missed her. Maybe even more than his daughter had.

Dani shocked him by rushing to Wynn for a hug.

Wynn didn't shock him a bit when she bent down and scooped Dani high, tossing her in the air and then hugging her close. "What have you been up to, munchkin?"

"You can eat peanut butter and jelly with me!"

Wynn glanced at Zack, saw the paper plate with the neatly sliced sandwich that he held in his hand, and said, "I *love* peanut butter and jelly. You don't mind sharing?"

"Nope."

When Wynn sat Dani down, she took her hand and stood staring at Zack. He cleared his throat. "How've you been, Wynn?"

"Busy. My folks are moving in tomorrow. I had to get everything put away and organized so they'd have a place to store their stuff. This moving on top of my moving is exhausting."

She snagged the sandwich, handed half to Dani and took a big bite of the other half. "Mmmm. Delicious."

Zack ignored that to ask, "Who are your guests?"

She gave a negligent shrug. "Guys from the gym. They wanted to see my new house and visit. They're also going to help me set up my patio furniture. I bought a picnic table with an umbrella and a glider and chairs and tables. I've got some plants, too. I can't wait to see it all together. The delivery truck should be here soon."

"It takes three giants to set up lawn furniture?"

Her eyes sparkled at the acrimony in his tone. Hell, he'd sounded almost…jealous.

Enunciating each word carefully she said, "They wanted to see my new house, too." Then she added, "You do have a problem listening to me, don't you? Or rather, you only hear certain selective parts."

Dani said, "I'll help, too."

"I dunno." Wynn pretended to study her. "I need strong laborers. Let's see your muscle."

Dani immediately flexed her skinny arm. She tucked in her chin and puffed out her cheeks and ground her teeth, with no visible effect.

Still, Wynn made approving sounds and squeezed the non-existent muscle. "Wow. All right, I think you're strong enough." She glanced at Zack. "That is, if your dad doesn't mind."

"He don't mind."

"Dani." She had jelly on her upper lip and a pleading look in her big blue eyes. He meant to reprimand her further, but she looked so cute...

"Please," Dani begged in her most hopeful tone.

Wynn chuckled at her theatrics, then leaned toward Zack, her hands clasped together now that she'd finished her half of the sandwich. Mimicking his daughter to a tee, she pleaded. "Pretty please, Zack. C'mon. We'll be careful. And I promise to watch her real close."

Zack eyed Wynn. She wore a baggy gray T-shirt today with denim cutoffs. She was barefoot, her frizzy flyaway hair in a ponytail on the very top of her head resembling a frazzled water fountain.

In a different way, a funny way, she was the most appealing woman he'd ever seen.

He gave up without a grumble and denied, even to himself, that he was using his daughter's wishes as an excuse. Dani wanted to be with her, so he'd allow it. But as her father it was necessary that he be there. That sounded plenty logical to him. "All right. But I'll help, too."

Wynn drew back. "You don't have to do that."

"I go where my daughter goes," he told her, letting her assume he didn't entirely trust her or her friends. She scowled in reaction, narrowing her beautiful eyes until they glittered golden with ire. He just grinned at her. Provoking her was way too easy.

"Fine." Then she said, "But you have to pass the muscle test, too."

"Don't be ridiculous."

"Hey, you're the one insisting. And fair's fair. Dani took the test."

Dani bounced. "Show her your muscles, Dad!"

"Yeah, show me, Dad," Wynn prodded, and Zack had the horrible suspicion that his neck had turned red.

Through his teeth, he said, "I promise, I'm strong enough."

Wynn shook her head. "Not good enough. I can see the muscles on my friends, and Dani proved herself." Her eyebrows lifted and her smile turned smug. "Now show me your stuff."

Zack knew he was in good shape. He had to attend daily workouts as part of his regimen for the station. He ate healthy food and his job was demanding, both mentally and physically.

But he wasn't in the habit of flaunting himself.

Wynn shoved his short sleeve up over his shoulder and said softly, "I promise this won't hurt a bit." She caught his wrist, locked her eyes with his, bent his arm at the elbow, and said, "Now *flex.*"

Tightening his jaw in annoyance, Zack dutifully flexed. His biceps bulged. His arms weren't enormous like the body builders', but still plenty defined and impressive if he did say so himself.

Wynn's gaze softened and her eyes darkened. The hand holding his trembled. "Nice," she murmured in a voice that was far too intimate. "You just might do."

Dani went on tiptoe to point at Zack's upper arm. "There's where Dad got shot."

"Shot?"

Wynn started to look more closely, but Zack pulled away and jerked down his sleeve.

In that instant the delivery truck arrived and began backing into Wynn's driveway. After a long look at Zack, which promised the topic was far from finished, she turned to face the men who were milling around her yard. They appeared to be checking out every blade of grass and especially the hammock. To Zack, they looked like concrete blocks with legs.

"The truck is here," Wynn called out to them. "The payment is in on my hall table. Will one of you go grab it and sign for the stuff? I'll be there in just a minute."

Almost as an entity, they nodded agreement and began a pilgrimage to the front of the house. Wynn turned back to Zack. "Is there a swallow of milk to go with the sandwich? I swear that peanut butter is hung up right about here." She pointed between her breasts, well hidden beneath the gray cotton shirt, but Zack still went mute.

Luckily, his daughter played the perfect hostess. "We always have milk. Come on." She took Wynn's hand and led her into the kitchen. Zack was forced to follow.

"You need to regulate your eating habits better," he grumbled.

She slanted him a look as he took a tall glass from the cabinet. "Do I look malnourished? Vitamin deficient?"

Since she was tall and strong and healthy, Zack ignored that question. He filled the glass to the top and handed it to her. "And I can't believe you're letting those men sign for your belongings. Or go through your house unchaperoned."

She'd already guzzled down half the milk when his words registered. With the glass tilted to her mouth, her gaze captured his and she blinked. Very slowly she lowered the empty glass and set it aside. She licked her lips. Two seconds passed before she said, "Marc and Clint and Bo are good friends. And they can be trusted."

Dani hovered near the door, watching the men. "They sure are big."

With an evil smile, Zack said, "Wynn evidently likes them that way."

Her smile was no less taunting as she leaned close and breathed into his ear, "But I wasn't in my backyard, on the ground, making out with any of *them*. Ever." Then she straightened and asked, "How'd you get shot?"

"By bein' a hero," Dani said, still with her head out the door.

Wynn turned to Zack. "Gunfire?"

How she managed to pack so much horror into one small word was beyond him. She acted as though the idea was ludicrous, as if he wasn't man enough... Deciding to nip that thought, and this conversation in the bud, Zack grabbed her arm and put his hand on his daughter's narrow back, urging them both forward. "If we're going to help we better get to it. No more time for gabbing."

Dani skipped ahead. "What should I do?"

"I have some new baby plants that need extra special care until I get them in the ground," Wynn told her. "You can move them from the back porch under the overhang to the yard so the men can set up the furniture without trampling them. I trust you more than I do all these big lugs."

Dani took off like a shot and Zack yelled, "Be very careful, Dani, and don't get in anyone's way."

Dani was no sooner out of hearing when Wynn asked again, "How'd you get shot?"

"It's nothing."

"Ohhh," she cooed in a dramatic voice, "I just love a humble martyr." She batted her eyes at him, laughed, then said, "No really. What happened?"

"You are such a pushy woman."

She stopped, which caused him to stop since he still had hold of her arm. Realizing that, he let her go and propped his fists on his hips.

"What?" he asked, when she continued to look at him.

For the first time that he could remember, she actually looked sheepish. "I didn't mean to be pushy," she muttered, and her face heated. She didn't blush well, Zack decided, seeing her entire face, neck and even her ears turn pink.

"It's a...well, a bad habit I guess. Sorry." She started to say more, shook her head, and stepped around him. Zack caught her arm again.

"Wynn."

She stopped, but rather than face him she looked down at her feet.

Zack stared at the back of her head where frazzled strands stood out on end, having escaped the band she'd used to contain her hair. The curls resting against her nape actually looked kind of cute, maybe even a little sexy. She had an elegant neck and broad, sexy shoulders...

Suddenly Zack felt a searing scrutiny.

He looked up and caught all three of the hulks watching him. One man had a large wrought-iron chair held aloft in his arms, which he continued to hold with seemingly no effort though the thing looked awkward and heavy.

The other two had a cumbersome settee between them, with yet another chair balanced in the middle of it. They, too, seemed more than comfortable with their burden.

Zack tugged on Wynn's arm. "That's some massive furniture you bought."

She shrugged, still staring at her feet. "I'm a big girl. I need big furniture to be comfortable."

"True. Those are also big, apparently protective guys you've got hauling it."

Wynn caught his meaning and looked up. Whatever dejection she'd been feeling fell away to be replaced by her natural arrogance. "Oh, for goodness' sake. Are you three going to stand there all day?"

One of the men, an artificially tanned behemoth, smirked. "Only until we see that you're all right."

Sounding incredibly surprised, Wynn asked, "You're worried about *Zack*?" And to compound that insult, she hitched her thumb over her shoulder toward him, then chortled. "Don't be silly."

One of the men holding the settee bared his teeth in what might have been loosely termed a smile. "Only Wynn would call us silly," he said to Zack, then added, "I'm Bo. A…friend."

The other two grinned at that, which made Wynn bristle, and Zack scowl. Just what the hell did Bo mean? Was it an inside joke? Did Wynn and Bo have some sort of understanding? Were they involved?

The guy on the other end of the settee said, "Bo, Wynn is going to get you for that," and then to Zack, "I'm Clint and that over there is Marc."

Zack nodded. "I'm her neighbor, Zack Grange."

"Yeah right." They all chortled again, looking between Wynn and Zack. "Just a neighbor."

Zack clenched his teeth. "The little one running around is my daughter, Dani."

Bo winked. "She's a sweetheart. And hey, Wynn just loves kids."

Wynn cast a quick look at Zack, then under her breath said, "You guys are in for it."

They pretended great fear, gasping and sharing worried glances—ludicrous considering their impressive sizes. Growling, Wynn took a threatening step forward and they quickly dispersed, rushing to the patio to put the furniture down.

Zack pulled her around to face him. She looked braced for his anger, until he asked, "Is Bo a boyfriend?"

Her eyes widened and she choked on a laugh before saying, "No! Of course not."

"Then what was all that inside snickering and shared looks?"

She waved that away. "Bo flirts with all women, sort of like your friend Josh. He's got about a dozen girlfriends and yes, he pretends to want to add me to the list, but it's all just in fun. I'm not an idiot and he knows it."

That brought up another issue that nettled, and Zack said, "You acted plenty interested with Josh."

"Ha! He's gorgeous and he took me by surprise. I'm used to Bo being outrageous, but not other guys. That's all." She looked Zack over and asked, "What about you? Any steady girlfriends?"

"No." But not for lack of trying on his part. He just hadn't met a woman yet who was right for him and Dani, and he saw no reason to get involved in a *wrong* relationship.

Except that with Wynn...he was tempted.

She looked skeptical, but said only, "You don't have to worry about those three. They're just a little overprotective, but now that I've assured them you're harmless, they'll let it go."

"Harmless?" He stepped closer to her, until they almost bumped noses. "One of these days I'm going to make you eat all these insults."

Her eyes brightened and filled with fascination. "Is that right? How?"

"A number of ideas are zinging through my head."

In the vein of being helpful, she suggested, "We could wrestle again. Next time you *might* win."

Damned irritating, irrational... He let her go and stalked away. He heard her satisfied snicker before she suddenly went quiet, groaned, and then began tromping after him.

And here he'd actually thought he'd missed her. Ha! He couldn't be that stupid.

But he *was* smiling.

The patio began to look just as Wynn had pictured it. She'd had the furniture rearranged three times, despite all the guys grumbling, but now everything worked. Including the beautiful new gas grill, which Zack had suggested she move away from the window, to keep smoke from coming into the house.

About half an hour ago at the hottest part of the afternoon, Zack had removed his shirt. His back and shoulders glistened with sweat, as did the straight, light-brown hair clinging to his nape and temples. His blue eyes looked even bluer in the bright sunshine, and the flex of his lean, athletic muscles made Wynn more aware of him than she'd ever been of any man.

She saw Zack lift his head and look around for Dani. He was good at doing that, at always being aware of his daughter and what she was up to. Wynn couldn't imagine a more attentive or caring parent.

Zack shaded his eyes until he located Dani sitting in the grass beneath a large tree. She was hunting for four-leaf clovers with Clint, who appeared suitably impressed with her skills while he drank an ice-cold cola.

Zack smiled, his face lit with so much love and pride, Wynn thought her heart might burst.

She needed to be with him again.

A week had gone by where she'd done her best to give him time and space, but she didn't think she could take it anymore.

Bo walked up and thwacked her on the behind. "I need sustenance after all my toils. You got any lunch meat?"

A quick peek at Zack showed his attention had shifted and he now had that scowling, disapproving look on his handsome face again. Resisting the urge to rub her stinging behind, Wynn huffed. It wasn't exactly her fault that her brother's friends were all too familiar. "I thought I'd order a pizza."

"No need, darlin'," Marc told her. "We can't stay that long. But a sandwich would hit the spot."

She flapped her hand toward the kitchen. "There's all kinds of lunch meat and fixings in the fridge. Go help yourself."

Bo thwacked her again, almost knocking her off her feet with the sharp swat. She was just irascible enough to give him a reciprocal punch to the shoulder, which he most likely didn't even feel despite his cringing facade of pain.

Clint called out, "Fix me one, too!" and Marc nodded as he went inside with Bo.

Wynn walked to the other end of the patio and dropped down into her settee. The forest-green-and-cream-striped cushions were soft and plush and she smoothed her hand over them with deep satisfaction. This was hers, all of it, the house, the tree-shaded yard, the hammock and…her neighbor. All hers.

She caught Zack watching her and she smiled. "It looks good, doesn't it?"

Zack appeared to be so annoyed she wasn't at all sure he'd answer. Then he sat down beside her. "It's very nice. You have good taste."

As he spoke, he stared out at the yard toward his daughter, giving Wynn his profile. She sighed, knowing his thoughts when he hadn't shared them. "Bo is just… Bo. I've known him almost as long as I've known Conan. They went through school together and stuff. He really doesn't—"

"Show any hesitation at touching your behind? Yeah, I noticed. I also noticed that you don't seem to mind."

Her lips tightened as her temper rose. "He treats me like a kid sister most of the time."

"Uh-huh." Zack turned to face her, his expression set. "I don't know why I'm even surprised, considering…" He made a disgusted sound and turned away again.

Her heart thumped hard and her stomach roiled. "Considering what?" When he didn't answer, she said, "Zack, don't you dare be a hypocrite. I wasn't the only one out there that night. We both got carried away."

He ran a hand through his hair. "I've never in my life done anything like that, so it had to be because of you."

He said that so casually, casting the blame without hesitation, that she wanted to throttle him. "*You* snuck up on *me* that night!"

"I did not sneak," he grumbled.

"Ha! I was asleep."

"Yeah, and what woman does *that?*" He jerked around to face her, looking angry and befuddled and very much like an attentive male. "What woman sleeps out in her backyard at night, exposed?"

"I wasn't *exposed*, you ass. You make it sound like I was naked or something." She shook her head, realized she'd just insulted him again, and wanted to bite off her tongue. She drew a breath and tried to sound reasonable. "Zack, I was just—"

He didn't let her finish. "I don't get carried away like that. Ever."

To Wynn, he still looked accusing, and all she could think to say was, "You did that night."

His eyes narrowed, then his gaze flicked over her. "Yeah. Bad judgement on my part."

Wynn sucked in a breath. *Damn, that hurt.* She wasn't sure if she wanted to punch him or cry. She wasn't much of a crier and seldom indulged, but now she felt dangerously close to giving in to tears. Her bottom lip even quivered before she caught it between her teeth.

For a brief moment, Zack looked guilty. "Look, Wynn, it's really none of my business what you do."

"I want it to be your business," she admitted softly.

His spine stiffened—and Bo shoved a sandwich into his face. "I figured you had to be hungry, too."

Zack studied Wynn a second longer, then warily looked up at Bo. "Thanks."

"No problem. 'A friend of Wynn's,' and all that." Bo pursed his lips and continued to glare down at Zack. "You *are* a friend, right?"

Wynn quickly stood and placed herself between the two men. "Back off, Bo. I mean it."

In the next instant, she yelped as she found herself yanked back down onto the soft settee. Zack had grabbed the waistband of her shorts and literally jerked her off her feet. She sat gawking at him while he stood and met Bo eye to eye. Zack wasn't as bulky as the bodybuilders, but he was all lean hard muscle.

"Actually," Zack said, "I'm more of an acquaintance at this stage."

"A friendly acquaintance?"

"You got reason to think otherwise?"

The male posturing had Wynn on edge. She would definitely strangle Bo later, and what in the world was wrong with Zack? She thought him to be a sweet, considerate, passive man. Not one to indulge in games of male one-upmanship. Yet he'd brought on as much attitude as Bo, and that was saying a lot.

A new voice intruded, full of good humor and mocking concern. "Making yourself the center of attention again, Zack?"

Wynn twisted in her seat, and found herself almost face-to-belt buckle with Josh, who stood just at the end of the patio, right behind the settee. He wore tight faded jeans and a white T-shirt that read: Firefighters Take The Heat.

Zack, too, turned to face him. "What are you doing here?"

Josh smiled and leaned down, bracing his arms on the settee back, looming over Wynn. She wanted to scoot away, especially with the dark frowns Zack sent her way, but she was a bit too surprised to move.

"I came to let you know that lunch is cancelled for

today," Josh said. "Mick insists on escorting Del to a coroner's for some research she's doing." He nodded at the sandwich still squeezed into Zack's hand. "But I see you'd forgotten all about our lunch."

Wynn lurched to her feet, feeling dreadful. "Ohmigosh. I interrupted your plans?" She looked between Josh who was smiling and Zack who was scowling. She ignored Bo.

Josh skirted the settee and again placed himself close to her. He even slipped his arm around her waist. She wasn't sure what to do. "Don't worry about it, Wynn. We meet nearly every week for lunch, so missing one now and then isn't a big deal."

Zack handed the sandwich to Wynn, who accepted it without thinking. Then he crossed his arms over his chest in a confident pose and said, "Josh, meet Wynn's erstwhile protectors. Bo and Marc and out there in the grass with Dani is Clint."

Bo and Marc nodded, but Clint was unaware of the additional guest. He was a grade school teacher with three daughters of his own and loved children in general. Wynn thought of him as a gentle giant, and smiled when she saw he was making Dani a flower garland out of clover buds.

Josh reached out to shake hands. He had his engaging grin in place, but his dark green eyes were alight with mischief. "Josh Marshall. How're you all doing?"

"They were just about to leave," Wynn said, trying for a not-so-subtle hint.

Bo just rolled his eyes. "Quit worrying, doll. We're not going to manhandle your neighbor."

Josh sputtered on a laugh. "Manhandle Zack? Of course not. You know he's a paramedic, right?"

Blank faces stared at Josh.

"Well, he is, and paramedics have to stay in great shape. So, don't let him fool ya. I've seen Zack lift three-hundred-pound men and carry them like they were infants. I've seen him work tirelessly through frozen snow for hours when cars piled up on the highway, and I've seen him go twenty-four hours without a single sign of exhaustion. He's got more dexterity and physical coordination than you can imagine, and he—"

Zack interrupted to say, "Can leap tall buildings in a single bound? Is faster than a speeding bullet?" His tone was dry, his expression chagrined.

Josh laughed. "I don't know about jumping buildings, but I've seen the bullet wound on your arm, so no, you're not all *that* fast."

Wynn jumped on that verbal opportunity. "I've seen it, too. How did it happen, do you know?"

"Sure I know. I was there."

"Josh," Zack warned, but now that everyone had redirected their attention from animosity to curiosity—all but Zack who still looked plenty defensive—Wynn wasn't about to back down.

And neither was Josh. "We were called to the scene of a riot. Buildings burning, glass everywhere, people down in the street."

"Dear God," Wynn muttered, easily able to picture the chaos. She'd never thought of Zack being involved in something so violent, and now that she did, fear swamped her.

Josh nodded. "Innocent people were cowering in alleys, afraid to move, *unable* to move. A woman had caught a stray bullet in the chest and she was just lying on the ground right in the middle of the worst of it, literally bleeding to death. Police were everywhere, SWAT teams were on the way. But we were afraid she'd die before we could get to her."

Wynn already knew what Josh would tell her, and in that moment she felt herself tumbling head over heels in love. To hell with logic or time or background. Her heart knew all it needed to know; she sank down onto the settee with her very first case of weak knees.

Zack shook his head. "It wasn't nearly so dramatic. Plenty of officers provided cover for me."

"Not well enough," Josh pointed out. "You took that slug to the upper arm. Actually," Josh continued, "he got shot when he covered the woman with his own body, trying to protect her from getting hurt worse. No doubt her body couldn't have sustained another serious injury."

"It was all fine in the end," Zack grumbled, and he started looking around for his shirt.

"Yeah." Josh grinned. "As I recall she was so grateful to Zack after that. Really grateful, if you get my meaning."

Marc and Bo chuckled in male understanding. Wynn rolled her eyes.

Zack said, "Shut up, Josh."

"My lips are sealed."

Zack finally found his shirt and pulled it on. Wynn mourned the loss of seeing his sexy naked chest, and she really wanted to examine that scar from the bullet more closely. "Dani said you were a hero."

He grunted. "Dani is four years old and adores me, which is only right since I'm her father. Truth is I just do my job, the same as anybody else."

Josh, still pretending to have zipped his lips, hummed a reply to that.

"Oh, knock it off," Zack snapped. He took his sandwich back from Wynn and took a healthy bite.

Wynn shook herself. "Since I interrupted your lunch, Josh, can I make you a sandwich, too?"

Bo clutched his heart. "You're going to make him a sandwich? Hell, we're the ones who worked for you all afternoon and you didn't offer to serve us."

Wynn elbowed him hard. "All of you behave," she said, and she encompassed Zack in that order, before heading toward the patio door. She caught Josh's arm as she went and dragged him along with her. "We'll be right back."

Chapter 7

Wynn got Josh inside the door, pulled him around the corner and flattened him against the wall. "I'm so glad you dropped in."

Josh, looking startled, said, "Uh," and clasped her upper arms to keep her from getting any closer. "Yeah, see, I sorta thought…well…" He looked around and to Wynn, he appeared hunted.

It took her a second to figure out what bothered him, and then she laughed. Men could be such big frauds!

"Look, Wynn…" He inched her a little farther away from him, while keeping his own body plastered to the wall. "Do you think it's safe to leave them all alone out there? I sensed some hostilities going on when I arrived."

"That's why you started defending Zack?"

"Hey, he's a friend. Besides, it's true. He can take care of himself. You know that, right?"

She shrugged, then daringly pressed closer, just to watch him squirm.

"The thing is," he blurted, looking all around again as if he expected someone to jump him at any second, "I thought you had a thing for Zack."

Wynn smoothed her hand over his very solid, very large shoulder and whispered, "I do."

"Because I'm not at all sure—" He did a double take. "You do?"

"Mmm-hmm." She looked him in the eyes, licked her lips, and continued, "That's why I dragged you in here." She patted his cheek and added, "To find out more about Zack."

"Oh. *Oh!*" Josh laughed and his confidence returned in his quirky smile and the way his shoulders relaxed. "Good. That's real good. Just what I wanted to hear."

"But Zack doesn't like me much."

"I think he likes you *too* much. That's the problem, at least as far as he's concerned." She stepped back and together they headed toward the kitchen. "Personally, I think you're perfect for him."

Wynn had never in her life been described as perfect. Her father harped on and on about her imperfect hair, and her mother harped about her lack of femininity and her brother drove her crazy telling her she was too aggressive while constantly challenging her. It was a rather nice compliment to hear. "No kidding?"

"Hell yeah." He pulled out a chair for her. "Look at you! You're attractive and healthy—being a paramedic, and having lost his first wife, Zack is big on health."

Wynn blinked at that sentiment.

"You're also fun and funny and you seem to like Dani." He frowned. "That's a must you know, that you like his daughter. And you can't fake that because plenty of women have tried and he's always seen through them."

Wynn fell speechless at such a wealth of verbal outpourings. She hadn't had to ask a single question!

He looked a little worried at her continued silence. "You do like Dani, don't you?"

Unwilling to lose this golden opportunity, she gathered her wits. "Of course. She's adorable. Smart, precocious, bold." She shrugged. "Beautiful like her dad."

Josh grinned. "Zack is beautiful, huh? What a hoot."

Wynn realized exactly what she'd said and blushed. "Don't you dare say anything to him."

"Oh, no, no, of course not."

Wynn didn't believe him for a second. "Josh…"

"Do you really have something to eat?"

One thing about men, you could always count on them wanting food—especially the big ones. Josh obviously spent his fair share of time in the gym pumping iron. His physique and looks were so impressive, he could have posed for a centerfold. "Sure. Help yourself."

He laughed at that. "So your muscle-bound friends were right, huh? You don't cater to men?"

Actually, she'd been so preoccupied formulating all her questions, she'd forgotten all about her manners. "Sorry." She stood. "I've had a lot on my mind."

Josh immediately pressed her back into her seat and then patted her shoulder. "Hey, you've been working all day and I'm a big boy, I can feed myself. It was just an observation."

Propping her head on both hands, she groaned. "This is awful. It's been so long since I dated, or since I tried to attract a guy, I'm going about it all wrong."

She heard the cabinets open. "You trying to attract Zack?"

"Without much success."

"Not true." The refrigerator opened and Wynn watched through her fingers as Josh poured out a glass of juice and hauled out sandwich fixings. She'd have to remember to stock up on more lunch meat now that she had her own home and had such big men living nearby and visiting.

Taking his own seat, Josh said, "Zack has noticed you big time. He's just in denial."

"You think?"

"I know." He piled enough meat on his sandwich to make a meal. "Zack hasn't acted this upside down about a woman since his wife."

Wynn wondered how to broach that subject, then decided against trying to dredge up tact she didn't have. It was pointless. She said simply, "Will you tell me about her?"

Josh popped a whole slice of bologna into his mouth and nodded. "Young, beautiful. Very sweet and very petite." He eyed Wynn. "Nothing like you, expect maybe the beautiful part."

Heat rushed into her face. Josh was such an outrageous flatterer! She decided the best thing to do was ignore it. "I'm only twenty-eight. Not exactly old myself."

"Ancient compared to Rebecca."

So, Zack was attracted to young, petite women? Just what she didn't want to hear. "That was her name? Rebecca?"

"Yep. She would have turned twenty-one a month after having Dani if she hadn't died."

Very young. Though Wynn didn't know the woman,

it hurt her to think of it. Dani and Zack had lost so much. She rubbed her forehead. "How long had they been married?"

"Only about seven months. The pregnancy was a surprise, and the reason for the marriage. Once Zack found out, he insisted, and Rebecca gave in. I'm not sure it's what either of them really wanted at the time."

Wynn did some math in her head and decided Zack was around twenty-five or so when he'd married, not much older than that when he became a father. Wynn swallowed hard. "How did she die?"

Josh laid the food aside and leaned back in his chair. He looked past Wynn, and he appeared more somber than she'd thought possible. "Rebecca had a hard time with the pregnancy. She was so small that it put a hell of a strain on her body. Her ankles swelled, her back hurt, her...well, you get the idea."

"Yes."

"She wasn't at all happy about the physical changes, so her emotional state of mind wasn't the best, either. She wanted Dani, no doubt about that, but she was pretty damn miserable those last few months. Physically and emotionally."

"I think that's pretty common, isn't it?"

Josh shrugged. "I suppose, what with hormone changes and all that." Then he shook his head. "Zack and I were both at a huge warehouse fire when she went into labor five weeks early. She called the station, and they immediately went to work on getting someone to replace Zack, but the destruction was huge and they were running short on manpower. Damn near everyone had already been called into service. Zack was working his ass off, dealing with a dozen different traumas, worried and anxious and madder than hell because he couldn't just leave. Leaving would have been a firing offense, though, which might not have stopped him except that he would never deliberately walk away from seriously injured people. And that's what he would have had to do. He thought Rebecca was okay, that she'd made it to the hospital and they were taking care of her..."

"But?"

Josh got up from the table. Like Zack's house, she had a window right over her sink, and that's where he went. He shoved his hands into his back pockets and stared out at the yard. "The contractions came too fast and she couldn't drive. She lost control of the car and it went off the road, flipping into a ditch. She took two other cars with her, but no one else was seriously hurt. By the time she was airlifted to the hospital, she'd died. They managed to save Dani."

Wynn nearly strangled on her own emotion. Her throat felt tight, her stomach ached and her heart beat painfully. She could only imagine what Zack had gone through.

"He's usually a rock," Josh said quietly. "Nothing rattles him. He's always calm and polite and reasonable. Always."

She looked up. *Zack* was calm and reasonable? Well, yes, he could be, she supposed. But he could also be forceful and outrageous and around her, he was seldom calm.

"That was the closest I've ever seen him come to losing it." Josh turned to face her. "That bullet wound he's got? Well, he knew he'd get shot when he went after that woman. I don't mean that he thought the odds would be good, I mean that he knew some of the rioters were firing *at* her, determined not to let her be saved, just to prove some fanatical point. Zack put himself between her and those bullets. He willingly risked his life for a person he didn't know from Adam. That's just how he is. He can't bear to see anyone hurt."

He drew a breath, then finished. "You can imagine what it did to him that he wasn't there for Rebecca."

"He blamed himself?"

"Yeah, he did. For a while. Then Dani got to him. For almost two weeks she was a perfect baby. Cooing when she was hungry, sleeping sound, and then bam, right out of the blue she became a tiny demon." Josh laughed. "Man, she put Zack through hell. He'd come in off a long shift and the sitter would say that Dani had slept and had been happy. Then she'd hear Zack and start making demands. When he was around, she wanted him to hold her. She wouldn't let him give her only half his attention."

Wynn considered all that. "You're saying he ignored her at first?"

"Hell, no. He made sure she was taken care of and he kissed her goodbye and hugged her hello, but he wasn't yet attached to her. He felt a responsibility for her, but he had so much grief, so much remorse, there wasn't much room for anything else, much less love. Till Dani took over."

"He's a good father."

"He's a *great* father. The absolute best. And he'd make a helluva husband, too."

Wynn was just digesting that not so subtle hint when Zack growled from the doorway, "I appreciate the accolades, Josh, but you're *way out of line*."

Josh said, "Uh, you didn't leave any dead bodies outside, did you?"

"Knock it off." He walked farther into the room. "You know I'm a pacifist."

"Right. Whatever you say." He skirted around Zack with theatrical fanfare, and said, "I think I'll talk to your friends, Wynn. They seem like very nice fellows."

The screen door fell shut a second later. Wynn slowly came to her feet to face Zack. "Nice fellows," he mimicked. "They seemed like possessive, jealous fellows to me."

"Protective, not possessive. I told you I haven't dated any of them."

"Did you? I don't seem to recall that conversation."

She cleared her throat. "Everything okay outside?"

He advanced on her, his gaze locked on hers. "If you mean has everyone played nice, yes. But your bully boys gave me the third degree."

"They didn't!" Dismay filled her. How could she make a good impression on a man like Zack if Bo kept behaving like an ass?

"They did."

As he reached her, she stepped behind her chair. She wasn't afraid of Zack, but she didn't understand his mood either. He seemed on edge, yet also sort of... accepting. But accepting of what? Something was definitely different, of that she was certain. "I'm sorry."

"They seem to think you have your 'sights set on me,' as they put it."

Oh God, oh God, oh God... She just knew her face was flaming. She only had one brother, and he was enough to contend with without his friends trying to take over the role, too. Hoping to excuse their bizarre behavior, she said, "I, ah, don't show a lot of interest in the opposite sex."

Zack cocked a brow. "What are you telling me? *Males* don't interest you?"

"No! That is, I meant that I don't show a lot of interest in *any* sex."

One side of Zack's mouth curled in an amused, mocking smile.

She bit her tongue, then took two long breaths. "I *mean*," she stated, "that I don't usually chase a guy. I've got friends, and that's it." And so she didn't sound pathetic, she added, "That's as much as I want."

His voice was oddly gentle when he quipped, "Glad to hear it."

He was now so close she felt his breath when he spoke. Just two inches and she could be kissing him again. She considered it, but held back because she didn't know if he'd be receptive to the idea. So far he'd acted really put out over their mutual attraction—even to the point of denying it was mutual.

Which, she realized, meant he was so close because he wanted to intimidate her. She frowned. "That was before meeting you, Zack. I want you. I haven't made a secret of that. But you should understand that what happened in the yard the other day was an aberration for me, too. I don't regret it, but no way has it ever happened before."

His mouth twisted, and she got the awful suspicion he didn't believe her.

Wynn lost her temper. "Just because I have big male friends—"

He rolled his eyes.

"—and I got carried away with you—"

"We *both* got carried away."

She completely missed his confession in the middle of her tirade. "—doesn't give you the right to assume I'm free with all men."

"It also doesn't give you the right to go snooping around in my private business. If you wanted to know about my wife, you should have asked me."

Her chin lifted so she could look down her nose at him. "Would you have told me anything?"

"No." Before she could finish her full-fledged huff, he added, "Because it's none of your business."

Wynn threw up her hands. "There, you see? Talking to you is pointless!" She realized she wasn't helping her case any, but really, what could she do? She couldn't change herself; she wouldn't even know where to begin. She let out a sigh and dropped her head. "Actually," she muttered, "I guess all of this is pointless, huh?"

Zack drew himself up. "What does that mean?"

"It means I'm beginning to accept that you're one hundred percent not interested." She lifted her shoulder in a halfhearted shrug. "I did hear all about your wife, and I know now that you're more attracted to petite women." She even snorted at herself in self-disgust. "God, I'm so far from petite it's laughable."

"Wynn." He said her name like a scold.

She held out her arms. "I'm a great big lummox of a girl and I know it. I'm not cute or petite or any of those nice things. You like little weak women who you can protect, and I don't need protection. I'm not even weaker than you."

His expression bemused, he rumbled, "Uh, actually you are. A lot weaker, damn it."

But she barely listened to him now. She was too upset

with the realization that Zack would likely never want to be involved with her. "I'm all wrong for you."

She paced around her kitchen, for the first time unmindful of the fine cherry cabinets and her new stainless steel sink and her side-by-side refrigerator, which just yesterday she'd kept touching because she loved it so much. Even the pleasure of getting her patio set up was now ruined.

Dejected, she turned to face him and said, "I'm sorry. I guess I've been a total pain in the butt."

"Yeah."

Though he said it gently, her shoulders slumped.

Then Zack stepped closer and he cupped her face carefully in his two hands and he said almost against her lips, "You are a pain in the neck, Wynn, and a pain in the ass and everywhere else. But you know why." And with a small laugh, "What bullshit, to say I'm not attracted to you."

She blinked at him, so startled she almost toppled over.

He shook his head. "You're not blind and you sure as hell aren't stupid. You *know* I want you."

"You do?"

"I do."

He briefly kissed her, but it was enough to make her breathless. "Even now," she questioned, "with us standing here in my kitchen and everyone else right outside? Even though I haven't just jumped you and dragged you to the ground?"

"Is that what you thought?" A sexy smile played with his mouth, making her heart punch. "That just because you took me by surprise and actually got me flat on my back was the only reason I acted as I did last week?"

Ignoring the part about taking him by surprise, Wynn nodded. The how and why of their interlude last week wasn't important. Not when right now, all she really, *really* wanted was for him to kiss her again. But he just kept staring at her mouth while his big rough thumbs stroked her cheeks and that was so nice, too, she held still and didn't dare complain or ask for more.

"Wynn, you did just take me by surprise, you know that don't you? You're strong, honey, but there's no way in hell you'd best me in a physical confrontation."

"Okay."

He laughed, a low husky sound, and shook his head. "You're placating me." And he kissed her again. "You're something else, you know that? I've never met a woman who wanted a man, yet continued to insult his manhood with every other breath."

"Your, ah, manhood?" Her gaze skipped down his body to his lap. He lifted her chin, keeping her from that erotic perusal while making a "tsking" sound.

"My machismo," he explained, "my masculinity." He tipped her face up and kissed her throat, the soft spot beneath her ear.

Wynn's toes curled inside her gym shoes.

"One of these days," he added while licking her ear and driving her insane, "I'm going to prove it to you."

"Yes." She had no idea what he wanted to prove, but whatever it might be, she was all for it.

His laugh was a little more robust this time. He looked at her, studied her dazed eyes and nodded. "All right. So, the challenge is made. What am I to do? I'm just a man after all, and I can only take so much without caving in."

He said all that with a wicked smile.

She said, "What?"

"Will you be at your hammock tonight?"

That caught her attention. Hope and excitement flared inside her. "Yes. Sure, of course."

"So anxious." He grinned and kissed her bottom lip. "I know this is wrong, I swear I do. But damn I want you. You're making me nuts, woman."

His machismo sounded just fine to her attuned ears. She smiled dreamily. "You're making me nuts, too. I tried to leave you alone, to let you get used to the idea of me..."

"Ha!" Shaking his head, smiling, Zack said, "That'd take a lifetime."

She liked the sound of that. A lifetime with Zack. With each day, with every damn minute, she was more attracted to him, in a million different ways.

Seeing her expression, his hands gentled and he waggled her head. "Wynn, I'm not making any promises about anything. If we meet tonight, it's strictly for sex."

Her hopes plummeted, but the excitement was still there. She bit her lip, undecided what to do. On the one hand, she'd never been one for casual sex.

But on the other, she'd never wanted a man like she wanted Zack.

And then suddenly there was a shrill yell from the yard and Zack moved with a blur of speed. He was outside before Wynn could catch her breath. Recognizing Dani's squeaky little voice, now filled with sobs, she quickly followed.

They found Dani held in Josh's arm, screaming her heart out. Josh, a study of frantic concern, blurted, "She got stung by a bee!"

Bo and Marc and Clint stood in a circle around Josh,

wringing their hands and fretting like old women. The sight would have been laughable if it hadn't been for the fat tears streaming down Dani's cheeks.

Zack took Dani and cradled her close to his chest. "Shh, honey, it's okay."

Josh lifted her foot and peered at it. "The stinger is out," he said, and his voice shook.

It amused Wynn that five large overgrown men would quake at a child's cry. Good grief, their panic would feed her own and the whole yard would soon be bawling.

"Is she allergic to stings?" Wynn asked, and both Zack and Josh said, "No."

She walked up to Dani and touched her tiny foot. In soft, soothing tones, she said, "If you think you're hurt, just think how the poor bee feels." She began steering Zack toward the patio. He hugged Dani so close she could barely get her head off his shoulder.

"I don't care about the dumb bee," Dani said, and hiccuped over her tears.

"That's good," Wynn told her, "because he's a goner now. Once they sting someone, that's all she wrote."

Dani looked mollified by that notion. "Really?"

"Yep. They can't grow a stinger back, and what good is a bee without a stinger? Zack, sit down here with her and I'll turn on the hose. The cold water will make it feel better." And to Dani, "You feel like soaking those little pink toes?"

Dani smiled and nodded, but her bottom lip still quivered.

Zack sat, rocking his daughter in his arms.

Wynn shook her head and fetched the hose. After about half a minute of freezing cold water running over her tiny foot, Dani struggled to sit up. She took one look at Zack, and patted his chest. "I'm 'kay."

He hugged her close, half-laughing, but still shaken. He also kissed her foot, then had to move so Josh could kiss it, too. Dani accepted the healing kisses as her due.

Zack kissed her one more time, then asked, "Dani, why did you have your shoes off?"

Evidently, this was something forbidden, for Dani summoned a pathetic, apologetic look, and then pointed at Bo. "I was tryin' on his shoes."

Bo took an appalled step back and his entire face darkened with guilt. "My shoes!"

"They're so big," Dani explained, looking down at her lap and giving another little sob. "Even bigger than Daddy's."

Everyone looked at Zack's feet. He muttered, "Size twelve."

Bo, still flushed with guilt, shrugged. "Thirteens," he admitted. "She's right, they are bigger."

Wynn had been stationed by the hose, watching the byplay, the way everyone looked from Zack's feet to Bo's and then to Dani's, doing some sort of bizarre comparison.

Her emotions had been on a roller-coaster ride since meeting Zack, keeping her on edge. Now the idea of a bunch of gargantuan men comparing foot sizes with a child who was so petite she barely reached any of their knees, just struck Wynn funny. She burst out laughing and couldn't stop. When everyone stared toward her, she laughed even harder.

On the edge of embarrassment, no doubt afraid he was the object of hilarity, Bo chuckled, too. Of course, that made Clint and Marc laugh. Dani finally started to giggle, drawn to the sound of the hilarity, though likely her humor wasn't for the same reasons. And with laughter being so contagious, within minutes everyone roared. Dani bounced on Zack's lap, her sting totally forgotten.

Watching Zack laugh was a special delight. Wynn had the feeling he didn't often give in to great displays of any kind of outward emotion. He wasn't, according to Josh, a man who lost his temper or his control.

Yet, with her he'd gone from one extreme to another. Surely that counted for something. What, she didn't know, but perhaps she'd find out tonight.

Now that she'd made up her mind, she could hardly wait.

Chapter 8

Zack checked on Dani one last time. Her tiny foot stuck out from under the sheet, and from the glow of the hall light he could just make out the rainbow print bandage she'd insisted on putting over her bee sting. He bent and kissed her toes, then tucked the foot away.

Dani stirred and stretched. "Daddy?"

A lump in his throat nearly strangled him. She only called him "daddy" when she was very tired, or hurt. He sat on the edge of the bed and smoothed her cheek. "Yeah, sweetie. It's me."

She yawned hugely, then reached for his hand. "We had a swell time today."

Smiling at the way she consistently phrased everything as a statement, Zack said, "Yes, we did."

"I really like Wynn."

"Do you?"

She nodded against her pillow. "You do, too."

Zack hesitated. His daughter had never played matchmaker in her life, so this particular statement totally took him by surprise. He said finally, "I like her fine."

"I like her more than fine. She's the funnest."

"Brat," Zack teased, and asked, "More fun than me?"

"The funnest *woman*," she clarified, and yawned yet again. "I'm gonna keep her."

Her voice had been faint, on the edge of sleep, but still he heard. "Dani? What do you mean you're going to keep her?"

"I want her to be mine," his half-awake daughter announced.

This was something totally new, like the feminine napkin discussion and Zack just knew he was going to start running into more of these torturous episodes. Heart pounding, he asked, "Yours, like as a friend?"

"Uh-huh. And a rela…retal…"

"Relative?"

"Yeah. That."

"She's not our relative, Dani. Remember, I explained relatives to you."

"I know. But she could be a wife and a mommy."

Zack stared at his daughter, and if he hadn't been sitting, he'd have fallen down. Dani's eyes were closed, her cheek nestled into her pillow.

Her sweet little mouth curled into a pleased smile when she said, "And we could have a brother." She peeked one eye open. "I want a brother."

"Honey…"

"A brother like Conan."

God forbid!

"I'd help with diapers and stuff."

"I know you would, sweetheart. But things like brothers take a lot of time."

She closed her eyes again and sighed. "Josh likes Wynn, too."

Zack froze, and found himself asking, "You think so?"

"Maybe he wants a brother." Her brow puckered. "I mean a son."

Zack had tried to talk to Josh about his interest in Wynn, but he hadn't had the chance. By the time Wynn's friends had left, which would have afforded some privacy, Josh had been ready to go, too.

He sat there thinking, recalling what Bo had told him. Wynn didn't date, and she very seldom showed sexual interest in men. Her reaction to Zack, according to those who knew her best, was extreme. Zack had been a little disconcerted to realize they all knew of Wynn's pursuit, but they said it was because she acted so differently with him. In the normal course of things, she pretended to be one of the guys.

Marc had warned him that Wynn was an uncommon woman, who looked at the world in an uncommon way.

As if he'd needed the warning! He'd already figured that out firsthand. Her flirting skills were nonexistent. She said what she wanted, and left Zack to deal with the shock.

Clint had added that she was a good sport, but still hated to lose. At anything. If she wanted Zack, then it'd be difficult to dissuade her.

And they all agreed, she wanted Zack.

He smiled. Wynn's approach was bold, but also refreshing. And now that he believed the reaction was as

unique for her as it was for him, his resistance had disappeared.

Zack sat quietly, contemplating all he'd learned today,
along with his daughter's sentiments until he heard her
breathing even into a light snore. He kissed her forehead
and stood. Her bedroom window was open, letting in a
cool breeze and plenty of fresh air.

Zack went to the window and looked out. As she'd
promised, Wynn sat in the hammock, waiting. At the
sight of her, he felt the rush of his blood and the swelling of muscles.

There was a lot to consider, especially his daughter's growing attachment to a woman totally unsuitable
for any type of permanency. But for now, none of that
seemed to matter.

For now, he had to have her.

He left his daughter's room in a silent rush, closing the door softly behind him. He'd already removed
his shoes so his bare feet made no sound as he moved
through the house and out the back door. The grass felt
soft and cool as he crossed through the darkness to
Wynn. As he went, he unbuttoned his shirt, letting the
evening breeze drift over his heated flesh.

What he planned, what *they* planned, felt wicked and
enticing and so sexual he was already hard.

She stood with her back to him, her arms wrapped
tight around her middle when he finally reached her.
"Wynn."

Whirling so fast she almost lost her balance, she
gasped, "I didn't hear you!" and in the next breath, with
relief, "I was afraid you'd changed your mind."

Her lack of self-protection shook him; she put her
heart on the line without reserve, and he felt her trust

like a deep responsibility—a responsibility he didn't want. "I had to get Dani settled down."

Her eyes a faint glow in the light of the moon, Wynn looked toward his house. "Will she be all right in there alone?"

"Dani sleeps like a bear hibernating. But if she should wake up, she'll look in the hot tub for me. We'd see the patio light."

With her arms still squeezed around herself, she nodded. "That's good."

"Are you nervous?"

"A little." She shifted her feet, moving a tiny bit closer to him. "I've never had a sexual assignation before."

Zack smiled. "Me, either."

"No?"

"I don't bring women to the house because of Dani. This is her home and I would never do that. My work schedule is crazy enough that when I get time to be with her, I don't generally like to waste it with women."

"Waste it with women," she repeated slowly, as if figuring out the meaning to his words. "You haven't dated much since your wife died?"

"More recently than ever before." He'd been bride hunting, so it had been necessary. "Not that more means very much."

"I know you haven't been celibate."

He laughed at her incredulity. "What is it about you, Wynn, that you can amuse me at the most awkward times?"

She frowned. "I didn't mean to amuse you. And what's awkward about now?"

Zack touched her cheek, let his fingers trail down to her throat and her bare shoulder. She wore a dark sleeveless cotton dress—like a long shirt—and she felt warm and very soft. "This is awkward because I'm so turned-on I can barely breathe."

"Zack." She rushed against him, clinging to him, her hands strong on his shoulders, her body pressed full length against his own. "How…how are we going to manage this? Not only haven't I had any assignations, but I've never made love in a hammock before either." She lifted her head and he felt her gentle breath on his jaw. "Have you?"

"No, but it doesn't matter." He kissed her, a light kiss to her temple, the bridge of her nose, the corner of her mouth. "Are you one hundred percent certain of this, Wynn?"

She offered a slight hesitation that just about made his heart stop, then nodded. "Very certain."

"Thank God." He kissed her, tasting her excitement and her urgency, which almost mirrored his own. Her lips were soft, and they parted for his tongue. Kissing Wynn was…well, it was definitely exciting. But it was more than that. Kissing her affected him everywhere, making his head spin and his abdomen cramp and his thighs ache.

He slid one hand down her back to her lush behind and pulled her in close, then groaned when she rubbed herself against his erection.

They both panted.

Wynn went to work on getting his shirt pushed off his shoulders. He shrugged it off, letting it land in the grass. With a sound of approval her fingers spread wide over his chest, tangling in his body hair, caressing his muscles, teasing over his nipples.

He backed her into the tree and briefly pinned her

there with his hips, grinding himself into her. He filled his hands with her breasts and their mouths meshed hotly, licking and sucking. Zack felt her pointed nipples, felt the lurch of her body as he gently rolled one sensitive tip. It wasn't enough. He caught the narrow shoulder straps and pulled them down to her elbows. She slipped her arms free and the dress bunched at her waist.

Moonlight made her breasts opalescent, made her nipples look dark and ripe. Shuddering with lust, he bent his head and drew her right nipple deeply into the heat of his mouth.

"Zack!"

"Shhh…" He licked and tasted and plucked with his lips. The husky sounds she made, hungry and real and encouraging, fired his lust. He lifted her dress.

She wasn't wearing panties.

"Damn." Zack stared at her wide eyes while his hands moved over the silky skin of her bottom. He closed his eyes, exploring her, relishing the feel of her, the carnality of the moment. "Damn, Wynn," he said again.

Her voice was a breathless, uncertain murmur. "I… I thought underwear might just be in the way, and I didn't know if…"

Zack went to his knees and pushed the dress higher.

Startled, Wynn tried to step away, but the tree was at her back and Zack held her securely. *"What are you doing?"* She sounded frantic as she pulled at his shoulders.

"It's dark." Zack glanced up, saw her embarrassment even in the night shadows and asked gently, "No man's ever kissed you here?"

She smacked at his shoulder. *"Zack,"* she hissed, and to his amazement, she looked around.

He couldn't help but laugh. "It's a little late to be worrying about voyeurs, Wynn."

"But…" She held his shoulders securely, as if she could keep him away. "You can't do that out here!"

"We can have intercourse, but not oral sex?"

She gasped, thoroughly scandalized by his words, and quickly looked around the deserted yard again. Zack loved it. For once he had the upper hand and no way in hell would he give it up. Especially since he was dying to taste her, to hear her moan out a climax.

He taunted her, saying, "You'll like this, Wynn. And so will I."

"I don't know…"

Knotting the dress in a fist, he anchored it high at the small of her back. He cursed the clouds that made the moon insufficient light. He wanted to see all of her, not just hints of her, curves and hollows exaggerated by the shadows. He wanted to see each soft pink inch of her sex, the dent of her navel, the dimples in her knees.

He groaned; what he could see was spectacular. Her thighs were beautiful, sleek and firm and now pressed tightly together as he stroked them each in turn. He looked up at her breasts, as large as the rest of her, full and white.

He couldn't tell the color of the hair on her mound, but he guessed it to be the same as her eyebrows, slightly darker than the honey brown hair on her head. He sifted his fingers through her curls and heard her indistinct whimper of excitement. Leaning close, he pressed his cheek to her belly as he touched her.

Her belly…well he'd always loved female bellies. To Zack, they epitomized femininity, soft and slightly rounded and smooth. Wynn's belly was extremely sexy.

He felt her quiver and turned his face, kissing her, licking her navel; all the while his fingers continued to pet her. Nothing more, just petting, but it made him so damn hot he felt burned.

Night sounds closed in around them, the hum of insects, the rustle of a soft breeze through the treetops. Clouds crossed the moon repeatedly, first softening the light, then obliterating it. The air felt thick, charged, damp.

"Zack, I don't know if I like this..."

"You'll like it," he assured her in a rough whisper. He trailed his fingers lower, cupping her, then working his fingertips between her clenched thighs. Her buttocks pressed back against his fist holding her dress. Zack urged her forward again.

He felt her. Her lips were swollen, warm and slick. He touched her gently, sliding back and forth until she grew even wetter, then he pushed one finger deep inside.

Her knees locked and she made a long, raw sound of surprised pleasure. "This," she rasped, "isn't at all what I expected."

Had she expected him to be *sweet*? Zack wondered. Had she thought to be the aggressor? The idea tormented him. Her misconceptions about him could be alternately amusing and enraging.

"Open your legs, Wynn."

Her head tipped back against the tree and she said, "The way you say that..." She looked down at him. "It really turns me on."

Zack stared up at her, his finger still pressed deep into the heat of her body, clenched by her muscles, and she wanted to talk? "Open them, Wynn."

After a long look and a shuddered breath, she obliged

him. Zack damn near came watching her long legs shift apart—for him.

"What will you do?" she asked, and she sounded almost as excited as he felt.

"This," he told her, sliding his finger deeper, then slowly pulling it out. Her muscles gripped him, held on tight. He worked a second finger into her. "You're tight, Wynn."

She reached above her head and clasped a branch for support, then moved her legs wider apart. "You expected something else from a big girl like me?"

"I never know what to expect from you." That was certainly the truth. Tired of talking, Zack kissed her thigh, her hipbone. "You smell incredible."

She groaned a protest when he pulled his fingers from her, until he began petting her again, spreading her wetness upward, over her clitoris.

She cried out, and her whole body jerked. He continued to touch her, circling and plucking and stroking. Her hips thrust toward him, her whole body straining. He could smell her, the fresh, pungent scent of aroused woman.

It had been so long, too damned long. He leaned forward, opened her further with his fingers, and drew her into his mouth, savoring her with a raw sound of hunger and satisfaction. The contact was so startling, so intense, she tried to lurch away, but he gripped her hips in his hands and held her pinned to the tree while he got his fill.

She gave up and with his support, her thighs fell open further, giving him better access, which he quickly accepted, licking and sucking at her hot sweet flesh. Her hands tangled hard in his hair, pulling him closer still.

Zack's heart punched hard in his chest and his cock strained in his jeans. He couldn't wait another second. He stood and turned her. "Hold onto the tree."

Panting, rigid, she looked at him over her shoulder and said, "What...?"

Zack had his jeans opened and the condom out in a heartbeat. He rolled it on, moaning at the sensation of the rubber on his erection, his teeth gritted with the effort of holding back. He stepped up to her, slipped his fingers under her to open her for his entry, and took a soft love bite of her shoulder while he pressed in.

Wynn flattened her hands on the rough bark, bracing herself, groaning with him. He wanted to touch her everywhere, and did. He felt her breasts, rolled her nipples, stroked her belly and below, fingering her until she cried and relaxed and he could sink deep into her.

"Oh yeah," he rumbled, finally where he'd wanted to be almost from the first second he saw her. He had to catch his breath and his control before he could start the rhythm they both needed. "Tilt your hips. Push back against me, Wynn. That's it, sweetheart."

He gripped her hips and helped her. When she caught the frenzied rhythm, he returned to pleasuring her, one hand on her breasts, one between her legs.

Sweat dampened his back though the night was cool. He squeezed his eyes shut and concentrated on not coming, on not giving in to the raging need to let go. He wanted her with him, wanted to know that she'd climaxed, that he'd satisfied her. He pressed his face into her shoulder while his every muscle grew taut and rippled and suddenly she went still, holding her breath.

"Yes, Wynn," he urged her, knowing he was a goner, that he'd last maybe two seconds more and that was it.

Her head dropped forward between her stiffened arms and her breath came out in a long, low earthy moan that obliterated any last thread of his control. She didn't scream, but at the end she said his name on a seductive, satisfied whisper of sound that licked along his spine.

He shuddered as he came, holding her tight and pounding into her, not the least bit worried about hurting her, not when she continued to roll her hips sinuously against him, continued to make soft sounds of completion and satisfaction.

A big woman was nice, better than nice.

He slumped into her, which made her slump into the tree. They both struggled for breath.

A few seconds later, she groaned and shifted the tiniest bit. "Zack?"

"Hmmm." Their skin felt melded together, her back to his chest, her sweet backside to his groin, the front of his hairy thighs to the smooth backs of hers. He didn't want to move, not ever.

"The tree isn't all that comfortable," she complained. "Do you think we can totter over there to the hammock?"

His legs were still jerking in small spasms. His heart hadn't completely slowed its mad gallop yet. There was a low ringing still in his ears.

He felt stripped bare down to his soul. His lungs burned. "Yeah, sure. No problem."

Determined not to crumble, he straightened slowly. He felt like an old man with arthritis, very unsure of his ability to stay on his feet. He removed the condom, dropped it into the grass with the mental reminder to dispose of it later, then tugged his jeans back up.

All that took more effort than he could spare and he nearly collapsed again. Wynn didn't help, not when she turned and leaned into him. She was a woman, but she was no lightweight. He remembered lifting his petite wife after sex and holding her in his arms. Ha!

Zack eyed the hammock that wasn't too far away considering they were against the tree supporting it at one end. He slung an arm around Wynn and fell into the canvas. She laughed as the hammock swung wildly, almost tossing them both, but when they stayed more in it than on the ground she snuggled around until she was mostly on top of him.

"Will the ropes hold both of us, do you think?"

"If not, I'll buy you a new one."

"You will not." She leaned up and looked at his mouth, then touched him with a gentle fingertip. In the most sweetly feminine voice he'd ever heard from her, Wynn said, "I really liked what you did."

Zack closed his eyes and grinned. She'd damn near yanked him bald with her enthusiasm, so he'd assumed as much.

He said, "I told you so."

"It seemed sort of...kinky."

Still grinning, he said, "It only seems kinky the first time. Trust me."

"Did you like it?"

He opened one eye. She looked uncertain. "My only complaint is that once again you pushed me over the edge."

"I didn't!"

"I wanted to spend more time tasting you. More time hearing you make all those sweet little squeaking womanly noises."

He was dead to the world, barely able to drum up a

little teasing, and she had the energy to slug him in the shoulder. Luckily, he was still numb so it didn't hurt.

"I do *not* squeak!"

He smoothed his hand down her back, discovered her dress was still hiked up, and patted her bare bottom. It was a nice big bottom, filling his large hand. "You squeak and you moan and I like it."

"You did your own share of moaning."

"Men don't moan," he informed her, "they groan. There's a definite difference."

"Whatever you say."

He smiled. "I like how you taste, too."

She ducked her head and rubbed herself against him.

Because he was too comfortable, too replete, he admitted, "At least I should finally sleep tonight."

"Are you saying you haven't slept well lately?"

He used both hands to hold on to her backside and anchor her close. "No. I've been as restless as a horny teenager."

That had her laughing, but she quickly sobered. "My parents are moving in tomorrow."

Zack yawned. "Yeah, I remember."

Turning shy on him, she curled her finger in and around his chest hair and said, "I was hoping we could maybe do this again."

Her meaning sank in and Zack stilled. Ah hell, he couldn't possibly be expected to get his fill of her in one lousy night! He'd been too primed and ended it too quickly. He hadn't luxuriated in her, hadn't explored her as he'd meant to, as he'd thought about doing.

A week, maybe two weeks, would take the edge off. But not one damn night.

"May I assume by your frown that you want to do this again?" Wynn asked.

Zack lifted his head enough to feast on her mouth in a long, slow, wet, eating kiss. When he released her, they were both panting again. "Yeah," he said, "you can assume that."

Wynn tucked her head into his shoulder. She had one leg bent across his abdomen, the other stretched out to the bottom of the hammock. Zack had one leg on the outside of hers, the other over the side with his foot firmly planted on the ground so he could keep them swaying.

He mulled over a few possibilities and then asked, "Are your parents the protective sort?"

She snorted. "No."

He didn't like how quickly she answered that. Parents should be protective, especially of a daughter living alone. But since he had his own plans, he didn't say so. "I've got stuff planned tomorrow and Tuesday. But Wednesday I should get home from work around eight. By nine-thirty I can have Dani tucked away." His mind conjured all sorts of erotic possibilities and he growled, "Is it possible you could come visit me, say to use the hot tub, and they wouldn't check up on you?"

Though Wynn didn't move, the rushing of her heartbeat gave away her excitement. "They wouldn't think a thing of it. They're used to me being pals with guys."

That made Zack chuckle. Damn, she tickled him with her strange replies and stranger relationships. "It'll be dark by then. I'll watch for you."

"Let's make it ten o'clock. My parents will be in bed by then."

Her position left her soft sex open and vulnerable to him. Zack trailed his fingertips over her bottom cheeks until he could feel the heat of her. He pressed. "Have you ever made love in a hot tub?"

"No." She reared up to glower at him, and the heat in her eyes was a combination of suspicion and arousal. Because of where and how he touched her, her voice shook when she demanded, "Have you?"

Zack thought she might be jealous, and oddly enough, he liked that. "No." He could see her face clearly now, the incredible hazel eyes, the long lashes and the very kissable mouth. "I've never made love against a tree before either. Or in a hammock."

He touched her tender lips, still swollen and wet from their lovemaking, then pushed his middle finger into her.

She panted. "Me, neither."

With her practically straddling his abdomen, Zack kicked the hammock again, making it rock. She grabbed his shoulders for support. He looked at her naked breasts bobbing and swaying before him and immediately grew hard. "I just might prove successful at all three."

Wynn made a low sound of agreement. "Based on what I've seen so far, I wouldn't be at all surprised."

"I have another condom in my pocket."

"A man who comes prepared. Incredible."

Zack started to laugh at that, but then she came down over him, her breasts pressing into his chest, and she kissed him and all he could think about was making love to her again. Wednesday seemed a long way off, so he'd have to make this last. And to do that, he'd have to slow her down.

"Wynn?"

"Hmm?" She continued to kiss his mouth, his chin, his jaw.

"Scoot up."

She stilled, lifted her head to stare at him. "Why?"

"Because I want to kiss your breasts. And then your belly—you have an adorable belly by the way. And then maybe I'll even nibble on this sweet rear end of yours."

Her eyes almost crossed; she swallowed hard. "Are you going to...do what you did to me again?"

He nodded slowly. "Oh yeah. You can bet I am."

Wynn froze, caught her breath, and with barely contained excitement, she attacked him. For Zack, it was the strangest sensation to laugh and lust at the same time. Strange, but also addictive.

It was well past midnight before he finally dragged his spent, satisfied body into his own house. And as he suspected, he no sooner collapsed onto the bed than he was sound asleep, with a very stupid smile on his face.

Chapter 9

"Darling!"

Wynn jerked so hard at the sound of that loud, wailing voice, she lost her footing on the ladder. It shifted against the gutter, making her yelp and attempt to grab for the roof, but it was too late. Her hands snatched at nothingness.

As if in slow motion, the ladder pulled farther away from the house and Wynn found herself pedaling the air for several suspended seconds before she landed in the rough evergreen bushes with a hard thud. The wooden ladder crashed down on top of her.

"Ohmigod! Wynn! Wynn!"

A flash of red satin blurred in front of her eyes as her father knelt in front of her. The sunlight caught his diamond earring and nearly blinded her. "My baby! Are you okay?"

Her head was ringing and her side hurt like hell. She had a mouthful of leaves and something sharp poked at her hip. Her father began picking debris from her hair, tsking and fussing until her mother showed up and shoved him aside.

"Dear God, you nearly killed her, Artemus!"

Wearing faded cutoffs and a colorful tie-dye smock, Wynn's mother leaned over her. "It's a good thing we're here, Wynonna. You look hurt."

Wynn could only stare. A good thing? She wouldn't be hurt if her father hadn't startled her so. She hadn't even heard their car arrive. Of course, her thoughts had been on Zack, on that mind-blowing episode the night before, not on her parents' extended visit. She'd slept little last night, too busy going over and over all the wonderful things Zack had done to her and with her.

Her mother sat back on her heels. "Artemus, will you look at her? I think she hit her head."

Artemus leaned down and waved his hand in front of her face. "Yoo-hoo, princess? Baby, can you hear us?"

Suddenly Artemus was shoved aside again, but not by her mother. Zack, wearing only jeans that weren't properly fastened and a very rugged shadowing of beard stubble, crouched down in front of her. "Wynn?" Unlike her parents, his voice was gentle and concerned. He touched her cheek, which she realized had been scraped raw by a bush. "No, don't move, sweetheart. Just hold still and let me make certain you're okay."

Sweetheart? She glanced at her parents and saw them both staring with speculation. Oh dear. Wynn blinked at Zack. "Um…what are you doing here?" It was very early still, not quite seven, and Zack should have been home getting ready for work.

"I was making my coffee when I saw you climb the damn ladder. Before I could get dressed and tell you how stupid you were being, you fell."

Her mother asked, "You were making coffee naked?"

Without looking at her, Zack said, "No, in my underwear."

A wave of heat washed over Wynn. Her parents began staring even harder.

Wynn cleared her throat. "My father startled me."

"Well!" Artemus took immediate exception to that accusation. "If your hair wasn't in your eyes, maybe you would have seen me coming and you wouldn't have *been* startled!"

Zack turned to him to say something, and went mute. Her father was in top form today. He wore a red silk shirt, open at the collar to show a profuse amount of curly chest hair. He had two rings on his fingers, a gold chain around his neck and the big diamond earring he almost never removed. His pressed dark-blue designer jeans were so tight they fit like his skin, and his low boots were polished to a shine. His golden brown hair, so unlike Wynn's, was parted in the middle and hung nearly to his shoulders.

At Zack's scrutiny, he tossed his head and huffed.

Zack snapped his mouth shut and turned back to Wynn without uttering a word. "Where are you hurt?"

"Nowhere. I'm okay." But when she started to sit up, she winced and Zack caught her shoulders.

"No, let me check you."

"Daddy?"

Dani stood there, still in her nightgown and holding a fuzzy yellow blanket. Wynn smiled at her. "I'm okay, munchkin."

"You're in the bushes."

"Luckily, they broke my fall."

Dani smiled. "I saw you on the roof. I wanna get on the roof, too."

Zack turned so quickly everyone jumped. "Dani, if I catch you even thinking such a thing you'll be grounded in your room for a month!"

"Wynn did it."

Zack ground his teeth together. When he turned to Wynn, his expression was no longer so concerned. Now he looked furious. "Wynn will tell you what a dumb stunt that was, won't you, Wynn?"

Everyone stared at her. Her parents looked particularly interested in seeing her response, and she knew it was because they expected her to chew Zack up and spit him out in little bits. Never, ever, did she let anyone speak to her as he did.

But there was Dani, watching and waiting, and the thought of the child trying to get on a roof made her skin crawl. "I should have waited until there was someone to hold the ladder steady for me, Dani. Sometimes I do things without really thinking about them. It's a bad habit."

Her mother gasped and her father pretended to stagger. After a long second, Zack gave her a thankful nod.

Relieved, Wynn said, "Mom, Dad, this is my neighbor Zack Grange and his daughter Dani. Zack is a paramedic."

"Well, that explains everything," her father said with facetious humor.

Wynn winced again as Zack pressed his fingertips over her side. She said quickly, "Zack, my mother Chastity and my father Artemus."

Dani said, "I like Wynn lots."

"We're rather fond of her, too," Artemus said, and he patted Dani's head, then frowned at her hair.

Zack paid no attention to the introductions. "Let me get your shirt up and see what you've done."

Chastity laughed.

"No, Zack, really I'm fine, I just… Zack, stop it…"

Chastity said, "Oh be still, Wynonna. Let the man have a look."

Zack looked.

A long bloody scratch ran up and over her ribs almost to her breast. Zack looked furious. "This needs to be cleaned."

"I'll take care of it as soon as you *let-me-out-of-the-bushes!*"

He began checking her arms, her legs. Wynn, peeved at being the center of attention, scrambled out of his reach, gaining more scratches in the bargain. Using the side of the house for support, she stood.

Her efforts ended in a gasp and she almost dropped again. Zack caught her under the arms. "What is it? Your leg?"

"No." She squeezed her eyes shut and whimpered. Damn damn damn. There was no help for it. Drooping, she said, "It's my toe."

"Your toe?" her father repeated.

"My baby toe." She was balanced on her left leg, so Zack rightfully assumed she'd injured her right toe.

"I'm going to lift you," he told her. "Tell me if I hurt you."

"Zack!" The whole situation was going from bad to worse. "You can't lift me."

"She weighs more than I do," her father said.

Wynn gasped. "I do not!" She tried to slap him, but he ducked aside.

In the next instant she found herself securely held against Zack's bare chest. His arms didn't shake and his legs were steady. He didn't appear the least bit strained.

Awareness mushroomed inside her.

She couldn't remember the last time anyone had lifted her up. Even Conan didn't do it anymore, claiming she was too big, and he could easily bench-press four-fifty.

It felt kinda nice. Dumb but nice.

She wrapped her arms around his neck, but said, "You can put me down, Zack."

He stepped out of the bushes. "Dani, come with me into Wynn's house. We'll get you dressed in just a minute."

"We'll be late," Dani predicted with an adult sigh, and skipped after him.

Wynn looked over Zack's shoulder and saw her parents watching the display with fascination. She groaned. "This is awful."

"Wynn?"

"What?"

"You'll notice I'm not even breathing hard."

She looked at him, his hair mussed and his eyes still heavy from sleep. His sleek, hard shoulders were warm and his chest was solid. He smelled delicious. "I did notice that."

"And I'm not straining, either."

Despite her humiliation at having fallen off a ladder, shocking her parents and making Zack run late, she smiled. "Superhero."

He grinned. "C'mon, Dani. You can open the door

for me. I think Wynn's parents are a little confused by all this."

"They're confused," Wynn responded, "by the sight of a male neighbor feeling me up in the bushes and toting me around with a lot more familiarity than has ever been exhibited in the past."

"I wasn't *feeling you up.* I was checking you over. There's an enormous difference."

"Yeah, well, I could tell by my parents' expressions, they considered it one and the same."

Zack paused to look down at her. His breath smelled of toothpaste and was warm. "I was watching you through that window, cursing you if you want the truth, and when I saw you fall, my heart almost stopped."

At the husky tone of his voice, something inside Wynn turned to mush—probably her brains. But it sounded as if he cared about her, at least enough to not want her to break her neck.

Wynn drew a breath. "I'm sorry," she answered, her voice just as husky. "I didn't hear them drive up."

"Mmmm." Zack stared at her mouth. "Had your mind on other things did you?"

"She was daydreamin'," Dani said and pulled the door open with exaggerated impatience.

"Is that right?" Zack stepped into the kitchen and went through to the family room. "Were you daydreaming, Wynn? About what, I wonder."

She muttered close to his ear, "As if you didn't know," and saw his small satisfied smile.

He lowered her carefully to the couch. "Let me get your shoe and sock off."

"I can do it."

Of course, he ignored her wishes and untied her laces.

"Zack, my feet are probably sweaty by now. I've been up and working since about five."

"Do you ever not work?" Pushing aside her fretful hands, he eased her sneaker off. "Sweaty," he confirmed as he peeled her sock away and began examining her toe.

Wynn stretched up to see. Dani stood beside her and patted her shoulder.

Her poor little baby toe was already black and blue and the bruising had climbed halfway up her foot. It was swollen and looked awful. Seeing it made it hurt worse, but she forced a laugh and said, "Big and sweaty. Betcha wish now you'd left my sock on."

"Damn, Wynn," Zack muttered, touching her foot with a heart-wrenching gentleness. "It's definitely broken. You need to ice it, then get it taped. Can your doctor see you today?"

"For a baby toe?" She snorted. "Don't be ridiculous." Wynn seriously doubted she could hobble her way to the doctor right now, the way her foot felt. How one small toe could cause so much pain was a mystery.

The kitchen door opened and closed and her parents joined them at the couch. Her father went straight for her head and began trying to groom her hair. Her mother asked, "Do you have any herbal tea? That always helps."

Zack looked pained, then resigned. "I need to be getting to work. But she has a broken toe, maybe even a broken foot, so it should be X-rayed. She's also got a lot of cuts and scratches that'll need to be cleaned."

Her father said, "Wynn, Wynn, Wynn."

She swatted his hands away from her hair. "I'm fine, Dad."

Chastity looked Zack over from head to toe and back

again. "Well." She smiled. "You run along, young man. We're here now and we'll take good care of her."

"You're a hippie," Dani said with awe.

Zack said, "Dani!"

But Chastity laughed. "Did my daughter tell you that?"

Dani nodded. "And you gots rings on your toes."

"Just two rings, but they're made of a special metal that has healing powers. Perhaps I'll put one on Wynn and it'll make her toe heal quicker."

"No!" Zack caught himself and stood. He looked frazzled and harassed and undecided. "No rings." Then, stressing the point by speaking slowly, he said, "She needs an X-ray."

"Zack," Wynn said, "I'm a big girl."

"Indeed." Her father moved from her hair to Dani's and Dani appeared to love the attention. She even gave Artemus a huge grin.

"I can take care of myself. I'm not an idiot!"

"No, just an intelligent woman who climbs a rickety ladder to the roof before the sun is even all the way up."

"If Dad hadn't snuck up on me…"

"Now don't go blaming me again, darling! Your young man is right. You had no business being on that ladder in the first place." He said all that without looking up, too busy working on Dani's hair.

Zack opened his mouth, then closed it. He shook his head. "Wynn, promise me you'll go get an X-ray."

"But…"

"It's likely just a broken toe and they'll tape it, but it's better to be safe than sorry. Being a physical therapist, you should know this."

She did know it. "Oh, all right."

As if making a decision, Zack said, "I'll check on you tonight. In the meantime, Mrs. Lane, why don't you get her some ice to soak her foot for the swelling? And, Mr. Lane, you could maybe get her a phone so she can make the call to the doctor?"

Her parents looked pleased with the direction. Artemus quickly finished fooling with Dani's hair and rushed off. Chastity followed him.

The second they were out of the room, Zack bent over Wynn. "I wish I had more time, but if I don't get going now, I'll be late."

"I understand. Really, I'm fine."

"When I get home I expect to find you taking it easy."

"Me and my large feet will make a leisurely day of it."

He touched her cheek. "Large feet for a large, beautiful woman."

Now her brain and her bones were mush. She managed a lopsided silly smile.

Zack straightened. "I'll see you tonight."

"I thought you had plans."

"I do." He didn't explain beyond that.

Wynn wanted to ask him what his plans were, but she was afraid he'd be out with another woman. And because she had no exclusive rights to him, she couldn't complain, so she was better off not knowing.

Dani kissed her cheek. "I'll see ya tonight, too. I'll even draw you a picture."

It was then that Wynn noticed Dani's fine, fair hair had been plaited into an intricate braid and tied with a tiny yellow ribbon. She shook her head in wonder. Did her father carry ribbons in his pockets?

She wouldn't be at all surprised.

Zack noticed his daughter's hair, too. He did a quick double take, then said, "Well I'll be."

Dani smiled and kept reaching back to feel it. She looked very pleased with the results. "It's pretty."

Wynn said, "Very pretty!" and meant it.

Chastity hustled back in with a big bowl filled with ice and several dishcloths over her arm. She dropped onto the foot of the couch, making Wynn groan. To Dani, she asked, "You're the artist who created that masterpiece on the refrigerator?"

Wynn managed a smile to help cover the discomfort of her mother's rough movements. "That's right. Isn't she talented?"

"Very much so." As Chastity wrapped ice in a towel, she said, "You'd love finger paints. Have you ever tried them?"

Both Wynn and Zack winced. "Mom, they're awfully messy."

"So?" She flapped a dismissive hand at Wynn. "You and your cleanliness quirks. She's a child! You can't stifle her creative spirit just because she might get a little paint under her nails." Chastity was gentle as she applied the ice to Wynn's foot.

Watching Zack, Wynn thought he might have jumped her mother if she hadn't shown what he considered adequate care. "I brought my paints with me, Dani. It'll be lovely, you'll see."

Beaming, Dani said, "Thank you!"

Artemus waltzed in with the phone. "Found it!" He handed it to Wynn, along with her small phone book, then turned to Dani. He patted her hair with pride. "Lovely." Then to his daughter, "Wynn," he said, "wouldn't you like for me to do something with your hair while you make your call?"

Wynn said, "No," and her father's face fell with comical precision.

Zack scooped Dani and her blanket into his arms. "We have to run. Wynn, remember what I said."

"Me and my big feet will follow doctor's orders."

There was a general round of farewells, and five seconds later, Zack was gone. Wynn fell back against the couch. Her foot throbbed and ached, her ribs pulled, she itched from all the shrub scratches and now her parents were standing there staring at her with tell-all expectation.

The day had started out being so promising, but now…

She doubted it had dawned on Zack yet, but after all they'd just witnessed, no way would her parents believe a simple visit to the hot tub. Nope, they were eccentric, but they were not dumb.

And they knew sexual chemistry when they witnessed it.

Her mother, pretending a great interest in Wynn's bruised and swollen toes, said, "My, my, my. What a hottie." She slanted Wynn a look and an I'm-onto-you grin.

"Quite virile," her father agreed, while tugging distractedly on his earring and eyeing his wife's legs. Despite years of marriage and the fact that he was more colorful, Artemus remained highly attracted to her mother. He made no effort to hide his sexual willingness, which pretty much started from the time Chastity woke in the morning and ran until she fell asleep at night. It was almost comical.

He visibly pulled himself back to the subject at hand. "I, ah, take it he's single?"

Wynn sank further into the cushions. "Yes."

Silence reigned for only a few seconds, and then her father clasped his hands together and sighed. "Well, the little girl has *fabulous* hair! Or at least she will when I finish with it. All in all, I say they'll be a wonderful addition to the family. What do you think, dear?"

Chastity smiled. "I think we got here just in time to watch the fireworks."

Zack heard the noise from Wynn's house the second he stepped out of his car. Blaring music competed with laughter and the din of loud conversation.

It was six-thirty and he was tired, hungry, worried and rushed. It seemed he'd been running late from the moment he woke that morning, and there'd been no let-up since.

He'd started the day by oversleeping. After the excesses of lovemaking the night before, he'd slept like the dead and hadn't even heard his alarm until it had been ringing for almost half an hour. When he got over that disquieting phenomenon, he'd washed his face and brushed his teeth in two minutes flat, then gone for coffee before attempting to put a razor to his throat.

He never had gotten around to shaving, he realized, and now he felt scruffy and unkempt. He rubbed his rough jaw, remembering the trials of the day.

It was as he'd measured coffee that he glanced out the kitchen window and spied Wynn precariously balanced on an old wooden ladder, attempting to clean her gutters. His hair had been on end, his eyes still gritty, his feet bare on the cold linoleum floor, and he lost his temper.

He ran upstairs to awaken Dani, hastily pulled on pants, then ran back downstairs and outside to confront Wynn before she fell and killed herself.

He'd been too late.

It still made him tremble when he remembered opening the door just in time to see her wildly flailing the air as she plummeted to the ground. His stomach cramped anew.

Damned irritating, irrational, provoking female! She was lucky she'd only broken a toe!

He thought about her parents and cringed. "Flaming heterosexual," she'd called her father, and now he knew the description was apt. He'd never met a more flamboyant, dramatic man; his every word and gesture had been exaggerated.

But he'd done a wonderful job with Dani's hair. She'd looked so cute…

Zack shook his head.

Wynn's mother was, as she'd claimed, a hippie. Her long blond hair had streaks of gray, but her figure was still youthful. Wynn had likely gotten her beautiful legs from her mother. Chastity's legs weren't nearly as long, and the rings on her toes were a distraction, but all in all, she was an attractive woman. Loony, but attractive.

After Zack secured Wynn's promise to see a doctor, he'd rushed back home to prepare for work. He left the house right on time. Unfortunately, when he reached Eloise's house to drop off Dani, he'd found the elderly woman ill.

With Dani hovering nearby, Zack did a medical check on Eloise. She was feverish and pale, her pulse too weak. Eloise claimed it was no more than the flu and she warned Dani to beware of her germs. She said she'd been sick off and on all night, so she'd called Zack that morning. But it must have been while he was at Wynn's house, and he hadn't thought to check his answering machine in his hurry to get out the door.

He called his supervisor and explained why he'd be late so one of the men from the shift before could stay over, then he'd bundled Eloise up for a trip to the emergency room. He wasn't willing to take any chances with a woman her age, especially when she looked so weak. While he gathered a few things for her, he'd called Josh, who was off that day.

A woman had answered.

Zack thought about hanging up and calling Del or Mick instead, but Josh retrieved the phone, discovered the dilemma and made plans to pick up Dani at the hospital.

En route to the hospital, Zack got hold of Eloise's granddaughter, who also agreed to meet them there in case Eloise needed to be admitted.

By the time he finally got to work, he was almost two hours late. The women he worked with teased him about his unshaven appearance and harried demeanor.

And throughout it all, he'd thought of Wynn.

She plagued him, making his brain ache and his body hot. He alternately worried about her and her broken toe, and contemplated making love to her again.

He glanced to the front of her house now where the driveway, just visible from his side yard, could be seen overflowing with a variety of vehicles.

A party.

She'd promised him she'd take it easy, that she'd prop her large feet up and rest. Instead, she was having a party.

Zack locked his jaw tight and stomped up to his kitchen stoop. Fine. Whatever. He'd simply ignore her and her irresponsible ways. It wasn't as if he wanted to worry about her, or even think about her.

No, he just wanted to take her again and again, in about a hundred different ways. He wanted to kiss her body all over, starting on her toes and working his way up those sexy shapely legs until he reached her...

"Oh hell." Zack jerked his door open, called out, "I'm home," and was greeted by silence. He suddenly realized there had been no extra cars in *his* driveway, which meant Josh wasn't here with Dani as he said he'd be.

But just to make certain, Zack went through the house. It was empty.

He was so tired he ached, and now he stopped in the middle of the living room and looked around, trying to decide what to do next. Where would Josh be?

He'd left the kitchen door open and now he heard a robust laugh carry across the yards. His mind cramped as he considered the possibilities. With deliberate intent, feeling ill-tempered and irked, he went to the kitchen to look out the window.

There in Wynn's yard were close to a dozen people, including Josh and Dani. A boom box blared from the patio and a badminton net had been set up. A woman he didn't recognize partnered Conan against Marc and Clint, while Bo leaned against a tree and shouted encouragement. It appeared to be a highly competitive game, given the viciousness of the play.

On the patio, he could see Chastity singing as she wielded a long-handled fork on the grill. Artemus, now dressed all in black except for a large silver buckle on his belt that glinted in the late-day sun, danced with Dani.

His daughter appeared to be wearing one of Chastity's tie-dyed shirts. It hung down to her feet.

Zack looked around without conscious thought and finally located Wynn. She sat on the settee with Josh, her foot in his lap.

Zack felt as though the top of his head had just blown off.

Before he'd even made the decision to move, he was halfway across the lawn, his gaze set on Wynn who was, as yet, unaware of his approach.

Today she was dressed in a pale-peach camisole that almost exactly matched her naked hide, and a pair of loose white drawstring shorts that showed every sexy inch of her long legs and put on display a tiny strip of her delectable belly.

Zack's lungs constricted. When he reached her, he'd—

Conan stepped in front of him. "Whoa, where ya going there, Zack?"

Zack heard a few snickers from behind Conan and knew he'd gained the players' attention.

Conan leaned closer. "The thing is," he whispered, "you look mad as hell and my sister's already been upset all day."

"Yeah," Zack said, still watching Wynn while she smiled and laughed with Josh. "She looks real upset."

Conan blinked, then laughed. "Jealousy is a bitch, ain't it?"

Zack snapped a look at Conan and the man backed up two steps. "Okay, okay," he said, swallowing down a laugh and holding up his hands as if to ward Zack off, "I take it back. You're not jealous."

Zack narrowed his eyes. "What reason would I have to be jealous?"

"None! No reason at all. I mean, believe it or not, Wynn's in pain and... Hey, wait a minute!"

Zack allowed Conan to pull him back around. Wynn was in pain? He couldn't stand it.

Conan laughed. "I'm sorry. Really, I am." Zack vaguely heard the other men laughing and offering comments, but he paid them no mind.

Over his shoulder, Conan shouted, "Shut up, Bo!" To Zack he said, "Ignore Bo. He's been giving Wynn hell all day for being *smitten*. I was about ready to flatten him myself when he finally realized she wasn't taking it well."

Zack drew a deep breath and attempted to ease his temper. Most times, he didn't have a temper, and he blamed the emergence of one solely on Wynn Lane. She brought out the worst in him.

She also turned him on more than any woman he'd ever known. "Why not?" he asked, hoping he sounded merely calm, not concerned. "What's going on?"

"Whew, finally you sound like a reasonable man." Conan clapped him on the shoulder hard enough to make Zack lose his balance. "At first you were looking like a charging bull. Nostrils flared, eyes red, steam coming out your ears. Bo told me, but I didn't really believe him. I mean, when I met you, you seemed so..."

"Conan."

"Sorry. The folks threw this surprise housewarming party for Wynn, but she's obviously not really up to it. I mean, her damn toe is broken in two places. Two! Can you believe that? Her feet are bigger than most, that's true, but it's still just a baby toe."

Zack closed his eyes and counted to ten, but he still heard the smile in Conan's voice when he continued.

"Your buddy has been fending everyone off, including my parents. He pulled Wynn's foot into his lap after the third person accidentally bumped her and made her yelp. Not a pretty thing to see Wynn yelping."

"Damn."

Conan rubbed his neck, looked up at the fading sun, then back at his teammates who were now clustered together and waiting. He faced Zack again. "The folks mean well. It's just that Wynn never complains much, and she never admits to being hurt, so they don't realize..."

"Dad!" His daughter ran hell-bent toward him, cutting off Conan's explanations. Not that he'd needed to continue; Zack already understood the situation and more than anything he wanted to shake Wynn for putting up such a ridiculous macho show. That was something a man would do, but it wasn't expected of a woman. And despite being hardy and strong, she *was* still a woman.

And damn it, he wanted to protect her.

Dani threw herself at Zack, and he noticed his daughter now wore sandals rather than sneakers. And she had a silver ring on her big toe.

He scooped her up and hugged her to him. "Look at you, Dani," he teased. "Wearing a dress."

She laughed, cupped his face and gave him a loud smooch. "It's not a dress. It's Chastity's. She let me wear it while I finger painted. Ain't it pretty?"

Zack didn't bother correcting her speech, not this time, not while she was so excited and happy. "Yes it is, especially on you."

"Conan said I was a flower child."

"But prettier," Conan clarified.

Zack hugged her again and started toward Wynn. He stopped, turned back to Conan and said, "Thanks."

Conan pretended great relief. "Yeah, anytime. I mean, she's a pain in the ass, but I still love my sister." His voice lowered to something of a warning. "And I wouldn't want anyone to upset her. Or hurt her." He stared at Zack, making sure Zack caught his meaning.

Zack nodded, which was the best reply he could offer, for the time being.

"So," Zack said to his daughter, staring at that silver ring on her toe, "you've had fun today?"

"I've had the bestest time! Artemus is teaching me how to dance and look what he did to my hair!" She primped, turning her head one way and then the other.

Her hair had been braided and then twisted into a coronet with tiny multi-colored crystal beads shaped like flowers pinned into place. Two curling ringlets hung in front of her ears.

Zack felt a lump the size of a grapefruit lodge in his throat at the sight of his daughter's proud smile. Artemus met him at the edge of the patio.

"I need your permission to give her a trim," he said before Zack could greet him. "She has *fabulous* hair, just fabulous. But God only knows how long it's been since it was shaped. It *begs* to be shaped."

Zack looked at Dani, who watched him hopefully. "Do you want your hair shaped?" *Whatever the hell that means.*

She nodded.

"You have my permission."

Artemus clapped his hands in bliss.

Chastity turned to Zack. "Hamburger or hot dog, Zack?"

He eyed this remarkable woman who had managed to birth Wynn. "Do hippies eat meat?"

"Honey, when they're my age, they do any damn thing they want to."

Artemus leaned close to nip her ear. "And there's a lot they want to do, too." He winked at Zack. "Hippies are a delightfully creative lot."

"Ah." Zack grinned, amused by the obvious affection between them. "In that case, I'll take a hamburger. Thank you, ma'am."

"Be ready in a moment."

Josh eased Wynn's foot out of his lap and stood to greet Zack. "How's Eloise?"

"I called the hospital before I left work today. She has bronchitis. With the medicine they gave her, she's feeling a lot more comfortable."

"Has she got anyone to take care of her?"

Zack nodded, not quite looking at Wynn yet. If he looked at her, he'd want to pick her up and pet her and coddle her. *Insane.* As she'd said, it was only a broken toe. "She's going to stay with her granddaughter for a week until she's had time to recuperate."

Dani and Artemus danced past them, moving to the tune of the Beach Boys. "A week, huh? What about the rat? Who's going to watch her?"

Zack glanced at his daughter as she threw back her head and laughed. "I finagled an early vacation week. It wasn't easy, but I got Richards to trade with me."

Josh looked pleased. "So you'll be around the house—" he glanced at Wynn "—day and night, for a week, huh?"

"That's what I just said." Done with that conversational gambit, he knelt down in front of Wynn. "How're you feeling?"

"Fine."

Zack could tell she lied. Her face looked pinched, her mouth tight. He gave her a frown that let her know he knew, and then took Josh's seat. He lifted her foot into his lap to examine her toe.

She wore no shoes and where the bandage didn't cover, he could see the dark, colorful bruises. Her foot still looked swollen and for some dumb reason, he wanted to kiss it. It's what he would have done for Dani, and now he wanted to do it for Wynn, too.

He manfully resisted the urge and met her gaze. "Have you taken anything for pain?"

"Aspirin."

Josh leaned on the armrest next to Wynn and peered down at them both. In a carrying voice, he said, "I'm sure you both know that ice for swelling is good, but soaking it in hot water is best for relieving the pain."

Zack rolled his eyes; Josh knew nil about subtlety, or medical matters.

Wynn just stared at him.

"I was thinking of your hot tub, Zack." Josh cleared his throat and forged on. "A good neighbor would offer to let her use it."

Without turning their way, Chastity said, "Oh, I'm sure he'd have thought of it sooner or later."

Artemus chortled at his wife's wry humor, and then swung Dani in a wide circle, ending their dance with a flourish.

Dani came over and, natural as you please, climbed into Wynn's lap.

Wynn positioned her comfortably, as if she'd been holding Dani since the day she was born.

Zack almost choked on another lump of emotion. Damn it, men didn't get lumps of emotion, and certainly not over something so simple as seeing a neighbor hold his daughter. But Dani was smiling and looking secure and confident in her welcome.

He silently cursed again.

Wynn was *not* the right woman for him. Whenever he'd envisioned the right woman, he'd pictured a woman who was discreet and circumspect and responsible. A woman who'd be a good influence on his daughter and the perfect domestic partner for raising a child.

Wynn was rash and outspoken and irresponsible. She didn't protect herself or think things out before doing them. She knew too many men who knew her too well... No, that wasn't exactly right and he felt guilty for even thinking it. But he found he was the jealous sort when he'd never been before. And that irked him, too.

Wynn dressed provocatively, didn't eat right, and her family was beyond strange.

She was big and beautiful and so sexy he couldn't stop thinking about her.

What the hell was he supposed to do?

"Eat," Chastity said as if she'd read his mind. She shoved a paper plate with a loaded hamburger, chips and pickles into his hand. She handed the same to Wynn, and gave Dani a hot dog.

Everyone came in from the badminton game and Conan introduced Zack to his girlfriend, Rachael. She was a pretty, slender woman of medium height. *She* was dressed reasonably in long tan walking shorts and a loose blue polo shirt. And none of the men swatted *her* behind.

However, the second Wynn said she needed to go inside a minute, the guys lined up to carry her. They jokingly compared muscles, trying to decide who was strong enough to bear her weight.

Not giving them a chance to get so much as a pinkie finger on her, Zack lifted Wynn into his lap and then stood. There was a general round of oohing and aahing and muttered respect for his strength.

"What do you bench?" Conan asked, and Zack rolled his eyes.

Wynn dropped her head to his shoulder. "This is totally dumb, Zack. I'm more than capable of walking, you know."

"I know. But no one else seems to." He turned to Dani. "Stay right here with Josh, sweetheart."

"I will!"

Zack headed for the back door. Truth was, she felt good in his arms, a nice soft solid weight. Warm and very feminine. He liked holding her. And no way in hell was he going to let any of her "friends" pick her up so they'd experience the same sensations.

"They're just nettling you," Wynn said, "and you're letting them." She reached down to open the kitchen door when Zack stopped in front of it.

"Where to?" he asked.

She sighed, then finally said, "The bathroom."

Zack grinned. The door closed behind them, shutting out some of the party noise. Now that they were in private, he nuzzled Wynn's ear, carefully because of his rough beard, and then asked, "Are you coming over tonight to…soak your foot?"

She looked up at him, surprised. "I thought you had plans?"

"I'll be free by eleven. It's been a total bitch of a day and I can't imagine a better way to end it than with a repeat of last night." He touched his mouth to hers and added, "That is, if you're up to it."

She said, "Ha! I sure wouldn't let a little broken toe keep me from it!"

Zack kissed her chin, feeling all his tension and aggravation melt away just from being near her. Leaving her behind this morning, knowing she was hurt, hadn't sat right with him. "And you called me a superhero," he teased gently.

Wynn hesitated, then made a face. "Okay, I give up. Just what are you doing tonight?"

They stood in the hallway outside the bathroom door. Wynn didn't ask to be put down, and Zack was in no hurry to release her. He looked at her mouth and wanted to groan. He could feel himself getting hard and ruthlessly brought himself under control.

"Del and Mick are coming over. They, Josh and I, are going to watch an interview Del did for her upcoming book. It's going to be on channel—"

They heard a thump and looked up to see Conan collapsed against the wall, a large fist pressed to his massive chest.

Zack was briefly alarmed before Conan wheezed, "Delilah Piper is going to be here? Right next door? Oh my God."

"Delilah Piper-slash-Dawson. Remember, I told you Mick's funny about that. And yeah, she is."

Conan's eyes rolled back and he wheezed some more. "A celebrity in our midst! Wait until I tell everyone else."

"Conan," Wynn said suspiciously, "what are you doing in here?"

Briefly taken off guard, Conan stammered, then looked much struck. "I brought Ms. Piper's books over to be signed and I was going to give them to Zack!"

Wynn said, "Uh-huh."

"But now I can just give them to her myself." He rubbed his hands together. "I can't wait."

Whatever Conan had really wanted—and Zack assumed it was to check up on his sister—was forgotten as he rushed back outside to share the news.

Zack looked down at Wynn, then readjusted her weight so he could kiss her throat.

She sighed. "I'm sorry, Zack, but I have a feeling your intimate little night with friends has just been ruined."

He kissed her throat again. "Conan is more than welcome. It'll tickle Del and it'll keep Mick on his toes. He gets rattled any time a guy looks at her with admiration—even if it's admiration for her work."

"Zack?"

"Hmmm?"

"You can set me down now."

"I'm not sure I want to."

Wynn hugged him, but said, "If you don't, Conan won't be the only one visiting us. My parents will come trooping through, too, and then the guys…"

Being especially careful of her injury, Zack slid her down his body. She kept her hands on his shoulders and her gaze on his mouth. "I like you in your uniform. It's sexy."

Zack grinned. "Is that right?"

She trailed her fingers over his jaw. "And this looks interesting, too."

"I didn't have time to shave this morning." He nuzzled her, letting her feel his whiskers. Then added in a gruff whisper, "But I'll shave before you come over tonight." He gazed down at her breasts and said, "I wouldn't want to give you a burn."

"Zack…"

The way she sighed his name was such a temptation. Zack turned her toward the bathroom. "Go, before I decide I can't wait until tonight."

She gave him a vacuous smile and hobbled in, favoring her injured foot while trying to strut like a man, just to prove she wasn't hurt. Zack shook his head and a warm feeling expanded inside him, making him hot and hard and filling him with tenderness.

Her ridiculous false bravado shouldn't have done that to him. *She* shouldn't have done that to him. But she did, and he knew he was in deep.

Problem was, for some strange reason, he just couldn't work up the energy to fight it.

Chapter 10

It was eleven o'clock and her parents had retired to their room half an hour ago. Wynn could still hear them talking and laughing, though. Because her parents remained frisky even after all these years, she made a mental note to run her ceiling fan at night for background noise, and slipped out of her room.

Unfortunately, she was almost to Zack's house when she realized the additional cars were still in his driveway; his company hadn't yet left. She was about to turn around when a female voice called out, "You must be Wynn."

Wynn froze. Zack had his porch light on and so did she, so she knew the woman could see her, but still she considered hiding.

The woman laughed. "I'm Del. Come on over and chat."

Wynn hadn't joined her brother and the others earlier when they'd gone to worship at the writer's feet. She wasn't much of a mystery reader, and beyond that, she hadn't liked the idea of forcing herself into Zack's company any more than she already had.

Her foot hurt and she was self-conscious in her robe, but she crept forward and even pasted on a smile. "Hello. Yes, I'm Wynn. A neighbor."

Delilah Piper-Dawson stood leaning against a tree admiring the sky. When Wynn got close, Del offered her hand. "I've heard a lot about you."

"Oh?" Who had talked about her? she wondered. Zack? What had he said? She stepped closer.

Though Delilah was tall for a woman, Wynn towered over her. Del had the type of slender willowy build that made Wynn feel like a lumberjack.

Delilah looked her over and asked, "You're ready for bed?"

"Oh, no." She fidgeted with the belt to her terry cloth robe and explained, "I have my bathing suit on. Zack invited me to use his hot tub. I, uh, I broke my toe today."

"That's right! I heard about that, too."

Wynn studied the smaller woman. "What exactly has Zack told you?"

"Well, not much. Zack, as I'm sure you know, is very closemouthed and private."

Wynn didn't know any such thing.

"He's also very calm and controlled."

"Oh?"

Delilah laughed. "Yes, but Josh and Mick have both told me that around you, he's just the opposite. Always losing his temper and grumbling and growling. I love it. It was so funny when he first started talking about getting a wife. He had all these absurd notions of what qualities he'd want." Delilah shook her head and her beautiful, very shiny and sleek inky-black hair caught the moonlight, making it look almost liquid. Wynn reached up to smooth her own hair, which she'd ruthlessly contained in a tight knot on top of her head.

When she realized she was primping and why, Wynn dropped her hand and said again, "Oh?"

Delilah nodded. "Let me warn you though, if you do marry Zack, they'll all expect you to get dressed up for the wedding."

She said that as if it were the worst fate possible. Wynn despised dressing up, too, so she understood.

Del made a face. "But it's not that bad, considering the end results."

Wynn looked around, wondering what the hell she was supposed to say to that. When Delilah just waited, she blurted, "We won't be getting married. Zack isn't all that serious about me. He just wants to…well, he just *wants* me." And to be completely clear, she added, "But not for marriage."

Delilah stared at her, then took her arm. "Come on. Let's sit down. Here you are with a broken toe and I've got you standing in the yard sharing confidences." She turned, holding on to Wynn as if she, with her measly delicate strength, could offer substantial support. "Let's be really quiet though. The guys are yakking and I escaped out here to get some fresh air. I don't want them to join us yet."

They stopped at the hot tub and Delilah sat on the edge, crossing her ankles. "The patio curtains are closed," she pointed out, "so they won't notice us. You can go ahead and get in if you want."

Wynn shook her head.

"Okay, but let's get back to this sex business."

"I didn't exactly mean to say that." Wynn had no idea why she'd confessed such a thing to a complete stranger. Delilah had just asked and she'd answered.

"That's okay. People are always confiding in me. I'm a writer, you know."

Wynn had no idea what that had to do with anything.

"Your brother told me a lot about you, too. He says you've never been this serious about a guy before."

"I'll kill him."

Delilah laughed. "Don't worry. No one overheard him. But you should know, it's the same for Zack. I thought Mick was a recluse when it came to women, but Zack is even worse. It's amazing considering they're both friends with Josh, and that man knows no moderation where females are concerned."

Wynn started to say, "Oh?" but caught herself in time. "I gather Josh is something of a lady's man."

"He likes to think so. Unfortunately, most of the ladies agree with him." Then she said, "Now back to you and Zack. I want to tell you, whatever you do, don't give up. I almost gave up on Mick, but luckily his family talked me out of it. Since we're like Zack's family now, I feel honor bound to do the same for you."

Wynn gave up without a whimper. She flopped down beside Delilah on the edge of the tub and hung her head. "It's no wonder Zack isn't interested in getting serious with me. Every time I'm around him, I end up doing something dumb. Like wrestling him to the ground—"

"No kidding?" Delilah looked very curious about that.

"And insulting him and then I fell and broke my stupid toe…"

"Why do you insult him?"

Wynn shrugged. "I've always been treated like one of the guys. It's all I really know. I speak my mind, tease and harass."

Delilah nodded. "Yeah, Mick and Josh and Zack do that all the time."

"So does my brother and the guys from the gym."

"Hmmm." Delilah got up to pace. She wore a tiny T-shirt with a smiley face on the front, baggy jeans, and strappy sandals, and still she looked utterly feminine. If the woman wasn't being so nice, Wynn might not have liked her. She sat again and took Wynn's hand. "I think you should tell Zack how you feel."

"Really?" Wynn winced even considering it. "Is that what you did with Mick?"

She laughed. "Too much so. Poor Mick didn't know what to think of me. But I'm not used to hiding my feelings, especially feelings that strong. I knew almost from the moment I noticed him that I wanted him for my own."

Wynn nodded in understanding. She'd felt the same about Zack. Almost from the first, she'd known what a wonderful person he was.

"Okay." Delilah stood. "Off with the robe and into the hot tub. I'll get Mick and Josh to leave and I'll send Zack out. What's your bathing suit look like?" Her eyes widened and she asked with scandalized delight, "Or are you wearing one?"

"Of course I'm wearing one!" Wynn almost sputtered at the idea of traipsing across two yards in nothing but a thin robe. "I wouldn't leave my house naked."

Delilah looked let down. "Okay, let me see the suit."

"It's…um, kinda skimpy."

"Because you wanted to entice Zack? Good idea, not quite as good as being naked, but still... Not that he needs any enticement, you know. He's been antsy and pacing and impatient all night. We all knew he wanted us gone so he could visit with you, so of course that made Mick and Josh more determined to hang around, just to watch Zack fret." Delilah shook her head. "They're all nuts, but I love them."

Once she finished talking, Delilah just waited. Then she cleared her throat. "Can I see the suit?"

Wynn hadn't had any really close female friends before. She hung more with the guys, and that had always suited her just fine. But Delilah, well, she was easy to talk to, friendly and open. Wynn liked her on the spot.

"Okay, but don't laugh."

"Why would I laugh?"

Wynn squeezed her eyes shut, gripped the lapels of the robe, and held it open. She wasn't naked, but the string bikini was as close as she could get.

Delilah whistled. "Wow. Zack'll be lucky if he lasts half an hour. You look great. Like a model."

Wynn snatched the robe shut. "The only time Zack and I made love it was pitch dark and he couldn't really see me."

"Well, that suit'll make up for it! I almost wish I could hang around for his reaction. Will you call me tomorrow and let me know how it goes?"

Dumbstruck, Wynn stammered, "Uh, well, yeah. Sure."

"Wait! Better still, let's have lunch. I just finished a book so I've got some free time. I need to let my brain recoup before I start plotting again. Where do you work? I could meet you there."

Overwhelmed by Delilah's enthusiasm, Wynn heard herself giving the address for her brother's gym. "Conan will wet his pants if you actually come and say hi."

"Your brother is a real sweetheart. It always makes my day to meet up with a reader. In fact, don't tell him yet, but I'm thinking of setting a book around a gym. Can you imagine? With all that weight equipment and the pool and the sauna, why, all kinds of stuff could go on there. Like maybe…" Delilah caught herself and laughed. "There I go, plotting again. Ignore me."

Wynn was charmed. "I think it's interesting. And I'm sure Conan would be thrilled to help out by showing you around and answering questions." Her brother would owe her big time for this one, Wynn thought, and smiled.

"That'd be great. So what time is lunch?"

Delilah Piper-Dawson had a quick mind and Wynn could barely keep up. "Eleven-thirty?"

"Perfect. I'll be there. Now into the tub and I'll send Zack out."

"It was nice meeting you, Delilah."

Over her shoulder, Delilah said, "Same here. And call me Del."

Wynn stared after Delilah, feeling like she'd gotten seized in a whirlwind. Then she caught herself and realized Zack could be out any second. She didn't want to have to disrobe in front of him! She dropped the terry robe over a chair and slid into the warm water. The jets weren't turned on yet, but the hot water felt heavenly— and it covered her mostly bare body.

She only hoped Zack appreciated her immodesty.

Zack stared at Josh and Mick, who stared back, and wondered how in hell he could get rid of them. The show featuring Delilah's interview was long since over, but still they hung around, drinking more coffee and chatting as if no one had anywhere to go. Delilah had tired of it and gone outside to stretch her legs, or so she said.

No sooner did Zack think of her than she reappeared. She walked to her husband, took his hands and pulled him from the couch. "Let's go."

"Go where?" Mick asked, teasing her.

"Home. Zack has company and we've overstayed ourselves."

All three men turned to stare toward the kitchen where Del had entered. Zack asked, "Wynn is here?"

"No, her dad."

"What?"

Del laughed. "Just teasing. Yeah, it's Wynn. And what a nice woman! I really like her, Zack."

Zack's eyes narrowed. "Just how long has she been out there, Del?"

"About ten minutes, that's all." She winked. "We were chatting and getting to know each other."

Mick shook his head. "Honey, why didn't you bring her inside?"

"She didn't want to come in."

"Why not?"

"She's in this teeny tiny little string bikini."

With arrested looks on their faces, the men all turned toward the kitchen.

Del caught Mick around the neck. "Oh, no you don't. If you want to see a mostly naked woman, you can just take me on home."

Mick grinned and his dark eyes heated. "That's a hell of an idea."

Josh took two steps forward and Zack stepped in front of him. He crossed his arms. "I don't think so."

Trying for an innocent look, Josh said, "But it wouldn't be neighborly of me to leave without saying hello first."

"I'll give her your regrets and tell her you said 'hi.'"

Josh almost laughed. "Ah, c'mon, Zack. You can at least appease an old friend's curiosity."

"Get out. And you can leave by the front door."

Josh sauntered over to Del and slung an arm around her shoulder. "Del, honey, I guess you'll just have to tell me all about it."

Del smiled. "She's gorgeous, Josh. I can see why Zack is hooked." Then she turned to Zack. "But she's also very nice."

Josh nodded. "Agreed."

Zack hastily bent to kiss Del's cheek as she stepped out front. "Do me a favor, will you, hon? Make sure neither of them sneaks around back."

As soon as he got Del's laughing promise, Zack closed and locked his front door then raced for the patio. Dani was long since asleep, his company was finally gone, and Wynn was already in the tub. Finally the day was beginning to improve.

He pushed the patio curtains aside and stared at Wynn for several seconds before opening the doors and stepping out. She looked beautiful, though he could only see her from the shoulders up. The rest of her was hidden beneath the water.

She had her impossible hair piled on top of her head, but the steam from the hot water had still affected it. Tiny curls at her temples sprang free, giving her the appearance of a newly hatched baby bird.

Zack smiled and he had to admit, it wasn't just lust making his stomach tight. "Hey."

Wynn lifted her head from the back of the tub and stared at him. "Hi."

Watching her, he began unbuttoning his shirt. "I didn't realize you were here or I'd have come out sooner."

"That's okay. I didn't mean to interrupt your visit with your friends."

"Did you and Del have a nice chat?" More than anything, he wondered what they had talked about. With Del, there was no telling.

"She's really nice, isn't she?"

"Del's a sweetheart." He dropped his shirt and sat in a lawn chair to remove his shoes and socks. "Mick's crazy about her."

He set his shoes aside and stood to unfasten his slacks. He heard Wynn squeak, and looked up. "I'm not going to bother with trunks. You don't mind do you?"

She stared at his abdomen and shook her head. Zack was already so hard there was no way she could miss his erection. He wanted her, even more now that he'd had her and knew how incredible it was.

They were behind the privacy fence, so no one could see them. Still he reached inside and flipped off the lights, casting the hot tub into shadows.

Wynn muttered a complaint, which made him laugh. "Your eyes will adjust, but I don't want to take the chance of your parents wandering over."

"They're in bed," she said. "Nothing short of a natural disaster would get them out of there now."

Zack removed his wallet from his pocket. He took out two condoms and put them close at hand, then pulled his slacks and his boxers off and put them over the back of a chair. He stepped into the tub. "Do you want the jets, or is this good enough?"

Wynn swallowed. He stood in front of her and he could feel her stare like a hot touch moving over his groin. He braced his legs apart and waited.

"Zack?"

"Yeah?"

"My eyes have adjusted."

He grinned and started to sit down, but she caught his hips. "No, wait just a minute. Let me…look. I didn't touch you much the other night. I kept thinking about that, you know, that I should have and wishing I had. Now I can."

Her hands slid down to his thighs then back up again. Zack watched her watching him, and it was so damned erotic he almost couldn't bear it. "I didn't give you much of a chance to touch me."

"You were remarkable." Without warning she leaned closer and cupped his testicles. Her hands were hot from being in the water, wet and gentle. His heart pounded.

She used her free hand to touch him everywhere, except where he most wanted her touch. His cock pulsed and flexed, but she ignored it as her wet palm moved over his lower back, his abdomen, his butt, with a gentle and exciting curiosity.

When she leaned forward and kissed his hipbone he groaned. "Wynn, you're a tease."

"No, I just want you so much. All of you."

Because she was always so open, so bold, he knew she meant it, every word.

He couldn't take it. He reached down, caught her wandering hand. "Right here, Wynn," he said, and curled her fingers around him.

Looking up at him, her beautiful eyes bright, she said, "Like this?"

A woman with large hands was a blessed thing, he decided. Her fingers circled him, firm but cautious, strong but soft. The contradictions made him wild. A sound of pleasure escaped his throat and he said, *"Yeah."*

Without releasing him, Wynn shifted to kneel in the tub. Zack caught sight of her barely contained breasts in the skimpy bikini top at the same time she indulged him with a long, slow, heated stroke.

Steam rose around him, expanded within him. He said, "That's enough," and reached for her hands.

"But..."

He hauled her up and held her in front of him. "Easy," he said, looking her over with hunger. "Don't hurt your foot."

She gave him a lopsided grin. "What foot?"

He smiled too, and reached out to cup her breast. "Christ, you're beautiful."

"I'm big," she said.

"And sexy."

"I've never worn a suit like this before."

"Thank God for small favors."

"My mother bought it for me when she was trying to get me married off."

His head snapped up. *"What?"*

Shrugging, Wynn explained, "I told you I don't date much. That bothers my folks. They hooked up young and they've always been happy and they want me happy."

Zack eased her closer, trying to quell the sick feeling in his stomach. "You need marriage to be happy?"

She looked away. "I'm in no hurry."

He wasn't at all sure he liked that answer anymore. "Why not?"

"Like you, I guess I'm looking for something special. That must be why I've never been that attracted to too many guys, right? And I did just get my own house. I want to have fun with it for a while before I start changing things again."

"I see." But he didn't, not really.

"Can we stop talking now?"

"You want to get on with it, do you?"

She moved her hands over his chest, and then lower. "Yes, I do."

Zack eased down into the water on the bench. "Come here, Wynn."

She stepped close and he reached around her to unhook her bikini bra. He draped it over the side of the tub. "One of these days," he said, "I'm going to get you laid out in the sunshine so I can see all of you." Before she could respond to that, he leaned forward and suckled her right nipple.

She clasped his head. "Zack!"

"Shh, sweetheart, keep it quiet. We don't want to wake anyone up."

He switched to her other breast, flicking her with his tongue, and she moaned low. "I'm ready now, Zack," she whispered urgently.

"Impossible," he said. "We're just getting started."

"But I've been thinking about it all day, even during that stupid party." She lifted his face to hers. "Please, Zack."

He stared at her while he slipped his fingers beneath the leg of her suit. Hot water swirled around her, but she was hotter still, wet and slick, her flesh swollen and soft. He removed his fingers and hastily pulled her bottoms off. Raising himself to the edge of the hot tub, he donned a condom, then eased back into the water to sit on the very edge of the bench seat.

"Straddle my hips, Wynn."

As she did so, her breasts moved over his chest, their skin wet and slippery and hot. He helped position her, taking care not to jostle her bruised foot.

"Brace your hands on my shoulders."

She did, and he eased up into her, hearing her soft moan, feeling the stretch of her inner muscles as she gripped him. He pressed his face into her throat, filled with so much emotion, so much pleasure, it was almost pain. He held her carefully and rather than thrust, he rocked them both, constantly kissing her and whispering to her; there was so much he wanted to say, but he didn't understand himself anymore. He only knew he wanted her, and now he had her.

When he felt Wynn tightening around him, he pressed his hand between their bodies and helped her along. She bit his shoulder as she came, and licked his mouth when he came seconds later.

Resting against him, she murmured, "Will we ever make love in a bed do you think?"

Zack wanted to say yes, that he wanted her in his bed right now. The more he saw her, the more he wanted to be with her. He didn't want to say good-night and send her back to her own home. He wanted to hold her all night, wake up with her in the morning, share breakfast with her and Dani, even argue with her.

But nothing was decided. All the issues still remained. He didn't have only himself to think about; he had to think of his daughter, too.

He said only, "I'm off for a week now. Dani has pre-school two afternoons so the house will be free. If you can get away then…"

She kissed his chin. "I'll get away. But, Zack?"

"Hmmm?" He'd just finished loving her, and already he was thinking of when he'd have her again. He felt obsessed.

"Are you seeing anyone else right now?"

"No, why?" He tried to see her face, but she kept it tucked close to his chest.

"You said you were looking for a wife. You said you had plans tomorrow night, too. I just wondered."

He smiled. "Tomorrow I planned to do my cleaning. That's all."

"Oh." She lifted up to look at him, winced when she bumped her toe, and finally got comfortable. "If you should decide to see anyone else, I want you to tell me."

Zack cupped her cheek, so smooth and sweet. "Why?"

"Because then I wouldn't see you anymore."

Just hearing her say it made him want to shout, made him want to drag her inside and keep her there. His chest felt tight, but he nodded. "All right." He smoothed his thumb over her bottom lip. "Same goes for me."

Wynn stared at him, then resettled herself on his chest. "All right."

Chapter 11

"Do you two realize we haven't been to Marco's in a month?"

Zack, sitting restlessly at his kitchen table, glanced up at Josh. Used to be he and Mick and Josh ate lunch at Marco's at least once a week. Now Mick was married and Zack...well, for the past three weeks he'd enjoyed spending his spare time with Wynn. She'd taken over his brain and his libido and probably even his heart.

That thought shook him and he stood to pace.

Mick chuckled. "There he goes again."

"Wynn has him on the run." Josh laughed. "Not that it'll do him any good. You were as bad once."

Mick just shrugged. "It's scary falling in love."

Feeling haunted, Zack turned to scowl at them. Love? *Love*. He hadn't known her long enough, only a little over a month, but he did know she wasn't what he'd always wanted in a female. She obviously had what he enjoyed, but that kind of enjoyment wasn't appropriate for the father of a little girl.

He said very quietly, "Shit."

"Oh give it up, Zack." Josh threw a potato chip at him and it bounced off his chest. "You walk around looking like a dying man, and there's no reason for it. Just bite the bullet. Tell her how you feel."

Even now, Dani was next door with Wynn. They were sitting in the grass, a giant roll of paper between them, finger painting. It had become Dani's favorite new pastime, thanks to Chastity. She and Artemus, with all their outrageous, oddball, delightful ways, had become surrogate grandparents and his daughter loved them. They hadn't yet found a place of their own, but Zack knew when they did move, Dani would miss them.

It was nearing Halloween and the fall air had cooled, breezing in through the open kitchen window and the screen door. But still Zack felt too hot, too contained. He dropped back into his chair and said, "I don't know."

Mick sipped his coffee. "Don't know what?"

"Anything. I don't know what to do, what I feel."

Josh offered, "She's a pretty special woman."

Zack propped his head on his open palms and tunneled his fingers through his hair. "She's not what I was looking for."

"I wasn't looking for anyone when I found Delilah. It doesn't make any difference."

"I can't just think about myself."

Josh tipped his head. "What the hell does that mean?"

"It means I'm a father. I have to consider Dani."

"Dani adores her, and vice versa."

Zack clenched his hair. "I wanted someone domestic, someone calm and reasonable."

Josh laughed out loud. "Domestic you got. Calm and reasonable? And you wanted her to be female right? Good luck."

"Having women troubles, Josh?" Zack asked suspiciously.

Mick grinned. "Woman—singular. Amanda Barker, the lady putting together the charity calendar? Well, they've already started shooting and Josh here still hasn't agreed. She's getting…insistent. Seems she won't take no for an answer."

"She's a pain in the ass." Josh shrugged. "Everywhere I turn, there she is. But I just ignore her."

Zack dropped his hands and shook his head. "Yeah, right. Like you'd ignore any woman."

Josh sat back and crossed his arms behind his head, a man at his leisure. "She's not like Del and Wynn."

Both Mick and Zack straightened. "What are you talking about?"

"They're real women, straightforward, funny, down to earth. They don't whine and cry and complain just to get their way, and they don't continually fuss with their nails and their hair. I doubt you'd catch either of them getting a facial. I like all that earthiness." He nudged Mick with his elbow and said, "They're both everything a guy could want—and more."

Mick glanced at Zack. "Do you want to kill him or should I?"

Zack shook his head. Everything Josh claimed was true. Wynn worked hard, played and laughed hard, and she never seemed concerned with the typical things women considered. Not in a million years could he imagine her whining. "I think your Amanda sounds responsible."

"She's not *my* Amanda, and yeah, so? Wynn is responsible."

Zack stood again. "Ha! Wynn is outrageous. She speaks before she thinks, acts before she's considered the consequences. She pretends to be one of the guys and dresses so damn sexy it makes me nuts."

Mick and Josh looked at each other. "She wears sloppy clothes."

"Sloppy sexy clothes that fit her body and show glimpses of skin and… How the hell would I live with someone like that?"

Mick stared down at his coffee mug. Very quietly, he asked, "How would you live without her?"

Zack drew back. Feeling desperate, he said, "Dani has all of us to teach her to do guy things. I wanted a woman who would be a good influence on her, someone who did all those female things you just mentioned, Josh. Someone to be a role model, ya know?"

"You're an ass, Zack." Josh shook his head in pity. "Wynn is terrific. She's independent and intelligent and honest. Yeah she's outspoken, but so what? You never have to guess at what she's thinking. And I like the way she dresses."

Zack's eyes nearly crossed. Josh had totally missed the point. He opened his mouth to explode with frustration, and noticed Wynn standing frozen just outside the open kitchen door. "Oh, hell."

Without a word, Wynn jerked around and hurried away. Zack took off after her, slamming the screen door open in his haste. Before it could slam closed again, Josh and Mick were on his heels.

"Wynn!"

"Go to hell!" she shouted over her shoulder. She all but ran—*from him*—on her not yet healed foot and Zack worried. The blasted woman hadn't even given him a chance to explain!

He stomped after her, cursing her impetuous reaction, worrying about her foot because he knew *she* wouldn't worry about it. Her legs were long and strong, but his were as long, and whether she wanted to believe it or not, stronger. He closed the distance between them.

From Wynn's yard, he saw his daughter and Chastity look up. On the patio, Artemus and Conan, along with Marc and Clint and Bo, all lifted their heads. He could hear Mick and Josh just behind him.

His jaw clenched. When he got hold of Wynn, he thought he might strangle her.

He reached out, caught her arm—and she whipped around on him in a fury, letting out a war cry that rattled his ears and totally took him by surprise. She jerked his arm, stuck her foot out and sent him sprawling.

For three seconds Zack lay flat on his back, staring up at the blue sky, hearing snickers and whispers and feeling his temper rise.

Wynn leaned over him, her eyes red and her mouth pinched. "Don't ever touch me again. You want rid of me, well, you're rid of me!"

In a flash, he grabbed her elbow and tossed her to her back beside him.

She yelled, "My foot!" and Zack froze at the thought of hurting her.

At the same moment he heard Conan call out, "It's a trick!" but it was too late.

Wynn landed on top of him, her knees on his shoulders, her hands pinning his wrists to the ground, her big behind on his diaphragm. He could barely breathe. "For the record, you miserable jerk, I never asked to be your wife. As to that, I wouldn't be your wife now if you went down on your knees."

It was hard, but Zack managed not to laugh. The fact that he couldn't draw a deep breath with her bouncing astride him helped. "You were eavesdropping!"

"Another of my less than sterling qualities," she sneered. "But don't worry." She leaned in, almost smothering him with her breasts—not that he was complaining. "I won't force myself on you anymore. You're free to go find your little paragon of domesticity! I wish you luck."

She started to rise, still a little awkwardly since her toe hadn't entirely healed, and Zack caught her with his legs. "Oh, no you don't!" He flipped her again and sprawled his entire weight on top of her. He heard her loud grunt, but paid no mind. "You don't get to just barge in in a huff after listening to a private conversation, just to give me hell and then leave."

Wynn bowed and jerked and, realizing she couldn't throw him off, she subsided. "I get to do whatever I please! It's none of your damn business." She looked him over with disdain, but Zack saw her bottom lip tremble. "Not anymore."

His heart hurt. Emotion swelled inside him. "Wynn."

She jerked again, but couldn't free herself. "I don't even know why I bothered with you," she muttered.

He wanted to kiss her, but figured if he loosened his grip at all, she'd run from him again. "Because I'm sweet?"

"Ha!"

"You're the one who said it, Wynn, not me."

He heard low voices and looked up to see everyone gathered around them wearing expressions of curiosity and expectation and anticipation. They blocked the sun.

He turned back to Wynn. "You're not walking out on me."

"I don't think she was walking," Bo pointed out. "Looked more like running."

"Did to me, too," Josh agreed. "Not that I blame her."

To hell with it, Zack thought, and he leaned down to kiss her. She almost bit him, but he laughed and pulled away. She looked ready to spit on him, and he said, "I love you, Wynn."

Her gorgeous golden eyes widened, and then they both *oofed* when Dani leaped onto Zack's back and began hopping up and down. "We're keeping her, we're keeping her!"

Laughing, Zack said, "Not yet, honey. She has to tell me she loves me, too."

Dani flattened herself on Zack's back and leaned over his shoulder into Wynn's frozen face. She put her tiny hand on Wynn's cheek and said, "I want you for my mommy."

Wynn drew a broken, shuddering breath and said, "Ohhh," and her face crumbled. She blinked hard, but big tears welled up.

Zack turned his head to kiss his daughter's cheek. "Move, Dani."

"'Kay, Dad." She scampered off and stood there fretting until Mick picked her up and whispered something in her ear. Then she smiled and nodded.

Zack nudged Wynn with his nose. "We need privacy, sweetheart. Don't fight me, okay?"

She nodded, attempting to duck her face against him. Knowing Wynn as well as he did, Zack imagined that to her, a spate of tears equaled the gravest humiliation. She would laugh heartily, yell like a fishmonger, and she loved him with enough intensity to leave him insensate. But she wanted to hide her upset.

He'd allow her to hide her tears from the others, but he didn't want her hiding anything from him.

Zack stood, hauled Wynn over his shoulder and turned away from everyone to head back into the privacy of his house.

Conan yelled, "For once in your life, Wynonna, be reasonable! Don't blow it."

Bo and Clint and Marc all laughed, offering suggestions to Zack on how to best her. They said, "Watch her legs!" and "She fights dirty, so protect yourself," and "If she gets the upper hand, just remember that she's ticklish!"

Zack waved his free hand in an absent "thank you."

Artemus called out, "Darling, I *will* do something with your hair for the wedding, so get used to the idea right now!"

At that dire threat, Wynn started to push up, but Zack put his hand on her bottom to hold her still. Grinning like a fool, he realized he felt better than good. He felt… incredible.

He went through the kitchen and the living room, took the stairs two at a time, went into his room and dumped Wynn on his bed. He rubbed his back and groaned dramatically. "Damn, you're heavy."

She held her arms out to him.

Amazing, Zack thought, loving the sight of her in his bed and knowing he wanted to see her there every day for the rest of his life. He lowered himself onto her. "I love you," he said again.

She squeezed him tight. "I love you, too."

His heart expanded until it nearly choked him. "Enough to marry me and be Dani's mommy?"

She pushed him away. "I won't change for you, Zack." Her eyes glistened with tears, but she still looked ferocious. "I am who I am, and I like me."

"I like you, too." He kissed the end of her nose and smiled. "You scare me to death, sometimes infuriate me and drive me to unheard of depths of jealousy, but I wouldn't want you to change, sweetheart. Well, except that I'm going to have to insist all other males keep their hands off you. Other than that..."

She laughed and swatted him, but her humor ended with a quiver. "I so badly wanted to be Dani's mommy. I love her so much." More tears gathered in her eyes and she groaned. "Oh God, this is awful." She used his shoulder to wipe her eyes.

Zack smiled. She so seldom said the expected. "How would you feel about giving Dani a brother? She mentioned that, too."

"She did?"

"Yes. Back when she first explained to me that she was going to keep you."

Wynn drew a shaky breath. "I'm twenty-eight. I'd like to have a baby before I'm thirty."

"In other words, you want me to get right on it?" He nudged her again. "I'm ready, willing and able. And I love you."

She choked back a sob and then viciously shook her head. "Josh would be appalled if he saw me snuffling like an idiot."

Zack kissed her wet cheeks and then the corner of her mouth. "Who cares what Josh thinks?"

"I care what Josh thinks. After all, he's the one who changed your mind about me."

Zack laughed. "I already knew I loved you and you can believe Josh didn't have a damn thing to do with it."

"Right. So what was all that in the kitchen about?"

He shrugged. "I was just mouthing off, fighting the inevitable, posturing like any respectable man would do." He eyed her and said, "*You* ought to understand that."

She made a face. "I heard you, Zack. I'm not at all who you wanted."

"But you're who I love. You're who I need." He cupped her face and kissed her. "Ever since meeting you, I've been thinking about leaving the field, becoming an instructor. I even took steps in that direction."

"You have?"

"And I've thought about moving Dani's room farther down the hall to the guest room—something she's mentioned before because that room's bigger, but I always wanted her close and until you, I never considered having a woman in the house with Dani. Then I started thinking about privacy."

Her brows lowered in thought. "You do get rather loud when you're excited," she remarked with grave seriousness. "You groan and if I touch you right here, you shout and—"

Zack drew away her teasing hand and quieted her with a mushy, laughing kiss. "Wynn, I know you won't be easy to control—"

"Control!" She reached for him again and he pinned her down.

"—but the upside to that is we'll get to spend lots of

time wrestling." He bobbed his eyebrows. "And now that I've made up my mind, you should know I'm not at all sweet. I'm actually ruthless when there's something— or someone—I want."

Wynn quit struggling and gave him a coy look. "And you want me?" He pushed against her, letting her feel his erection. She grinned. "Well, since we love each other, then I suppose we should get married."

Zack collapsed on her. "Thank God. You do know how to drag out the suspense, don't you?"

"There's something you should know, though."

He opened one eye.

"My parents have already told me that if we marry, they want my house." Zack made a strangled sound, but she quickly continued. "I think they suspected this might happen, which is why they let you carry me off and why they've only been halfheartedly looking for another place to stay." She pressed back so she could see his face, and with a crooked impish grin, added, "But I know how you feel about awkwardness with neighbors…"

He pinched her for that bit of impertinence, then grunted when she pinched him back.

Zack rolled so that she was atop him. "I like your folks and so does Dani. As long as you live with me, the rest doesn't matter." They kissed and it was long minutes later before Zack again lifted his head and looked down the long length of his future wife. "We're going to need a bigger bed."

Wynn immediately asked, "Do you think Dani would like to be a flower girl?"

Zack laughed. "At least it'd get her into a dress."

* * * * *

Also by Brenda Jackson

HQN Books

Catalina Cove
Love in Catalina Cove

The Protectors
Forged in Desire
Seized by Seduction
Locked in Temptation

Harlequin Desire

The Westmoreland Legacy
The Rancher Returns
His Secret Son
An Honorable Seduction

Harlequin Kimani Romance

Bachelors in Demand
Bachelor Untamed
Bachelor Unleashed
Bachelor Undone
Bachelor Unclaimed
Bachelor Unforgiving
Bachelor Unbound

For additional books by
New York Times bestselling author Brenda Jackson,
visit her website, brendajackson.net.

IN THE DOCTOR'S BED

Brenda Jackson

To the love of my life, Gerald Jackson, Sr.
To all my readers. This one is for you.

Let love and faithfulness never leave you;
bind them around your neck,
write them on the tablet of your heart.
—*Proverbs* 3:3

Chapter 1

The moment Jaclyn Campbell stepped off the elevator she felt her nerves kick in. Tension stirred in the pit of her stomach, and her pulse throbbed at the base of her throat. It was as if she was back in high school and had been called to the principal's office. The only difference was she wasn't sixteen anymore, but a twenty-six-year-old woman, an intern at Hopewell General Hospital, and she had gotten summoned to the office of the chief of staff, Dr. Germaine Dudley.

Taking a deep breath and inserting her sweaty hands in the pockets of her slacks, she paused at the desk of Dr. Dudley's administrative assistant, Mona Wells. The older woman glanced up from the paperwork just long enough to say, "Go on in, Dr. Campbell. They're waiting on you in the conference room."

They? The pit of Jaclyn's stomach nearly dropped to the

floor. Who were "they"? She wondered just what kind of trouble she had gotten into. Granted she and Kayla Tsang, E.R.'s head nurse, never saw eye-to-eye on much of anything. Jaclyn had known from the first day of orientation it would behoove her to stay out of the woman's way.

Nurse Tsang was a stickler for rules and had the attitude of an old sourpuss, which was sad for someone who was only thirty-five years old. Jaclyn smiled to herself upon recalling what her roommate and fellow intern, Isabelle Morales, had told her just last week. "Miss Thang"—as other staff members called the nurse behind her back—needed to get laid.

Quickly wiping the smile off her face and drawing in another deep breath, Jaclyn knocked on the door.

"Come in."

Jaclyn entered the room to find three individuals sitting at a long table. Her gaze first went to Dr. Dudley who was seated at the head of the table, and as usual his gaze raked over her. It wasn't the first time she'd thought the man had a roving eye. Isabelle also had caught him ogling her and other young female interns the same way. That was probably the only mark against the man. The married, sixty-something father of three was well-respected in the medical field, and he had some political clout as well because he and the governor were college chums.

Her gaze then swept across the length of the table. The woman seated to the right of Dr. Dudley was Camille Hunter, the attractive public relations director of the hospital. Although Jaclyn didn't know Camille that well, she'd always found the young woman friendly enough when they'd passed in the halls or met in the elevator.

And last but definitely not least was the man who'd

captured Jaclyn's heart her first day at Hopewell. Dr. Lucien De Winter, chief resident.

She wasn't ashamed to admit to herself that she had a crush on the man and had for months. Her mother had warned her that it would be that way when she met her true mate. Jaclyn wasn't sure how Dr. De Winter would fit into her future, but right now he was just a nice specimen of a man that any woman would love to lay claim to.

Even while sitting down, Dr. De Winter was tall, and had a muscular build. His black hair was cropped short and he had the sexiest brown eyes any man had a right to have. And that neatly trimmed mustache and goatee only accentuated a pair of sensuous lips.

Their gazes met briefly before she swiftly moved her eyes back to Dr. Dudley. "Nurse Tsang said you wanted to see me, sir," she said.

"Yes, come in and join us, Dr. Campbell. We won't bite."

She nervously crossed the room and sat in one of the chairs that happened to be directly across from Dr. De Winter.

"Now, Dr. Campbell, the reason you were summoned here today was to first thank you for your bravery as well as your loyalty in reporting the drug abuse of one of your fellow interns. I know that wasn't an easy decision to make, and I want to assure you that you did the right thing and you are appreciated for doing so. We were hoping we would be able to handle this matter rather quietly, but it seems that won't be the case."

Jaclyn nodded, trying to follow what Dr. Dudley was saying, but her close proximity to Dr. De Winter was distracting her. Was that heat she felt radiating off the man? She wouldn't be surprised given how drawn she was to him. It was an attraction she'd constantly tried to downplay, thanks to the hospital's no-fraternization policy regarding managers and those reporting to them.

"The Matthews family has threatened the hospital with a lawsuit."

Jaclyn blinked. *Lawsuit?* That one word pulled her attention back to Dr. Dudley. "I don't understand, sir."

"And neither do we, Dr. Campbell. Thanks to you reporting to Dr. De Winter what you knew regarding Dr. Matthews and our own proof of certain events, we'd hoped the matter could be handled discreetly. However, we have been notified that the Matthews family has decided to sue the hospital."

Jaclyn raised a brow. "On what grounds?"

"That we reacted in the extreme and that Dr. Matthews was wrongfully terminated."

Jaclyn frowned. "How can they say that?" Although she'd asked the question, in a way she already knew the answer. The Matthewses just happened to be one of the richest families not only in Alexandria but in all of Virginia. It was a known fact they were Hopewell's biggest benefactors. They even had a wing named after them. Their son Terrence had also been an intern. Jaclyn hated being the reason for Terrence's termination, but she felt she'd done the right thing when she'd witnessed his attempting to steal drugs from the hospital pharmacy more than once.

"The hospital feels we had sufficient grounds to release him. And although we are faced with a lawsuit as well as the withdrawal of the Matthewses' support to the hospital, we will deal with it," Dr. Dudley said assuringly.

He then glanced over at Camille. "As public relations supervisor it will be your job, Ms. Hunter, to make sure the hospital maintains its stellar reputation through all of this. I can just imagine the type of image the Matthewses will try painting us with."

Camille nodded, her expression sober. "I will."

Dr. Dudley smiled at Camille, a smile that made Jaclyn's flesh crawl. She wondered if she was the only one who'd caught on to it. She glanced over at Dr. De Winter and their gazes met, and not for the first time she thought she felt something emitting from the dark eyes holding hers.

Knowing she was just imagining things, she drew in a deep breath and shifted her attention back to Dr. Dudley as a question suddenly burned in her mind. "Now that there's a lawsuit pending, does that mean I will be named as the person who was…"

"The whistle-blower?" Dr. Dudley finished for her. "You won't have that to worry about. Your name will be held in the strictest confidence and protected by hospital policy. It has been proven that Dr. Matthews does indeed have a drug problem and it will be up to the Matthews family to prove otherwise."

Jaclyn was glad to hear that. She knew that once the news broke everyone would wonder who had snitched on Terrence because he was well-liked and had a promising future. It hadn't taken her long to figure him out and she'd been able to read the signs mainly because her older brother had had the same problem before he'd gotten help. Now he was married with a little girl and volunteered a lot of his time trying to help others kick the habit that had nearly destroyed him eight years ago.

"And because of the sensitive nature of the matter and the Matthews family's association with this facility, we have decided to hire someone to handle the suit that is not one of our regular hospital attorneys. In other words, we've decided to bring in the big guns."

"But we can assure you again, Dr. Campbell, that your confidentiality won't be compromised," Dr. De Winter interjected.

Jaclyn nodded while trying to ignore the warm, husky tone of his voice that seemed to caress every inch of her skin. She glanced over at him, met his gaze, felt her heart rate quicken. "Thank you."

"That will be all, Dr. Campbell," Dr. Dudley said, reclaiming her attention.

"All right." She stood and turned to leave. Although she was tempted to glance back over her shoulder to look at one person in particular, she was fully aware that doing so would be foolish as well as risky, so she continued to move toward the door.

Lucien entered his Georgetown row house at close to eight that night, hours later than his schedule at the hospital dictated. But then when was the last time he had what he considered a bona fide schedule? Certainly not since he'd taken the role of chief resident at Hopewell. At least this group of interns was halfway through this leg of their training. He had high hopes they would become good physicians one day. Some more so than others. There were a few he still needed to work on.

And one in particular he needed to keep his mind off.

Scowling, he paused and rubbed his hands down his face. Jaclyn Campbell would be his downfall if he wasn't careful. He of all people knew the hospital's non-fraternization policy and the consequences if it wasn't obeyed. Yet that hadn't stopped him from remembering every single thing about her whenever he saw her.

Take today, for instance. A surge of desire had rushed through him the moment she had entered the conference room. And when their gazes had connected it seemed that every nerve ending in his body had awakened.

Drawing in a deep breath, he forced one foot in front of the other as he made his way into the kitchen. Tonight would be one of those nights when dinner would be a guessing game and frankly he wasn't in the mood. He could have stopped somewhere to eat before coming home, but this was one night he wanted to put as much distance between him and the hospital as he could.

The day hadn't gotten off to a good start. The moment he'd entered the hospital and been told Dr. Dudley needed to see him immediately, he'd gotten a clue how things would be. Because Lucien had been the one to actually terminate Terrence, his name would come under fire as well. The thought of the Matthewses actually filing a suit against the hospital when they knew their son had a drug problem was ludicrous. It only went to show that people with money thought they could do just about anything.

Lucien opened his freezer and pulled out a microwave dinner. Moments later while waiting for his meal to heat up he decided to switch his thoughts to more pleasant things.

Namely, Jaclyn Campbell.

After the morning meeting with Dr. Dudley, they had met again when one of her patients, Marvin Spencer, had presented with shortness of breath and she needed approval to increase the dosage of the man's medication. As usual she was precise and right on point. There was no doubt in his mind that she would become an outstanding physician. On her previous rotations she'd received nothing but compliments from patients and fellow doctors alike. Patients felt she listened to what they'd had to say, and doctors remarked on her professionalism.

His thoughts shifted back to their time in Mr. Spencer's room. They had worked well together, adjusting the intravenous line, asking the patient questions.

Jerome Stubbs, a male nurse who usually worked in O.R., had also been in the room. But even while Lucien was checking Mr. Spencer's vital signs, the only person he had been aware of was Jaclyn. The first time it happened had been her first day at Hopewell, over a year ago. He'd gotten upset with himself for his immediate attraction to her, and he still wasn't sure what had brought it on. For some reason the sight of her in her pale blue scrubs had been a total turn-on.

Later that week, when the staff had joined the interns offsite at a nearby bar and grill for a casual get-acquainted session, all it had taken was seeing the way her body had been shaped by a pair of denim jeans and a pullover sweater, and his mouth had watered for days.

And then he had run into her at a grocery store one Sunday. She had been dressed for church and he'd gotten a chance to see the most gorgeous pair of legs any woman could own. She had looked so good in her peach-colored fashionable two-piece suit that he had only narrowly avoided running his grocery cart into a display of canned goods in the middle of the aisle.

Never had any woman been able to dominate his attention like she had, especially in the workplace. And no matter how much he'd tried, he hadn't been able to lick his inappropriate attention for the female doctor who was reporting to him directly. And that wasn't good.

The bummer was that the attraction was one-sided. There was not one incident he could cite as being deliberate on her part. She had the type of beauty a woman didn't have to flaunt. It was just there and he honestly doubted she knew the effect she had on men.

Hell, he'd even seen Dr. Dudley eye her down more than once and had to bite down the jealousy that had consumed him. But then the old man was known to have that bad-ass habit with the female interns. Lucien was surprised no one had filed a sexual harassment complaint against him. Lucien wasn't blind. He'd seen the looks and heard Dudley's offhand comments to several of the female interns. He'd even confronted his superior about his behavior, which hadn't gone over well.

As he sat down to dine alone, his thoughts shifted back to Jaclyn Campbell. He'd assumed he had fixed his problem when he'd sent her to work the nightshift in E.R. for a while. Usually she would have left the hospital by the time he would arrive. But on one particular morning there had been a school bus accident resulting in a number of injured kids. E.R. had been quite busy that day and everyone, even off-duty personnel, had been called in to assist.

And he had seen her. He had worked alongside her that day, and finally admitted to himself that he didn't want distance between them again. He would just have to learn how to control his attraction. So far he had. However, there were days, like today, that could test him to the fullest.

While they were in Mr. Spencer's room together, he had looked at her face and thought she was the most beautiful woman in the world. He'd seen the long dark lashes and how they'd fanned across her face, her beautiful hazel eyes, her chin-length, straight brown hair and creamy fair skin. Although she'd never confirmed or denied it, he'd heard that she was the product of a biracial marriage. Her father's family hailed from Scotland and her mother was African-American.

After completing his meal, he stood to stretch his body when his cell phone rang. He smiled when he pulled the iPhone from his back pocket and saw the caller was his sister.

"Yeah, kiddo?"

"Everyone, especially Nana, will be particularly glad to hear you're coming home for Christmas. Tell me it's true, Lucien."

He chuckled. Although both he and his sister were naturalized citizens of the United States, "home" was their birthplace of Jamaica. He, his sister, Lori, and a slew of cousins had all left Jamaica about the same time to attend college in the United States and had eventually made it their home. But for the holidays everyone tried returning for what they considered a family reunion. Due to work obligations he'd missed attending the last two years.

"It's only August, Lori. Any reason you want to know so soon? You've got four months."

"Four months will be here before you know it, Lu. Besides, we need time to plan and to prepare Nana for the disappointment if you aren't coming again. It will be three years. I wish you can make it this year."

Lucien didn't have to be reminded. His grandmother did that every time they spoke. He hadn't been home since he'd taken the position of chief resident at the hospital. With the job came new obligations as well as a number of sacrifices.

He smiled. "You'll get your wish, Lori. I'm going home for the holidays. The time off is already on the hospital schedule."

Not wanting to risk getting a busted eardrum, he held the phone from his ear when she began screaming in excitement. He was older than his sister by a year and they had always been close, although they now lived thousands of miles apart. She was an attorney working and living in Los Angeles.

He placed the phone back to his ear when he felt it was safe to do so. "Doesn't take much to get you excited, does it?"

"Oh, you," she admonished softly. "This is great news, so don't try to downplay it. Nana is going to be counting the days."

And he would, too. As far as he was concerned his grandmother was the wisest women he knew and always had been. And she was the kindest and most motivating. Not only had she raised Lucien, but she had also supported everything he'd ever wanted to do and had extended this same support to his sister and his two cousins whom she'd also raised. That's why one of the first things the four of them had done after achieving their goals in America was to build Nana a beautiful and spacious home in Kingston, Jamaica, that had a picturesque view of the Blue Mountains from every room.

A short while later Lucien ended the call with Lori, looking forward to the two weeks he would be home. But he had a lot to do before he left Alexandria for Kingston. He had to get some normalcy in his life. And the way to achieve that goal was to get a handle on his attraction to Jaclyn Campbell. He'd tried it before and it hadn't worked. This time, no matter what, he couldn't fail.

Because he knew if he did, he was headed for deep trouble.

Chapter 2

"Have you given any more thought to my suggestion that we get a puppy, Jaclyn?"

Jaclyn glanced across the stretcher at her roommate Isabelle Morales as they quickly rolled a pregnant woman down the hall toward the delivery room. A Jennifer Lopez look-alike, Isabelle wanted to go into pediatrics when her residency ended, and Jaclyn considered her friend one of the brightest interns at Hopewell.

"I honestly don't think a puppy is a good idea, Isabelle. With the hours we spend at the hospital who's going to make sure he's fed properly?" she replied.

Before Isabelle could respond, the patient, who'd been enduring her labor pains quietly, suddenly screamed. She had been in labor for the past ten hours and, last timed, her contractions were less than three minutes apart. Her obstetrician was already in the delivery room waiting.

"The two of you are talking about puppies and I'm about to die here," the woman snarled at them.

"You're not dying, Mrs. White, you're having a baby."

Ignoring what Jaclyn said, the woman then added, "And where is my husband?"

"He's washing up. He'll be in the delivery room when we get there," Isabelle added.

"I don't want him there. He's the one responsible for my condition."

Jaclyn cast a glance over at Isabelle and fought back a smile. She pitied Mr. White about now.

As soon as they wheeled the mother-to-be through the double doors, several nurses took over. One of them was Jerome. "It took both of you to bring her here?" he asked grinning. "Better not let Miss Thang see you. She'll think you're goofing off with nothing better to do."

"I was on break," Isabelle said smiling. "Besides, I needed to talk to Jaclyn about something."

At that moment Dr. De Winter walked out of the operating room and Jaclyn had to quickly compose herself. The man did things to her without even trying. Not that he would try because he didn't have the same interest in her that she had in him.

He stopped before them. "Dr. Morales and Dr. Campbell. How are you two doing?"

"Fine," they responded simultaneously.

He looked solely at Isabelle. "Dr. Morales, Dr. Thornton has requested that one of my interns be ready to assist him tomorrow. He's performing an advanced surgical procedure on the throat of a six-year-old boy. Is that something you'd be interested in?"

Jaclyn thought the smile on Isabelle's face was priceless. "Yes, sir. Very much so," she said in an excited voice.

"Then be here ready to scrub up at eight in the morning."

"Thanks. I will."

"Good." And without saying anything else, or giving Jaclyn a second glance, he walked off.

Jaclyn's gaze followed him until he was no longer in sight. She then switched her attention back to Isabelle who was grinning from ear to ear. Dr. De Winter's recommendation that one of his interns be present during surgery was a big thing and every intern under him knew it.

"That's a good opportunity, Isabelle. Congratulations."

"Thanks. I can't believe he chose me."

Jaclyn chuckled. "I can. He recognizes how good you are and knows you're planning to go into pediatrics. You deserve it."

The smile slowly faded from Isabelle's face. "Not everyone will think so."

Jaclyn knew that to be true. Not all the interns were supportive of each other. Some were competitive and a few were downright cutthroat.

"Hey, don't worry about it. A few might bitch and moan, but I doubt any of them will question Dr. De Winter about it," Jaclyn said.

"You're right, but—"

"No buts, Isabelle."

Later, when Jaclyn made her rounds, she turned the corner and collided head-on with Dr. De Winter, sending the charts she was carrying flying across the floor. "Oh, I'm sorry. I wasn't looking where I was going."

"Apparently, Dr. Campbell," he said in what she thought was an ultra-sexy voice. It was the same voice that she'd heard in her dreams last night, the night before and the night before that.

He knelt down and began picking up her charts and

she knelt to join him. "You don't have to do that, Dr. De Winter. I can get them."

"No problem," he said, handing her the charts he'd collected.

Their gazes connected the moment their fingers touched and she felt a deep stirring in the pit of her stomach. As she stared into his eyes she thought she saw them darken, but when she blinked he'd already straightened and was standing back up.

She stood as well. "Thank you," she murmured, clutching the charts to her chest like an armor of steel.

"You're welcome. And how are your patients? Any problems or concerns?"

Because he'd asked... "There is this one thing. We're still trying to determine the reason behind Mr. Aiken's high fevers."

Dr. De Winter nodded. "I understand he had another one this morning."

"Yes. We took more blood, but there's nothing abnormal. The fever means there's infection somewhere in his body, but nothing is showing up in his blood."

"So you're dealing with an FUO?"

Fever of unknown origin. "Yes," she said, clearly disturbed.

"Any other signs and symptoms, Dr. Campbell?"

"None."

"Let me see his chart for a second."

She pushed a lock of hair behind her ear and then flipped through the charts to find the one belonging to William Aiken. She handed it to Dr. De Winter, grateful their fingers did not touch this time.

Her pulse thudded as she stood there and watched him peruse the man's chart. She couldn't help noticing how his long lashes fanned across his cheeks and how sensuous his mouth looked. He then glanced up and caught her staring at his mouth. *Good grief.*

"May I make a suggestion, Dr. Campbell?"

"Yes, sir, you may." The one thing that was different about Dr. De Winter compared to other doctors in an authoritative position was that he didn't project a brash, all-knowing demeanor. He liked getting input from the interns he supervised and always solicited their opinions.

"Have blood drawn from his toe, preferably the big one, and have it checked."

She raised a brow. Probably any other intern would have accepted what he said without question, but unfortunately she wasn't one of them. "Why, if I may ask?"

He chuckled and the sound seemed to whisper across her skin. "Yes, doctor, you may. When I was an intern at a college in Boston, I had a patient with FUO and drawing blood from the big toe was suggested to me by the chief of staff. He explained that often bad blood will find places to settle and can't easily be detected."

She nodded as understanding dawned. "Which was the premise behind bloodletting," she said, thinking out loud and seeing his point. "Which is the draining of bad blood out of a person's body. And if there's bad blood not detected, it might be confined in one of the body's peripheral points. A premise we have now put to sound scientific use."

"Exactly."

She smiled. "Thanks, Dr. De Winter. I'll have that done immediately." She then quickly walked away.

Lucien watched Jaclyn hurry off and drew in a deep breath. When they had accidentally touched moments ago, it had taken everything within him to control the urge to pull her into his arms and mesh his lips with hers. That encounter had been too close for comfort. Way too close.

No matter how much he tried to control himself around her, he was finding it hard to do so. When they had knelt facing each other and he'd looked into her eyes and gazed upon the lushness of her mouth, heat had flared inside of him. He could imagine them kneeling facing each other, but the setting hadn't been the hall of the hospital. In his mind they were in the middle of the bed. Naked.

Those were the last kind of thoughts he needed lodged in his brain. He tried forcing them out. The hospital's nonfraternization policy had been put in place for a reason and he intended to abide by it. But God, he was attracted to her. And if knowing that wasn't enough to shake his world, then he didn't know what would. At that moment he thought he could even feel the floor shift under his feet. Yes, he was definitely standing on shaky ground.

Jaclyn nibbled on her bottom lip as she read Mr. Aiken's most recent lab report. Dr. De Winter had been right in suggesting that blood be drawn from the man's toe. The report clearly indicated bacteria in Mr. Aiken's body. Bacteria of an unknown source.

Now she had to determine what was causing it. As she read the report again the main question circling around in her head was why the bacteria hadn't shown up in a routine lab test.

"You're too pretty to be frowning."

Jaclyn glanced up and smiled at Ravi Patel, another

intern. With his tall, slender build, long wavy black hair, dark eyes and dark skin, he made a reality of the old cliché tall, dark and handsome.

All the female interns, nurses and patients alike drooled over the American-born East Indian. Even Miss Thang seemed taken with him and would blush like a silly schoolgirl whenever Ravi was near. What Jaclyn most admired and respected about Ravi was that he was quick to let the admiring ladies know that he was an engaged man. His fiancée, a woman from India, was an intern at a hospital in Miami. The two planned to marry in a few years.

"Hi, Ravi. I was going over one of my patient's charts."

"His condition is serious?"

"FUO earlier, but thanks to Dr. De Winter I was finally able to find something in his blood. There are bacteria. Now I'm trying to determine the cause."

"If you need help, this might be something to bring before the others in our group session with Dr. De Winter in the morning."

Jaclyn nibbled on her bottom lip. She of all people knew when the group of interns would meet with Dr. De Winter in a classroom setting. She looked forward to those once-a-week sessions when he would take center stage at the front of the class. Those were the times when she could sit in the back and ogle him to her heart's delight and come across only as a very attentive student.

More than once he had glanced her way and caught her staring and she appreciated that he wasn't a mind reader. He would have been appalled at some of the things she'd been thinking at the time. "I might do that. Thanks for suggesting it, Ravi."

Ravi glanced over her shoulder and smiled. "There's Dr. De Winter. We can ask him now."

Before Jaclyn could stop him, Ravi had gotten Dr. De Winter's attention. Jaclyn released a deep breath. She hadn't quite recovered from their earlier meeting when they had touched. Now he was about to get all into her space again.

"Doctors Patel and Campbell. Is there something I can help you with?" he asked, his gaze passing between them.

"Yes, sir," Jaclyn said. "Thanks to your suggestion I was able to pinpoint bacteria in Mr. Aiken's blood. But now I'm concerned with the cause. I've done tests to rule out several abnormalities, but these bacteria are determined to remain in certain areas. I'm still concerned that we could not detect it in a routine blood test."

"I thought this would be something she could bring before the group in the morning," Ravi interjected.

"I agree with Dr. Patel. This is something we can give the group as a think tank question, Dr. Campbell. In the meantime, how is Mr. Aiken? What are we doing for him?"

Before Jaclyn could respond, Ravi glanced at his watch and then said apologetically, "Sorry, I need to go check on one of my patients."

He then quickly walked off leaving her alone with Dr. De Winter. She forced her gaze from Ravi's retreating back to Dr. De Winter. For the next few minutes she provided him with the answer to his question. He didn't interrupt and every so often he would nod slowly. It was hard not to get absorbed in the tingles of aware-

ness that were going through her body from his standing so close to her.

At one point while she was talking, their eyes held
for a moment. Her mind went completely blank and it
was only when he'd said in a warm tone, "You were saying, Dr. Campbell?" that she realized she had stopped
talking in mid-sentence. She swallowed hard and began
talking again, knowing with her fair skin that her blush
of embarrassment was easy to see.

So okay, now he knew one of his interns was taken
with him. The man was sexy and handsome so there was
no doubt in her mind she wasn't the first and wouldn't
be the last. Although flattered, he was a professional
who wouldn't encourage her. He probably considered
her one of those silly little interns with hormonal problems. For her it went beyond that. Oh, she would love
to jump his bones if given the chance, but her crush on
him was growing by leaps and bounds each day.

When she finally finished her spiel, he met her gaze
and asked in what she thought was a husky voice, "Why
did you zone out on me a few moments ago?"

She hadn't expected him to ask her that. Did he honestly expect her to tell him the truth? Even worse, did
he suspect the truth? She drew in a deep breath and decided to lie through her teeth. "No reason, sir. I merely
lost my train of thought for a second." *And please don't
ask me why.*

He slowly nodded and as if he could read her mind
and was privy to her last thought, he took a step back.
"I'll see you at the group discussion in the morning,
Dr. Campbell."

And then he walked away.

Chapter 3

Jaclyn had known the moment she entered the meeting room the next morning and saw how everyone was clustered together and talking in whispers that word was out about the Matthews lawsuit.

It had been bad enough when everyone had found out about Terrence's termination last month. Speculation had run wild as to the reason for it. Now his family was bringing things out in the open and letting everyone know what was going on and that the hospital would pay for what they saw as a grave mistake.

"Hey, what's going on?" she asked a fellow intern by the name of Tamara St. John as she slid into the seat beside her. She'd liked Tamara from the first day they met and found her to be a down-to-earth person.

Tamara leaned closer and whispered, "Word is out as to the real reason Terrence was kicked out of the program. Rumor has it that he had a drug problem. His family is suing the hospital and saying the charges against him are false."

Jaclyn swallowed deeply. "What will the hospital do?"

"I hear they feel they have a good case against Terrence. Someone on staff came forward with the goods on him and provided enough proof to make the hospital take action. Now everyone is trying to figure out who among us talked."

A muscle tightened in Jaclyn's stomach. "Does it matter, especially if the allegations are true?" she asked.

"Doesn't matter to me. I can't help admiring the person for doing it. Some people who are born into wealth think they can get away with anything. Terrence acted like too much of a snob to suit me anyway."

Tamara glanced beyond Jaclyn and smiled. "Here comes Dr. De Winter. We'll talk later." Tamara then straightened in her seat to chime in with the others when they said, "Good morning, Dr. De Winter."

"Good morning, everyone," the husky voice replied.

Jaclyn hadn't been one of those to coo out the greeting, yet she thought his gaze deliberately settled on her as he passed her seat to walk toward the front of the room. It was then that she overheard a female intern sitting in front of her whisper to another woman, "That doctor is way too fine. I just love watching him strut his stuff."

Jaclyn thought the same thing. She liked seeing him strut his stuff as well, but that was something she wouldn't dare share with anyone. She watched and listened as he went through the regular routine of asking how things were going and if anyone had had any challenges for the week to share with the others.

She knew that was her cue and she raised her hand. He glanced over in her direction. "Yes, Dr. Campbell?"

She spoke up and presented Mr. Aiken's situation to everyone. Some fellow interns asked questions while jotting down notes. Several threw out possible diagnoses for her to consider and she wrote those down as well. It was nice getting feedback from her peers. More than once she glanced at Dr. De Winter and saw him watching and listening with interest. He was letting them work as a team. A few times it seemed after scanning the room his gaze would come to settle on her. And each time it did, her breath would get caught in her throat and she would swallow deeply to force the air down.

"So, Dr. Campbell, do you think you have enough possibilities to work with?" he asked, his eyes homing in on hers in a way that made blood rush through her veins.

She took a deep breath and then responded, "Yes, and I'm going to narrow it down to the best three."

He nodded. "Time might not be on your side," Dr. De Winter then said. "I understand Mr. Aiken's fever spiked overnight."

She wasn't surprised that he was well aware of what was going on with each of the intern's patients under his charge. How he kept up with it all she didn't know. There were fifteen of them and each had been assigned five to seven patients.

"Yes, sir, but so far we're keeping the temperature down."

He nodded. "But what we want is to get rid of it all together."

Jaclyn moistened her lips with her tongue thinking she could have taken his words as a put-down. Instead she took them as a challenge. A patient's health was on the line and her job as a doctor was to not make him comfortable but to get him well. "Yes, sir."

He straightened from the podium he'd been leaning against and then looked out over the group. "Good job, team. Now go out there and take care of your patients."

Lucien remained behind in the empty meeting room. Things with Jaclyn Campbell were still not going well. Hooking up with a woman, getting to know her, developing a relationship both mentally and especially physically, was one of those simple pleasures in life that all men looked forward to experiencing.

He dated, although it had been a while since he'd dated anyone seriously. He always enjoyed a female's company, but in most situations he tried avoiding dating women in his own profession. More often than not their conversations would center too much around the medical cases they were up against.

The last woman he'd dated had been in the education field and he enjoyed learning about her work and the challenges she faced. The only bad thing about Shawnee Powers was her inability to stop placing herself on some sort of pedestal. There was nothing wrong with someone believing in themselves, but for Shawnee it had begun getting downright ridiculous. He'd put up with it until he'd noticed her jealous streak. She had begun questioning him when he didn't call or when he didn't immediately text her back. It had been ten months since they'd broken up and at no time had he been tempted to call her.

Ten months.

That had been when he'd seen Jaclyn for the first time. He would always remember that day. There had been twenty residents and now they were down to fifteen. One had gotten seriously sick and had to leave the program, three hadn't been able to cope the first six months and one he'd had to terminate.

His mind shifted to Terrence Matthews, the one he'd had to terminate. The young man, although somewhat brash at times, had had a promising future. He had started off sharp as a whip, up on every assignment and possessed a bedside manner all the patients appreciated. Then Terrence began being late to group meetings, going MIA when he was supposed to be visiting patients and falling asleep during group discussions.

Lucien had mentioned Terrence's behavior to Dr. Dudley who at first hadn't wanted to rock the boat; after all the man was a Matthews. But Lucien had been making his own notes and observations when Jaclyn had come to him about Terrence's drug use.

Without Terrence aware he was being observed, she had witnessed him stealing drugs from the hospital pharmacy. A replay of the pharmacy's surveillance camera had backed up her claim, and a random drug test confirmed Terrence's drug use.

Lucien shook his head when he recalled the day he had summoned Dr. Matthews to his office. The man didn't deny the charges. Instead he said because he was a Matthews and his family had given so much to the hospital, he felt anything he did should and could be overlooked.

Even the offer that he take a temporary leave and go into drug rehab was laughed off with Terrence saying to do such a thing would be an admission of guilt. Lucien had ending up terminating Terrence's association with the hospital that day.

Although he'd backed up Lucien's actions, Dr. Dudley had predicted there would be a backlash from the Matthews family. The old man had been right.

Drawing in a deep breath Lucien walked to the window and glanced out at downtown Alexandria. Below, the brick-paved streets were lined with shops and boutiques of early eighteenth and nineteenth century architecture. And in the distance, across the Potomac, was the nation's capital in all its glorious splendor. He enjoyed where he worked and loved living in Georgetown, far enough from the hospital on the D.C. side to appreciate the days he had off work.

He knew Jaclyn lived in Virginia, and the only times their paths had crossed after hours had been that Sunday when he'd decided to do his grocery shopping at a store in Alexandria.

He rubbed his hand down his face and turned away from the window. Although she had been sitting in the back of the room today, his gaze had sought her out anyway. He had looked for her. Found her. And had felt his attraction to her intensify. When she'd opened her mouth to speak, his pulse had accelerated and his ability to breathe had become affected.

What the hell was wrong with him?

It had taken all of his control to keep his features neutral, void of expression. Each and every time he was around her he risked the possibility of giving something away. The interns under his charge were bright, observant and astute. They would hang on to his every word, decipher his every action.

Jaclyn made it hard for him to think straight at times. Like today when she had been explaining Mr. Aiken's condition to everyone. While she talked about the man's fever, Lucien had begun imagining a fever of a different kind—the type generated in the heat of passion between a man and a woman. Namely, him and her. He could envision her lush body, naked and hot, extremely hot, writhing beneath his while he thrust in and out of her making nonstop love to her.

Those thoughts had been the last thing that should have been flowing through his mind, but they weren't. Even now those kinds of thoughts were uppermost in his mind and determined to get the best of him. It might be wise to consider placing as much distance between him and Jaclyn as possible, and the only way he could do that was to suggest she transfer to another hospital. He knew there was no way he could do that. It wouldn't be fair to her to disrupt her position here just because he was the one with a libido problem.

As he gathered his belongings, Lucien knew what he had to do. He had to get a grip. No matter what, he could not lower his guard around her.

By lunchtime Jaclyn had heard so many versions of what was going down with the Matthews lawsuit that she wondered where was rumor control when you needed it. The only good thing was that so far no one knew the identity of the person who'd snitched on Terrence and for that she was grateful.

She hadn't known what to expect when she'd made the decision to come forward to report Terrence's drug abuse. But her parents had raised her to do the right thing, and knowing about the abuse and the harm it could cause her fellow doctor had been the determining factor in making her talk. No one knew she was the one responsible for Terrence losing his job. Not even her roommate Isabelle.

No one except Dr. De Winter.

Just the mention of his name made a picture of him flash in her mind. He was so drop-dead gorgeous. Most of the other female staffers felt the same way, too. She'd heard the comments, and she'd noticed that several of them would cook up any excuse to go up to his office, only to return with what they considered the same disappointing news. Dr. De Winter had suspected them from the first. In other words, he'd seen through their attempt at shrewdness and wasn't having any of it.

Thoughts of Dr. De Winter still took up residence in her mind hours later at the end of her shift. But they'd been pushed to the background after she'd overheard some interns trying to figure out who had nailed Terrence. They had what they termed a snitch among them.

They'd claimed if they'd known about Terrence, they would have implemented a "don't ask, don't tell" policy. Who in their right mind would want to go up against the Matthews family? they'd asked. Hadn't the snitch caused the hospital more harm than good now that the family was withdrawing its financial support?

As far as Jaclyn was concerned things were getting out of hand. What if Dr. Dudley was wrong and she was identified as the person who'd come forward about Terrence? She could see some of the interns turning on her and making her life at Hopewell unpleasant.

She knew the one person she needed to talk with and found him standing at a nurse's station writing in a patient's chart. Taking a deep breath she walked over to him. "Excuse me, Dr. De Winter, may I speak with you privately?"

Lucien stopped writing at the sound of the soft feminine voice. He didn't have to glance up to see to whom it belonged. He forced the air from his lungs as he turned and looked into Jaclyn's face. He immediately saw from the look in her eyes that she was troubled by something. But he had to play it cool, remembering he couldn't jump at the chance to be alone with her any more than he would any of the other interns.

He stuck his pen into his pocket and lifted a brow. "I'm about to call it a day, Dr. Campbell. Is it something that can wait until tomorrow?" he asked in a no-nonsense, very professional tone, knowing his words had been overheard by Nurse Tsang who was all ears. As usual her radar was on high alert. The woman had a tendency to mind everyone's business but her own.

"No, sir. It can't wait."

He glanced at his watch. "Very well, then. We can go to my office."

They walked side by side toward his office at the end of the corridor. And with every step he took he inhaled her scent. The tropical fragrance of jasmine reminded him of the night-blooming flower from the island where he'd been born. She was wearing it well and it made him recall sultry summer nights.

As he walked beside her, he racked his brain for something to say that wouldn't come out as too forward. He glanced over at her. With her exotic features and dark hair, she could pass for an island girl if it wasn't for her fair skin. She was a beauty. He'd thought so the first time he'd seen her and he thought so now.

He increased his pace and she managed to keep up

with him. Lucien could imagine those long legs beneath the slacks could do so with ease.

It had been a quiet day, no emergencies that had needed his attention beyond the norm and for that he was grateful. He had been about to call it a day, had hoped he could quietly slip out without seeing her more than he already had that day. But now it seemed he would be in close quarters with her. As long as he kept things on a professional note he would be fine.

At least that was his prayer.

But his prayer didn't help him a few minutes later when they'd reached his office and he held the door open for her to enter. She brushed past him and her scent had made him tremble.

He knew at that moment he had no business bringing her to his office. The space was tight as it was and having her in it would make it even more confining. And as he stepped into the cramped room behind her and closed the door, he knew he was in trouble.

Deep trouble.

Jaclyn glanced around the office, remembering the first time she had been here. That had been her first week at the hospital and Nurse Tsang had reported to Dr. De Winter that she hadn't turned in her end-of-the-day report on time. Jaclyn had argued that her report had been turned in on time, but Nurse Tsang's watch had been set two minutes early. Dr. De Winter had calmly suggested that to eliminate confusion in the future she get her report in five minutes early. What he hadn't said and what she clearly understood that day was that the head nurse enjoyed making everyone's lives miserable and she'd have to avoid getting caught in her trap.

Jaclyn took a deep breath when she remembered the last time she'd been in his office. It was last month when she had reported Terrence's drug use. She had done a lot of soul searching before requesting a meeting with Dr. De Winter and now it looked like the decision she'd made that day might be coming back to haunt her.

"Please have a seat, Dr. Campbell."

"Thank you." She sat in the chair next to his desk and she watched as he sat down as well.

"If you're here regarding the remark I made earlier today in the group session, it wasn't made to call you out or to make it seem as if you didn't know what needed to be done."

She shook her head. "Yes, I know, but that's not why I'm here," she said softly.

He nodded. "Then why are you here? You said whatever you needed to talk to me about couldn't wait until tomorrow."

She inhaled deeply again, wondering why the man had to look so heartthrob sexy. She'd been around good-looking men before, but there was something about Dr. De Winter's looks that could literally take a woman's breath away. She wondered if he knew the effect he had on women and decided yes, he had to know.

"Dr. Campbell?"

She blinked, realizing he was waiting for her to say something. "They are talking."

He raised his brow and a guarded look appeared on his face, and she wondered the reason. "Who's talking?"

"Everyone. They know. Or they think they know and those who don't are trying to figure it out."

He leaned back in his chair and simply stared at her, but it was a stare that made tiny flutters appear in her stomach. "I think you need to tell me just what you're talking about," he said in a gentle tone, so gentle it made her want to tell him everything, especially her misgivings about letting him know about Terrence and how everyone was trying to figure out just who told. But she wanted to go even farther and spill her guts about how she felt about him, how she dreamed about him at night and how she often envisioned him naked. Most important, how her desire and love for him kept taunting her day in and day out. However, she knew she couldn't tell him any of those things. She wouldn't dare.

"I'm talking about the Matthews lawsuit," she finally said. "That's all everyone has been talking about all morning. They're determined to find out who snitched on Terrence."

"They won't."

"Can you be absolutely sure of that, Dr. De Winter?" she asked in frustration, fighting back tears that threatened to fall any minute. When she'd come to him to report Terrence's problem she had hoped that in addition to protecting the hospital in the long run she would be protecting Terrence as well. He needed help. She knew firsthand what drugs could do to a person and didn't want an addiction to rule his life like it had ruled her brother Kevin's.

"Yes, I can be absolutely sure of it, Dr. Campbell. You are protected by the privacy act. What you told me was in confidence and that is equivalent to doctor-patient privilege. I don't have to reveal my source to anyone. Besides, it doesn't matter. He didn't pass the random drug test that was given to him that day."

"I know, but what if their attorneys force the issue? Then what? I thought I was doing the right thing in telling you about it, but now I—"

"You were doing the right thing. You knew one of your fellow interns was involved in something unethical and you brought it to my attention. I repeat, you did the right thing."

There was something in his gentle and understanding tone that pushed her to the edge. There were so many emotions she was trying to deal with. The issue with Terrence was just one of her problems. But beside all that, her feelings for the gorgeous doctor was another issue all together. She'd always been pretty level-headed when it came to men, but she felt way out of her league with Lucien De Winter, mainly because she knew she'd fallen in love with him the moment she'd set eyes on him. She was too old to consider it merely a schoolgirl crush. She'd stop thinking of it in those terms months ago. She was experiencing the wants, desires and needs of a woman with the man she loved.

Now there was no telling what would happen. Once word got out she was the snitch, the hospital would probably have to send her away to downplay all the negative publicity. That meant she wouldn't see Lucien ever again. She would leave without his having a clue how she felt about him. But what did it matter? she asked herself. Her feelings weren't reciprocated.

"Look, maybe I should not have requested this meeting today," she said standing, unable to fight the tears any longer. The do-gooder didn't always save the day, she reminded herself. Not all the time. "I have to go," she said swiping at the tears falling from her eyes.

He stood as well. "No, not this way. Not with tears. I don't want to see you cry."

In a move that surprised her, he stepped around his desk and pulled her into his arms. The moment he wrapped his arms around her, giving her a shoulder to cry on, she took it and began sobbing.

"Shh, things are going to be all right. You're going to have to trust me. The Matthewses will eventually discover that money can't buy everything."

Jaclyn knew for her to be standing here sobbing her heart out in her supervisor's arms was inappropriate, but she couldn't pull away. He smelled good and the way his hand was gently stroking her back felt wonderful.

And then, as if he realized where they were and what he was doing, his hand stilled. She swallowed and lifted her head from his chest to take a step back. But instead of letting her go, he reached out and tenderly cupped her chin in his hand and forced their gazes to connect.

The look she saw in his eyes had her senses reeling. At the same time sexual tension, as thick as it could get, began surrounding them, capturing them in a mist that was saturated with desire. She felt it and knew he had to feel it as well. If it wasn't for the beat of her heart marking the passage of time she would not have known how long they'd been standing there, staring at each other with deep hunger entrenched in their gazes and heat radiating between them.

He moved closer and slowly began lowering his head until his warm breath fanned across her lips. She wanted to blink but couldn't. His hot, possessive gaze was keeping her eyes wide open and glued to his. Her pulse quickened with every inch closer to her mouth that his lips came.

The room was charged with something she'd never experienced before, a kind of static electricity that increased the flow of blood rushing through her veins, made her world turn upside-down, then right-side up. His hand on her chin began moving, allowing his knuckles to tenderly caress the side of her jaw. Her vision blurred when a heated sensation took over her senses and every part of her body.

He lowered his head still more and his mouth came within a breath of taking possession of her lips. Suddenly the alarm on his desk sounded and they knew what that meant: 911 in E.R.

Without saying anything they both rushed toward the door.

Chapter 4

Lucien glanced around. E.R. was in chaos. Doors were flying open with people being wheeled in on stretchers. He stopped one of the nurses. "What do we have?"

"Twelve-car pileup on the interstate. There were four casualties on impact—three of them children in different families. Life flight is on its way and rescue is unloading others as we speak," she said.

"We need all hands on board. Contact all medical staff, even those off duty," Lucien said. He then raced off to assist an injured teenager. Jaclyn was right on his heels. Lucien treated one patient after another, seeing to everyone's needs, and making sure those needing surgery were taken care of.

He glanced over at Jaclyn and saw she was busy as well and couldn't help admire how she was handling things. He had a feeling this would be a long day.

* * *

It was close to four in the morning before things had settled down in the E.R. Jaclyn thought it was so quiet the place appeared eerie. Of the thirty-four people who'd been involved in the twelve-car accident, six hadn't survived and four were still in critical condition. The others had been fortunate to receive minor injuries.

She couldn't help but be proud of her fellow doctors and how they had handled each patient swiftly, confidently, compassionately. Then there had been the media who had swarmed inside looking for a story. And then the family members who'd come to see for themselves that their loved ones were all right. Through it all, she admired the way Dr. De Winter had handled himself and the entire situation. Now she knew why he was one of the top physicians at the hospital and especially why he was in charge of the interns. They respected him and when it counted they had pulled together to make it happen and had saved lives.

She felt good. Exhausted but good. This was the career she had chosen and helping others gave her a high.

A shiver ran through her when she recalled what had almost taken place in his office, right before the alarm had sounded. She refused to believe she had imagined the heat and the desire she had seen in his eyes. It had been real. And he had come within seconds of kissing her.

She pulled her tired body out of the chair beside a patient's stretcher. Ten-month-old Stacia Minestrone, the youngest survivor of the multicar accident, had only minor injuries but was waiting for a bed in Pediatrics. Even though she was presently under Tamara's care, Jaclyn had agreed to observe the precious little girl while Tamara touched base with family services. Stacia's mother hadn't survived and the little girl's father who lived in Wisconsin had been notified and was on his way.

Jaclyn glanced up when Tamara returned. "Thanks for watching her for me. I guess you're ready to leave this place about now."

Jaclyn stood, stretched her muscles and glanced at her watch. She was to have gotten off work more than eight hours ago. Tamara had been spared the initial arrival of E.R. patients because she'd been assisting in O.R. But like the others, once she'd arrived she had quickly joined in to do what was needed to be done.

"Yes, I can't wait to get home to my bed," Jaclyn said. "I'm going to the locker for my backpack and then I'm out of here."

It didn't take her long to gather her things. She was on her way out the hospital's revolving doors when Dr. De Winter called out, "Dr. Campbell, wait up."

She turned around and the moment she did so, her pulse quickened at the sight of him jogging toward her. He had removed his lab coat and was wearing jeans and a shirt. She wondered if he was aware of the effect he had on women, especially the effect he had on her.

The man exuded so much raw masculinity that she simply stood there while memories came flooding down on her. She couldn't help but recall that moment in his office when they'd almost kissed. Now that the crisis in the E.R. was over, she fully understood her predicament. No matter what almost happened in his office, which she still hadn't gotten over, she was an intern and Dr. De Winter was her boss. She would do well to remember that and not do anything to put her job and her career in jeopardy. That was probably why he was in such a hurry to talk to her.

She knew what he was probably going to say. She'd been crying and he'd only taken her into his arms as a way to comfort her and nothing else. Anything else that she assumed she saw or thought transpired was a figment of her imagination.

When he came to a stop in front of her a lock of hair fell in her face and she pushed it away at the same moment she shifted her backpack to another shoulder. "Yes, Dr. De Winter. Is there something you need me to do before I leave?"

Lucien thought that was a loaded question if ever there was one. He could easily respond by saying yes, there was something he needed her to do before she left. Returning to his office so they could finish what they'd started earlier would be nice.

Then he could take her mouth, make love to it, mate with it without any distractions or interruptions. Or if she didn't want to go to his office, they could go anywhere. She could name the place and he wouldn't hesitate to take her there.

"No, there isn't anything I need for you to do," he said, studying her features. She looked tired, but exhaustion in no way detracted from her beauty. "You did a hell of a job in there today. I appreciate everything you and the other interns did. The group was awesome."

One thing Lucien subscribed to was that it didn't pay to bully his group of interns. He was not one who believed in group spankings. He dealt with those individually who did not pull their weight. On the others he didn't mind bestowing compliments when they were due. After what had gone down in E.R., praise was certainly called for. He would tell her now and the others when he saw them again.

Although he'd given her a compliment, what was on his mind more now than anything else was the kiss they'd almost shared in his office. A part of him knew in a way he should be grateful it didn't happen and regret that it almost did. But the truth of the matter was that the memory of holding her in his arms, inhaling her scent, bringing his lips so close to hers sent a flood of heat rushing through his veins and made his breath catch in his throat.

"Thanks," she said. "You did an outstanding job yourself. It amazes me how well you do what you do and know just when to do it, seemingly without thought."

He chuckled. "It comes with practice, trust me. Don't forget I was an intern once and made my share of mistakes. Thankfully none of them cost anyone their life, but still. One day you'll look back at these years and smile and accept them as your growing period."

She smiled. "I hope you're right."

"I am." He glanced at his watch. "I can't believe how late it is—or how early, depending on how you look at it. We never did finish our discussion from earlier today. I know a coffee shop across the bridge that stays open twenty-four hours. This time of morning there won't be a lot of people around so we'll be able to hold a private conversation."

He paused when she hesitated in accepting his invitation. He didn't want to make her feel uncomfortable and think she had no choice in meeting with him, so he added, "Of course I'll understand if you prefer going home. You've pulled a double today so I'm sure you're tired."

Jaclyn couldn't help but smile. She doubted she could ever be tired enough to not want Lucien's company, regardless of the reason. "No, I'm fine and yes, we can finish our conversation from earlier."

In a way finishing up their conversation wasn't what she really wanted. She believed she had done the right thing in turning Terrence in, and she figured the stress, frustration and all kinds of emotions had gotten the best of her earlier and had driven her to a mental meltdown. The activities in E.R. had revived her, given her an adrenaline rush.

"You sure?" he asked.

She felt her heart slamming against her ribcage with his question. Was she absolutely, positively sure when she didn't know what he would say to her? For all she knew he might criticize her for giving in to a crying spell earlier today. But she would take her chances. "Yes, I'm sure."

He smiled. "We can take my car."

"All right."

Lucien wasn't surprised they couldn't make it out of the hospital and to the parking lot without encountering someone he'd rather not have seen. Nurse Tsang was walking toward them as they were leaving. She stopped, causing them to do the same.

"Good morning, Ms. Tsang," he said, his tone formal.

"Dr. De Winter." The woman then glanced over at Jaclyn with a speculative eye. "Dr. Campbell."

"Good morning," Jaclyn acknowledged.

"The two of you are leaving?" the woman then asked.

Lucien lifted a brow. "Yes, we're going to get coffee. I think we've earned the right because we've been here for the last eighteen hours. We had one hell of an emergency."

"So I heard," Ms. Tsang said drily. She then looked over at Jaclyn and then back at Lucien. "Need I remind the two of you of the hospital's nonfraternization policy when it comes to managers and their subordinates?"

Lucien looked down at the woman. He smiled a little, but the smile didn't quite reach his eyes. "No. Just like I'm sure I don't have to remind you of the hospital's contact policy whenever an emergency occurs. I understand no one could reach you yesterday, Ms. Tsang. Nor did you call in."

Her gaze sharpened. "It was my long weekend and I caught the train to New York. That's why I couldn't be reached."

"I'm sure you had a nice time," he remarked.

"Yes, I did."

"Glad to hear it. Now if you will excuse us." He didn't wait to see if she would excuse them or not, nor did he care. He and Jaclyn walked off, leaving the woman standing there staring at them.

The woman had a problem with sticking her nose where it didn't belong. He had mentioned it several times to Dr. Dudley, especially when the interns had come to him complaining, but it seemed the chief of staff always found some excuse or another for Ms. Tsang.

"If you want to cancel our having coffee, I'll understand, Dr. De Winter," Jaclyn said.

He glanced over at her and he knew the smile he gave her was a lot different than the one he'd bestowed upon Ms. Tsang earlier. This one not only reached his eyes but it also spread throughout his entire body like a beacon of light. "There's no way I'm going to let Nurse Tsang's nosiness dictate what I do and how I handle my business."

He opened the car door for her, paused a moment and then asked, "I guess I'm the one who should be asking you if you still want to share a cup of coffee with me."

She smiled up at him as she slid onto the leather seat of his car. "Yes, I still want to share a cup of coffee with you."

He held her gaze. "You sure?"

She nodded. "I'm positive."

Jaclyn knew without a doubt that Lucien had no idea just how positive she was. Regardless of Nurse Tsang's remark, she had no intention of turning down Dr. De Winter's invitation to go someplace where they could talk. It didn't matter that the only discussion they would have was about the Matthews lawsuit. All she cared about was that she would be sharing his space again somewhere across the bridge that hopefully wasn't frequented by their colleagues.

"I like your car," she said after she'd buckled her seat belt and waited for him to do the same. It was a silver 1980 Trans Am, all shiny and clean and expensively upholstered.

"Thanks."

"And it sounds good. So what's under the hood?"

He glanced over at her and chuckled. "This baby was a limited edition Indy car. Turbo, 210 horsepower, 4.9 cubic inch motor and it rides like a dream."

"I hear. What's the torque?"

"Three hundred forty-five pounds."

"Um, four speed manual, V-8 and an 8-trac player that plays CDs. Very impressive, Dr. De Winter," she said.

He took his eyes off her to return to the road. "Thank you, and because we're away from the hospital a first-name basis suits me just fine." He glanced back over at her. "Is that okay with you?"

She nodded, swallowed deeply and said, "I have no problem with it."

"Okay, so tell me, Jaclyn, how do you know so much about muscle cars?"

"My dad made a living as an auto mechanic, but not just any auto mechanic. Back home people came from far and wide just to get him to look under their hoods. He was known as the Muscle Car King."

"Now I'm impressed. Where is back home?"

"Oakland, California."

"Any siblings?" he asked her.

"A brother who's four years older."

"The two of you are close?"

She chuckled. "Yes, but he stopped counting when he married a woman who became the sister I never had and they gave me a niece who everyone thinks is mine. It's uncanny, but she looks just like me when I was her age."

"Then she must be cute as a button."

"Thanks." Had he just given her a compliment? Was he insinuating he thought she was cute? She shifted positions in the seat while thinking she should probably take a chill pill because all her thoughts were wrong. *He's probably being nice to you because he doesn't want to say anything to make you burst into tears on him again.*

"Are both your parents still living?"

She chuckled. "Are they? They take the word *living* to a whole new level. At fifty my father bought a Harley and he and Mom think nothing of hitting the road crossing state lines. And then at fifty-five he bought a boat and we can't keep them off the water. He'll be sixty in a few years and my brother and I are bracing ourselves for what they'll get next."

"They sound like a fun pair."

"They are. They were high school sweethearts who married before either of them were twenty. Then they took turns going to college while raising me and my brother."

She paused a moment and then asked, "What about you, Dr….I mean Lucien. Any siblings? Your parents still alive?"

"I have one sister. We're a year apart. And I understand both my parents are alive…somewhere."

She glanced over at him. "Don't you know?"

"No. I haven't seen my mother since I was five. She left Jamaica and swore she would never return. I was raised by my grandmother. My mother had me when she was fifteen and I never knew my father," he said quietly.

"Oh." She couldn't imagine growing up and not knowing her father because he had always been a part of her life. Although she was close to both of her parents, everyone knew she'd always been a daddy's girl.

Deciding to change the subject, she said, "I'm glad they were able to contact the father of Stacia Minestrone. I understand he and his wife divorced last year and he moved away. Her neighbor said they were trying to make a comeback and now she's gone. It's sad."

He nodded. "And what's even sadder is that according to one of the police officers involved in the investigation, the accident was caused by a twenty-year-old college student texting her boyfriend."

He paused a moment and then added, "In the end six people died, four are still critical and she was able to walk away with a few scratches. Then again maybe she won't be walking away from everything. I saw the police place her in the patrol car."

Jaclyn had seen it as well, but at the time she hadn't known why. It was sad. No, it was worse than sad. It was a sin and a shame. That text message had ended up probably being the deadliest the young woman had ever sent.

A few minutes later, Lucien pulled into a parking spot in front of a quaint-looking café of red brick with shutters at every window. Day was breaking and the sun was just coming up over the horizon. Although her budget dictated that she live outside the nation's capital, she enjoyed whenever she crossed the bridge over to D.C. And this neighborhood was the one she enjoyed the most. Georgetown, one of the oldest sections of town. She loved the tree-lined streets of old row homes drenched deep in D.C.'s history. She loved the numerous upscale boutiques, restaurants and cafés that lined the narrow cobblestoned streets. What she liked most of all was being surrounded by the beautiful flower gardens, where the cherry blossoms and gladioli were in full bloom.

Moments later they were walking through the door of a café that had only a couple of patrons sitting at the counter sipping coffee and tea. Lucien led her over to a booth in the back, and a waiter, an older man with a beard who greeted Lucien by name, quickly gave them menus.

"Nice place," Jaclyn said, deciding that in addition to a cup of coffee she'd like to try an omelet on the menu called the George Washington. It had all the ingredients she liked. Lucien told her she would not be disappointed.

Within minutes a waitress appeared to take their order. He ordered the George Washington, with coffee as well. After the waitress left, Jaclyn glanced at Lucien and smiled. "I take it you come here a lot."

He chuckled. "Practically every day. I live in the area."

"You live in Georgetown?"

"Yes. My sister lived with an older couple while attending Howard. When the couple decided to retire to Florida they gave Lori the option of buying their home before anyone else. They even financed it for her. When she got a job offer to move to L.A. she talked me into relocating here from Atlanta. At first I thought she was crazy to even suggest a thing. Why would I want to leave Hot-Lanta for docile D.C.? But I came and stayed a week and fell in love with the area. Then I knew I had to live here. And I fell in love with the house. I thought it was just what I needed, real nice although at times I think it's way too big for a bachelor. I ended up convincing her to sell it to me."

She bet his house was nice. Too bad she probably would never get to see it. "I need to apologize to you, Lucien," she said, deciding not to put off saying what she needed to say any longer. Besides, that was the reason he'd brought her here. "I'm usually more together than that. I didn't mean to start crying earlier today."

"It's okay. You were frustrated and needed to let it out. It can happen to the best of us."

"Yes, but—"

"But nothing, Jaclyn," he said softly. "I can understand your frustration. I don't know what the Matthewses are trying to prove by filing that lawsuit. The hospital will suffer unnecessarily when what they should be doing is getting their son the help he needs. Denying that Terrence has a problem isn't helping the situation or him."

"But what if their attorneys demand to know who told you about Terrence?"

"Like I told you, they can't force us to give them the information. And as far as the staff trying to figure out who told, sounds to me they have too much time on their hands. But realistically, there's no way to stop them from talking. Your secret is safe."

She certainly hoped so. They refrained from talking when the waitress returned with their food and set the plates in front of them. She hadn't known the omelet was so huge and told Lucien so.

He lifted an amused brow. "Didn't you know that George was an important man in this town? Anything representing him can only be big."

"Then explain the dollar bill, Lucien."

With a very serious expression he said, "It was a lost bet. I understand that George and good ole Ben Franklin tossed coins to see who would get top dibs and George lost."

Jaclyn couldn't help but laugh. It felt good to laugh and it felt good, for whatever the reason, to be sharing breakfast with the man she had fallen in love with. If anyone saw them it would appear as if they were on a breakfast date. But she knew they were not on a date. They were just colleagues sharing coffee and a meal.

"So, do you get to go home often?" she asked him, trying not to notice how his mouth moved while he chewed his food. There was something downright sexy about it. He waited until after he swallowed his food to respond.

"Not as much as I would like, and my grandmother and sister remind me of that every time we talk. Because of my work at the hospital, I haven't been home in two years. I plan to go to Kingston for the holidays, though."

"I bet that will be nice."

Lucien nodded slowly as he sipped his coffee. "Yes, it will be and it will get my sister off my back for a while."

"The two of you are close?"

"Yes, very. My grandmother raised me and my sister, as well as two of our cousins. We're all close. My sister Lori is a practicing attorney in L.A. My cousin Martie is a surgeon in Seattle and my other cousin Danielle is an accountant in New York."

"All of you are spread out," she noted.

His mouth curved in a smile. "Yes, but we enjoy traveling to visit each other when we can get together. The four of us became naturalized citizens our second year in college, but we still consider Jamaica home."

"I bet it's beautiful."

"It is."

He'd said it in a voice filled with love for the place where he was born. He might be a citizen of the United States now, but she could tell Jamaica was a part of his heart.

The waitress materialized to clear away their plates and to see if they wanted more coffee, and because

Jaclyn was enjoying their conversations and he hadn't shown an inclination to leave just yet, they had refills.

"You worked up an appetite during the past eighteen hours, so if you're still hungry we can order you another George Washington," he said over the rim of his cup as he took another sip of coffee.

"You got to be kidding. If I eat another omelet you'll have to roll me out of here," she said chuckling. "I should not have eaten all of that. Now instead of going home and going straight to bed I'm going to have to find some physical activities to get into."

"And what kind of physical activities do you think you might be interested in, Jaclyn?" he asked silkily.

The words flowed across her skin like a physical caress and her nipples suddenly felt tight and erect. She didn't have to glance down at her chest to know they were probably poking through her blouse, a telltale sign that she'd gotten aroused by his question.

He proved that point when his gaze slowly moved from her face to shift downward. She quickly picked up her coffee cup to hold it in front of her, trying to act natural, but from the look in his eyes, she knew she'd failed. She couldn't help but shiver under the intensity of his gaze.

His eyes then returned to hers. "There is something else I think we need to discuss, Jaclyn," he said in a voice so low and sexy that it seemed to rumble out each and every syllable.

"And what is that?" she asked thinking the coffee was only making her feel hotter. She needed something cold like lemonade or iced tea to cool her off.

He continued to hold her gaze and she felt her pulse rate increase when he said, "The kiss that almost happened in my office yesterday."

Her mouth instantly dried and she struggled to swallow. She'd hoped he had forgotten about that. But there was no reason for her to deny it when she'd known the moment had been real. Had the 911 alert not gone off, they would have shared a kiss and they both knew it. If he could own up to it, then so could she.

"I need to apologize for that, too," she said softly.

"Why?"

His question surprised her. "Because I'm the one who called the meeting and I'm the one who let it get out of hand. The only reason you were comforting me was because I broke down in tears."

Lucien had been listening to her with his cup half-way to his lips. "Yes and no." He set down his cup.

She raised a brow. "Yes and no? What do you mean?"

"It's true you called the meeting, but I'm the one who made the move to hold you in my arms."

"Because I was crying," she said.

His gaze darkened with a heat she felt in every bone in her body. "Because I wanted to hold you," he corrected.

Her nipples acted up again and felt achy as they rubbed against both her bra and blouse. And even worse, when his gaze shifted to her mouth, she felt tingling sensations in her lips. Was he saying what she thought he was saying? Was he admitting that he'd held her not because she was crying but because he'd wanted to?

She must have had a confused look on her face because he then said, "I just wanted to clear that up."

She shook her head. If he honestly thought he'd cleared anything up, he was sadly mistaken. He'd only opened up a can of worms. Maybe this wasn't the time or the place to ask, but he had brought it up. "Lucien,

why would you want to hold me?" she asked in a whispered voice. The café was a lot more crowded now than
when they'd first arrived, filling up with students and
workers who needed a cup of coffee and breakfast to
kick-start their day.

He glanced around and noticed the crowd. When he
looked back at her a smile played around his lips. That
same smile played her insides like a string guitar. And
his dark eyes had latched on to hers, almost making
breathing difficult. "Let's go and finish this discussion
someplace else," he suggested.

She nodded. Would he invite her to his home? He did
say he lived in the area. But no, that wouldn't be right.
Being alone in his office was one thing, but she had no
reason to visit his home. "Someplace like where?" she
heard herself asking.

"I know it's still early, but there's a nice park nearby.
The Georgetown Waterfront Park. I go there a lot when
I need some me time."

Jaclyn thought it was good to know others needed
alone time as well. She was definitely a stickler for it.
Spending so much time in the hospital, tending to the
physical and sometimes emotional needs of the patients
could be somewhat draining and made her appreciate
solitude. There was nothing like getting away for a few
quiet moments.

"So will you go there with me, Jaclyn? If you prefer not
to, I'd understand. You pulled a double shift yesterday."

Yes, she had and so had he. There was something about
being here with him that had her adrenaline flowing, and
she wasn't ready to put a cap on it. She smiled at him and
said, "Yes, I'd love to go to the park with you."

Chapter 5

Lucien knew he had no business spending time with Jaclyn Campbell, let along asking her to spend time at the park with him. What in the world was he thinking?

He drew in a deep breath as he put the key in his car's ignition, knowing just what he'd been thinking. How good she'd looked sitting across from him, with her creamy smooth skin, gorgeous hazel eyes and chin-length straight brown hair. And how good she'd looked when he'd seen her about to leave the hospital in a pair of khakis and a pretty pink blouse. But most of all he'd thought about making nights of endless love to that lush body of hers.

He came to a stop at an intersection in the H Street Corridor and glanced over at her. He couldn't help remembering the moment she had become aroused by something he'd said. Her body had responded right be-

fore his eyes. He had just finished asking her what kind
of physical activities she might be interested in. He wondered if her mind had followed the path his had taken.
The thought of that possibility gave him some wicked
pleasure he shouldn't be experiencing.

What was it going to take to make him think ratio-
nally where she was concerned? He should be thinking
with the head connected to his neck and not the other
head that throbbed each and every time he glanced over
at her.

"It's going to be a beautiful day."

He glanced over at her, finding it hard not to say
that the beauty of his day had begun with her. The moment he'd seen her about to leave the hospital he was
pushed into motion to do something. The E.R. situation
had kept him busy, focused and concentrated on saving
lives. But when he'd taken a moment to breathe when
all the injured patients had been cared for, his gaze had
immediately sought her out. She had been busy sutur-
ing a cut on a man's forehead, concentrating intently
on her patient. He hadn't been surprised. When it came
to taking care of those who came to Hopewell General,
she was always on top of her game.

"Yes, it is." He smiled. "A great day to have a boat
race."

She lifted a brow. "A boat race?"

His smile widened. "Yes, but relax. I'm talking about
remote-operated toy boats. A friend of mine and I like
putting them in the pond at the park to see who is king
of the waterways."

"And you have these boats with you?"

He chuckled. "Just so happens that I do. Both his
and mine are in the trunk. I'm sure he'll feel that any

woman who knows anything about what's under the hood of a car is entitled to use his boat. So what do you say, Jaclyn?"

Jaclyn couldn't help but return Lucien's smile. He'd conveniently forgotten that they were supposed to be discussing the kiss they'd almost shared in his office yesterday. Evidently he wasn't ready to go there again just yet, so she would indulge him for the moment.

"Should I warn you that in addition to being an auto mechanic, my father loves boats as well? I did mention he bought one a few years ago and taught me how to operate it."

He parked the car in the park and glanced over at her as if he was sizing up the competition. "Should I remind you we're talking about toy boats?" he asked, clearly amused.

"And just for the record," he added. "Maybe I should also remind you that I came from a place literally surrounded by water. Knowing how to swim and how to operate a boat were a must-do. In fact I worked on a boat dock from the time I was fourteen. I saved my money to apply for college in America."

"Impressive. So this friend of yours whose boat I'll be using, are you sure he won't mind?"

"If he thought for one minute you'd use it to beat me, then I can tell you he won't. And you happen to know him."

She lifted a brow. "I do?"

"Yes. Dr. Thomas Bradshaw."

She nodded. There wasn't a person at Hopewell who didn't know Dr. Bradshaw. A pure workaholic if ever there was one, he was the youngest person ever to be

named head of surgery at Hopewell. That made him the
envy of a number of other surgeons. And she'd heard
he was as arrogant as he was handsome. On the other
hand, in comparison, she thought Lucien didn't have an
arrogant bone in his body. They were like day and night.

"Dr. Bradshaw is a close friend of yours?" she asked
surprised.

He chuckled. "Yes. Why do you find that hard to
believe?"

Jaclyn would rather not say. She could see him and
Dr. Bradshaw being colleagues. But close friends?
Friends who would share time racing toy boats? "No
reason. Okay, Lucien, bring on the race."

There was something about Georgetown Waterfront
Park that reminded Lucien of parts of Kingston. Maybe
it was the way the waterways stretched from one har-
bor to the other, or the flowering trees that lined the
boardwalk.

"Will we be racing our boats in the river?" Jaclyn
asked, pulling his thoughts back to her, not that they'd
fully ever left. The wind was blowing and her hair was
like silk fanning around her face.

"No, there's a small pond on the other side that will
be perfect," he said, taking the boats out of the trunk of
his car. She was standing beside him looking on and he
thought she smelled good, definitely not like someone
who'd pulled a double shift.

"This one is yours," he said, handing her a twenty-
eight-inch toy replica of a speed boat.

She took it and their hands touched. He had the same
reaction that he had the other day when he'd handed
her back the charts. Their gazes met and he felt a heat

flow through him. He was aware of the intense ache in the lower part of his body and decided to pause a moment. Inhale and exhale. He did so while desire coursed through his veins in a way it had never done before.

"Let me see the boat you'll be using, Lucien."

The sound of her voice invaded some outcropped part of his brain, made him realize he needed to get a grip. He hadn't explained why he had wanted to kiss her yesterday and already he was fighting the urge to kiss her again. He knew she was probably aware of it and was trying to bring him back around. Let reality invade.

Taking another deep breath he pulled his own boat out of the trunk. "So what do you think?" he asked, showing it to her.

She smiled up at him. "It's cute, but I like mine better."

"Cute? Hey, you won't be saying that in a little while," he said, closing down the trunk and trying to force back the desire he felt just from her smile.

She shrugged. "We'll see." And without saying anything else she fell into step beside him.

At that moment her presence next to him felt right.

She liked walking beside him, Jaclyn thought as they made their way to the pond. She didn't want to think of the way he had looked at her a few minutes ago. It was the same way he had looked at her yesterday after she'd dropped those charts on the floor and he'd helped her gather them up. The same way he'd looked at her just before he'd almost kissed her. The same way he'd looked at her at the café.

He led her over toward a grassy bank. It was a small pond surrounded by flowering plants off the side of a boardwalk. "I hope the ducks and geese don't mind sharing today," she said when she saw how many were in the pond.

"Once we put the boats in the water and start them up, the birds will start scattering."

Jaclyn glanced over at him. "You sure?"

"It happens each and every time."

Moments later after they set their boats in the water, the first sound of the humming from the boats sent the geese and ducks flying. "Do you ever feel as if you're invading their turf?" she asked him.

He chuckled. "Not at all. They have the entire sky, so they should not mind if we use their water." He then said, "The rules of the game are simple. The first boat to the other side wins."

A smile curving her lips was her only response.

He hunched down and set the boats next to each other and she knelt down beside him with her remote in her hand. "On your mark…get set…go."

The boats took off and at some point they were even as they crossed the pond. But then suddenly hers took the lead. He glanced over at her, saw the smirk of victory on her face. "I wouldn't get cocky so soon." And then suddenly, his boat took the lead. They stood there, cheering their boats on. In the end his boat made it to the other side first.

He glanced over at her smiling. "Well, what do you think?"

"My mom was right."

"About what?"

"Men are boys who like playing with more expensive toys."

He threw his head back and laughed. "You're going to be a sore loser?"

"No, but you do know I want another race."

"I think I can accommodate you."

It took a few minutes to get the boats back to their side of the pond to start the race up again. She won the next one and he took the lead, winning the next two. "We've raced our boats enough for today. Let's sit down and talk," he said, gesturing to a bench that faced the pond.

"All right."

There weren't a lot of people about and the geese and ducks, Jaclyn noticed, flew back the moment they'd taken the boats out of the pond. It was a beautiful day in August and numerous boats could be seen out on the Potomac.

He sat beside her and they didn't say anything for a few moments. She knew they were both enmeshed deep in their own thoughts. Moments later, his soft chuckle drew her attention.

"What's so amusing?"

"You. Me. The boat race," he said, stretching out his legs. "When we left the hospital this morning after pulling a double, you should have gone to your place and I should have gone to mine."

Jaclyn nodded slowly. "Why didn't we?"

A grim smile curved the corners of his mouth. "That would have been way too easy. Besides, we needed to talk."

And it was a conversation they still hadn't had, at least not fully. "Okay, Lucien, let's talk."

Silence lingered between them for a moment .Then he said, "The reason I almost kissed you in my office yesterday was because I wanted to kiss you. It had nothing to do with your tears, although they provided the perfect opportunity, an advantage I didn't waste any time taking."

Jaclyn made no reply. All she could do at the moment was to listen while her body responded to the husky sound of his voice.

"And the reason I wanted to kiss you," he continued to say, "is that in case you hadn't noticed, I'm attracted to you."

He hesitated, as if he expected her to make a comment and when she didn't, he said, "And being attracted to you isn't a good thing considering the hospital's policy and your position and mine."

She looked down for a few moments and then looked back at him. She saw the intensity in his eyes and thought it was time she said something. It was time for her to let him know the attraction was not one-sided. "I'm attracted to you as well, Lucien."

She decided it was best not to let him know her feelings had moved from mere attraction to love. There were still a lot of things she didn't know about him, but it didn't matter. At least not to her heart.

She loved him.

She swallowed hard when she saw the impact her confession had on him. It was there in his features, in the way the muscles tightened in his jaw, the way the pupils of his eyes darkened even more. "Had I met you at a medical convention, research seminar or just passing by on the street, I would welcome the attraction. But considering the hospital's policy… Well, it is what it is."

"Yes, it is what it is," he agreed slowly in a husky tone.

She hesitated a moment and then said, "I know you

aren't married. At least the word among the interns is that you're not. But are you involved with anyone?"

A smile curved his lips. "No. I haven't been seriously involved with anyone for close to a year. In fact I haven't dated anyone since October of last year."

She wondered if he'd intentionally told her that period of time because it was when she'd begun working at the hospital. Was it his way of letting her know he hadn't dated a woman since they'd met?

"What about you, Jaclyn? Is there some serious guy in your life?"

She tried not to frown when she thought about Danny, the guy she had dated seriously while in her first year of med school. She could clearly remember when he had graduated from law school and had accompanied a group of friends to England for a summer vacation well-earned. Jaclyn couldn't forget how he had returned to the States and dropped by to see her just long enough to break things off with her. He had explained he had met someone in London and it had been love at first sight.

At the time she had been too hurt to consider that such a thing was possible, but now after meeting Lucien, she knew better and could appreciate Danny for not stringing her along. Instead, he had followed his heart. According to her brother who still heard from Danny from time to time, he went back to London, married the woman he loved and the two were now living in Rhode Island where Danny was working at a law firm and was the father of a little girl.

She glanced over at Lucien and saw he was waiting for her response. "No, I'm not seeing anyone seriously. At least not now. My boyfriend and I broke up a little over a year ago and I've been too busy to become involved in another serious relationship."

What she didn't add was that even if she hadn't been busy she probably would have not become involved again. She had put a lot of time into her relationship with Danny and in the end he'd still walked…right into the arms of another woman.

"What about Marcus Shaw? He seems to like you."

Was that a tinge of jealousy she heard in his voice? She shook her head, finding the notion ridiculous, especially when she thought of the playboy intern. "Marcus likes to flirt with all the ladies. If you notice I never flirt back."

He nodded. "No, you don't." Then he stood, held out his hand to her and said, "Come take a walk with me."

"What about our boats?" she asked.

"We can leave them here for a minute."

The moment she placed her hand in his, she felt it. A tingling sensation all the way to her toes. Suddenly his hand tightened on hers in what seemed to be a possessive grip as she stood on her feet while forcing the cozy awareness from her mind. Standing up brought them so close that there was barely any breathing space between them. Up close she could only marvel at the breadth of his wide shoulders and powerful chest, and a face that could make a woman drool.

"Ready?" He leaned over and whispered close to her ear.

She swallowed and wondered what she was supposed to be ready for. "Yes."

His hand continued to hold hers as they began walking along a grassy path that led away from the pond toward an area shrouded by huge cherry blossoms and magnolia trees. The area would be perfect for a picnic with the lush lawns and the Potomac River as a backdrop.

He stopped at a huge maple tree and he perched his back against the bark. She followed his line of vision and saw he had a good view of where they'd left the boats. And then his gaze moved over her features. "Do you know what I thought when I first saw you?" he asked her.

She smiled. "Probably the same thing you thought of all the other interns. That we had a lot to learn before we could call ourselves doctors."

He chuckled. "Yes, that too, but I'm talking about when I first saw you specifically. You might not have noticed, but my gaze stayed on you a minute too long."

She had noticed but assumed she had imagined it because her gaze had remained on him even longer than that. "No, I didn't know what you were thinking," she whispered when she realized just how close they were standing.

"I thought you were more than just pretty. I thought you were strikingly beautiful, which is something I should not have been thinking. I also thought, less than a few minutes later, that with you I was going to have to keep my distance. I had immediately felt an attraction to you and I knew that was not going to work."

"Is that why you transferred me to nights for a while?" she decided to ask him.

"Yes," he responded honestly. "That, and I thought the E.R. could use a person like you. You have a way with patients. You have a lot of patience."

With some things, she thought, knowing her patience was being stretched at this very moment. They were talking, true enough. And he had admitted to being attracted to her. But he hadn't explained what had made

the attraction so great he'd been willing to risk breaking a hospital policy by kissing her.

"I can't explain it, Jaclyn," he said softly, as if he'd
read her mind. "Nor do I fully understand it. All I know
is that at that moment, I had to taste you." Then in an
even lower voice he added, "I had to know the sweetness
of your mouth, and how your tongue would feel wrapped
around mine, with me sucking on it, devouring it."

Whatever she'd assumed he would eventually get
around to saying, that wasn't it. His words made her
heart start racing in her chest at the same time that
her breath caught in her throat. Luscious and succulent
images filled her mind while sensations crammed her
body in a heated rush. She could feel her eyes darken
as she watched his do likewise. And then of its own accord, her body leaned into him and his head lowered
and swooped down on her mouth to finish what they'd
started before the interruption yesterday.

It had to be the most focused kiss she'd ever experienced. It seemed he was putting everything into it. His
every thought, all five senses and a flood of emotions.
And when she felt his arms wrap around her, she automatically sank into him. At that moment she couldn't
think and was relying on him to do all the thinking for
both of them. All she could do was give herself over to
a kiss she was feeling all the way to her toes.

Lucien felt his mind and body unleash turbulent emotions that he'd held back for the past eighteen months.
Now he was giving in to a hunger he hadn't known possible. There was this ravenousness that was invading
his body and obliterating any kind of control. And he
was giving in to it. Letting it dominate.

Her tongue tasted just as he'd known it would with a sweetness that was turning his bones to jelly. There was a faint taste of the spiced coffee she'd drunk earlier, but mostly it was all woman and it was so captivating that he couldn't imagine how it would be not to kiss her.

He pushed that thought out of his mind as he continued to devour her mouth, lips, tongue. There wasn't a part of her mouth he hadn't invaded and sampled. And she was kissing him back with a hunger just as greedy as his own.

The sound of people approaching had them breaking off the kiss, but Lucien was intent on feasting on her mouth anyway and began licking the corners of her lips, tracing the outline with the tip of his tongue, leaving a wet trail from corner to corner. And when she moaned the word "Oh" and her mouth formed into the shape of a bow, he licked around that as well.

When the voices came closer his hold around her waist loosened and he shifted slightly while taking a step back. Their gazes held while a couple with a child walked past. Lucien had a gut feeling when reality returned they would realize just what line they had crossed. They were treading on forbidden ground, but he needed her to know he wasn't remorseful in any way.

"I don't regret kissing you, Jaclyn," he said. "This was personal and our relationship at the hospital is business. I can separate the two." But he knew the officials at the hospital wouldn't agree, which was why they had the nonfraternization policy in place.

"And just so we're absolutely clear about something. I'm not a boss who makes it a point to hit on one intern out of every group I get. Nothing like this has ever happened to me before. You are the one and only woman

I've been this attracted to." He hoped she knew that he was being completely honestly with her because he was.

"And nothing like this has ever happened to me before. I didn't intentionally set out to draw your attention either," she said.

He believed her. Like he'd said earlier, there were some things that were hard to deny and for him it was an attraction of this magnitude. He leaned in and kissed her again. He couldn't help it. It seemed her lips had parted just for him.

This kiss was gentler than the first but just as ravenous on both their parts. He didn't just want to kiss her, he wanted to lay claim to every inch of her mouth and he was doing so inch by inch and second by second.

The sweetness of her mouth was holding him captive and he surrendered easily with a hunger he couldn't deny. But when a plane flew overhead the noise nearly causing the ground beneath them to vibrate, he accepted that as his cue to release her mouth.

"You can become habit-forming," he whispered against her moist lips.

"If only things could be that easy," was her quick response and he knew exactly what she'd meant. They'd crossed over to forbidden grounds and weren't sure how to go back. Things wouldn't be easy between them from now on, no matter what route they chose to take.

He saw the desire in her eyes and he saw something else, too. Weariness. She had to be tired. "Come on," he said, taking a step back and reclaiming her hand. "I'm taking you home." Her hand felt so right enclosed in his.

She glanced up at him when they began walking back toward the area where they'd left their boats. "You mean you're taking me back to the hospital for my car, don't you?"

"No, I'm taking you home. You're exhausted." When she parted her lips to protest, he quickly said, "Don't argue about it, Jaclyn. If you need me to take you to get your car tomorrow I can do that."

"That won't be necessary. My roommate can take me to get it later today."

They gathered the boats with the remotes and walked back to the car. She had gotten silent on him and was probably wondering where their kiss would lead. He had no answer to that question. They didn't even have the luxury of taking things one day at a time. Whatever was going on between them needed to end now. But he couldn't make himself do that.

When they were in the car with seat belts in place, he decided to engage in conversation about anything and everything but the kiss they'd shared. They talked about recent movies they'd seen, mostly on DVD, because their time was limited when it came to going to the theaters. He wasn't surprised that they enjoyed the same movies and actors. It should have been a simple matter to ask her out on a movie date, but he knew doing something like that was only asking for trouble.

He didn't know about her, but he considered their day in the park as a date and the thought that it would be the only one they could have made sadness well up inside of him. The one thing he wanted—a relationship with her—was the one thing he could not have.

Once he crossed the Francis Scott Key Bridge, it didn't take them long to reach where she lived. She had given him good directions. He brought his car to a stop in front of a nicely landscaped town house. "Nice place."

"Thanks. It's owned by friends of my parents who spend most of their time out of the country since retiring. They offered me the use of it. I have a roommate to defray the cost because it's in a nice part of town."

He nodded. "Dr. Morales is your roommate, right?"

"Yes, that's right."

He figured the reason she wouldn't be inviting him in was because Dr. Morales would have come home from the hospital by now. Chances were she was sleeping off the long hours spent at the hospital because she'd stayed on duty most of the night. That was a risk neither of them needed to take.

"Thanks for such a fun day, Lucien. I had a wonderful time…even if you did best me three out of four on the boat race."

He smiled. "There's always another time, Jaclyn."

He wasn't sure why he was putting ideas into her head that they could spend another day together when they both knew they couldn't. They had too much to lose. He had the position he wanted at the hospital and she had her entire future as a doctor to protect.

Instead of responding to what he'd said, she proceeded to unbuckle her seat belt. When he began unbuckling his, she glanced over at him and asked, "What are you doing?"

"Walking you to the door."

She nervously gnawed on her bottom lip. "You don't have to do that."

"Yes, I do." He had to do it for more reasons than one. Most importantly because this was probably the last date, official or otherwise, they would ever share. And although he figured they both had to be exhausted, he wasn't ready for their day together to end.

He waited to see if she would present some sort of argument and gave a sigh of relief when she didn't. Together they disembarked the car and began walking toward her front door.

Upon reaching their destination, she pulled the key from her purse and glanced up at him. "I would invite you in, but my—"

"Yes, I know. More than likely Dr. Morales is home," he finished for her.

Her mouth curved in a slight smile. "Yes."

He slanted her a smile. "I'll see you back at the hospital but no sooner than Friday. If I recall, you have the next two days off."

"Only if they don't need me."

"They won't. You deserve to get some rest. Got that?"

She chuckled. "Yes, I got that. And you don't have to worry about me showing up before then," she said. "After I take a shower I'll probably fall face down in my bed and sleep for the next forty-eight hours."

A sudden vision jerked his brain to life—that of her stepping out of the shower, naked, with water glistening all over her body. The thought had goose bumps prickling his skin while blood rushed fast and furious through his veins.

"I'll be seeing you, then," she said, and made a move to open the door.

"Yes, I'll be seeing you."

He turned to leave and had even taken a few steps. But something made him turn back toward her. All it took was a look in her eyes and he was a goner. Without any thought he retraced his steps to her and pulled her into his arms. She parted her lips invitingly.

The moment his tongue touched hers, like before,

passion ripped through him and he deepened the kiss as hunger took control. For all he knew her roommate could have been standing at the window staring at them, but for the moment he didn't care. The only thing he cared about was kissing her, tasting her, claiming her mouth this way once again.

Never had he found kissing a woman so deep-in-the-gut pleasurable. Never had he been so caught up in a kiss. Her lips were soft and pliable; her tongue was just as aggressive and greedy as his. He detected a need within her that was just as great as his own. So he deepened the kiss, continued a thorough sweep around the insides of her mouth like he had all the time in the world. He was taking it whether he had it or not.

She was the one who pulled away from the kiss to gasp for air. And as he watched her battle short breaths, a tiny voice inside his head scolded that he should not have kissed her again. But he knew there was no way he could have left without doing so.

He slowly ran his tongue around the upper part of his lips, enjoying the taste of her still lingering there. He reached out and gently rubbed the pad of his thumb across her chin wondering what he could say to free himself from a moment that would forever be trapped in his mind. And he knew there was nothing he would say. "I'll be seeing you."

She nodded. "All right."

Forcing distance between them he turned and jogged back to his car. One thought rang in his mind: What had he gotten himself into?

Chapter 6

Jaclyn took a shower and fell into bed. The moment her head touched the pillow she should have been fast asleep. But that was not the case. Her lips were still tingling and her body was still keyed up from the kiss she had shared with Lucien.

They hadn't kissed just once but twice, not counting the nibbles in between as well as the encore at her door. She could definitely say her mouth had gotten quite a workout. She had never been kissed so soundly by a man in her life. He hadn't just kissed her, he had literally consumed her.

The one thing she had been grateful for was that Isabelle had slept through it all. That meant her friend and roommate knew nothing about the sensuous exchange on their doorstep. She was also relieved that as far as she knew, no other employee of the hospital lived in their neighborhood.

She had two days off and hopefully by the time she returned to work she would be on solid ground, ready to put the time she'd spent with Lucien behind her.

Fat chance!

She changed positions on the bed wondering if counting sheep would help and quickly figured that it wouldn't. So she flipped on her back and stared at the ceiling to think. How was she supposed to act when she saw him again? How could she manage to look at him, gaze at his mouth and not remember how that same mouth had wiped all her senses clean with a smooth stroke of his tongue?

And they had been the smoothest strokes, with such thorough possession that she got butterflies in her stomach at the mere memory. Just like the interns referred to Ms. Tsang as "Miss Thang" behind her back, a few of the interns had taken to calling Dr. De Winter "De Man" behind his back. Well, he had shown her today that he was definitely *the* man.

She was about to close her eyes when her cell phone went off and she quickly recognized the ring tone. It was one or both of her parents. She quickly picked it up. The last time one of them called was to tell her that her grandmother had taken a fall. "Hello?"

"Hi, precious. How's my favorite girl?"

Jaclyn smiled. She and her father always had a close relationship. She wasn't ashamed to admit she was a daddy's girl. "I'm fine, Dad. How're you, Mom and Gramma doing?"

Jaclyn's grandfather had died the year she had started medical school. Childhood sweethearts, her grandparents had been married over sixty years. After he died, everyone had wondered how her grandmother would handle the loneliness. But Gloria Campbell had surprised everyone by joining a senior citizens' club where the over-seventy group did a number of activities each day.

"Everyone is fine. We heard about that multicar pileup on CNN. A reporter said all the injured people were taken to the hospital where you work."

"Yes, that's right. I had to pull a double."

She and her father talked a little while longer before he passed the phone to her mother. Hearing the exhaustion in her voice, her mother gave her instructions to get rest, told her that her grandmother was at the senior citizens' center playing bingo and then ended the call.

They were great parents, Jaclyn thought as she hung up the phone. She couldn't imagine growing up without them, and her brother.

Kevin had always been a clean-cut kid until he went away to college. It was there when he began experimenting with drugs and eventually got addicted. He had returned home in his junior year of college with a drug habit. A year later her parents had to Baker Act him when his illegal drug use had gotten out of control. It had taken some time, but with the family's support he had pulled himself together, gone back to finish college and met and married a wonderful woman. Trish was just the person her brother had needed in his life.

She wouldn't be surprised if Kevin called her as well to check up on her. Although she would love hearing from him she needed to sleep and hoped her parents passed the word that she was fine and just needed to rest.

Kevin would be the first to tell anyone that upon

admitting he'd had a drug problem the best thing he'd gotten was support from his family.

That was why she found the Matthewses' lawsuit so confusing. Terrence had a drug problem and the worst thing his parents could do was stick their heads in the sand and pretend that he didn't. He needed help, and with the right type of counseling there was no doubt in her mind that Terrence would one day become the gifted physician she believed he could be. But the route his parents were taking was one of denial. They were going after the hospital for revenge. It didn't make any sense.

Jaclyn shifted positions in bed and her thoughts moved from Terrence back to Lucien. She didn't want to face the fact that today she had gotten her first and last kisses from him. As she closed her eyes and drifted off to sleep she still had the taste of Lucien on her tongue. And she liked it. She liked it too much.

Lucien left his bedroom in his bare feet and walked to the kitchen to grab a beer out of the refrigerator. He popped the bottle cap and took a huge pleasurable gulp. What a day, he thought. What a woman. What a kiss.

Before coming home he had gone back to the hospital to check on the patients who had been brought in through E.R. yesterday. He hadn't run into Dr. Dudley, but he had seen Nurse Tsang, who had locked her gaze on him like she'd known he was hiding something. He couldn't help but smile. If only she knew… And he was so damn grateful that she didn't. It was bad enough that he did.

He rubbed his hand down his face thinking of the predicament he was in. But instead of trying to come up with a way out of it, his mind was conjuring a plan to get further into forbidden territory. It made no sense. First and foremost he was Jaclyn's boss, which meant he had no right dating her even if the hospital didn't have a policy against it.

He dropped down in a chair at the kitchen table remembering the last time he'd gotten involved in a workplace relationship and how badly it had ended. What he'd told Jaclyn was true. He wasn't involved with anyone and hadn't been seriously in quite a while. He'd also been honest when he'd said he'd never been involved with an intern under his supervision.

But what he hadn't told her was that years ago when he had been a intern himself he'd dated another med student by the name of Nikki Stinson. Both he and Nikki were very competitive and when he earned a better intern placement than she did, the affair ended badly. That was when he'd decided never to mix business with pleasure again. So why was he so into Jaclyn? Not only was he breaking the hospital rule, but he was also breaking his own rule.

Granted, Jaclyn was nothing like Nikki. Nikki had grown up in the Bronx and was tough as nails. There were times he thought there wasn't a compassionate bone in her body, which made him question her choice of profession. More than once Nikki's bedside demeanor with patients had been so atrocious that she had gotten written up by their superiors. Jaclyn, on the other hand, had a gentle, calm nature, a kindness that gave him the impression she was emotionally fragile. Not weak but vulnerable. She had a way of bringing out the very essence of his protective instincts.

A short while later, even though it was still daylight outside, Lucien was in his bed lying flat on his back and staring up at the ceiling. He had truly enjoyed spending the day with Jaclyn. When he'd mentioned the boat race, she hadn't given him a funny look or made a wisecrack about a grown man who would like doing such a thing. Instead, she had smiled and joined in an activity that he enjoyed, one that always relaxed him.

Being around her had relaxed him as well. She was the type of woman a man could open up to, the kind of woman a man could get attached to if he wasn't careful. He drew in a deep breath. Who was he kidding? He was already a goner. If he was smart he would put Jaclyn and the kisses they'd shared not only to the back of his mind but out of his mind completely. But for some reason he couldn't do that.

When he'd kissed her he had been caught off guard by how delicious she tasted. Intense heat had circulated in his stomach and moved lower to his groin. It had filled him with desire so thick and potent that he'd succumbed to the very power of it by deepening the kiss. He hadn't experienced anything so erotic in his entire life.

Lucien knew he had felt every luscious curve of her body when he had held her close to him. It had been a beautiful day and he had been lucky enough to hold a beautiful woman in his arms. But he had done more than just hold her. He had kissed her with a possession that he'd felt all through his body. And the strange thing about it was that he still felt it.

And when she had shivered in his arms, he had felt each and every vibration in a way that made his gut rumble with need that has been so urgent and vital that his pulse rate had raced out of control. His mind had suddenly filled with possibilities of just how far that kiss could take him, and he'd known it would be beyond anything in his wildest dreams. In other words, each kiss had shaken him to the very core of his being.

Even now his pulse was accelerating just remembering their day together. A day he hadn't wanted to end. He was surprised he had won the race those four times because he hadn't been able to take his eyes off her. The sun had been shining bright in the sky and the rays had hit her at an angle that had made her look gorgeous from the top of her head to the soles of her feet.

He couldn't help wondering what she would be doing with her free time over the next two days. He hadn't mentioned it to her but he had the next two days off work as well. Imagine that. He drew in a deep breath, not wanting to imagine it. If they had been free to date he would call her in a heartbeat and suggest they spend their days off together.

But they weren't free to date and that was the crux of his problem. He knew the limitations, the boundaries and the risks, yet today he had outright ignored all three and today he had done just what he'd wanted to do where Jaclyn was concerned. And a part of him knew tomorrow wasn't going to be any better. Already he was contemplating calling her and asking that they spend their two days off together. Now if that wasn't asking for trouble, what was?

Doing something like that would be the most irrational thing he'd ever done. However, at the moment he wasn't strong enough to resist her. He wanted to see her again, spend time with her and taste her once more.

Before he could talk himself out of doing it, he reached for his cell phone on the nightstand. He had every intern's number in his phone and the moment he punched in her name he could hear the ringing sound.

What if he was waking her up from a sound sleep? She had mentioned she planned on going straight to bed after taking a shower. Just because he was too wired to sleep didn't mean she was, too. On the third ring he'd made up his mind to hang up when she answered the call.

"Hello?"

His heart slammed in his chest at the sexy, husky and sluggish sound of her voice. He had awakened her, but damn, she sounded so good. That same pulse that had been giving him fits all day began to thud almost mercilessly in his chest. He was so caught up in how she sounded that it was only when she said hello a second time that he realized he needed to say something. His reaction to her wasn't normal, but for him normalcy had gotten tossed to the wind the moment he'd laid his eyes on Jaclyn that day at Hopewell.

He closed his eyes and then reopened them, knowing what he was about to ask would change the course of their relationship forever. "This is Lucien. Sorry if I woke you, but I need to ask you something."

"What?"

He decided to jump right in. The worst she could do was tell him no. "I'm off work the next two days as well. I plan to get away and go sailing on the Chesapeake and wanted to know if you'll go with me."

And just so she understood the depth of what he was asking, he quickly added, "And I'd like to make it an overnight trip, so we won't be returning until sometime Thursday."

Jaclyn jolted wide awake. Had she dreamed what Lucien had just said? What he'd suggested? "Sorry, could you repeat that? I think I misunderstood you."

His soft chuckle sent heat flowing through her body and her lips suddenly felt dry, so she licked them. "I'm asking you to spend two days with me. I'd like for us to take a drive over to Annapolis, then spend the day sailing on the Chesapeake. I know the perfect place where we can stay for the night."

She swallowed thickly. After two kisses did he just assume she would sleep with him? She sat up at the edge of the bed. Don't jump to any conclusions, she told herself. All he'd said was that he wanted her to spend the day with him tomorrow. He hadn't come right out and said they would be sharing a bed. He would expect them to get separate rooms, wouldn't he?

"Jaclyn?"

"Yes?"

"We can get separate rooms, if you'd like."

She wondered if he had read her thoughts. She hadn't missed the way he'd made the suggestion. He would leave it up to her to decide whether there would be one room or two.

"Will you spend your off days with me?" he asked when moments slipped by and she hadn't said anything.

She began nibbling on her bottom lip. He sounded as if he was in his right mind, which meant he was well aware of the risks if they were seen together, regardless of the sleeping arrangements. "Lucien…"

"I know what you're thinking and yes, I know the risks. I knew them today as well. But that didn't keep me from wanting you, wanting to hold you in my arms and kiss you. And knowing the risks isn't keeping me from wanting to spend the next two days with you. I know it's crazy, but I want to be with you."

Jaclyn inhaled slowly. If it was crazy, then he wasn't

the only one affected by this madness because she wanted to spend time with him as well. For the past eighteen months they had shared an intense attraction but had resorted to pretending the other hadn't existed. At least they had tried to pretend. But for the next two days he was giving her a chance not to pretend and by golly she would take it. "What time will you pick me up?"

He didn't say anything for a second, as if surprised by her decision. Then he asked, "Will ten o'clock be okay?"

"Make it eleven. Isabelle would have left for work by then."

"All right. I'll see you tomorrow around eleven. Goodbye, Jaclyn."

"Goodbye."

She held the phone in her hand long after the call had disconnected. She sat there a moment and recalled everything that had transpired between her and Lucien beginning yesterday in his office. Then she thought about their morning at breakfast and the day they'd spent at the park. When she'd closed her eyes to get some rest earlier, she had convinced herself the relationship building between her and Lucien was more her imagination than anything else. But now that phone call from him proved otherwise. He wanted to be with her just like she wanted to be with him.

She stood and strolled in bare feet over to the window. It was close to seven yet it hadn't gotten dark yet. Should she have turned down his invitation? She knew deep down there was no way she could have done that. Wanting to be with Lucien and his wanting to be with her was a fantasy she refused to deny, no matter the risks. And as ludicrous as it sounded, she intended to enjoy the fantasy as long as it lasted.

But she had to be careful that Isabelle didn't find out. She didn't want to place her roommate and best friend in a comprising position by covering up for her. So the less Isabelle knew, the better off she was.

Just like Jaclyn had felt it was her duty to report Terrence's drug use to her superiors because he was breaking a hospital policy, she didn't want to place Isabelle in a position of having to do the same. The nonfraternization policy was in place whether she liked it or not. And for her and Lucien to see each other in spite of it meant they were clearly breaking hospital rules and regulations.

She told herself they would have these two days and no more. But as she walked back to the bed and slid under the covers she had a feeling those two days were just the beginning.

Chapter 7

"Okay, Jac-O, what's the reason for that silly grin on your face?"

Jaclyn resisted the temptation to burst out laughing. She had been trying so hard not to let her excitement show but couldn't help it. The last thing she needed was for Isabelle to start asking questions…like she was doing now. Her best friend was known to weasel anything out of her she wanted to know. "I have no idea what you're talking about."

Isabelle lifted a dubious brow. "Yeah, right. And I guess there's no reason why you're up at the crack of dawn when you don't have to go in to work today, or there's no reason why I heard you humming in the shower earlier."

Isabelle then crossed her arms over her chest and looked at her pointedly when she added, "And no reason why your car is missing. I noticed it was still at the hospital when you left yesterday which was before me. However, when I got off work at noon your car was still there. How's that?"

Jaclyn swallowed under the intensity of Isabelle's gaze. In as calm a voice as she could muster, she said, "I was tired and got a ride home."

Isabelle nodded slowly, still keeping her gaze on her. "And where did you go? You weren't here when I got home."

Jaclyn took a sip of her coffee. "Why the questions?"

"Why the secrecy? Are you seeing someone behind my back?" Isabelle asked in a voice laced with humor.

Jaclyn wasn't sure what gave her away. It could have been that she didn't answer quick enough to suit Isabelle or that she had a blush of guilt on her face. Regardless, Isabelle's mouth dropped open and she pointed a finger at her. "You are seeing someone," she exclaimed.

Jaclyn knew she was in hot water. When Isabelle wanted to know something she was like a dog with a bone. She wouldn't let up until she got her fill.

"Don't you think you're getting carried away, Belle?"

"Um, you tell me, Jaclyn. I've never known you to be so secretive about a man. To be quite honest, I've never known you to get serious about a man period."

What Isabelle said was true. "We're taking things one day at a time and until we test the waters to make sure it's going to work for us, I prefer keeping things private."

Isabelle sipped her coffee and then said, "So in other words you're not going to tell me a thing about him."

"No, for now it's best." Like Jaclyn had decided last night, the less her best friend knew the better. "You're just going to have to trust me on this one, Belle. And before you ask, no, he isn't married."

Isabelle shrugged. "Hey, I couldn't stop that possibility from running through my head. But for once I'll mind my own business until you decide to let me in on what's going on."

"Thanks."

"And if you ever need me for anything, let me know. From what you told me you haven't dated much since that guy you broke off with a few years back. Things have changed. Men have changed. They are more of a dog than ever."

"All of them aren't that way, Belle."

"True, but finding a good one these days is like looking for a needle in a haystack. So I hope you know what you're doing."

She hoped she knew what she was doing as well. But all it took was the memory of their time together yesterday to convince her that although she might be doing the wrong thing, it was for the right reason…if that made any sense.

Jaclyn glanced over at Isabelle who was studying her over the rim of her coffee cup. It took all her willpower not to squirm under her best friend's scrutiny. "There is something I might need your help with, Belle."

Isabelle placed her cup down. "What is it?"

"I'm going out on a date and would like your opinion on an outfit to wear." Jaclyn watched the smile spread over Isabelle's face. She of all people knew that next to practicing medicine Isabelle's other love was clothes. She could hook an outfit together like nobody's business. Even though Jaclyn wasn't a total flop when it came to working an outfit, she knew for this date she needed help. First of all, she'd never been on a boating date.

"Sure I'll help. Where are you going?"

"Sailing on the Chesapeake and possibly dinner later. And…"

Isabelle lifted a brow at her hesitation. "And what?"

"And I might need an overnight outfit. You know, a nice piece of lingerie."

Isabelle covered her face with her hands and literally groaned. "Please don't tell me you're planning to spend the night with this guy."

Jaclyn stood to place her cup in the sink. "Okay, I won't tell you, especially because I haven't decided. Right now we're getting separate rooms. But I want to be prepared just in case."

Isabelle crossed the room to where she was standing and placed her coffee cup down on the counter. "What do you know about this mystery man of yours? Are you sure you want to go that far already? I think we need to talk about this," she said with a scowl on her face. "Sounds to me you're moving too fast, letting your hormones get out of control."

Jaclyn chuckled. "Possibly, but last time I looked at my driver's license I was twenty-six and you don't look like Hattie Campbell to me. Even if you did favor my mom, I'll tell her the same thing I'm about to tell you. I'm a grown-up."

"Yes, but you know so little about men. You're like a fish out of water. A shark is getting ready to gobble you up."

Jaclyn smiled. "And how do you know I won't be gobbling him first?"

Isabelle stared at her, speechless, for a moment and

then she threw her head back and laughed. "Okay, you got me there." She slowly shook her head. "You've become a bad girl right before my eyes."

Jaclyn grinned. "No, I'm finally going after something that I truly want."

"If I didn't know better I'd think you're trying to get rid of me."

Lucien couldn't help but chuckle at the accuracy of his sister's words. She had called right after he'd gotten out of the shower. Last night had been the best sleep he'd gotten in months—at least since the nightmare with Terrence Matthews had begun—and all because he'd known he would be spending the next two days with Jaclyn.

"Not that I'm trying to rush you off the phone, kiddo, but this is my day off and I've made plans."

"What kind of plans? You sound excited."

He pulled the belt through the hoops of his jeans while cradling the phone against his face with his shoulder. "I'm going sailing on the Chesapeake."

"Mmm, nice. It would be even nicer if you had female companionship on this voyage of yours."

He smiled. Lori was always trying to hook him up with someone. "And what makes you think that I won't have someone with me?"

He heard his sister's sharp intake of breath. She was surprised. "If I'm wrong, then by all means correct me. I'd love for you to do so."

He chuckled. "Yeah, I bet."

"Is it serious?"

"I would love for it to be serious, but already there are roadblocks and they're almost insurmountable."

"Then come up with a plan to get them out of the way. If anyone can do it, you can."

If Lori was here with him, he would have hugged her. She always had more confidence in him than he had in himself. "I hope you're right because failing is not an option for me."

Lucien thought about those words again a short while later as he drove across the Francis Scott Key Bridge on his way to pick up Jaclyn. Failing wasn't an option for him. He wished he could explain what was compelling him to spend the next two days with her and basically risking everything to do so. And he was risking everything. Dr. Dudley could make things pretty damn difficult for him as well as for Jaclyn if word got out about them.

He had called her before leaving home to make sure her roommate had left for work as scheduled. Jaclyn had answered the phone in an excited voice, one that had stirred emotions inside of him the moment he heard it. He'd known at that moment, short of death, nothing would keep him from spending whatever time he could with her.

Because it was well after the morning rush hour, it took no time at all to reach Jaclyn's home. He pulled his car into the parking space in front of her town house. As he got out of his car he glanced around to make sure the coast was clear. He didn't like the fact that he had to sneak around to see his woman.

His woman?

He stopped walking and inwardly grimaced. Why would he think of her as such? Hell, if you wanted to count yesterday as an official date, that meant this was only their second. She hardly belonged to him. She was merely someone he was intensely attracted to, but they both knew the attraction had a dead end.

Then why are you here? he couldn't help asking himself. *Why are you willing to put your career on the line for an attraction that's a dead end?*

He forced himself to start walking again, refusing to answer that question just yet. He rang her doorbell and felt the rate of his pulse increase when he heard her fiddle with the lock.

And when she stood there after opening the door, he knew the answer to his questions. He knew why he was there the moment he felt heat emitting between them in a connection so electrifying that they could only stand there and stare at each other.

Without saying anything, she took a step back, and drawing in a deep, steadying breath he followed, entering her home.

He filled her doorway and for the life of her, Jaclyn couldn't avert her gaze from his. Nor could she stop the way her pulse was thudding as he stared at her. His eyes were darker than usual and she continued to feel heat—the kind that was giving off an erotic energy. It was an energy she wasn't used to.

She held her breath when he closed the door and slowly covered the distance separating them. He reached out and brushed loose stands of hair back from her face before cupping her chin and tilting her eyes up to his.

It was then that he said, "Good morning, Jaclyn," before slanting his mouth over hers.

She wasn't given the chance to respond when his mouth began mating with hers with a possession she felt in every part of her body. Instead she returned his greeting in a physical way. She wrapped her arms around his neck and drew her body flush with his. This kiss was more powerful, forceful and ignited more passion within her than anything she'd ever experienced, and that included the kisses they'd shared yesterday. She'd thought nothing could top them. But there was something about this one, a confidence or determination or possibly both, that seeped through to her bones.

And just when she thought he had released her mouth to end it, he took her mouth again, deepening the kiss as a low, guttural hum vibrated in his throat. She heard it. She felt it. And she responded to it, letting him take charge of her tongue while she all but melted into his arms. The way his wet and greedy tongue was sliding against her own made her moan. Desire filled her unlike anything she'd ever felt.

And then he suddenly released her mouth. He continued to hold her while his breathing calmed, regained a semblance of control. So did hers…at least it tried to anyway. She felt his hands gently stroke her back, and all she could do was stand there and rest her head on his shoulder and draw in deep, rapid breaths.

"Around you my control gets blown to hell," he whispered in a low, husky voice close to her ear.

She figured whenever she was able to catch her breath, she would admit her control around him wasn't much better. She lifted her head and her breath got lodged in her throat when she looked into his features. The rays from the sun shining through her living room window hit him dead in the face and made him appear even more devastatingly handsome. She wasn't sure what she liked the most—his sculpted cheekbones, his sensual lips or the tempting darkness of his eyes.

Jaclyn decided she liked all three, but his sensual lips had the ability to make her panties wet just looking at them. And she didn't want to remember how they'd tasted.

"We're getting deeper and deeper into this, aren't we?" he murmured softly against her lips.

Ignoring the shiver that lapped at her nerve endings, she said, "Yes, but don't ask what we can do to stop it because I haven't a clue." Was Isabelle right? Was she moving too fast? Thinking with hormones raging out of control?

After his call inviting her to spend the next two days with him, she hadn't gotten much sleep. Anticipation had overtaken her senses. And when she had opened the door and seen him standing there, it had hit her just how far gone she was where he was concerned. He was right when he'd said they were getting deeper and deeper into it.

"You look nice, Jaclyn. Extremely nice."

His compliment made her smile and she glanced down at herself. "Thank you."

With Isabelle's help they had rummaged through her closet and drawers and found an outfit appropriate for sailing—a pair of white shorts and an aqua blue top. And she had prepared an overnight bag. Once Isabelle had seen her mind was made up about the overnight trip, her roommate had gotten naughty in selecting the outfit to wear this evening and another to sleep in tonight. Although Jaclyn had tried convincing her that sharing a bed with her mystery man wasn't a done deal, Isabelle hadn't wanted to hear it. She'd even put a couple of condoms in the bag, saying it was always best to be prepared.

"Ready?"

"Yes, I just need to grab my overnight bag," she said turning to quickly go to her bedroom.

When she returned he was still standing in the same spot but was glancing around. He looked at her and smiled. "Nice place."

"Thanks."

He then crossed the room to take the bag from her hand. Their fingers touched during the transfer and something inside her rocked. Every sense she possessed was in tune only to him. He met her gaze and she was held captive once again by the darkness of his eyes.

A horn blast from a passing vehicle made her jump, and her lips firmed as she drew in a deep breath. This was crazy. When had an attraction affected her to such a degree? When had it gotten so potent?

"I think we need to get the hell out of here."

She couldn't agree with him more. If they stayed even a second longer there was no telling what they might be tempted to do. "All right."

As they headed toward the door to leave, she had a feeling when she returned in two days her life wouldn't be the same.

"I see you got your car from the hospital," Lucien said as he steered his vehicle toward Annapolis. It was a beautiful day and although the sky appeared filled with dark clouds, the weatherman had indicated there was no rain in the forecast.

"Yes, I got it late yesterday. Because Nurse Tsang saw us leave together, I didn't want to give her any ideas about us. Had my car stayed there all night she would have assumed..."

When she didn't finish what she was about to say, he glanced over at her and asked, "Assumed what?"

He saw the blush staining her features when she said softly, "That we spent the night together."

He didn't say anything for a minute and then, "Yes, I can imagine her assuming that."

For a long moment he tried not to think of the implication of that. Not only would the woman think it, she would tell others of her assumptions. He'd worked at Hopewell long enough to know that for some reason Kayla Tsang had Dr. Dudley's ear when it came to hospital gossip. If Ms. Tsang concentrated more on what she was supposed to do rather than what the hospital personnel were doing, things at Hopewell would run a whole lot better.

"Do you go sailing a lot, Lucien?"

He nodded and smiled while keeping his eyes on the road. It was tempting to look at her, glance down at her pair of gorgeous legs. She looked good in shorts. "Yes, whenever I can get away. The guy who owns the marina where I rent the boat teases me about being his best customer."

"It must be nice getting away from the hospital every now and then," she said softly.

"It is."

He knew as an intern that first year was grueling for them. Most of the time the interns spent the night at the hospital and rarely got to sleep in their own beds at home. Working a double shift was routine. He could remember those days.

"If I don't escape somewhere, I'll find an excuse to drop in to the hospital to check on my patients like I don't think someone else can take care of them besides me." He shrugged his shoulder. "Everyone needs a life outside the hospital to do the things they enjoy. You deserve it. Your patients deserve it. There's nothing worse than a doctor in a bad mood."

"You're a good doctor, Lucien."

He glanced over at her when the car came to a stop at a traffic light. "You think so?"

She chuckled and he liked the sound of her voice. "Yes, and I'm not just saying that because you are my boss. Getting brownie points isn't my style."

"And what is your style, Jaclyn?" he asked, letting his gaze leave her face to trace a path down her body to her legs. He didn't want to think of all the things he would like doing with those legs.

"Mmm, I'd like to think my style is pretty straightforward. I learn not only by observing but by listening as well. I know to ask questions when I don't understand something and won't hesitate to disagree if I truly believe I'm right and someone else is wrong."

She didn't say anything for a moment and then said, "And I don't think there is anything wrong with a person being wrong sometimes. Nobody is perfect. So I guess my style is to always remember that everyone should be treated with respect. When a person comes to the hospital it's because they need us to do what it takes to make them better. We should tend to their needs individually and not collectively and not think we don't need them because we do. I think a dedicated doctor knows that."

Lucien remained quiet as he dwelled on what she'd just said. Her beliefs were going to make her a good doctor, a cut above the others. He had observed certain things about her from the first. In addition to just how good-looking she was, he'd known that she had compassion for those she treated, wasn't quick to diagnose anyone and didn't mind going the extra mile to see to her patients' comfort.

"Sorry, I didn't mean to get on my soapbox," she said apologetically.

"You didn't. I asked a question and you answered it the best way you knew how. I don't have a problem with that."

"Thanks. And what do you see as your style, Lucien?" she then asked him.

He thought about her question for a moment. "I don't think you need to be a drill sergeant to get the best out of anyone, so I don't use that approach with the interns, as you well know. I tell them what is expected and make sure they deliver. I don't bully and neither do I beg. All the interns are well aware of why they're here and what it takes to cut the mustard. Some will make it, while others, like Terrence Matthews, will fail."

He hated bringing up the man, but whether he wanted him to be, he was there right in their faces. He knew the Matthewses were out for blood, mainly his because he was the one who'd fired Terrence. The one good thing was that he had evidence on his side. And for the time being Dr. Dudley. Faced with such evidence his boss couldn't do anything but back him with the firing.

Lucien decided to change the subject. "So how did you meet Isabelle Morales? The two of you seem to be pretty close friends."

"We are. We met years ago at one of those medical student seminars while in college. She was attending University of Florida Medical School and I was at Johns Hopkins. We kept in touch and were ecstatic to discover we'd both landed slots at Hopewell. Her main concern was housing and luckily I had that taken care of. She's a lot of fun as a roommate."

He heard the soft sigh escaping from her lips after she paused briefly and added, "And in case you're wondering but not asking, the answer is no. She doesn't know you're the person I'm spending time with over the next two days."

She chuckled. "Of course Isabelle wouldn't be Isabelle if she wasn't curious. Especially when she knows I haven't dated anyone seriously since we've become friends. But she does respect my privacy."

A part of him should have felt relieved about that, but for some reason it didn't head his list of concerns.

"What about your friendship with Dr. Bradshaw?"

He knew why she was asking. "I haven't mentioned anything to Thomas about spending time with you."

Being confined with her in the car made him very much aware of her scent. It was a sweet yet arousing fragrance that was getting next to him. "So for now this is between only us, Jaclyn."

She nodded. "And I prefer it that way."

His hands tightened on the steering wheel. A part of him should have felt relieved that that was her attitude, but that was not the case. She was a woman any man would be proud to be seen with, but as long as she was his intern there was no way that would be happening. Why was he willing to be with her any way he could, even if it meant behind closed doors?

As he continued the drive to Annapolis, that question weighed heavily on his mind.

When they arrived at their destination it didn't take Lucien long to rent a boat. Jaclyn could tell from the friendly exchange of conversation between him and the manager of the marina that Lucien was a frequent customer like he'd said.

While the two men conversed she glanced around and took in the beauty of her surroundings. She had been so busy at the hospital with so little free time to spare that she hadn't gotten around to checking out all the beautiful places around Alexandria.

The sun was shining brightly overhead in this part of Maryland. It was the perfect day for activities on land or on water and she looked forward to going sailing.

Her lips were still throbbing from the kiss she'd shared with Lucien earlier. Each time she would try to convince herself that maybe Isabelle was right and things might be moving too fast, he would do or say something to make her think that everything was moving at the right pace.

She enjoyed everything about Lucien. He was a great conversationalist and a gentleman at heart. And although she was fully aware of the degree of his desire, she was in no way frightened by it. For her to have fallen in love with him so quickly and easily spoke volumes. But then, according to her parents, things had been that way for them.

"Ready?"

She glanced over at Lucien. He was holding the basket filled with lunches they had grabbed from a restaurant near one of the piers. She didn't have to inhale deeply to appreciate the aroma of fried chicken, reminding her it was past lunchtime and she hadn't eaten anything since that morning. "Yes, I'm ready."

Together they walked on the pier to the boat they would be using. It was definitely a beauty. And it was huge. She glanced over at Lucien. "It's bigger than I thought it would be."

He chuckled. "Relax, I'm a capable captain."

She smiled. "That might be true, but I'll probably fail as your mate. I know nothing about sailing."

"Then I'll look forward to teaching you a few things."

He made good on those words when less than an hour later he not only proved what a great captain he was by his handling of the sailboat, but also just how patient he was when he showed her how to assist him. When he had shown her how to put the life jacket on correctly, she had given him what she hoped was her most appreciative smile, while fighting all the sensations rumbling in her stomach.

And when he had glanced down at her to make sure the jacket was just how he wanted it, she had glanced back up and met his gaze. She had actually felt the heat in every part of her body. Even with all the sexual tension surrounding them she was glad she was spending time with him and couldn't help wondering what tonight would bring.

He had placed her overnight bag in the trunk of the car next to his and it had looked natural for them to be side by side. Ever since then, she couldn't stop anticipating their time together later.

"Daydreaming isn't allowed."

His words interrupted her thoughts and she glanced over at him and chuckled. He was sitting down operating the tiller and keeping the sailboat from sailing directly into the wind. Like her, he was wearing a pair of white shorts and he had a pullover jersey sporting the name of his favorite NFL team.

"Sorry. It's such a beautiful day, I can't help it," she said.

"Then maybe I need to give you something else to do."

She lifted a brow. "Something like what?"

"Like bringing that lunch basket over here. I think it's time for us to eat. I'm starving. What about you?"

Jaclyn was starving as well, so she didn't waste any time grabbing the basket. Taking the tablecloth out of the hamper, she spread it over the small table and emptied the contents of the carrier—a container of fried chicken, pickles, bags of chips and a bottle of wine.

She tried ignoring the shivers of pleasure that raced up and down her spine when she sat beside him. When he inched closer to her, leaned over and placed a kiss on her lips, she couldn't help the goose bumps that formed on her arm.

"I doubt anything in that basket," he said in a low husky voice, reaching up and pushing a lock of hair from her face, "will taste as good as you do."

She wished he hadn't said that. She'd been kissed before, but no man had ever said such a thing to her. She swallowed deeply noting her breathing pattern had changed. And she and Lucien were sitting so close that she could feel his muscles tensing.

She nervously licked her bottom lip and asked, "You think so?"

The smile he gave her could wet a woman's panties. "Baby, I know so."

Jaclyn smiled. "Are you always this complimentary?"

"No, but I always speak the truth."

He was good for a woman's ego and she enjoyed having him around. He was definitely a keeper. "I think we should try tasting something more filling."

He chuckled and leaned back. "Okay, then, woman. Feed me."

Sharing lunch with him was fun. While they ate what she thought was the best fried chicken she'd ever eaten and sipped wine, they talked about anything and everything other than work.

He told her more about his life in Jamaica and some of the pranks he and his sister had pulled on their cousins. She could tell by the sound of his voice that he missed seeing his grandmother and looked forward to the trip he'd planned for the holidays.

She was enjoying being with him and getting to know the man her heart had already claimed as hers. After a while she noticed they had fallen into silence. As she glanced over at him, she realized he'd been staring at her. "Is something wrong, Lucien?"

He shook his head slowly. "No, I think everything is just right. Things couldn't be more perfect at the moment."

A smile touched her lips. She felt the same way.

Chapter 8

Jaclyn's breath caught when Lucien brought his car to a stop in front of the most beautiful bed and breakfast she'd ever seen. The hour drive from Annapolis to the Eastern Shore had definitely been well worth it. Nestled on a hundred and twenty acres, Wades Point Inn was huge and spacious and provided a scenic and picturesque view of both the Chesapeake Bay and the Eastern Bay.

"So what do you think?"

She glanced over at Lucien and figured she dared not tell him what she thought. They would be here only one night, but already she could imagine all the things they could do together in such a romantic setting. She could envision their seeing the sun rise and set from their room and could picture their holding hands while exploring the nearby quaint, historical towns of St. Michaels and Easton. And she could definitely see their sharing a glass of wine tonight while watching the boats go by on the bay.

She drew in a deep breath knowing what those thoughts meant. He had left the decision regarding their sleeping arrangements to her and she had made it. They would definitely be sharing a room tonight. She glanced over at him. "I think this place was meant for us, Lucien. It was meant for us to be here. Together."

She knew he had purposely taken them far away from Alexandria and she appreciated his doing so. No matter how the future unfolded for them, she was convinced that this was their time to be together.

His smile was priceless and she knew he'd gotten the meaning of her words. She saw the simmer of heat already forming in his gaze at the thought of what tonight could possibly hold for them. But she wasn't surprised by his next question. "Are you sure, Jaclyn?"

She knew why he was asking. If they carried through with their plans there would be no turning back. Each was making a leap into forbidden territory, regardless of what tomorrow would bring. They were concentrating on only today. Temptation teamed with anticipation and rippled all through her when she said, "Yes, I'm sure, Lucien."

Lucien studied Jaclyn carefully when the receptionist at the front desk handed over their room key. He was looking for any sign that she had changed her mind and didn't want to share a room with him after all. But he didn't see any. What he did see was a woman, a very desirable woman, with a made-up mind.

"Ready to go up?" he asked softly.

She looked over at him and smiled and at that moment he felt like the luckiest man on earth. And when it came right down to it, he was probably also the horniest. Just being with her was making sexual urges hit him from just about every angle.

"Yes, I'm ready."

They had left their overnight bags with the bellman, so he was free to tuck her hand firmly in his as they headed for the elevator. Anticipation lapped at his heels with every step he took. Being with her had basically turned his world on its ear. She had decided that they would share a room tonight. But even if she had asked for her own room, he still would have appreciated this time they were spending together. He knew at that moment, although he wanted her with a passion that he felt to his gut, there was more between them than just sex. A part of him knew it even though he didn't fully understand it.

He was still pondering what was there about her that made him risk everything just to be with her. What had made being with her the ultimate surrender more than a supreme sacrifice was the woman whose hand was firmly tucked in his. The woman who in just two days had opened his eyes to things they had been closed to for years. Besides work there was play and what made it enjoyable was the person you were with.

They stepped into the elevator alone and automatically she turned to face him. It seemed the most natural thing to do when he pulled her closer to him, wrapped his arms around her waist and lowered his mouth to hers.

Her lips parted the moment his touched hers and in the back of his mind there were imaginary fireworks exploding all around them. He delved deeper in her mouth and couldn't help the groan that slipped past his throat. Red-hot sensations rushed through his bloodstream as his mouth continued to not only explore hers but claim it.

The elevator came to a stop so suddenly that it almost jerked them apart, and her sigh of disappointment equaled his moan of frustration. They stared at each other, fully aware that their desire for each other had escalated out of control. Stripping her naked the moment they got to their room seemed like a good idea about now. But it wasn't what he wanted. It wasn't what she deserved. He hadn't brought her here just to jump her bones. Their time together had more meaning than that. Although he would be the first to admit he was getting used to kissing her, getting used to tasting her. Kissing a woman had taken on a whole new meaning. And he didn't want to recall just how she felt in his arms. How her body had automatically curved into his. How soft she felt and just how good she smelled.

He shoved his hands into the pockets of his shorts and walked beside her as they exited the elevator. There was no way he could touch her now. Doing so would be suicide. They needed to make plans to get out of their room rather quickly or they wouldn't be going out tonight.

"The lady at the front desk mentioned something about a concert in the square tonight," he said.

The older woman had explained to them that in the historical town of St. Michaels tonight was jazz night, and suggested they check out the concert that would be followed with a magnificent fireworks display. It had sounded like something he wanted to see and do…until he had kissed her. Now all he wanted to do was get her in that room and kiss her some more.

"Yes, that would be nice," she replied.

He smiled, thinking that she didn't seem too excited about it. "Or if you'd like we can take a stroll around the grounds and then call it an early night," he suggested.

He watched the smile that touched her lips and at the same time temptation pricked up his spine. Hell, forget about the stroll. It would suit him just fine if when they got to their room they didn't come out until checkout time tomorrow. But he knew he couldn't let that happen. He had to remember that as much as he wanted her, it was more than just sex between them.

"Okay, then, we'll take a stroll around the place before dinner," she said.

He expelled a huge breath. He was still reeling from the kiss they'd shared in the elevator, and when they finally reached their room and he inserted the key and opened the door, he had a feeling he was in big trouble.

It should have been relatively simple, Jaclyn thought. She could have turned on the television and watched the news until the bellman delivered their luggage. And Lucien could have moved around the room and checked out the menu on the desk, counted the number of hangers in the closet or studied the design of the bedspread. But that was not the case. As soon as the door closed behind them, she was pulled into a pair of strong, masculine arms.

The second his mouth touched hers she knew they were finishing what they had started in the elevator. A wave of longing washed over her and she felt any control she might have had come tumbling down. The depth of passion that overtook her wreaked havoc on her senses and opened floodgates of emotions she'd kept at bay for eighteen months.

His mouth went still on hers when there was a knock at the door. Then he gave one final sensuous lick of his tongue around her mouth before breaking off the kiss and taking a step back. He frowned at the door, and when he spoke his voice was laden with frustration. "Who is it?"

"Bellman with your luggage, sir."

He glanced over at her. The look in his eyes pretty much made her suspect that he would tell the man to go away and pull her back into his arms. She figured she needed to intercede. "We need our clothes, Lucien," she said, reasoning with him.

"No, we don't."

She laughed. A part of her knew he was serious. "Behave." She immediately moved to the door when she saw he would not.

The bellman entered. As soon as he deposited the bags on the bed Lucien gave him a tip and the guy wasted no time leaving. She had a feeling the man had known he had interrupted something.

Lucien inclined his head toward the door and gave her an innocent smile. "Was it something I said?"

She chuckled. "Your look gave you away, Dr. De Winter."

He slowly crossed the room to her. He placed his hands in his pockets as if he needed them there or else he would reach out and touch her. "And how do I look, Dr. Campbell?"

For some reason she loved it when he referred to her as such. It made her feel like his equal in the professional realm of things. She paused a moment as if to study him. *You look like a man any woman would want.* Those were the words on the tip of her tongue, but she wouldn't utter them. They were thoughts she preferred keeping to herself for now.

Instead she said, "Like a man with a plan."

His brow rose and he frowned slightly as he seemed to study her features. "Do you think the only reason I asked you to come here with me was to seduce you?"

Without missing a beat, she reached out and placed her arms around his neck. "If that *was* the reason I'm not complaining."

She knew that they had pretty much crossed the line when they'd kissed at the park yesterday. And now they were about to spend two days together. She knew what was happening between them, so why did it seem as if he was stalling now?

"I know what this is costing us, Lucien," she said quietly.

He searched her features. "Do you?"

She looked him squarely in the eye and said, "Yes, but I'm willing to take what I can. Whatever you offer."

"Why? Why are you so accommodating to me? I see the other male doctors and the interns and how they look at you, how they check you out. Unlike me they have been free to make their interest known. I know a couple have asked you out, yet you've turned them down. I overheard their disappointed whispers when you did so. But you didn't hesitate to go out with me. Why me and not them?"

She shrugged. "I could say I get a thrill coming on to my boss."

"You could but you won't."

Jaclyn glanced down at the floor. He was right. She wouldn't. Nor would she tell him the real reason. The truth. That she had fallen in love with him the first day they'd met. He would probably find the whole concept of love at first sight ludicrous.

"I like mature guys," she heard herself say, knowing he was waiting for her response. "I like a guy who knows where he's going. A guy who is respected. A guy with whom I know where I stand. I like a guy who I believe won't lead me on. A guy who will give it to me straight."

She dropped her arms from around his neck. Now was the time to tell him more so he could understand. "The last guy I was seriously involved with I dated for almost two years. I thought I knew him. Then a group of his buddies decided to tour England. He had finished law school and it was going to be the last chance he got before he went to work at some law firm or another."

When she paused, longer than she planned to, he asked, "What happened?"

She held his gaze. "He returned at the end of the summer as planned, but..."

"Why did I know there was going to be a but somewhere?"

She smiled slightly. "Mainly because you're perceptive."

She tossed her hair from her face and said, "But he returned just long enough to tell me he was going back to England for a while. He had met someone and he was going to get her and bring her to the States."

"He dropped you?" Lucien asked in an astonished voice.

"Like a hot potato."

"For another woman?" he asked as if the thought of such a thing happening was above his level of comprehension. She saw the way his jaw tightened as if what Danny had done was an insult to him as well as to her.

"Yes, but I got over it and him soon enough." There was no need to tell him that in a way she'd been relieved because she'd realized soon afterward that she hadn't truly loved him anyway.

"Now I only live for the moment," she said, as if she preferred something casual to a committed relationship, which was so far from the truth. But because she knew they could never have such a relationship, she wasn't bothered by the little white lie she was telling.

"So," she said, placing her hands on his broad shoulders. "You know my position. What's yours?"

She stole a look at him from underneath her lashes, saw the heated gaze staring at her. Then in a low, seductive voice he said, "I have several positions, Jaclyn. And I plan to show you all of them. Starting now."

He then lowered his mouth to hers.

Chapter 9

Lucien slanted his mouth possessively over Jaclyn's as desire swept through him. He told himself to slow down, not be greedy but to savor not only the moment but also the woman. However, the deeper he took the kiss, the more he wanted her, the more the need to make love to her became as elemental as breathing.

Her lips were softer, more delicious than anything he'd ever tasted. And as he continued to kiss her he detected it again, in the recesses of her mouth—her unique flavor, a potency he tasted, absorbed and was convinced he was addicted to.

Lucien traced every inch of her mouth with the tip of his tongue before using that tongue to tangle with hers. Sensation after torrid sensation swamped his body. He hadn't wanted to go this far this quickly. He had wanted them to take a stroll around the property, to appreciate their surroundings, to enjoy the bay. But it seemed all those things would be placed on the back burner as they enjoyed each other.

He deepened the kiss while his hands slid up and down her back in leisurely strokes, and he shifted his stance to bring her closer to his hard, masculine frame. She was soft to his hard, but from her kiss he could tell she was just as ravenous as he was. Just as overtaken with desire so arousing that he felt it in his bones.

He tried to draw on the strength he truly didn't have to end the kiss here and now. But the only thing he could do was let his mouth cling to hers and not let go. He'd known he was a goner the moment he had arrived at her house and seen her in those white shorts and blue top. She'd looked more than just cute in the outfit. She'd looked tantalizing with a capital T.

There wasn't anything indecent about the way she looked, but all her lush curves had sent blood rushing through his veins, had ignited sensations he'd tried reining under control but couldn't. The only reason he finally released her mouth was because they both needed to breathe.

But that didn't stop his tongue from sensuously licking the sides of her mouth or playfully tasting the bow of her lips as she drew in sharp intakes of breath. There was just something about her mouth—the shape, taste and texture—that could render him mind-bogglingly delirious with need.

And if that wasn't bad enough, he had eased his hand beneath her shirt to roam up and down her back, stroke the softness of her skin. She was wearing a bra without a back opening which meant the clasp was in the front. The thought of freeing her breasts from the bra had heat flowing all through him and sensations tugging low in his gut.

He pulled his hands from beneath her shirt and went for her hair. From the first day he'd seen her he had wondered how it would feel to run his fingers through it. Now he reveled in the silky feel of her brown tresses.

He took her mouth again. Never had he made love to a woman's mouth the way he was doing hers. It was as if he was paying homage to it. And Jaclyn's mouth deserved the honor. She had lips made for kissing and a mouth made for tasting, and he was doing both.

He had known the more he kissed her the weaker to resist her he would become. But the last thing he had expected was this raw hunger, this intense desire that he felt in every part of his body. There was no organ spared, no sensation missed or muscle neglected. All were working simultaneously to give him the Jaclyn Campbell effect. He was getting it in large doses and had no control of what was happening to him at that moment.

"Lucien," she groaned his name, slowly pulling her mouth away and looking up at him.

His gaze snagged hers and the degree of desire he saw embedded in the dark depths almost took his breath away, almost brought him to his knees. He fought back both reactions as he swept her off her feet and into his arms. Moving toward the bed, he thought of the words he could possibly say to make her know just how he felt. He was good with a stethoscope, but when it came to expressing himself where a woman was concerned, he was at a loss for words. Never had he been so overwhelmed.

He gently placed her on the bed, but that was where

his tenderness ended. He began undressing her with a need so fierce that he sent her clothes flying everywhere. His intent was to strip her naked. And he wasn't wasting any time doing so.

He paused and raked his gaze over every inch of her bared flesh. Each part of her was so tempting that he had to force his hand to remain by his side, hold his tongue hostage inside his mouth and shift his body to ease the pressure of his erection straining against the zipper of his shorts.

His gaze then zeroed in on her mouth, a mouth that had been thoroughly kissed by him and that tempted him to do so again. His eyes moved up to hers and held her gaze, watched the magnitude of emotions that flickered in their depths.

"You are simply beautiful," he said in a soft, unsteady voice, one filled to the brim with need of the most intense kind. The smile that appeared at that moment on her lips made his gut clench.

"I think you're beautiful as well," she said, letting her gaze roam all over him.

He chuckled. Because he was still fully clothed she didn't really see much skin, but she would and he hoped she thought the same thing when she did. He slowly skirted around the bed to sit in the wingback chair to remove his shoes and socks, not taking his eyes off her. He saw she was paying attention to everything he did, taking it all in.

After tucking his socks into his shoes and placing them aside, he stood and went to the belt on his shorts and slid it through the loop. Placing the belt aside he pulled his shirt over his head and tossed it away.

He glanced over at her when he heard her sharp intake of breath as she stared at his bare chest. Moments later he eased both his briefs and walking shorts past his thighs and down his legs and the look that flared in her eyes sent red-hot sensations sweeping through him.

He knew at that moment their lovemaking would not only be intense, but it would also be special. The entire room oozed with sexual chemistry. When he picked up his shorts to get a condom packet from his wallet, he had a strong feeling they wouldn't be leaving their room anytime soon.

Jaclyn fought to regulate her breathing as she stared across the room at the man who had the body of an Adonis and wore the most beautiful smile she'd ever seen. Even when a nagging voice inside her mind was saying she should really question being here with him and that maybe things were moving way too fast, she couldn't help the heated desire that seemed to overtake her senses.

She would never forget the first day she'd met him, when he had walked into the auditorium and introduced himself to all twenty interns. She'd heard the feminine whispers that had wafted through the room. Like all the other women she had been checking him out, but unlike them, she saw beyond a handsome face and a well-built body.

When he started to speak, his words momentarily weren't the focus of her attention. She concentrated on the man as a strange phenomenon took place and it was just as her mother had said it would be. She'd discovered that day that love at first sight, as crazy as it sounded, was as true as true could be for her.

The strange thing was that she had known nothing

about him other than his name and the fact that during the period of her internship at Hopewell he would technically be her boss. But a part of her had known something else. It had known love in a way she'd never had with Danny. Stranger still was that Lucien had had no idea what she'd been thinking. He hadn't had a clue.

But now he was here. They both were. Totally naked and about to connect in an intimate way. She watched while he encased his manhood with a condom and she couldn't help but lean back on her haunches in the middle of the bed and take it all in, not quite believing the size of him. *And I'm supposed to handle that?*

From somewhere she was suddenly entrenched with confidence that she could and she would. Maybe it was the way he was looking at her watching him. Or maybe it was the fantasy of him tucked away in the back of her mind. Whatever the reason, her body began tingling all over, causing a delicious ache to start throbbing at her center. And when he slowly began moving his naked body toward her, she could only look at him and be totally consumed by him.

He came to a stop at the edge of the bed and said in a deep, husky tone, "I want you."

Okay, so it wasn't the L word, but she would take it. And the meaning, spoken with such profoundness made her tremble. "You're shivering," he said.

She released a deep sigh while thinking that wasn't all she was. She felt as if she was a heated mass of desire and all for one man. Before she could respond to his observation, he reached out and pulled her into his arms.

More than anything, Lucien thought, this was what he wanted. This was what would often make him toss and turn, and keep him up late at night. Thoughts of sharing a bed with Jaclyn, of kissing her this way, of participating in racy foreplay before their bodies joined in lovemaking. His fantasies had been so profound that he would wake up in cold sweat.

Now he was about to experience the real thing.

Her taste was luscious on his lips and while his tongue toyed endlessly and hungrily with hers, he wanted more and tilted her head back to get it. The low moan that escaped her throat when he deepened the kiss made his heart beat that much faster, and caused goose bumps to form on his arms.

His hands smoothed over her back before moving lower to clutch twin cheeks in his hands while easing her on her back. He broke off the kiss long enough to say, "I love kissing you."

The words tumbled from his throat easily and he knew he hadn't experienced anything quite like what he was sharing with her. When he had her flat on her back, he began tasting her from her lips to her breasts. The twin globes were high, firm, and the nipples were dark and inviting and he couldn't resist the temptation to taste them.

He heard her deep sigh and felt her clutch the back of his head to hold his mouth in place when he began sucking earnestly on a nipple. Her scent conveyed her readiness, but he wanted to taste her all over and he slowly left her breasts to move his mouth lower to her stomach.

He was consumed with a hot hunger, a deep desire to lick her all over, taste her and absorb every inch of her into his mouth and the scent of her into his nostrils. Wanting to know just how ready she was for him, he lowered his hand to the wet spot between her legs, slipping his fingers between the damp womanly folds. His body began shivering knowing just how much she wanted him and how her body had prepared to have him.

Desire, as potent as anything he'd ever felt before, rushed through his body as he lowered his mouth, kissing a path downward. When he reached his destination and his tongue entered her, the quivering of her thighs sent a tidal wave of sensations through him.

Never had he enjoyed loving a woman this way more. *This* woman. And he took his time to savor her as well as to bring her pleasure. When she moaned he deepened the intimate kiss, determined that she partake of the dose of rapture overtaking him. And when she called out his name after an orgasm took control of her body, he locked his mouth to her, determined to feast on her to the max.

Moments later when he finally pulled his mouth away, he sat back on his haunches to stare down at her. She wore pleasure well. Satisfaction was carved into her features and she seemed to inhale an air of bliss with every intake of her breath. She held his gaze and he knew from this moment that when he brought her home tomorrow that would not, could not, be the end of things for them. If he'd ever thought that this could be a two-day affair and that when it was over he would return to his senses, he was totally wrong.

"You're ready for me, sweetheart?" he asked, feeling the deep throb of his erection overtake his senses.

Jaclyn could only lie there while toe curling sensations oozed from her body, leaving her feeling bone tired and weak. But she wasn't too weak to respond to what he'd asked. Because although she had just experienced one whopper of an orgasm, all she had to do was read the look in his eyes to know there were more where that one came from and he intended for her to enjoy every single one of them.

"Yes, I'm ready."

A smile curved his lips. Evidently he liked her response. Then he slowly began easing toward her, and her heart began beating more furiously with every inch he took toward her, his warm breath getter closer and closer to her lips. Anticipation was eating away at her, renewing her desire and kicking her hormones into overdrive once again.

And then he was there, touching his lips to hers. No matter how often they kissed she would always look forward to mingling her tongue with his, eagerly, hungrily, willingly. And when he covered her body with his, she felt the heat of him from shoulder to thigh, especially from his center. It was almost burning her alive.

She felt him fit right between her open legs. The intensity of his kiss deepened and suddenly he thrust inside of her as he held tightly to her hips so she would take him fully. Pleasure ripped through her the moment their bodies connected, and then he began moving in and out while she arched her body to meet his every stroke.

She'd made out with Danny many times, but until today she hadn't known how it felt to be so in tune to a man. The more he thrust, the more she wanted him. His strokes deepened, and so did her need for him.

Finally, she couldn't take any more, couldn't handle the expert precision of his lovemaking another moment. Sensations slammed into her, pushing her over the edge. She broke her mouth from his to scream out his name.

There was not a single disillusionment in how she felt. Every bone in her body felt pulverized, every cell energized, and she knew that no matter what the risks of having a relationship with him might be, it was all worth it. Here, in his arms, was where she belonged.

Lucien soothed Jaclyn's hair back from her face as she slept. She looked beautiful awake or sleeping. He couldn't help but think about what they'd shared moments ago. Never had making love to a woman meant so much. Never had he gotten just as much as he'd given. He had wanted her badly and she'd given him just what he'd wanted.

He momentarily closed his eyes, just to decipher what kind of future the two of them could have if they continued on this path. And the answer wasn't one he was ready to accept just yet. She was a woman any man would be proud to be seen with. A woman a man should cherish and not sneak around with. She deserved better than that.

He opened his eyes and gazed around the room. They weren't supposed to be here together like this. They were taking a huge risk doing so. But the sexual chemistry, the need and the desire had been too keen, too overpowering. They hadn't been able to resist such temptation.

"Lucien?"

He glanced down at her. Although the room was dark, he could see her gaze. He held it. "Yes?"

She reached up and touched his cheek, traced a line around his lips with her fingertip. "Any regrets?" she asked in a soft whisper.

"None," he whispered back quickly. "It was everything that I imagined it would be. Even more so."

And he meant it. When he'd slid into her body and her inner muscles had clamped on to him, pulled everything he had to give out of him, he had willingly surrendered his all.

He studied her features while breathing in her scent. It was a fragrance he doubted he would be able to forget. "What about you?"

He watched as she drew in her breath slowly before saying, "I wish…"

When she paused, he lifted his brow. "And what do you wish, Jaclyn?"

Her gaze connected with his. "I wished we didn't ever have to leave here."

He wasn't sure if she meant the bed or the inn. Regardless, he was still feeling her. "I wish we didn't have to leave, either."

Beyond the door were things he wasn't ready to deal with. Realities he preferred not to face. He much preferred being here, in this room, in this bed, with her.

But he knew that was impossible. They had a life beyond that door. In another day they would return to their jobs. And it was a job he rather liked doing and he knew for her it was the same. They were who they were. They had simply met at the wrong time.

When he'd left Jamaica many years ago his life plan had been set. From a child he had always known two things: he would one day make a life for himself in America and he would be a doctor. He had worked hard, finished top in his class and he'd played by the rules, refusing to break any.

Until now.

He wanted his job and he also wanted her. He wanted it all, but life decreed that wasn't possible and they both knew it. And it was something he wasn't ready to talk about right now. He just wanted to hold her in his arms and relish the memories.

Moments later he heard her stomach growl and couldn't help smiling.

"Sorry," she said apologetically.

He shook his head. "I'm the one who should be apologizing. We missed dinner. I'll call and have something brought up to us."

"Thanks."

"And I still want to take that stroll tonight. I hear the grounds of the inn are beautiful at night."

"And I'd love to see it…but at some other time." And then she pulled his head down to hers. When she slid her tongue inside his mouth, he moaned deep in his throat and deepened the kiss.

And just like that, she had stoked his desires once again.

Jaclyn opened her eyes to the sunlight shining through the window. She heard Lucien moving around in the bathroom and shifted to lie on her back and gaze up at the ceiling.

It didn't take much to remember last night. It had started with Lucien's mouth on hers and things had moved quickly from there. When it came to kissing, he was a master, but then it was her opinion he was a master lovemaker as well. His strokes and his thrusts had been precise and had aroused her to a point of no return. Never had she been made to feel like that before. In the end they had both lost control. They had both got-

ten what they wanted. At that moment she didn't want
to think about the fact that yesterday and today were
all they would have.

"You look beautiful in the morning."

She glanced across the room. He was standing in the
bathroom doorway, shirtless, with a pair of jeans hanging low on his hips. The man epitomized sex appeal.

She sat up in bed and smiled. "And you don't look
bad yourself, Doc."

He chuckled as he began slowly moving toward her
in what she thought was one sexy stroll. He sat on the
edge of the bed and pulled her into his arms and she
was ready for the kiss she knew was coming.

Moments later when their lips parted, she could only
moan in protest.

"Hey, I need to feed you breakfast," he said, joking.

She shook her head. "No, you don't. We ate dinner
late last night, remember?"

And they had. They had made love again before
they'd finally ordered dinner delivered to their room.
After eating they had gone out on the balcony to watch
the fireworks over the bay. The way the prism of color
had burst across the water, lighting up the skies, had
been nothing short of spectacular. They had slipped
into thick terry cloth robes, compliments of the inn, and
Lucien had stood with his arms around her waist. She
had leaned back into him and had felt like she was the
most cherished person on earth. When the fireworks
had ended, they had returned to their room, stripped
and made love again.

"I still want to go for a stroll around the inn, Jaclyn."

She rolled her eyes. "You're back to that again?"

He chuckled. "You're going to thank me."

She blushed, knowing exactly what he meant. Her body was sore and he knew it. If they remained in their hotel room all day, the soreness would only increase. "Okay, we'll go walking."

Surprisingly it didn't take long for them to get dressed once they got out of the shower a while later. She'd known for them to take a shower together was a mistake as soon as he'd suggested it. But like everything else with him, she'd been tempted and the weakling in her had given in to it.

They enjoyed breakfast on the huge screened-in porch and then they walked around the inn, hand-in-hand, taking in the various sights and sounds. The inn was magnificent, the lawns well kept and the trees and shrubbery neatly trimmed.

Checkout time was at noon, but instead of driving directly back to Alexandria, they had decided to stop along the way and enjoy lunch in the quaint historical town of Evans. After they ate, they walked around the town, and they fell into silence, each one seemingly caught in their own thoughts.

"You're quiet," she said softly.

He glanced over at her and a smile touched his lips. "I was thinking how much I've enjoyed my time with you."

"And I've enjoyed these stolen moments with you as well," she replied.

"Stolen moments…" He seemed to test the words on his lips.

"Yes. Tomorrow we will be back in the real world."

"At the hospital?"

"Yes." They kept walking and then he stopped and turned to her, reached out and tenderly stroked a thumb across her cheek. "And what if I said I still wanted to see you away from the hospital?"

She met his gaze. "Then I would say you would be asking for trouble. You would be taking chances neither of us needs."

He didn't say anything for a while and momentarily broke eye contact with her to glance over the bay. When he returned his gaze to her, he said, "Can you look at me, Jaclyn, and say all you wanted was yesterday and today, and that our time together meant nothing but an affair to you?"

She drew in a slow breath and shook her head. Jaclyn knew her true feelings for him, knew there was no way she could say that. Although the past two days might not have been a turning point for him, it definitely had been for her. She loved him more now than before.

"No, but it doesn't matter what we might want," she said. "The hospital isn't going to change its policies just for us. It is what it is."

"But if I can come up with a plan, would you continue to see me?"

He was gazing at her with such tenderness and longing in his eyes that she knew what her answer would be. She would risk all to continue to see him. "Yes, I would continue to see you."

He nodded. "That means we will have to keep our secret."

She nervously nibbled on her bottom lip. Isabelle would be asking questions when Jaclyn returned. Her best friend was relentless when she wanted to know something.

"I know how you probably feel and what you're thinking," he said, interrupting her thoughts. "I don't like sneaking around any more than you, but that's how it will have to be to protect our careers at Hopewell, Jaclyn. The only other solution is one I'm not ready to do. I'm not ready to give you up and walk away. I'm not prepared to pretend the last two days, especially last night, didn't happen. No matter the cost. You mean more to me than that and I refuse to treat it like it was some cheap hotel-room affair."

Jaclyn didn't say anything. He'd said she meant something to him. Granted it wasn't what her heart declared he meant to her, but at least it was something.

"Jaclyn?"

"Yes?"

"So we are in agreement to continue what we started here?"

His mouth was set in a grim line and she knew he wasn't overjoyed with his suggestion any more than she was, but for them that was the only way. They had their careers to protect and there was no doubt in either of their minds what would happen if word got out they were involved in an affair.

But then she knew what would happen if they weren't involved in an affair. She would be miserable. "Yes, we are in agreement. I'll continue to see you."

With her words she knew a commitment had been made. And it was one she intended to keep. No matter what.

Chapter 10

"Good morning, Dr. De Winter."

He raised a brow as he passed the nurses' station. Was that a smile on Ms. Tsang's face or was it a smirk? He wasn't sure and he really didn't care. The woman was known to cause trouble and he didn't have the time or the inclination to wonder what she was up to now.

"Morning, Ms. Tsang," he said as he kept walking. His day had started off badly. He had to change a flat tire before he could get to work and then got caught in traffic on the Francis Scott Key Bridge. The only good part of his morning was that sitting idle in traffic had given him the chance to relive moments of the two days he'd spent with Jaclyn.

He had taken her home around six yesterday evening and luckily for him her roommate's car was gone, which meant Isabelle wasn't home. But Jaclyn hadn't invited him in because they hadn't known how soon Dr. Morales would be returning. He'd had to kiss her goodbye in a corner of the doorstep where a huge plant had shielded them from possible prying eyes.

He checked his watch as he rounded the hallway to his office. He was eager to see how the patients from the multicar accident were doing. He hadn't gotten beeped on his days off, which meant no emergency had come up while he was away.

Lucien was about to place his key into the lock of his office door but found it already unlocked. He frowned, wondering who'd been in his office. He opened the door to find Dr. Dudley sitting in one of the chairs. He wondered what would have the chief of staff waiting for him at nine in the morning. Had there been some new development regarding the Matthews lawsuit?

"Dr. Dudley, is anything wrong?" he asked, entering his office and closing the door behind him.

"I think we need to talk, Dr. De Winter," he replied in a gruff tone.

Considering that his morning had gotten off to a bad start anyway, Lucien knew he should not be surprised that something was brewing with his boss. Although he hadn't liked the fact that Lucien had fired Terrence Matthews, Dr. Dudley had been backed in a corner where he had no other choice but to support Lucien in his decision. Lucien hoped like hell that given the pressure the Matthewses were exerting on the hospital by withholding funding that Dr. Dudley wasn't thinking about backing down on the stance the hospital had taken.

Lucien went to his desk and sat down. When Dr. Dudley didn't say anything, Lucien glanced over at the picture of the older woman framed on his desk. His grandmother. He smiled before turning his attention back to his visitor. "I take it this meeting has something to do with the Matthews lawsuit."

Dr. Dudley crossed his arms over his chest and leaned back in the swivel chair. "No, I'm here for another matter altogether."

"Oh? And what matter is that?" he asked.

"Your behavior with one of your interns."

Lucien's stomach plunged. Keeping a poker face, he searched his mind to recall if at any point during the two days they'd spent together he and Jaclyn had run into anyone who worked at the hospital. When he couldn't, he figured the man didn't know anything but was merely fishing for information.

"And just what is supposed to be my behavior with one of my interns? And what intern are we talking about?" he asked in a remarkably calm voice. He leaned back in his chair, hoping there wasn't anyone who had valid proof of his affair with Jaclyn.

"I understand you and Dr. Campbell were seen leaving the hospital together two days ago and her car was still here late in the afternoon."

He inclined his head, seeing clearly now. He shouldn't have been surprised that Ms. Tsang had run to him with her suspicions, just like he shouldn't be surprised that he was acting on it. A part of him wondered again why Dr. Dudley always followed up on whatever gossip that particular nurse tossed him.

"And my leaving here with Dr. Campbell is supposed to be a crime?" he countered trying to keep the anger from his voice.

"It is if the two of you are breaking the hospital's nonfraternization policy."

"We're not. Like a number of my interns she'd worked a double, taking care of the injured from that multicar collision. But before we got beeped for the accident, she'd come to see me to discuss the Matthews lawsuit. Rumors were going around and she was afraid somehow she would get connected to it. I felt I needed to assure her that wasn't the case and preferred meeting her off-site."

He paused a moment and then said, "And as far as her car being left here for a long period of time..." *Like it's really anybody's business,* he thought. "I offered to take her home when I saw how tired she was. End of story."

Dr. Dudley didn't say anything for a long moment as he studied Lucien. And then, "I hope for your sake, Dr. De Winter, that's the end of the story. You have a promising future at Hopewell. You came highly recommended by Dr. Benjamin Norris, for heaven's sakes. It would be an injustice for you to risk ruining your career by becoming involved with Jaclyn Campbell. I admit she's a very attractive woman and all, but you need to ask yourself if she's worth it."

Lucien returned the man's stare. He would never admit it to Dudley, but he had asked himself that same question last night when he'd gone to bed and this morning when he'd awaken. The answer had been the same: Yes, she was.

Lucien inhaled deeply. He didn't fully understand what there was about his attraction to Jaclyn that he was willing to risk it all to be with her. But it was a risk for her as well.

Yesterday they had agreed to continue to see each other. It was their secret and he intended to protect it any way he could. Even if it meant lying outright to his boss and taking the position of the victim wrongly accused. The one thing that was genuine was his anger. First at the hospital for having such an outdated policy, and then at Dr. Dudley for believing everything he heard.

Besides, his boss, of all people, should not be calling him out on anything. Although Dudley hadn't been accused of any extramarital affairs, he was known to have a roving eye, and Lucien had caught him checking out Jaclyn more than once.

The thought made his nostrils flare in anger and he leaned forward in his chair. "I appreciate your concern for my career, Dr. Dudley, but like I said, it's the end of the story. Unless you have valid proof of any wrongdoing on either my part or Dr. Campbell's, as far as I'm concerned this conversation is over. Now, if you don't mind, sir, I have rounds to make."

He stood up and walked around his desk, grabbed his lab coat off the rack and slid it on before opening the door and walking out. He didn't have to look over his shoulder to know Dr. Dudley hadn't appreciated his exit.

"If I didn't know better I'd think you were avoiding me," Isabelle whispered to Jaclyn as they sat up in the viewing room watching surgery being performed.

Jaclyn inwardly cringed. Yes, she had avoided Isabelle, which was why she had been pretending sleep when her best friend had come home last night and why she'd left early this morning long before Isabelle had awakened. The last thing she'd needed was her best friend grilling her about anything. Although she figured Isabelle's questions would come sooner or later, she wanted to put them off as long as possible.

"I'm not avoiding you. Was there something you wanted?" she whispered back.

Isabelle glared at her. "Of course there's something I wanted. I want to know how about your rendezvous with your mystery man. How was it?"

Jaclyn glanced around. Although Isabelle had whispered the question, Jaclyn needed to make sure no one had overheard. She knew how much people enjoyed eavesdropping. Something was going on today, although she wasn't certain what. She had been at work half a day already and hadn't run into Lucien anywhere.

When Jaclyn had left home early this morning she had gone first to the gym to work out and had showered and changed. Lucien's car was not in the regular parking spot when she arrived at the hospital which meant he hadn't arrived yet. That was unusual because typically he was at work at seven every morning.

Dr. Bradshaw had needed an intern to assist him with surgery and she had volunteered. The surgery was supposed to last a couple hours and ended up lasting four. She'd heard from one of the other interns that Lucien had already made his rounds and was in some sort of meeting on another floor.

"Jaclyn?"

Jaclyn met her friend's curious stare. "It was nice. I enjoyed myself."

"I bet, but I'm not letting you off the hook that easily. Why are you still being so secretive about him?"

If only you knew, she wanted to say. Instead she said, "It's complicated but I promise once I work things out to my satisfaction you'll be one of the first to know."

Isabelle looked at her strangely for a moment, as if she was a puzzle she needed to put together real quick.

Then she smiled. "Okay, I'll wait because I know you wouldn't deliberately put me in misery." Isabelle's features went serious when she added, "But you better give me the scoop as soon as you…"

She stopped talking when her gaze latched onto something or someone beyond Jaclyn's shoulder. Then she smiled and whispered, "Don't look now but Dr. De Winter just came in. I swear that man looks hotter each and every time I see him."

Jaclyn's heart started beating furiously in her chest just knowing Lucien was near and she fought the temptation to glance over her shoulder to look at him. Because her back was to the door, turning around would be a sure indication that he'd been the topic of her and Isabelle's conversation.

"You think he's hot, too, don't you?" Isabelle asked when Jaclyn didn't give a response.

Jaclyn shrugged. "He looks all right."

Isabelle frowned and leaned closer to whisper, "Just all right? Girl, you must be blind. Even wearing a lab coat I can tell he has a nice body."

Jaclyn gnawed her bottom lip to keep from saying Isabelle didn't know the half of it. Not only did Lucien have a nice body, but the man also certainly knew how to use it. It didn't take much for her to recall just what that body had done to hers for the past two days.

She was grateful when Isabelle shifted her concentration from Lucien to the date she'd had the night before. From the sound of it, Thurston Reynolds, an attorney Isabelle had met at Cup O'Java Coffeehouse, a hangout for the hospital staff, was a real cutie.

It didn't take long for the doctors to wrap up surgery, and when she stood to leave her gaze automati-

cally went to Lucien. His gaze met hers and she felt a
tingling sensation all the way to her toes. She quickly
made her way to the door, but of course Isabelle had to
make sure they were seen.

"Hello, Dr. De Winter," Isabelle said.

He nodded in greeting. "Dr. Morales. Dr. Campbell."
The expression on his face was serious, more so than
it had been the last two days. She searched his gaze
for some indication of what was wrong. A part of her
knew he was bothered by something because he didn't
even smile.

Her gaze lingered on him while Isabelle thanked him
for recommending her for the pediatric surgery a few
days ago. He didn't even glance over at her. They'd said
it was their secret and he was definitely doing his part
in keeping things undercover.

As she stood there, the only thing she could think
about was that her eyes hadn't played tricks on her for
the past two days. Lucien was as handsome as she remembered. And she could pick up his aroma even from
where she stood.

Moments later Isabelle finally ended the conversation and they turned to leave. Like before, although she
was tempted to do so, she didn't look back.

Lucien stood watching as Jaclyn left the viewing
gallery. It had taken all the control he could muster not
to say "career be damned" and reach out and pull her
into his arms.

He had felt her gaze on him the entire time he'd been
engaged in conversation with Dr. Morales. More than
once he'd been tempted to glance over at her, but doing
so would have been unwise. Perhaps even fatal.

"Hey, you okay?"

He glanced up to see his friend, Dr. Thomas Bradshaw, had entered the room from the other side. "Yeah, I'm fine. What about you? I understand you had a pretty complicated surgery this morning."

"Yes, one of the accident victims took a turn for the worse, and he had to be rushed to surgery before eight this morning. One of your interns assisted and she did a real good job."

Lucien lifted a brow. "Who?"

"Dr. Campbell."

He nodded approvingly. "She's good and catches on easily."

"You're right about that." Dr. Bradshaw checked his watch. "I think I'm going to go and grab lunch. You want me join me?"

"No, they served breakfast at that meeting I attended this morning. I'm good. Besides, I need to make rounds and check on my patients."

"All right, I'll see you later."

Lucien breathed in deeply as he made his way out of the viewing room and down the hospital corridor. He needed to check on the patients still under his care from the multicar pileup. The surgery he'd just seen involved one of them—a married father of two who was still fighting for his life. The surgery had been a success, but the road to recovery for the man would be a grueling one.

As Lucien continued walking, his thoughts shifted to Jaclyn. He hadn't been able to concentrate on the surgery like he should have because he was thinking about her. In his mind he could imagine his nostrils picking up the scent of sex mingled with the most luscious perfume, namely hers.

Today, even with her hair tied back in a ponytail and wearing very little makeup she looked beautiful. Then there had been those few rebellious curls protesting confinement that had fallen in her face. He had been tempted to take his hand and brush them back like he'd done several times these past two days, but doing such a thing would have been a dead giveaway to anyone watching, especially someone as observant as Dr. Morales.

He'd seen the questioning look in Jaclyn's eyes before she had walked off. She had detected something was wrong with his attitude toward her, especially when he'd barely acknowledged her presence just now. He needed to contact her to let her know they were being watched and needed to remain as neutral toward each other as possible.

As he caught the elevator back up to his floor, he thought about Dr. Dudley. The chief of staff would make things hard on both of them if his suspicions were proven right. So right there and then Lucien vowed he'd do whatever he could to make sure that didn't happen.

Jaclyn sighed and rubbed the back of her neck as she looked at the older woman lying in the hospital bed who was trying to be difficult. Even with the shortage of rooms, Nora Allen had insisted on a private one with the view of the Potomac. She had told anyone and everyone who wanted to hear that the famous country singer Jay Allen was her nephew, using that connection to throw her weight around. And it seemed everyone was jumping to her commands in hope they would at least get a glimpse of the singing legend when he flew in to visit his aunt.

Jaclyn glanced down at the woman's chart again. "Ms. Allen, you are scheduled for surgery in the morning. Therefore, your nurse was instructed to remove the polish from your fingernails."

The older woman, whose features showed signs that she was a Botox recipient many times over, gave her a mutinous look. "There's not that much surgery in the world for which I would deliberately take away any armor of beauty I wear."

"Not even when the intent of the surgery is to save your life?" Jaclyn couldn't help but ask.

The woman's glare deepened. "First of all, I can't see anything life threatening about removing a tiny little mass from my stomach. In fact I'm sure there's another way it can be removed without surgery. Can't one of those doctors give me something to drink to shrink it and dissolve it away?"

Jaclyn bit back the response she wanted to give the arrogant woman, whom she'd heard had caused nothing but grief to the staff since being admitted two days ago. That tiny little mass she was referring to had the woman looking nine months pregnant. And from the lab reports, chances were the tumor was cancerous.

"Sorry, Ms. Allen, there's no way around the surgery. It's needed."

"So you say. However, you're nothing but one of those student doctors, so your opinion doesn't mean a thing."

Jaclyn took the insult well. "I understand Dr. Meadows met with you last night."

The woman rolled her eyes. "And I'm supposed to

believe that old man who looked like he had one foot in the grave and should have retired from practicing medicine at anyone's hospital ages ago? I think not."

"Is there a problem, Dr. Campbell?"

Jaclyn didn't have to turn around to see to whom the ultra-sexy voice belonged. But she did so anyway because he'd asked her a question. "No, Dr. De Winter, there's no problem. However, Ms. Allen has decided she doesn't want her nail polish removed for her surgery in the morning."

She glanced back over at the woman. To Jaclyn's surprise, the glare that had covered Nora Allen's face all day had disappeared. In its place was a smile filled with blatant feminine interest. Lucien was probably young enough to be the woman's son, yet she was lying there and all but licking her lips.

"You're a doctor?" the woman asked Lucien as if surprised.

He chuckled and walked farther into the room. Jaclyn felt heat emitting from him when he came to stand beside her. "Yes, I am. I'm Dr. De Winter."

"Well, Dr. De Winter, I must say that you're a cutie. Where have you been hiding the past couple of days?" Nora asked, still licking her lips.

Lucien smiled. "I had two days off."

"Did you enjoy yourself?" the woman then asked.

"Yes, very much so."

Jaclyn felt an immediate rush of sensations when his response reminded her of what he'd done those two days. Desire thudded through her with a force that nearly knocked her off balance.

He moved closer to Nora Allen's hospital bed, took the woman's hand in his and gazed down at her fingers. "Nice color of polish, but you do understand why it needs to come off, don't you?"

Jaclyn stood there thinking that even if the woman did know she would make sure Lucien told her again anyway just to hold his attention. She was proven right when the woman said, "I think so, but I want to hear it directly from you, Doctor."

Lucien smiled, and the way his lips curved would have taken any female's breath away, so Jaclyn could understand why Nora Allen was lying there with her gaze glued to Lucien's lips. They were lips that had kissed Jaclyn more times than she could count over the past two days. Lips belonging to a mouth that had given her earth-shattering orgasms when it had licked her feminine core. A day later and aftershocks were still flitting through her system on occasion.

Like now.

Jaclyn shifted her stance to tighten her legs together when she felt a tingling sensation between them. And she breathed in deeply trying to get her heart rate under control. She knew now was not the time or place to recall such thoughts, but when the object of your desire was standing less than five feet away from you, there was no help for it.

Jaclyn saw Lucien try releasing the woman's hand, but she held tight. A part of her couldn't blame the woman too much for wanting to share his touch. Jaclyn could only sigh in appreciation that she'd been able to share a lot more than that.

"The reason the nail polish has to be removed," Lucien was saying as Ms. Allen seemed to hang on his every word, "is because during surgery your surgeon will need to check your fingertips from time to time to determine your blood flow. We don't want to take any chances where you're concerned. I want you to get the best of care."

The woman beamed. "And I appreciate that, Dr. De Winter. I have no problem with the polish coming off now that it has been explained to me."

Jaclyn shook her head. Things had been explained to the woman before, although the deliverer probably hadn't looked as yummy as Lucien. Her gaze moved from Nora Allen to see that Lucien had turned to look at her. Had he said something? "Yes, Dr. De Winter?"

"You can call Nurse Sampson back in to remove the polish from Ms. Allen's fingernails."

He then moved to leave the room. She waited, hoping that he would say something—some parting remark—or at least glance over her way. And when he kept walking out the door without looking back, her heart dropped in disappointment.

A few hours later Jaclyn was at her locker to get her things to leave work for the day. She pulled out her phone to see if she'd gotten a call from her parents or brother. She saw she'd received a text message...from Lucien.

Her heart began beating rapidly as she read his brief but meaningful text:

Meet me at our park at five.

Our park. She glanced down at her watch. That would give her just enough time to go home and change clothes before meeting him at *their* park. Grabbing the items she needed from her locker she closed it back and then quickly headed toward the elevator to leave the building.

Chapter 11

Lucien glanced down at his watch for the umpteenth time. Never had he been so anxious to see someone. Jaclyn's car was not parked in her usual spot when he'd left the hospital to come directly here, so he hoped she was on her way.

He adjusted his car seat to further accommodate his long legs and leaned back to enjoy the view of the Potomac from his vehicle. His day had started off badly and it didn't help matters when he'd walked into his office and found Dr. Dudley sitting there.

The man's accusations had definitely struck a nerve, not because they were true but because they reminded him of his wrongdoing. By right he should be meeting with Jaclyn to advise her they shouldn't see each other again because the stakes were too high. But that was the last thing he wanted. However, she deserved to know this new development. It would be her decision if she wanted them to end things.

He turned his head and saw Jaclyn arriving, pulling into the parking lot and claiming the spot directly in front of him. She killed the engine and then got out of the car, one leg at a time.

Immediately his body went into arousal mode as his gaze roamed over her when she closed her car door. She had taken the time to go home to change. She was wearing a printed skirt and matching blouse with a cute pair of sandals on her feet. He couldn't help his appreciative perusal of her entire outfit. There was something outright charming about it. His gaze then returned to her face. Against skin the color of rich creamy cocoa, her hazel eyes seemed to sparkle when she saw him. Her hair was down and flowing around her shoulders and she was wearing a touch of makeup. He especially liked the clear gloss she'd added to her lips.

He thought she looked absolutely radiant. And seeing her someplace other than Hopewell made an abundance of sensations roll along his nerve endings. When she reached his car, he unlocked the door on the passenger side and he watched her slide in. He drew in a deep breath when she unintentionally flashed a creamy brown thigh.

Then she flashed him a smile. "Hi."

Instead of responding to her greeting, he leaned over and captured her lips. Something he'd wanted to do each and every time he'd seen her earlier today. His pulse accelerated when she began playing hide and seek with his tongue, and then quickly tired of the game and began sucking on his.

They shouldn't be kissing like this. They were in a parked car in a public place, for heaven's sakes. Thanks to him, they were yet again taking chances. Pulling his mouth away, he drew in a deep breath and leaned back in his seat and momentarily closed his eyes. How could a woman be so tempting?

"That was some greeting, Lucien."

He chuckled. "Did you like it?"

"Most definitely."

"I'm glad." He kept smiling as he started the engine and looked over his shoulder and backed out of the parking spot.

"Where are we going?"

He glanced over at her. "Someplace where we can talk."

Earlier he had dismissed the idea of taking her to his place, especially with Dudley's suspicions and Ms. Tsang being the nosy person that she was. He wouldn't put it past the woman to find out where he lived and do a drive-by. But suddenly a part of him was willing to risk it. He wanted her in his home. Besides, even if Tsang did a drive-by, Jaclyn's car wouldn't be there.

"Sounds serious."

He glanced over at her when he brought the car to a stop at a traffic light. He hesitated a moment and then said, "Thanks to Ms. Tsang, Dr. Dudley suspects something."

She frowned. "Did she tell him she saw us leave together that morning?"

He nodded slowly. "Yes, and he was in my office first thing this morning to ask me about it."

He turned his attention back to the road. However, he didn't miss the nervous gnawing of her bottom lip. "We need to make decisions." He was sure he didn't need to tell her what about.

Because they were already in Georgetown, it didn't take them long to reach his home. When he parked out front, he couldn't miss the smile that touched Jaclyn's face. "You live here?"

"Yes."

"Your house is beautiful. But then I shouldn't be surprised. This is one of oldest sections of D.C. and my favorite."

Lucien was pleased because this was his favorite section of town as well. He loved the tree-lined streets and the row homes that had been renovated in such a way as to retain their historical significance. "Thanks. Hold tight. I'll get the door for you."

He got out and jogged to the other side to open her door. He glanced around. Because of his hours at the hospital he didn't know a lot of his neighbors and vice versa. In a way he liked the privacy. However, every once in a while he would get an invitation to join the neighborhood potluck night at someone's home. He had yet to show up for one of those.

Lucien opened the door for her and she brushed against him when she adjusted the straps of her purse on her shoulder. The fragrance that drifted from her was arousing, reminding him of the scent of her that he'd carried with him since the time they'd spent together.

They walked side by side up his walkway and inside his house. Luckily for him, today had been one of his neat days. The last thing he'd want was for her to think he was a slob.

"Your home is beautiful, Lucien."

A lazy smile touched his lips. "Thanks, but you've told me that already."

She smiled as she turned around to face him. "Yes, but at the time I was talking about the outside. I like the inside as well. Nice furniture."

"Thanks, but I won't take credit for it. When my sister sold me the place, she left everything behind. She had a new job and wanted a new beginning." There was no need to tell her that Lori's heart had gotten broken here and that she needed to leave and start fresh elsewhere, or that even after three years she hadn't returned once.

"Would you like something to drink?" he asked her.

"No, I'm fine. But you're right. We need to talk, although I'm pretty sure you've made up your mind about things."

He lifted a brow. "You think so?"

"Yes."

He absently picked up a large seashell off an end table. He could remember the very day he'd found it on the beach in Jamaica. He'd been fishing when he'd stumbled across it. Later that day he'd received word he'd been accepted to attend college in America on a full scholarship. After that he'd considered the seashell his lucky charm and it had been with him ever since.

He placed the seashell back down to glance over at her. "And what do you think is my decision?"

"To end things between us. You've decided the last thing you really want is to risk your career at Hopewell to become involved with me."

He didn't say anything for a moment, thinking that ending things between them *would* spare both of them any unnecessary risks. But no matter what she thought, there was no way he could do that. There was no way he could turn his back on what he saw as a developing relationship between them. No matter the risks.

He still wasn't sure what this thing between them was, why was there such intensity and why was he willing to risk everything for an unknown. He just knew he had to. "So you think those are my thoughts," he said quietly. "What are yours?"

He watched her, studied her features. And then he skimmed a glance down her body and felt heat simmer through him. *Keep focus, De Winter,* he admonished, returning his gaze back to her face. He saw her nervously gnawing on her bottom lip and was tempted to cross the room to her, pull her into his arms and gnaw on that lip for her. Then he would lick it a few times before capturing it with his. That would be when the real deal would begin.

He'd discovered on those two days they were together that his desire for her was nonstop and all-consuming. At times, like now, it could take his breath away. Since when, he'd been asking himself lately, could a woman leave him breathless? He knew the answer without much thought. Ever since Jaclyn Campbell had come on the scene and been introduced as one of his interns.

And there lay the crux of his problem.

Jaclyn stood there, not only trying to figure out what to say but also how to say it. Bottom line was that she loved him and had from the first. But that wasn't anything she could share with him. This wasn't about love…at least it wasn't with him. It was about desire, need, attraction and yes, of course, sex.

She had accepted that. More than anything she wished they could end up like her parents. But she was realistic enough to know that wouldn't be the case. However, she would risk all to be with him because of the love she had for him even though she didn't expect him to feel the same way. She didn't like seeing him each day and pretending there was no real emotion between them, but it was what it was.

She saw he was waiting for her response. "My thoughts might be a little more complicated," she said honestly.

"And why is that?"

She drew in a deep breath, not surprised he would ask. "You've made me feel things I've never felt before. This attraction between us is almost bigger than life and in a way it's bigger than my common sense. I'm willing to take my chances and any risks right along with it to be with you."

She had deliberately made it seem that what was between them was merely physical, when for her it was a whole lot more. But he didn't have to know that. A girl had her pride.

"Are you sure, Jaclyn?"

"Yes. However, I'd understand if you want to end things," she said, trying not to be distracted by the way he was looking at her from across the room. Her breathing accelerated when he began walking toward her in that sexy stroll that often had all the young single nurses and interns talking.

When he came to a stop in front of her, he reached out and settled his hands at her waist. "This," he said, leaning so close to her that she could feel his breath on her lips, "is what I want. A chance to hold you, kiss you, get to know you, make love to you and claim you as mine. Even if it's behind closed doors. Ending things between us is certainly not what I want. Maybe it's something I should want for both our sakes, but it's not. I'm willing to risk all for this."

And then his mouth captured hers. His tongue mingled with hers and she couldn't help but release all the desire she'd been holding. He'd said he didn't want to end things and this kiss he was giving her let her know he was dead serious. Passion had erupted, sending them both in a tailspin, and she wasn't sure who began taking off whose clothes first.

All she knew was that when he drew back from the kiss, her skirt was in a heap by her feet. Her blouse was unbuttoned and the front clasp of her bra was undone. His belt was out of the loop and his jeans were unzipped. She licked her lips. Had she done that?

Before she could even think about what she had or had not done, she found herself swept off her feet and into his strong arms.

Lucien walked down the hall to his bedroom while telling himself he needed to slow down. He was thinking with the wrong head, the one below his gut and not the one connected to his neck. But at that moment nothing mattered because what he wanted more than anything was to make love to Jaclyn. He needed to feel his manhood ease into her wet warmth. He needed to feel her muscles clamping down on him hard before milking everything out of him. He needed to revel in the thrusts he would make into her body and appreciate the feel of her moving against him, stroke for stroke.

He reached his bedroom in record time. Before placing her in the center of his bed, he glanced down at her and the look he saw in her eyes sent a flash of blazing heat and desire through him. And when she tightened her arms around his neck and drew his mouth down to hers, he knew how it felt to become obsessed with someone.

When she finally broke off the kiss, he sat down on the edge of the bed with her in his arms. "Don't think when you saw me today that I hadn't remembered what we'd shared over the past two days. But I couldn't be certain no one was watching us or listening to our conversation. Dudley's accusations caught me off guard and of course I denied everything. Tsang is all eyes and all ears and we can't give her anything to work with. As much as I wanted to find you today and pull you inside one of those closets with me and get the kiss I've been craving all day, I couldn't. Right now they're just speculating about us. We have to be careful that we don't give them a reason to do more."

Jaclyn nodded slowly. "All right."

Lucien rubbed a hand down his face in frustration. "Even asking you to meet me at the park and bringing you here was taking a big chance. But I needed to see you outside the hospital. Alone. I needed to kiss you, taste you, let you know I remembered our time together because being with you those two days is something I can't and won't forget."

And then he stood and proceeded to finish undressing her. She then watched as he undressed himself as well as put on a condom to keep her protected. He thought it was something totally arousing to see her watch him do it.

He sauntered back over to the bed and reached out to touch her, tracing a path along the sides of her body before letting his fingertips glide over her firm and uplifted breasts. He remembered them well. Could distinctively recall how they tasted on his tongue.

His pulse pounded at the same time his manhood hardened even more. And at that moment, something inside of him that had dimmed when he'd returned her home yesterday flared to life again.

His breath caught at the thought she could do this to him, that she had that much influence. That much power. But then he'd known after their time in Maryland not to underestimate the power of a woman in control. And as far as he was concerned Jaclyn was in control because she constantly dominated his mind as well as his body.

When it came to stroking him into a tizzy of desire, she could do it instantly. Not knowing when they would have another chance to slip away from prying eyes again, he wanted to make this time between them last a while, give them both memories to savor when they were alone, miles apart in their individual beds.

He began tracing a path downward to the center of her and he could tell she was wet for him. A sharp moan escaped her lips the moment he touched her. "You like for me to touch you there, don't you?" he asked huskily, stirring up her sensual scent as he continued to stroke her.

"Yes, I like it," she responded in a voice that sounded strained to his ears.

He smiled. "Do you want me to stop?"

"No, please don't stop," she implored quietly in a sensual plea.

His fingers moved beyond the springy curls to slide a lone finger between her womanly folds. And then he began caressing her there, stroking her while hearing the sharp intake of her breath. He stroked her into deep, heavy passion. He glanced up at her, studied the intensity of her features, heard the moans from deep in her throat.

"Mmm, you okay?" he asked, thinking her arousing scent was getting the best of him. His mouth watered and his manhood throbbed.

When she stared at him through glazed eyes, her pupils were drenched in yearning. "I want you, Lucien."

He decided this time he would let her be in control, do the leading and call the shots. "Then take me, Jaclyn. Any way you want."

Chapter 12

*A*ny way she wanted.

Lucien's words gave Jaclyn pause. Their gazes held for a long moment as ideas flowed through her head and she liked each and every one of them. She took a moment to study the handsome contours of the face staring at her. Every angle, every sensual plane displayed strength.

Her mother once told her that you could tell a lot about a man not only by the strength of his features, but also the strength of his character. She knew the man looking at her had both.

And she knew something else as well. He was someone she could not only enjoy spending time holding conversations with, but also someone with whom she could indulge her fantasies. There wasn't a single night that she didn't go to bed dreaming about him, basically making love to him in her sleep. Some of those sessions were so brazenly hot that she would wake up in the middle of the night sweating. But now she was here with him. They were both totally naked and completely aroused. And he had offered himself to her—any way she wanted.

She leaned up and slowly slid her hand up his thigh while holding his gaze. "That's a nice offer, Lucien."

"Glad you think so," he said, his voice showing signs that he was getting more aroused by the minute and that her hand touching him was only adding to his torture.

"I do. No man has done that before. You're my first. But then I've never wanted a man with the intensity that I want you," she said honestly.

His breath quickened and she knew why. She had taken hold of his thick erection. She could feel it thickening even more in her hands. "Nice piece of work you have here, Lucien."

He chuckled, at least he tried to, but to Jaclyn's way of thinking his chuckle sounded more like a groan. "Glad you like it."

"I do, and do you know what I wonder about each and every time I watch you remove your pants and free yourself in front of me?"

He groaned again and she responded by stroking him with her fingers. "No, I don't know what you wonder about when I do that," he said, his breath sounding ragged.

She lowered her gaze and watched for a second as her hands continued to grip him, to stroke him slowly, and automatically she licked her lips before returning her gaze to his face. "I wonder how you taste. You know my taste and I think it's such an injustice that I don't know yours. And because I can have you any way I want, I want to have you that way." With that said, she then rolled the condom off his erection.

She pushed him back on the bed and straddled him, leaned down to place a kiss on his lips. When he tried deepening the kiss, she pulled back but returned to use the tip of her tongue to lick him along his jaw, throat and neck. She liked the taste of his skin and knew she would enjoy the taste of another part of him as well.

"Do you plan on torturing me?" he asked, his voice almost a hushed and husky whisper.

"Not intentionally," was her response. "I like to think we'll be sharing the pleasure. I'll make sure you enjoy it when I get what I want."

His eyes, she noted, were simmering in desire, the red-hot kind, and she thought that was good. He had shown her what he could do with his mouth; now it was time they both found out what she could do with hers. She'd never done this before to a man—not even to Danny. Once when she'd mentioned wanting to do it, he'd seemed to have gotten turned off by the very idea and she'd never brought it up again. But it seemed Lucien was just the opposite and she was glad for that.

Her tongue left his chin and began moving lower toward his chest. After placing kisses there it moved on down but stopped long enough to prod around his belly button. She thought he had a cute one. She smiled upon feeling the way his abdominal muscles clenched beneath her mouth.

Her mouth was on the move again, going lower, and she lifted her head slightly when she noted his thick erection was stiff and jutting straight up as if waiting for her tongue's visit. Her breath quickened at the sight of something so beautiful. He was hot and he was ready.

So was she.

She leaned forward and slid him into her mouth, liking the taste of him, and it seemed her mouth automatically stretched to accommodate him. Grabbing hold of his hips she began working her mouth on him and she could tell from the sounds he was making that she was stirring pleasure within him of the most intense kind.

She felt his fingers run through her hair and the feel of his doing so aroused her even more with a wantonness that was new to her. "Jaclyn." He called her name in a voice that was throatier than anything she'd ever heard from him. She thought there was something special in savoring the heat of him this way, tasting all of him— every engorged muscle, every thick vein. When his body jerked and he gripped her hair to pull her mouth away from him, she locked her mouth tighter, refusing to let go.

"Jaclyn!"

He came hard as his body exploded. Just knowing what they were sharing sent sensations flooding through her the same way he was flooding her mouth, and she still did not let go. She wanted this as much as he did. And when he didn't have anything left to give, she slowly loosened her grip on his hips.

It was then that he took over and flipped her on her back, quickly donned a condom he grabbed off the nightstand and, with his gaze holding hers, he entered her in a hard thrust. He began moving inside of her in sure, rapid strokes with such precision that she cried out.

But he kept on going, shifting various times and in several ways to provide the ultimate penetration. Their gaze met each time and the look that held them together was another kind of arousing factor that was seeping into their bones.

And then their world exploded and they were tossed

into a sea of ecstasy that had them clinging to each other for life, for pleasure. Jaclyn's heart began beating too rapidly and she had to take long breaths to get it back in sync.

For long moments they lay beside each other with labored breathing. To say Lucien had pushed her over the edge was an understatement. She glanced over at him and couldn't say anything. There was nothing to say. She had gotten what she wanted.

"You hungry?"

His question reminded her she hadn't taken the time to eat anything before rushing off to meet him. "I guess I have worked up an appetite."

He smiled. "Good. Although I don't think it would be wise for us to go out any place, I know my way around the kitchen and would love to prepare something for you here," he said, caressing the line of her jaw.

"You would do that for me?"

He chuckled. "Haven't you caught on yet, Jaclyn Campbell, that I will do anything for you?"

And knowing the risk they were taking by being together, she couldn't help but believe him.

Lucien glanced across the patio table at Jaclyn. He had enjoyed preparing dinner for her and having her help. At first he'd been kind of leery to accept her offer because he remembered the times he and Nikki had tried doing that same thing and failed miserably due to her competitive nature. She'd taken his suggestions as orders and stated more than once she didn't like being bossed around.

It hadn't been that way with Jaclyn. She had taken his suggestions as suggestions and they had worked well together in the kitchen. He bit into the steak he had grilled outside in his backyard and appreciating his pri-

vacy fence more than ever. At least he wasn't looking
over his shoulder wondering who was watching them.

"This place is like a beautiful flower garden. It's so
peaceful out here, Lucien."

He smiled. "I think of this as my peace zone. Lori
planted a lot of the flowers herself. Most of them are
common in Jamaica. During winter the harsh cold usually does them in, but in the spring they miraculously
come up again. All I do is water them and sometimes I
even forget to do that." He chuckled. "Lori's known to
call from time to time and remind me."

"She sounds like a nice person."

He smiled. "She is. You'll like her and I know she's
going to like you." He leaned back in his chair. "I wished
you didn't have to go home tonight." Earlier he had mentioned the possibility of her spending the night, but they
both finally agreed doing so would not be a good idea.

"I wish I could stay, too, but it is what it is."

He knew she was right. They had agreed to continue
their affair and take the risks. After making love they
had redressed and gone into the kitchen to prepare dinner. They had used that time to talk. They knew how
they would have to react toward each other at work.
They also knew even when they met at their secret
hideaways they would need to be careful as well. You
never knew who you might run in to.

So they figured getting away together for out-of-
town trips would be best. They had enjoyed the time
they'd spent together at Wades Point Inn and discussed
the possibility of going back again soon.

"I have a trip to Florida coming up. One of those
medical conventions," he said, missing her already. But
then maybe it would be good to put distance between

them for a week. It was going to be hard to see her each day at work and not let anyone know they were involved. He didn't like the thought of their sneaking around, but there was nothing they could do about it.

"When do you have to leave?" she asked him.

"A couple of weeks." He paused for a moment and then said, "I know things are going to be crazy for us, Jaclyn, but I believe that no matter what, we're going to make it work." *And then what, De Winter? What can you offer her other than more clandestine meetings? More behind-closed-door affairs? Secrets kept hidden? Lies to people you and she cared about?*

"I believe that as well, Lucien."

She didn't say anything else as she continued to eat her food and he couldn't help wondering what she was thinking and how she was feeling. She had agreed to continue their affair and the selfish person in him should have been glad. But the part of him who knew she deserved better than sneaking around with him felt bad about it. And the last thing he wanted was for her to think or even consider the possibility that he was taking advantage of her. Because he wasn't. But would others who knew the situation see it that way? He knew for a fact his sister would not. She was a romantic at heart and would want to read more into his and Jaclyn's relationship than what was there. That was one of the main reasons he hadn't told Lori anything about Jaclyn.

"You're not eating. You're picking at your food."

Lucien glanced up. "I was just thinking."

"If it's on my behalf, please don't."

He wondered if she was a mind reader. "Why not?"

"We've talked. Made decisions. And we know what we want to do and need to do. I'm fine with it."

"But—"

"Please, Lucien," she interrupted by saying. "No buts. Buts can begin leading in regrets and regrets then become doubts, qualms and misgivings. And I don't want that."

He stared at her and she stared at him. "You're sure?" he asked her for the second time that night.

"I'm positive."

They changed the subject to talk about other things. He told her more about his life in Jamaica and she told him about her life in Oakland. When he updated her on the Matthews lawsuit she shared with him her own brother's bout with drugs and subsequent rehabilitation and how he was doing fine now and happily married.

"So you think there's hope for Terrence?" he asked her after taking a sip of his wine. Dusk had settled and he'd already lit the decorative lanterns to light up his backyard. They were sitting on his screened-in patio which was keeping out uninvited mosquitoes. It was a beautiful night and he was enjoying it with a beautiful woman.

"Yes, but first he and his family have to admit he has a problem."

Hours later after she had finished helping him clean up the kitchen, she glanced down at her watch. "It's late and although I left Isabelle a note, she's going to worry. I need to leave now."

He walked over to her. "All right." But neither of them made an effort to move. They just stood there. Then within seconds they were kissing like there would be no tomorrow and he knew at that moment he couldn't fight this. And when he swept her into his arms and headed once again toward the bedroom, he knew from the way she was returning his kiss that she couldn't fight it either.

And at this point in time, he didn't want to.

Chapter 13

"If you happen to be on Corridor C tomorrow, please check on Mrs. Canady. She's such a sweetheart," Isabelle said of one of her patients as she downed the last of her coffee before grabbing the handle of her luggage.

It was Isabelle's parents' thirtieth anniversary and she was returning home to the Bronx for a huge celebration and wouldn't return until late Sunday. "I'm going to miss you," Jaclyn said, walking her to the door.

"Yeah, right. I don't believe you as long as you're keeping the identity of your mystery man hidden from me."

Jaclyn gave her best friend a wry smile. "You're not going to let up with that, are you?"

"No, not until I meet him. You claim he isn't married, so there has to be a reason you're keeping him well hidden."

Moments later Jaclyn stood at the window and watched Isabelle pull off, thinking about her best friend's parting words. She hadn't given a response because she wasn't sure what response she could give.

It had been a little more than three weeks since she had first gone to Lucien's house that day where they'd made love and then later made dinner. Even now she could remember how it felt sitting across from him on his screened patio while jazz music played in the background and lanterns cast a dim light on all the beautiful flowers in his backyard.

For her it had been the most romantic evening and even now she could still get goose bumps remembering how they'd made love again before she'd left. That night had been the beginning of many more to come.

During the day at Hopewell, although it was becoming more and more difficult, they played their parts as Dr. Lucien De Winter and Dr. Jaclyn Campbell—both very much aware they were being watched by Nurse Tsang. On more than one occasion she had caught Dr. Dudley eyeing them suspiciously as well. They made sure they didn't take the same days off and on those occasions when they did, they made sure they left town, far away from accusing eyes.

Although Isabelle teased her sometimes about her "mystery man," for the most part Isabelle didn't ask questions anymore and Jaclyn appreciated her for that. Still, it was getting harder and harder to keep her secret from her best friend; especially those times when Jaclyn would smile for no reason after spending time with him.

And they were spending time together. Sometimes they would travel all the way to Baltimore to meet and stay for the night. One weekend they had gone to New York. Right before he'd left town they'd returned to Wades Point Inn, which had become their favorite secret hideaway. The more time they spent together, the more they wanted to be together. It was getting harder and harder for her when they were apart.

She moved away from the window and headed toward the laundry room to sort out her clothes. Lucien had left a week ago to attend that medical conference in Florida and would be returning sometime in the morning. Although he had called her every night, she still missed him. She couldn't help but do so because they'd begun spending more and more time together.

Jaclyn knew he was still bothered about the situation they were in and the secrets they were keeping from the people they cared about. But they had agreed they had too much at stake to trust anyone right now.

Jaclyn had put in her first load of clothes when she heard the doorbell. Wondering who it could be, she made her way to her front door. She figured after doing her laundry she would curl up with a good book.

She glanced out the peephole in the door and her breath caught. It was Lucien. She quickly opened the door. "Lucien? When did you get back? What are you doing here?"

Instead of giving her answers, he reached out and pulled her into his arms.

How could any man miss the taste of a woman so much? Lucien wondered as he pressed his mouth to hers and then as soon as she parted her lips, he slid his tongue inside her mouth. He needed to kiss her with a desperation he wasn't aware that he could experience.

And just as he knew she would, she reciprocated and her tongue began dueling with his as a rush of heated desire skirted through his system. He'd known to expect that as well. He was convinced he was incapable of ever getting enough of kissing her, of tasting her, of making love to her.

He automatically deepened the kiss and pulled her closer to him. Not only did he need to kiss her, but he also needed to feel her all over. His hands ran down her back before cupping her backside. She felt so damn good in his arms and a part of him wished he would be able to touch her like this forever.

Her heart was beating fast and he felt it, pressed against his own that was pounding just as furiously. Her taste could spur him to do some of the most outrageous things and it wouldn't take much to push him over the edge. He wouldn't hesitate to make love to her right where they stood.

But now he just wanted to take his time to savor what he'd missed. And he definitely missed this, the feel of her soft and compliant lips beneath his that were goading him with an urgency that he felt all the way to his toes, stirring up sensations inside of him. She could ignite his passion in a way it had never been lit before he'd met her.

Moments later when he finally pulled his mouth away, he heard her sigh of both disappointment and pleasure and it mirrored his own. He gently cupped her chin in his hand so their gazes could meet, and he whispered in a deep, husky voice, "I missed you."

He wasn't sure just how much he'd missed her until now. When she had opened the door it seemed as if a weight had been lifted off his shoulders. Although they had talked every night while he'd been away, it hadn't been the same. Even during the day when they were at the hospital, pretending to be no more than associates, at least he would see her. But for an entire week he had to endure the hardship of not seeing her at all. And now that he was here, he didn't want to let her go.

"And I missed you, too, Lucien."

His breath shuddered on her words. The last couple weeks with her had been the best he'd ever shared with a woman. Because they were limited as to where they could go and just what they could do, a lot of their time— in and out of bed—was spent talking. So he felt that he'd gotten to know her pretty well. And everything he had assumed about her in the beginning was true. Besides being devastatingly beautiful, she was smart, kind, a great conversationalist, confident, sharp, gifted...

He could have gone on and on as he looked at her, standing before him with lips that still glistened from his kiss. Last time they were together he'd placed passion marks all over her body. He doubted they were still there, which meant it was time for him to place a few new ones on her.

"Lucien, you took a chance coming here."

Her words reclaimed his attention. "You told me last night that Isabelle would be leaving around noon. It took all I had to wait until then to get over here."

"But—but what about your car parked outside?"

A smile curved his lips. "I didn't drive here. I caught a cab a few blocks from my house. And I had the cabbie put me off one street over from here."

She shook her head as if she was utterly amazed. "You went through all that trouble?"

He reached out to snag her around the waist and brought her closer to him. "Yes, I missed you and had to see you. I hadn't planned on coming home until tomorrow, but when we finished early, I got an early flight back."

He paused a moment and then asked, "Isabelle did leave, right?"

She chuckled. "If she hadn't, you'd be in a world of trouble. What were you thinking?" she admonished.

"I told you. I was thinking of seeing you and being with you." And then he leaned over and captured her lips.

When Jaclyn tried to ease out of bed in the wee hours of the next morning, an arm reached out and grabbed her around the waist. Lucien then shifted on his back. "Where do you think you're going?"

She chuckled as she glanced over at him thinking the shadow on his chin made him appear sexier. "Some of us have to go to work today. Go back to sleep."

He reached out and grabbed the back of her neck to bring her face close to his for a kiss. He finally released her mouth and smiled at her. "You'll come see me before you leave?" he asked in a deep, husky voice as he shifted to his side.

"Only if you promise to keep your hands to yourself," she said, trying to regain her equilibrium. His kisses could do that to her. "If you don't, I'll be late," she added.

By the time she had come out of the bathroom after showering, she saw he had drifted back to sleep. Not wanting to wake him, she left a note letting him know she would be home today around six. She was glad she and Isabelle had stocked the refrigerator that week. She knew that Lucien would wake up hungry.

Jaclyn knew something was going on the moment she arrived on her floor at Hopewell. There was a buzz in the air and several doctors and nurses were in groups talking. She hoped there wasn't any new negative development in the Matthews lawsuit.

She saw Tamara St. John and quickly walked up to her. "Hey, what's going on?"

Her fellow intern pulled her off to a private spot. "I got here an hour ago and the hospital was swarming with security. It seems someone has hacked into the hospital's fertility clinic database to get the sperm bank records."

Jaclyn lifted her brow. "Why would someone do something like that?"

Tamara shrugged. "Who knows? But I understand the real concern is that back in the day a number of the med students and interns hard up for money sold their sperm to the clinic. I guess those guys are now wondering if they will be exposed as some baby's daddy."

A short while later Jaclyn was heading to Corridor C to check on Mrs. Canady like she promised Isabelle when she encountered Ms. Tsang coming out of a patient's room. She hadn't seen the nurse for the past couple of days and she hadn't been missed.

"Ms. Tsang," she greeted in a formal voice.

"Dr. Campbell." The woman paused and then said, "Is Dr. De Winter back from his medical seminar? The patient in C5, Nora Allen, has been asking about him. It seems he made somewhat of an impression on her."

Jaclyn lifted what came across as a nonchalant brow. "Really? And why would you be asking me about Dr. De Winter?"

A smirk appeared on Ms. Tsang. "He's your boss."

"And Dr. Dudley is yours. Do you know where he is twenty-four seven?" Her question actually made the woman blush. Jaclyn found that interesting.

"No, of course not. I just assumed..."

"And what did you assume, Ms. Tsang?" she asked, her annoyance with the woman clearly evident.

"Nothing."

The woman quickly walked off and Jaclyn watched her go while easing out a deep breath. Kayla Tsang was determined to unravel something on her and Lucien, but neither of them intended to give her the chance.

As she kept walking toward Mrs. Canady's room she couldn't help but think about what Tamara had told her. Lucien had been an intern here some years ago. Was he one of those men who had sold their sperm to the fertility clinic? Was there a woman out there who'd had his baby?

Jaclyn felt a sudden jab of jealousy at the very thought and tried to shrug it off but couldn't do so easily. She knew that what he did before he met her was none of her business. In truth, what he did now was no business of hers, either. Her only comfort was that he had labeled theirs an exclusive relationship. Secret but exclusive.

She smiled when she thought how unknowingly Ms. Tsang had come to the truth. Not only did Jaclyn know Lucien's whereabouts, but he'd also been in her bed all night. She didn't want to think about what would happen if Ms. Tsang or anyone else found out about that. She guessed Ms. Allen would just have to pine for Lucien a couple more days because he wouldn't be returning to work until then. She smiled at the thought of what Lucien would be doing on his off days.

"You have such a pretty smile, Dr. Campbell."

She inwardly cringed when she glanced up and saw Dr. Dudley. "Thanks, Dr. Dudley."

She kept walking. There was something about him that made her uneasy. Maybe it was the way he looked at her with lust-filled eyes. And the man was married, for heaven's sakes. Some people, especially men who were evidently going through some sort of midlife crisis, never ceased to amaze her.

* * *

Lucien hung up his cell phone after talking to Thomas Bradshaw who'd called to inform him that someone had hacked the fertility database. Thomas was one of the men who'd once donated sperm and like others was concerned the information might get in the wrong hands. Fortunately, Lucien was not worried. Although a lot of interns had gotten together and gone over to the clinic that day, he hadn't been one of them. The thought of his child out there without his knowing the mother hadn't sat well with him. Possibly because he had thought of his own predicament while growing up without a father in his life.

Thomas was hoping security found the culprit. Lucien was certain most of the men who'd donated sperm wanted to remain anonymous and he hoped that continued to be the case. He didn't want to imagine the purpose of someone obtaining those records.

He walked over to the oven to check what he had cooking. Jaclyn would be surprised when she got home to discover he had dinner already prepared for them. He glanced around thinking he really liked her kitchen. It wasn't as large as his, but he liked how she had things arranged, all within easy reach.

By the time she got home she would have put in at least twelve hours today. He of all people knew how hectic an intern's schedule was, but he worried about her. He glanced up when he heard the key in the door and moved quickly to be there when she opened it.

"Hi."

"Hi, yourself," she said, entering the house and closing the door behind her.

That was all she was given a chance to say when he

pulled her into his arms. "Dinner's ready," he said, after releasing her mouth.

She lifted a brow. "You cooked?"

He chuckled. "You asked like you've forgotten that I can."

"No, I was wondering why you did. I figured you'd want to rest. We could have ordered out."

"But I wanted to do that for you. You've put in a long day. Interns' hours are too long."

She grinned. "You're the boss. Change it."

He gazed at her thoughtfully. "I would if I could, believe me. It's hospital policy to cram all your training into two years."

"I understand. I was just teasing," she said, taking her purse straps off her shoulder and placing the bag on the table. "Give me a minute to freshen up and I'll be back. I'm hungry."

Then she said, "Ms. Tsang asked about you."

He frowned. "Any reason she did that?"

"Just her typical nosy self. I think she was hoping that I'd slip up and say something I shouldn't. And Nora Allen in C5 has been asking about you."

"The patient who didn't want her nail polish removed?"

Jaclyn smiled. "Yes, she's the one. She's back in the hospital. I think you made quite an impression on her."

He slowly walked over to her. "And what if I said that you made an impression on me?"

She lifted her mouth to his after saying, "Mmm, that sounds rather nice."

He then lowered his mouth to kiss her.

"As usual this is delicious, Lucien," Jaclyn said as she took another forkful of mashed potatoes. Neither hers nor Isabelle's ever got this fluffy.

"Thanks. Anything interesting going on at Hopewell?"

"Yes, I forgot to mention that someone hacked into the fertility clinic database. I understand a number of doctors who were interns at the time were donors. They're beginning to freak out at the thought that someone might come after them as their baby's daddy."

She paused and then looked across the table at him curiously. "Anything you want to tell me?" Jaclyn hoped she didn't sound like a jealous woman, although she inwardly felt like one now.

He shook his head. "No, because I wasn't one of those interns. I didn't ever want a child who didn't know I was its father."

Jaclyn released a deep breath of relief. She appreciated how he valued the thought that a child deserved both parents and she knew why he did so. He'd told her that he grew up never knowing his father.

"Earlier you mentioned my hours at Hopewell, so I might as well tell you I found out that all the interns' hours are increasing over the next few weeks."

He frowned. "I didn't approve that."

"Dudley did. And from what I understand it was Nurse Tsang's suggestion. She thinks we have too much of a life and all of us think she needs to get one."

He got up from the table with his plate. "I don't agree with any of you working additional hours," he said with anger in his voice. "You work enough hours already. I intend to let Dudley know how I feel when I return to work in a few days."

"What if he starts wondering why you give a hoot about how many hours an intern works? He might try putting two and two together, Lucien. Thanks to Nurse Tsang, he already suspects something is going on with us."

His frown deepened. "They can't prove a thing."

Jaclyn got up from the table thinking he was right. They couldn't prove a thing...unless they saw all those passion marks under her scrubs.

"Did I tell you how much I like your bed?" he asked, breaking into her thoughts.

"I figured you did." Last night was the first time he'd slept in her bed and she had slept like a baby knowing he was there. At least she had slept like a baby when he hadn't been making love to her.

"How long will Isabelle be gone?"

"Till Sunday night." She smiled across the table at him. "That means you're free to stay here until then... and especially because you like my bed so much."

He chuckled. "Thanks for the invite. I definitely plan to take you up on it. I want to hang around and pamper you on my days off, assuming an emergency at Hopewell doesn't call me in."

"When you do return to work it's pretend time for us again," she said, trying not to sound as disappointed as she felt.

"Yes, it's back to pretending again."

As she carried her plate over to the sink, she thought that for them the pretense would probably never end.

Chapter 14

"Not so fast," Lucien ordered in a teasing voice.

He couldn't hide his chuckle while watching Jaclyn quickly rip into what had been a nicely wrapped gift. Her lips then spread into a smile and she glanced up at him.

"This is for me?" she asked with awe in her voice when she stared back down at the diamond solitaire necklace.

He laughed. "Who else would it be for? We've been seeing each other for a month today and I wanted to give you something."

She glanced back up at him. "But when did you have time to go shopping for anything?"

He knew why she was asking. Since returning from the medical seminar in Florida two day ago, other than the time he'd caught a cab back to his place to gather a few of his belongings, he'd been camped at her place.

If anyone had the inclination to be nosy and ride by his place, his car was parked out front and a timer would turn his lights on and off at certain times to make it appear he was there. But where he had been was here spending every possible moment with Jaclyn when she wasn't at the hospital.

"I bought it while I was in Florida. There was a jewelry store in the hotel. I saw the necklace in the window one day, liked it and thought it should be worn around your neck."

What he hadn't told her was that it had been his third day there and he'd been thinking of her, missing her like crazy. Talking to her every night hadn't been enough.

"That was so sweet of you," she said softly. "I'll cherish it forever and it will always remind me of you and our time together."

His lips thinned. Why did she make it sound like a parting gift?

"Will you fasten it around my neck?" she asked, too busy taking the necklace out the box to notice the scowl on his face. Maybe that was a good thing because he couldn't explain the reason for it.

Honestly, De Winter, do you really expect her to subject herself to a secret affair forever? It will be just a matter of time before she decides she wants better. She wants more. And rightly so because it will be just what she deserves.

She turned and presented her back to him and tilted her head to the side while pushing her hair out of the way. After fastening the necklace, he couldn't resist kissing her there.

"What are you doing?" she asked over her shoulder.

"Tasting you," he said, leaning down and kissing that spot on her neck again while tugging her back against him.

To balance their bodies he braced his legs apart which only cradled her hips into the confines of the lower part of his body. He sucked in a deep breath when her bottom brushed against his zipper. That was all that was needed to make his erection start throbbing.

"Stay still," he warned, tightening his arms around her.

"Why?"

"Because I said so," he answered. What he didn't tell her was that he liked the feel of his erection nudging her backside. His jeans and her shorts weren't a barrier from the heat they were generating.

"Lucien," she said in that voice that did crazy things to his pulse.

"Yes?"

She turned around in his arms to face him. "I'm going to miss you when you return to your place later."

Her words reminded him that he would have to leave today because Isabelle would be returning tonight. To play it safe he had decided to leave not long after lunch. "I'm going to miss you, too. But you know where I live. And you're welcome over at any time."

After dark. By taxi. In disguise. He then felt anger that those were the only choices he could offer her when she deserved so damn much more. She needed to be involved with someone who could take her places, be seen out in public with her.

"What's wrong, Lucien? Why the frown?"

His gaze lingered on hers a moment before he simply said, "You deserve more."

She chuckled. "More? You don't think this diamond is big enough or something?"

She was trying to make light of the situation and they both knew it. "I'm serious, Jaclyn."

"Yes," she murmured softly. "I know you are and that's what makes you truly special. I told you a month ago today my decision about us, Lucien. Nothing has changed."

His heart began beating hard in his chest. That's where she was wrong. Something had changed, but he wasn't certain what. All he knew was that whenever he would dwell on the state of their relationship he would feel as if he was drowning in guilt. He would feel something else, too. Emotions he couldn't put a name to just yet. Then again, maybe he could and he was just afraid to do so. Those thoughts made him remember the conversation he'd had with Dr. Waverly one night in Florida over a few beers. Dr. Waverly was the new chief of staff over on the E.R.

"Lucien?"

Jaclyn recaptured his attention. "Yes?"

"You've gotten quiet on me," she said softly.

He regarded her for a moment and then said, "Didn't mean to." His lips quirked into a smile. "I guess I'm just going to have to make up for wasted time."

He lowered his head and his body shivered inside and out the moment their lips touched. And then it was on when he proceeded to kiss her, taking her mouth with searing intensity. He had enjoyed kissing her from the first and now four weeks later that hadn't changed. The power in her kiss could overwhelm his senses, make every cell in his body respond and every muscle in his body quiver.

She was returning his kiss in such a provocative fashion that he felt his erection pressing hard against his zipper. It wouldn't take much to take her here, standing up. Or over there on the sofa, lying down. Or on the kitchen counter kneeling before her while he—

"Ahem."

The loud clearing of someone's throat had them jumping apart. Too late. They turned and found Isabelle standing there with a combination of shock and humor on her face.

And then with a smirky grin on her face, she said, "Mmm, maybe it wasn't a good idea for me to catch a ride and come home early after all."

A hour or so later Jaclyn leaned back against the front door after seeing Lucien out of it to catch a cab. After her surprise appearance, Isabelle had beat a hasty retreat to her bedroom, pulling her luggage behind her, and hadn't been seen or heard from since.

Jaclyn knew her friend was giving herself time to absorb what she'd walked in on and what it all meant. Jaclyn could just imagine what Isabelle was thinking about now. She pushed away from the door deciding now was the time to find out.

The two bedrooms were separated by attached baths, both off halls from the living room in different directions. It was a good setup for privacy. That gave Isabelle her own space while Jaclyn had hers.

She knocked on Isabelle's bedroom door. "Come in."

Jaclyn squared her shoulders, opened the door and stepped in. Isabelle was unpacking and from the looks of things, she'd been shopping while in New York. "I owe you an explanation," she said quietly, not sure where she should begin.

Isabelle glanced over at her but didn't stop unpacking. "No, you don't. What you do is your business. I just hope the two of you realize what can happen if you're caught," she said point blank.

Isabelle then threw a shopping bag on the bed and gazed at her, drawing her in the full scope of her eyes. "For crying out loud, Jaclyn. Your mystery man is Dr. De Winter. He's not only your boss but he's also mine."

"I know. That's why I didn't want to tell you. I didn't want you involved in our deceit. And you would never have found out if you hadn't come home early."

Isabelle lifted a chin and crossed her arms over her chest. "And just how long did the two of you plan to keep it a secret? Until some big executive at Hopewell decides that the nomfraternization policy isn't needed anymore? You and I know that won't happen, so why are you risking it all, Jaclyn?"

Jaclyn breathed in deeply and met her friend's confused gaze as she said, "Because I love him. I know it might sound crazy, but I had fallen in love with him the moment I saw him my first day at Hopewell. Even before he opened his mouth to say a single word."

She could tell by the weird look Isabelle was giving her that her best friend found that hard to believe. "Does he love you?" Isabelle wanted to know.

Jaclyn turned and glanced out the window. She tried to deflect the magnitude of Isabelle's question by thinking that her best friend had a better view out her window than she did.

"Jaclyn, ignoring me won't work. Does he feel the same way about you that you do him?"

Jaclyn turned back to Isabelle. "I'm not sure. He's never said he did, but then I've never told him how I feel, either. Right now we're just enjoying each other's company."

"And is his company—although you can't convince me it's not more than that from the looks of that kiss—worth it? Is it worth being kicked out of your internship program because you want to play doctor, literally?"

"Yes, it's worth it because I believe my love is worth it, regardless of how he feels about me. And now you know. But I'm asking something that I probably don't have a right to do and that is for you to keep our secret as well. Asking you to do so makes you a part of our deceit."

Isabelle waved off her words. "Hey, although I wish your mystery man was someone else, my lips are sealed—you know that. I promise to keep your secret."

Jaclyn drew in a deep, relieved breath. "Thanks, and just so you know, Nurse Tsang suspects something. She saw us leave one morning together and has put a bug in Dr. Dudley's ear. Lucien and I have been careful."

Isabelle frowned. "Miss Thang needs to go somewhere and sit down. That woman has nothing to do with her time other than to go around gossiping. I would love to get something on her so she could see just how it feels."

Jaclyn nodded her head. "Stand in line. I don't think there's an intern in our program who wouldn't like to get something on her, especially after she suggested that Dr. Dudley give us more hours."

Jaclyn then told Isabelle about the increase in their work hours starting tomorrow.

"Are they crazy?" Isabelle all but screamed. "We work too many hours now. I didn't know how tired I was until I slept that entire first day at my parents' home. I was totally drained."

Jaclyn knew exactly how she felt. "Well, just be prepared." She turned to leave the room.

"Jaclyn?"

She turned back around. "Yes?"

"I didn't have a clue about you and De Winter. How have the two of you managed to keep it a secret?"

Jaclyn thought about her question as well as what her response would be. Then she said, "Because we wanted to be together and were determined to make it work. It hasn't been easy, trust me."

"I can imagine. I doubt I could pull off something like that."

Jaclyn gave her a warm smile. "Yes, you could if your heart was at stake. And trust me when I say my heart is so full of love for him that I can't imagine a time when we won't be together, although such a time will eventually come. That's why I need to absorb all I can get now."

She chuckled quietly and added, "Whoever said that love will make you do foolish things knew exactly what they were talking about."

Chapter 15

Lucien pretended to be reading a patient's chart when he saw Jaclyn out of the corner of his eye. Anger twitched in his jaw. She, along with all the rest of the interns, had been working extra long hours. They were all tired and he knew it.

He had tried reasoning with Dudley and the man just wouldn't discuss it, saying the interns needed to prove they could handle things under extreme pressure. Lucien had tried to get him to see that an extremely tired intern was just an accident waiting to happen. He could just imagine one of them slipping up and giving a patient the wrong medicine. The thought of that happening gave him the shivers.

He placed the chart in the rack and glanced over at Jaclyn. She was talking to a floor nurse and he could tell by the lines around her eyes that she was tired. She had pulled a sixteen-hour shift yesterday and a twelve-hour one the day before. On top of that he knew she'd been battling flu-like symptoms for a week.

"Is there anything wrong, Dr. De Winter?"

He glanced over at Nurse Tsang. "What makes you think something is wrong?"

She gave him a rueful smile. "Because you're just standing there staring at Dr. Campbell."

Damn! Had he been that obvious? "I'm waiting for her to finish talking with Nurse Atwater. I need to ask her a question about one of her patients," he lied.

"Oh, I see."

Lucien frowned. The woman saw too much. When Nurse Atwater walked off, he began walking toward Jaclyn. They had been busted a couple of weeks ago when Isabelle had walked in on them. According to Jaclyn, her roommate would keep their secret and he was grateful for that. The next time he'd seen Isabelle he had expected her to pull him to the side and read him the riot act for what she saw as a sleazy backdoor affair, but she hadn't. In fact, if he hadn't known for certain the woman had walked in on him and Jaclyn kissing, he would wonder if he'd imagined it. Not only had she not said anything, but she also hadn't acted any differently toward him.

"Dr. Campbell, wait up," he said when he saw Jaclyn about to get in the elevator.

She turned toward him and his heart almost dropped. Not only did she look extremely tired, but it was also evident she wasn't feeling well. Why was she doing this to herself? "Yes, Dr. De Winter?"

"It's obvious, Dr. Campbell, that you aren't feeling well. I think you need to take a few days off."

She blinked. "I can't take time off. I just caught a bug. I'll shake it in a few days."

"I'm not taking any chances, Dr. Campbell," he said in a firm voice. "It's not good for you to be around the patients. I'm sending you home."

She glared at him and lowered her voice. "Really, Lucien, that's not necessary," she whispered.

"I think it is, Doctor. I want you to leave here immediately." He frowned. "And why are you holding your stomach?"

"No reason," she all but snapped before turning to walk away.

Lucien watched her go and when he turned around he saw Kayla Tsang standing at her station staring at him. He then asked her the same question he had asked earlier. "Is something wrong, Ms. Tsang?"

A smirk appeared on her face. "No, Dr. De Winter, there's not anything wrong."

"I can't believe he's sending me home," Jaclyn said angrily to Isabelle as she walked toward the break room to grab a snack out of the vending machine.

"Hey, don't look for any sympathy here," Isabelle was saying. "I told you this morning that I thought you needed to stay home and get some rest."

Jaclyn rolled her eyes. "Why do I need rest?"

"Because you're sick. And I agree with Dr. De Winter, you don't need to be around patients."

Jaclyn glared at her. "Whose side are you on?"

Isabelle smiled. "Yours. When you're well. Otherwise I'm in with Dr. De Winter. You need to take better care of yourself. I heard you moving around last night with stomach pains. You need to get checked out."

"I'm fine. I'm just experiencing flu-like symptoms."

Isabelle rolled her eyes. "I can't stand a doctor who tries to diagnose their own condition."

"Whatever."

Jaclyn was about to step in the elevator when suddenly she felt dizzy at the same time a sharp pain ripped through her stomach. She heard Isabelle call her name when everything began turning black and she felt herself tumbling to the floor.

Lucien had just left a patient when he got paged. He went to the nearest phone, punched in a couple of numbers and said crisply, "This is Dr. De Winter."

"And this is Dr. Isabelle Morales. Jac… I mean Dr. Campbell…just passed out."

Lucien's heart dropped. He forced himself to stay calm. "Where is she?"

"She wouldn't go down to the E.R. like I suggested, but she did give in and agreed to be seen by a doctor on staff."

He was moving although he wasn't certain which direction he should go. "What floor?"

"The fifth."

"I'm on my way." And not caring who saw him, he all but took off running toward the nearest elevator.

"Acute appendicitis?" Jaclyn said, staring at Dr. Bradshaw like he had two heads. "There must be some mistake. I have the flu."

Dr. Bradshaw shook his head. "Trust me, I know what I'm taking about. You might have flu-like symptoms, but you don't have the flu, Dr. Campbell. You have acute appendicitis and it needs to come out immediately."

"But—"

"No buts. You're a doctor, so you know the dangers of a ruptured appendix."

Jaclyn began nibbling on her bottom lip. Yes, she did know and that's what scared her. Now the shoe was basically on the other foot. Treating patients was one thing, but becoming the patient was another. "I need to think about this."

Dr. Bradshaw glanced up from filling in his chart. "There's nothing to think about. You need the surgery immediately."

Jaclyn opened her mouth to say something, but suddenly the curtain was pushed aside and she literally caught her breath when Lucien walked in. And she could tell from the look on his face he was both angry and worried.

"Jaclyn, are you all right? What happened?" he asked quickly moving toward her and pulling her into his arms.

She went willingly and gazed over his shoulder and met the surprised look in Dr. Bradshaw's gaze. She immediately knew her and Lucien's cover had gotten blown to smithereens. Lucien then touched her chin to bring her gaze back to him and placed a kiss on her lips. "Sweetheart, what happened?"

Before she could say anything, Dr. Bradshaw cleared his throat. "Hey, you two, remember me?" he asked teasingly. Then he added in that same teasing voice, "And remember the hospital's nonfraternization policy? So if I were you, Lucien, I would shield my reaction to Dr. Campbell's health issue so it won't be apparent what the two of you have been up to."

Lucien glanced over at his close friend. "Go to hell, Thomas."

"Yeah," Dr. Bradshaw said chuckling. "But not until Dr. Campbell is doing better. She needs surgery."

"Surgery?" Lucien echoed.

"Yes," Dr. Bradshaw said. "She has acute appendicitis and her appendix needs to come out immediately. She's being difficult."

Lucien raised a brow. "Difficult in what way?"

Dr. Bradshaw smiled at Jaclyn and ignoring her frown he returned his gaze to Lucien. "When I told her she needed the surgery she said she needed to think about it."

Jaclyn's frown deepened. The two men were conversing like she wasn't there. It was her medical issues they were discussing. "Excuse me, Dr. Bradshaw, but isn't there a privacy law prohibiting discussing a patient's medical situation with a nonfamily member?"

"That was before Lucien kissed you," the man replied seriously, all manner of teasing gone from his voice. "I know Lucien. He's a close friend who loves his job as much as I love mine. And for him to risk that by breaking a hospital policy tells me a lot."

The man paused a moment and added, "And it tells me a lot on your behalf as well, Dr. Campbell, because I'm sure your career is important to you, too. But the most important issue at the moment is your health. Like I said, you need surgery immediately."

Jaclyn nervously nibbled on her bottom lip and she glanced over at Lucien. Before she could say anything, the curtain was pulled aside once again. Dr. Dudley walked in. He glanced at everyone in the small room before looking back at her. Jaclyn was certain he'd taken note of how close Lucien was standing to her bed.

"I understand one of our interns passed out, Dr. De Winter," he stated in an authoritative voice.

Lucien took a step back. "Yes, and I needed to see how she was doing," he said as if to explain his reason for being there.

Dr. Dudley glanced over to Dr. Bradshaw. "What's the diagnosis?"

"Acute appendicitis. She needs surgery immediately."

Dr. Dudley nodded. "Then let's get it scheduled," he said as if Jaclyn's decision wasn't needed.

He then glanced over at Lucien. "Don't you have a conference call with that attorney they hired to handle the Matthews lawsuit in less than ten minutes, Dr. De Winter?"

Before Lucien could blow their cover, Jaclyn quickly spoke up. "Thanks for dropping by to check on me, Dr. De Winter. I really appreciate it."

Lucien turned to her and she hoped he could read the plea in her gaze. He did. Without saying anything, he nodded and then left the room.

Lucien hung up his phone, grateful the conference call had lasted only ten minutes. And more grateful that the attorney had only a few questions to ask him because his mind hadn't been able to function worth a damn.

He stood and began pacing the room. He knew he needed to pull himself together, but how was he expected to do something like that when the person he cared about, the one woman who had come to mean the world to him, could be in danger?

It didn't take much to remember nine-year-old Brittney Adams whose parents had brought her to the hospital last year, hours too late. Her appendix had ruptured and she had died on the operating table. He had been the one to deliver the news to her parents.

The thought of losing Jaclyn that way made him shiver from the inside out and he didn't have to wonder why he felt that way. He loved her. For a while he'd suspected he had but hadn't wanted to own up to it because he'd known what that meant: choosing the woman he loved over the position he had worked so hard to achieve.

But the choice had been taken out of his hands. It was technically a no-brainer. Jaclyn meant more to him than his career. He wanted her no matter the professional cost. He was tired of their sneaking around for stolen moments to be together. She deserved more. They deserved more.

And a part of him refused to believe she hadn't fallen in love with him, as well. No woman could give herself to a man the way she gave herself to him without love.

He crossed his office to the window and looked out. But it seemed he could have it all thanks to that conversation he'd had with Dr. Waverly back in Florida. The man had been so impressed with the way Lucien had handled the emergency involving the multicar accident that he had told him if Lucien ever wanted to switch departments he'd love for Lucien to come over to E.R. and take the position of head doctor.

Lucien had been thinking seriously about accepting the man's offer. No longer being Jaclyn's boss meant they wouldn't have to sneak around anymore. Without wasting any time he moved back to his desk and picked up the phone to make a call.

"This is Dr. Waverly."

"Yes, Dr. Waverly, this is Dr. De Winter. Is that offer you made in Florida still out there?"

"Most definitely. I'd love to have you as a part of my E.R. team. I've seen you in action. I can't think of anyone else I'd want as my head doctor."

"Thank you and I accept your offer. How soon can we make the change?" Lucien asked. He preferred working with Dr. Waverly than Dr. Dudley. It was time for him to break camp and move on.

"I'll put in the paperwork today. Are there any special requests?" Dr. Waverly chuckled. "Now is the time to make them."

"I have two weeks off around the holidays this year. I promised my grandmother I'd be home in Jamaica for Christmas."

"That's not a problem. I'll approve those days off for you now as part of your lateral-move package."

"Thank you," Lucien said.

"No, I want to thank *you*. And I'm looking forward to working with you."

After he hung up the phone Lucien glanced at his watch. Thomas had texted him earlier to say Jaclyn's surgery was scheduled for three, which gave him ten minutes to get to the surgical floor. He planned to watch from the gallery and hoped and prayed nothing went wrong. He loved her and knew there was no way he could go on without her.

"How is she, Thomas?"

Thomas Bradshaw smiled at Lucien as he exited the O.R. "Hey, man, I know you were watching, but I'll answer anyway." All amusement was removed from his features when he added, "She was lucky. Had we waited any longer her appendix would have ruptured. Passing out was in her favor. She had to have been in tremendous pain and working all those hours didn't help. Her body was extremely exhausted. I'm going to give her a generous amount of recovery time away from here. She needs it."

Thomas then looked at him curiously. "What about your relationship with her? You can't keep taking chances. If Dudley finds out you can kiss your career here goodbye."

Thomas glanced around to make sure they weren't overheard when he added, "Personally, I think although you did the right thing in firing Terrence Matthews, Dudley is holding it against you, anyway. Especially in light of all the problems the Matthewses are causing the hospital. I know how much your career means to you, so I hope you have a plan B."

"I have. I've accepted the position as head doctor of E.R."

Thomas smiled. "Hey, that's wonderful and Dudley won't go up against Waverly, especially when the hospital moved mountains and courted him like the dickens to bring him here. Obtaining someone with the credentials of Waverly is the only stellar thing Dudley has done lately, and he knows it. Trust me, he'd want to keep Waverly happy."

Lucien nodded slowly. "When can I see Jaclyn?"

"In a few. They're wheeling her to recovery now." Thomas paused and then asked quietly, "You love her, don't you?"

Lucien pulled in a deep breath. "Yes, with all my heart. I didn't realize just how much until the thought of losing her became a reality. Then I knew I could no longer sneak around with her. She deserves more. We both do."

Jaclyn slowly opened her eyes while several jumbled images floated through her mind. She was still at the hospital, but she wasn't standing up and moving around; she was the one lying flat on her back in a hospital bed. She was now the patient. With that realization she felt the pain which made her remember why she was there. Acute appendicitis… Surgery…

"You're awake."

She blinked at the sound of the deep, husky voice and shifted her gaze to her side. Lucien was sitting beside her bed. She opened her mouth to speak, to ask what was he doing there. He would blow their cover if he didn't leave. There was no reason he should be sitting at her bedside and holding her hand. What if Dr. Dudley or Nurse Tsang walked in?

"Shh, don't try to talk, sweetheart. Just listen to what I have to say."

He paused a moment and then said quietly, "I love you. I think I've known it for some time but wasn't sure what to do about it, how to go about handling the situation we'd boxed ourselves in with the hospital's nonfraternization policy. But none of that matters now. Your medical issue made me realize it doesn't matter. It's time we live our lives for ourselves and no one else. And I believe you love me, too. Thanks to you there's no way I can think otherwise."

Jaclyn felt the tears spill out of her eyes. Lucien loved her! She couldn't speak, so she moved her lips to say, "I love you, too."

He smiled. "And don't worry about our careers. We'll be able to work things out and have it all."

Jaclyn didn't understand what he meant and wanted to ask him, but she felt sleepy all over again and could barely keep her eyes open.

"Go back to sleep, Jaclyn. You need your rest. I'll still be here when you wake up. I'm not going anywhere."

Jaclyn held his gaze. And looking into his eyes and seeing the love so blatantly shining in them was the last thing she remembered before sleep took over once again.

Just like he'd promised her, Lucien was still there at her bedside a few hours later when he saw Jaclyn open her eyes. He had gotten off work more than five hours ago but had refused to leave her side. Isabelle had dropped by several times and so had several other interns. No one questioned his reason for being there, although he'd seen some curious glances. He was certain there would be some buzz about it. Both Dr. Dudley and Nurse Tsang had come by, although he doubted it was out of concern and not out of just plain nosiness.

"Welcome back," he said, gazing over at Jaclyn. "Feeling better?"

"Yes."

He was glad she had her voice back although it sounded kind of raspy. "Is there anything you want? Anything I can get you or do to make you more comfortable?"

"Lucien, what are you doing here?"

By asking him that question he wondered if she had remembered their prior conversation. He decided to jog her memory. "I'm here because I love you and I can't imagine being any place else."

He saw the frown settle on her beautiful face and knew she was remembering. Moments later she said, "But what about our careers? I love you too, but—"

"I have it all taken care of. In a few weeks I will become head doctor in E.R."

"You're changing departments?"

"Yes. That means I will no longer be your boss. And as for your remaining under Dudley, he is smart enough not to hassle you because he has no proof of anything between us before today. I'm sure he and Nurse Tsang have put two and two together, but he can't prove anything. And he knows what kind of trouble he can get into if he files any kind of report based on speculation. That means your career is safe as well."

"And you think he will let the matter go just like that?" she asked.

"Knowing Dudley, I doubt it, but he can't and won't try doing anything about it. Dr. Waverly approached me about the position while we were in Florida. Dudley knows the hospital considers Dr. Waverly the golden calf. It took a lot of hard work to get a doctor of his caliber here and Dudley's not going to do anything to piss him off."

"But will you be happy in the E.R.?" she asked and he could tell by her tone that she truly needed to know.

"I'll be happy practicing medicine, sweetheart. But it's really a blessing for us. I couldn't keep you behind closed doors any longer. I wanted to be with you and be seen with you. It would have only been a matter of time before our secret got out and both of us risked losing our careers. This way our careers are safe and we can be in love out in the open."

"And you want that?"

"Yes," he said, and he meant it. He eased closer to her bed. "And there's something else I want."

"What?"

"To marry you. Make you my wife. I love you. Will you marry me, Jaclyn?"

He saw tears form in her eyes and saw the way her lips trembled. "I fell in love with you, Lucien, that first day I met you, even before you said a single word to me," she said brokenly. "My mom said it would probably be that way for me because it was that way when she met my dad. She said she'd known all along that Danny wasn't the man for me and that I'd know him when I saw him."

A smile touched her lips when she added, "Although I knew you were the man for me, I just wasn't sure I was the woman for you."

He leaned over and placed a kiss on her lips. "You are. I can't imagine living my life without you. You don't know just how scared I was during your surgery. I watched from the gallery while thinking I could lose the most precious person in my life. I would not have been able to go on without you, sweetheart."

"Oh, Lucien," she said, swiping at her tears.

"And I want you to go home with me for Christmas, to meet my grandmother, my sister and all my cousins." He chuckled. "Although I think I need to warn you that I told Lori about us earlier today and she's already making plans to come here to meet you."

He paused and then said, "And if you want we can have a small wedding in Jamaica and another one here in the States. And just so you'd know, I called your parents."

She lifted a surprised brow. "You did?"

"Yes. They needed to know about your surgery and I also told them what you mean to me. I asked your dad's permission to marry you and he gave it."

Jaclyn drew in a deep breath, thinking she doubted she could love him any more than she did at that very moment. He had worked out everything for them to be together, and that meant all the world to her.

"Thomas said you'll be able to go home tomorrow if you continue to improve. I've talked to Isabelle and she knows you'll be staying with me. Your parents are flying in tomorrow and I have plenty of room for them to stay at my place."

He slid her hand from his and got up and went to lock her hospital room door. He didn't want any interruption while they sealed their marriage agreement. He returned to stand by her bed. "I love you, sweetheart, and when you get better we'll go shopping for a ring."

And then he leaned down and kissed her and he knew for them it would be a new beginning. One filled with plenty of love.

* * * * *

We hope you enjoyed reading
TREAT HER RIGHT
by *New York Times* bestselling author
LORI FOSTER
and
IN THE DOCTOR'S BED
by *New York Times* bestselling author
BRENDA JACKSON

Both were originally Harlequin® series stories!

From passionate, suspenseful and dramatic
love stories to inspirational or historical,
Harlequin offers different lines to
satisfy every romance reader.

New books in each line
are available every month.

Harlequin.com

I have a new boss—and he's hot but irresponsible, a
youngest son. If he thinks he can march into this office
and act like he owns the place, he needs to think again…
If only I didn't want him as much as I hate him…

Read on for a sneak peek of
Boss
by New York Times *bestselling author Katy Evans!*

My motto as a woman has always been simple: own
every room you enter. This morning, when I walk into
the offices of Cupid's Arrow, coffee in one hand and
portfolio in the other, the click of my scarlet heels on
the linoleum floor is sure to turn more than a few sleepy
heads. My employees look up from their desks with
nervous smiles. They know that on days like this I'm
raring to go.

Though it sounds bigheaded, I know my ideas are
always the best. There's a reason Cupid's Arrow swept
me up at age twenty. There's a reason I'm the head of
the department. I carry the design team entirely on my
own back, and I deserve recognition for it.

The office doors swing open to reveal Alastair
Walker—the CEO, and the one person I answer to
around here.

"How's the morning slug going, my dear Alexandra?" he asks in that British accent he hasn't quite been able to shake off, even after living in Chicago for a decade. He's adjusting his sharp suit as he saunters into the room. For his age, he's a particularly handsome man, his gray hair and the soft creases of his face doing little to steal the limelight from his tanned skin and toned body.

At the sight of him, my coworkers quickly ease back.

"The slug is moving sluggishly, you might say," I admit, smiling in greeting.

When Alastair walks in, everyone in the room stands up straighter. I'm glad my team knows how to behave themselves when the boss of the boss is around. But my own smile falters when I notice the tall, dark-haired man falling into step beside Alastair.

A young man.

A very hot man.

He's in a crisp charcoal suit, haphazardly knotted red tie and gorgeous designer shoes, with recklessly disheveled hair and scruff along his jaw.

Our gazes meet. My mouth dries up.

And it's like the whole room shifts on its axis.

I head to my private office in the back and exhale, wondering why that sexy, coddled playboy is pushing buttons I was never really aware of before. Until now.

Don't miss what happens when Kit becomes the boss!
Boss
by Katy Evans.

Available March 2019 wherever
Harlequin® Desire books and ebooks are sold.

www.Harlequin.com

HARLEQUIN® *Desire*

Family sagas...scandalous secrets...burning desires.

Save **$1.00**
on the purchase of ANY
Harlequin® Desire book.

Available wherever books are sold,
including most bookstores, supermarkets,
drugstores and discount stores.

Save **$1.00**

on the purchase of any Harlequin® Desire book.

Coupon valid until April 31, 2019.
Redeemable at participating outlets in the U.S. and Canada only.
Not redeemable at Barnes & Noble stores. Limit one coupon per customer.

52616277

5 65373 00076 2   (8100)0 12413

® and ™ are trademarks owned and used by the trademark owner and/or its licensee.

© 2018 Harlequin Enterprises Limited

BACCOUP80427

Love Harlequin romance?

DISCOVER.

Be the first to find out about promotions, news and exclusive content!

Facebook.com/HarlequinBooks

Twitter.com/HarlequinBooks

Instagram.com/HarlequinBooks

Pinterest.com/HarlequinBooks

ReaderService.com

EXPLORE.

Sign up for the Harlequin e-newsletter and download a free book from any series at **TryHarlequin.com.**

CONNECT.

Join our Harlequin community to share your thoughts and connect with other romance readers!
Facebook.com/groups/HarlequinConnection

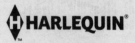

HARLEQUIN®

ROMANCE WHEN YOU NEED IT